MURDER
ON THE
SMALL
FARM

MURDER
ON THE
SMALL
FARM

*AN IT'S NEVER
TOO LATE MYSTERY*

DONNARAE MENARD

Reagan Rose Billodeau, our rising star.

Praise for Murder on the Small Farm

"Murder at the Small Farm drew me into the characters and their exploits.
It's a fun read." — Bellamy Gayle, author of the Sazerac Series

"This book is strong. Katie's struggling with her demons was realistic, if a
bit dark like real life. This is a terrific book."— Deb Well

Chapter One

The fence rails between the granite uprights were iron pipes. The top rail on the orchard side had a shallow, V-shaped dent where, long ago, a toppled pine had left its mark. Katie sat in the crux of the V; feet hooked on the lower rung.

She had been there for a while, contemplating the colorless grass and matted thickets of last season's weeds. A hawk, returned early from southern climes, drifted across the meadow on currents from Camel's Hump. His dark shape and wing tips lifted and held steady to feel the winds caught her interest for a few seconds.

"It's been a damn cold winter." Katie's attention returned to the tiny family boneyard. "There was so much snow. I don't know how you made it through before, Gram. If it hadn't been for Rick finding that old wood-burning furnace, we'd have had to leave."

Behind her, the pig shuffled in the dry grass. Not a single cat had been willing to tramp through the slushy winter waste to follow. The few sprigs of green near the uprights seemed to excite the young pig but did nothing to raise Katie's spirits. She had returned to the place of her youth in a past spring, planning a trampoline visit and then a bright, party-like future somewhere else. She was still here.

"The cats are good, Gram, and you know about the pig," Katie said. "How about the well? Um, yeah. With three of us here, laundry, showers, and twelve cats, the dug well used for the house gave up." She looked for the hawk, but he had moved on. "I forgot how much I hated the laundromat. We tried pumping up from the barn well, but there's not enough pressure to create a constant flow."

The pig had moved to the fence, rubbing her sensitive disc on the back of Katie's boots.

"I was just getting to where I had fifty cents in my pocket. Then this." Katie sighed. "It was so embarrassing. I had to go to the bank, and they wanted a co-signer. I had to ask Rick to step up." She shook her head, heat rising in her cheeks at the memory. "The drilling company will be here tomorrow."

The pig prodded her again. Katie slid off the rail. She had no more words. Tossing a kiss to her people, she followed the fat black rump towards the barn. Behind her, the hawk made one last pass, but with her head bowed in defeat, she didn't see it.

* * *

Bonnie, the pig, led the way. It was late afternoon, close enough to the end of the day that she was willing to be tucked away with supper laid out before her. Before the snow had set in, she had left Katie's care at one hundred pounds. There had been no warm place for her on this farm, so she had moved south one-eighth of a mile to Raymond Dean's barn. But now his two sows were ready for farrowing. They would need a separate enclosure, and there wasn't room for a guest. So, at a nice, round one-hundred-seventy-five pounds and with the threat of a long freezing period past, Bonnie had come back to take her place in the stall in Katie's empty barn. They had a connection, the two of them. Not just because Bonnie was a pet or that she, like Katie, was an orphan, but because she had been left tied to the sheriff's cruiser. At a tender age, she had developed a dislike equal to that of her human companion for the man.

Snuffling happily, Bonnie tossed the hay into a comfortable pile while Katie filled her trough. Then, with the pig settled and snug, Katie climbed the six-foot embankment to the house. The width of the old stagecoach inn away, she saw Rick, an arm wrapped around his fiancée Ruth, hobbling toward the porch. Even from that distance, Katie could tell Ruth was in pain. Pushing her toes hard against the sodden ground, the young woman rushed forward.

"What happened?" she demanded, circling the pair. Together, she and Rick made a cradle of their arms and lifted the elderly woman off the ground.

"Damn woodchucks." Ruth's voice was more a sob than a moan. "I'm going to shoot them all."

"You shouldn't have been tramping around out there in the meadow," said Rick.

Both were over sixty and being asthmatic, he had developed a wheeze for his effort to try and bear Ruth's weight. Though he had loved her for a long time, it was only recently he had been honest about his feelings. They'd been engaged since Christmas, cohabiting like feral hippies because Ruth refused to give up her social security to Uncle Sam, and life was short.

"I didn't see the hole," Ruth said with another sob. "I just went down to check if the fiddlehead ferns were ready to pick."

"Yeah, like you need to be near the brook when it's flooding its banks." Katie kicked the door open, turning to edge sideways into the stagecoach inn-turned-farmhouse, which she had inherited from her grandmother. Dismayed at the feel of Ruth's wet clothing, she wondered how long the old woman had been on the ground.

"It's a good thing I was watching and saw you go down." Rick's words answered her thoughts.

With Ruth on the sofa, Katie whirled from one place to another, getting dry clothes, a basin of hot water for the woman's feet, four-inch strips torn from a bed sheet to hold the frozen venison flank steak against the sore place, and finally an over-sweetened cup of tea. She had just stopped to draw a breath when Rick came back through the front door. He had driven down into the village to where the new doctor lived above her office. With the offer of supper to follow, he had brought Ann Gillian M.D. back to the farm.

While Ann examined Ruth, Katie hustled together a supper meal for the group. The pickings were slim because most of the food they had put up the previous fall was gone. It was just another thing that dragged Katie down.

Depression had always been an enemy; running away from it was her usual manner of recovery. Now, with the farm, her growing emotional bond with the old couple, and the faint possibility of stability on the horizon, she vainly sought a new coping mechanism.

"We'll have breakfast for supper," Katie stage-whispered to Rick.

Peeling and dicing the potatoes small, she parboiled them before dumping them in a skillet with chopped ham, onions, and some leftover peas. Every Sunday morning, in lieu of attending Mass at Saint Jude's, Katie spent time meditating and kneading two loaves of bread. Today had been no exception. With the early dark of evening setting in, the golden loaves rested on the sideboard, waiting for Rick to slice pieces for toast.

"We've got six eggs," said Katie. "Go check the hen house, but if you don't find anymore, Ruth, Ann, and Charlie can have scrambled eggs and you and I will have just potatoes and toast."

Rick came back with a single goose egg, which Katie was grateful for. They and the doctor sat to eat in the living room, where Ruth rested. As luck would have it, Charlie, who dropped in regularly for a meal, was a no-show for supper, so there was plenty for all.

"I heard you had a mess of cats," Ann said, eyeing the scratched surfaces of the stair newel and door frames. The conversation rotated to the Feral Cat Society, and Katie's job as the animal control officer. Ruth was doing all the talking.

Listening to her elderly friend list all the stumbling blocks they were working to overcome and how they had all come to live here together, sank Katie back into her earlier depression. She left Ruth, who seemed to be feeling better, to entertain the others while she cleaned up. After softly closing the last cupboard door, she took her shaking nerves to her hidey-hole. More and more often, she was thinking how a little nip might make her feel better. In the past, booze had made her dependent, then proven not to be a friend. The space she had secretly staked out to be hers, and the knowledge she'd have to drive to the village to find any alcohol, kept her sober by default.

The pantry was a long, narrow room that had many years before been half of the borning room. Its use had been for pregnant women or stagecoach customers too feeble to make it upstairs to the dormitory-style bedrooms. Now the space was halved, shared with an abutting bathroom. Doors to both rooms opened into the kitchen. In the pantry, shelves lined one wall just beyond the washer and dryer. The old and very noisy freezer brought in from its now-boarded-in nook on the porch took up space on the other wall. There was barely room to turn around between the two. The half of the back room, which hadn't been taken up, opened into the living room and was kept closed off from the cats.

At the far end of this space, a tall, old-fashioned eight-pane window let in late afternoon light. Through the rotted screen, patched and stitched with heavy upholstery thread, she was offered a slightly blurred view from the back of the house off over the fields toward the west and the ridge separating Parentville from Charlotte. Between the freezer and the window, was an empty space. Well, empty except for the ironing board, an extra coat tree, and an ancient kitchen chair with a broken bottom rung. Its color might have been green with cream trim, or maybe cream with green trim—so yellowed and dirty it was hard to discern the original pattern. For Katie, the chipped paint and cracked seat meant no one would be looking for the chair, making it a safe place to park her butt and remain undiscovered. The pantry was one of three invisible places she had found as a child in the stagecoach-turned-farmhouse.

Katie let her mind wander, hoping for calm. She gazed out over the sloping rear lawn down to the barn. At the end of the structure was the holding yard where the milk cows used to wait for Poppa twice a day like clockwork. In the fading light, she could just barely see across the hay field that surrounded the duck pond and right to the edge of the Gypsy Copse. Katie had loved the Gypsies. Many folks hadn't, including Gram. But Poppa had always welcomed them, allowing the wandering band to park their caravan wagons over in the copse. She knew at one time those tall wooden conveyances, like seafaring three-masted schooners, had sailed the country's highways and byways pulled by proud horses. But in her memory, each gaily painted caravan was towed behind an old station wagon or a beat-up pickup truck.

She remembered waiting, confined to the porch by Gram, watching with Poppa. The Gypsy men would come strolling down Lovers' Lane. One would be playing a Selmer guitar, and maybe a few would be singing, but all were laughing. The elders came to the house, standing in the yard and greeting Poppa, offering a tall, dark green bottle of wine. There was no begging or exchange of coins, just the bottle and a handshake. *As long as you leave it like you find it*, Poppa would say. Katie had heard him repeat those words each and every year when the Gypsies pulled in. The next morning, some young scrapper would be down in the barnyard tinkering with whichever piece of farm equipment was balking. Gram would pour off two galvanized steel pails of raw milk, and the women in their long black skirts and bright shawls would walk back up Lovers' Lane, turn off at the far end of the duck pond meadow, and head down the long length to the copse. There were no shortcuts taken across the hay until Poppa's two Canadian hired men and the younger Gypsy men and boys had it mowed, baled, and stowed up in the loft.

Katie smiled. It was the kind of memory that popped up now and again, helping her deal with having left Gram in the heat of anger, and now, with her death, unable to make amends. The scene running through her mind made her happy, warming her from the inside out. She continued her letter to Marlie, her love, whose way home after an altercation with Geofrey Ash had her working in Pennsylvania. Katie could only hope she described on paper the momentary joy in her heart.

They would be here for a week, busy every minute. We all worked together, cutting the hay, picking the apples. They'd help slaughter the two pigs and a cow, taking their quarters and whatever bits we didn't use. I remember the old ladies always had a sour look because Gram kept parts of one of the pigs to make her own hog's head cheese. Katie's pen raced to keep up with the memory as it spilled out of her mind. But by this time, Marlie was used to the cross-outs and missing words.

There would be five to eight caravans, maybe a few Gypsies living in old tag-a-long campers. I bet some years there were up to thirty people. They had a lot of mouths to feed and wanted to make their own hog's head cheese. While the men went from farm-to-farm, trading work for what they needed or a few dollars for gas, the women helped harvest and put the gardens to bed for the winter. We canned vegetables together. There was singing. It was beautiful to listen to. Like cathedral music, or maybe warblers. The way they talked was exciting. Up and down, no quiet spaces, lots of laughter.

I thought they were wonderful. I asked Gram why she'd get edgy, but never got an answer. Maybe I'll ask Ruth.

Katie had grown up in this house, raised by her grandparents after the loss of her parents. Each landmark, every acre, was as permanently tattooed on her gray matter as was the certainty of the sun rising in the morning. Ten years hadn't shaken her feelings for the land out of her bones, the respect, the guardianship. She'd tried to forget, but memories kept rising, drawing her back. The Gypsies returning twice a year—late spring for the fete and early fall for the harvest—was just such a memory.

Katie continued her letter to Marlie, expressing her love, never mentioning how the missives coming back to her seemed to be coming fewer over time. If she hurried, she'd have this letter ready to drop off at the post office the next morning on her way to work. With her head bent over the pages, she missed the three little sparkles of sunlight that glinted off steel and chrome from way off across the duck pond in the Gypsy Copse.

* * *

There was a narrow passage left open among the cedars and saplings, over beyond the duck meadow. Like a telescope, it narrowed the vision of any in the copse to Katie's yard. The farmhouse seemed far away. Most of its windows were dark. The man and dog walking toward the front corner were barely discernible. Well, that's the way it would have appeared if the two people emptying the blanket-wrapped bundle from the car trunk had bothered to look up. One was more intent on what could be seen from where O'Neil Road entered Shelbourne Road. The other walked gingerly, trying to protect an expensive pair of shoes from a messy demise in the slime and rotten leaves.

The trunk was slammed shut. Mud from the thaw, and leaves, ground and mixed in from the previous autumn, was spewed up as the wheels spun, leaving long, spindly streamers of grime behind. Then the automobile toiled back along the rutted road.

At the mouth of the road, the driver paused only for a moment, eyes flicking toward a single light burning in the kitchen of a small house further along Route 3. That was the way they needed to travel. Once out on the tarred surface, the driver turned on the headlights, and the car sped by the house. No one was the wiser.

Chapter Two

Three days later Katie was having a busy day at Baldwin's Feed and Hardware. New spring and summer merchandise was coming in daily. Keeping the displays filled kept Katie running between that and her register.

"I heard Ruth got hurt Sunday." Charlene, the town librarian, laid her sacks of bird seed and cat chow on the feed store counter. "I hope she's doing better. Will she be at knitting club?"

"No," Katie said, fingers running over the cash register keys. It was a busy day at Baldwins Feed and Hardware. Two sunny days and a balmy wind had everyone thinking of planting days ahead. She hesitated, distracted as her thought process split between the price of seed and Ruth home alone on the couch. There was a tired sigh.

Pulling money out of her wallet to settle her bill before moving on, Charlene asked, "How bad is it?"

Instinctively, Katie clamped her mouth shut. Then, she considered this woman was the axis for all the women's groups in the community. It would be good to have someone help keep Ruth busy and still so she would heal. She had also proven herself to be a kind friend to Katie.

"Dr. Gillian doesn't think it's a torn ACL. A sprained knee, maybe. Ruth is pretty much confined to the couch. Grace Dean from across the road, checks in with her at noontimes. It gives Ruth plenty of time to get in all her complaining about what she needs to do."

"Mm," said Charlene. "She probably has lots of work to get caught up on now that the water is running back into your house. How did that go?"

"We're not using the water yet." Katie felt like laughing. No matter what your business was, in a town like this, everyone knew. "It took two days to get the well drilling done and another two to flush the line. We should be able to use the water tonight."

Before Charlene could reply, the loudspeaker squawked, cutting off Kenny Rogers' crooning. Loud and sharp, Stan said, "All firefighters report to my office immediately."

There was a scramble in the store as several employees and customers hustled into the small area outside the office door. Stan came out and spoke with them. Katie, behind her cash register, was just far enough away behind the wall of bodies to not be able to hear what was said.

"What's going on?" Davidson Cormat, age twenty, and in-training as second cashier, asked Katie as the group turned as one person and rushed out of the building. Those who were employees hit the time clock and streamed out the rear door.

Katie, watching the exodus, felt the flesh crawl on her back. "No idea."

Just then, the air raid siren at the firehouse near the center of town gave off a deafening blast. The warning, used only in the gravest emergencies, sent a further shiver down her body.

Charlene grabbed her bundles and sprinted for the door.

"Katie! Pull your drawer!" Stan yelled from his office.

While Davidson peppered her with questions she couldn't answer, Katie pressed the release catch and pulled the till out of the open cash register, then hurried into the office.

"What's up?" she asked Stan, sliding the cumbersome cash drawer into the floor safe.

"Two little boys have gone missing from one of the housing developments." Stan was pulling on the assistant fire chief jacket hanging next to the door. "Fire and rescue have been called out to search for them. Cindy is coming in to close the store. She'll be here in a couple of minutes. Get ready. As soon as she arrives, go home. Grace Dean called. She's picking you up there." He stopped moving around and exhaled, his face sorrowful and pained. "One kid is five, the other three. They've been missing for four hours."

Chapter Three

Katie pulled into the dooryard and was already on the porch when the pickup truck door banged shut behind her. In the kitchen, shoving a thermos of water, a sandwich bag of snacks, and a sweatshirt into her backpack, she explained to Ruth, still lying on the living room sofa, what had happened. Grace called to her from outside. Grabbing the backpack, Katie ran out the door and stopped so quickly she almost slid off the edge of the porch.

Grace was waiting right beside Katie's truck. She was seated on top of Red Man, a big roan gelding, and held the reins for Duncan, a smaller dappled gray, that her own boys rode.

"You have to be kidding," Katie said, gawking.

"No." Grace had the same hurt look Katie had seen on Stan not all that long ago. Both of them were parents and were suffering with those of the small lost boys. "The LaPlatte Brook is running high, and those missing kids live just on the other side." She looked at Katie, who hadn't moved. "You do ride, don't you?"

"Yeah," said Katie, "but I haven't in years." She moved down the steps to where Duncan stood, ears forward. "Hi, baby. Are you ready for this? Are you a good boy?"

She exhaled into his face, one hand caressing his cheek, the other holding the bottom of the bridle. His ears flicked as his muzzle stretched out, inhaling her scent. Katie spent a few moments standing in front of the horse, letting him get a good sniff of her. His lips mouthed her hand and the shoulder of her jacket. Finally, he let out a lip-fluttering sigh. They were good to go. Katie moved around to the left, put her foot in the stirrup, and, after two skipping steps, heaved up into the saddle. Other than a small side-step, when she pulled on the horn and the back of the saddle, Duncan stood still.

"I adjusted the stirrups for my height," said Grace. "Are they okay?"

"Yes, they're fine," said Katie. Though she still wasn't so sure about being astride, she also felt the need to get to where they had to be.

But Grace was already turning Red Man away from the house. No tarrying to make adjustments.

"So," Katie whispered to Duncan, allowing him to follow his buddy, "if you have to dump me, let's try not to break any bones. And maybe wait until after those babies show up."

They rode around the house, past the workers finishing up with the well-drilling rig, and through the holding yard. Single file, they moved down the short lane beside the orchard. When they came to the heifer pasture, where Poppa had kept the cows soon to freshen and heifer stock, they rode through the broken gate and on to the area the Deans rented to harvest hay. Katie stayed directly behind Grace, trying to do as little damage to the new green stalks as possible. Once they were at the gravel riverbank, Grace stopped.

"Okay. If I remember right, there's a shallow place a little upstream where we can cross to the other side." She chewed her lip, studying the fast-moving water.

"We're going to cross?" Katie's mouth felt dry. "What happens if I fall off?"

"Don't worry about it," said Grace. "Duncan will go home for his supper."

"That's not what I meant," Katie sputtered, slightly irritated she wasn't being taken seriously.

Grace turned to her with a grin. "You'll be fine. The kids' family lives on the other side. We need to go to that side." Then she pointed downstream. "Some of the searchers are walking down the bank that way, so we'll go upstream." At Katie's quizzical look, she added, "Matthew is five, Lenny is three. They may have gotten this far and walked up toward the ridge. We'll cover more ground on horseback than the searchers will afoot. That's where we're assigned to look."

They could have gotten this far? Katie looked at the rushing water and swallowed hard. She sincerely hoped not.

Once again, Grace turned Red Man without waiting for an answer. Katie followed, allowing Duncan to find his best footing. The water made her nervous, and his ears kept twitching back.

"I'm okay," she whispered to console the horse and convince herself. "I'm just fine."

When they reached a place where the LaPlatte Brook ran wide and fairly shallow over the gravel plains, Grace urged Red Man down the bank and into the cold water. Duncan followed with no urging, and Katie held on. The worst part of the crossing was the four-foot climb up the bank on the far side.

After that, they rode along, taking turns calling out to the missing boys, listening for small voices calling back. Katie had gotten into the rhythm of the rocking ride much faster than she would have believed. Off to the right, she could see the back tip of the barn at the Small Farm. She hadn't remembered it being this close. Then, she spotted a man walking through the rough pasture. He was headed in the same direction they were, but closer to the Gypsy Copse. She knew he was searching as well and raised her hand in greeting when he turned.

"Grace, what about checking at the Small Farm?" she asked, pointing the way.

"Rescue is going door-to-door getting property owners out to search," Grace answered.

On both sides of the LaPlatte, the land this far up towards the ridge was wild, filled with big stones and stalks from the previous summer's weeds. Among the cockle burr and thistle bushes, Katie saw the remnants of barbed wire fencing. Once, this had been farmed land. Rough, but still used, and dotted with Scotch Highlanders, stocky, long-haired cattle.

Barely a mile into their journey, the ground edged higher, becoming steep and rocky. At one point, Katie held Duncan back as Red Man bunched up his haunches and leapt to climb up a place where the grade was steeper.

They were following a deer track. Katie exhaled, but before she could do much more, Duncan followed. She gave him his head, leaning low over the saddle horn and holding on for dear life.

At the top, after they came to a small, flat area filled with serious boulders, new grass, and tiny yellow flowers, Grace suddenly launched herself off Red Man. Katie wasn't sure if her friend had fallen or if the maneuver was an illegal dismount. Then she saw the blue jacket lying beside one of the bigger stones. She jumped off as well, holding Duncan's reins and grabbing Red Man's. Fortunately, both horses were more interested in the graze than whatever had snagged the women's attention.

Still wrapped in the jacket was a small red-headed boy, barely more than a toddler. He lay on his stomach in the sun, his eyes closed. Grace moved closer, hands reaching out.

"He's taking a nap," said another child's voice. Leaning against the rock on the other side was the boy's elder brother, Matthew. "We walked a long way and got tired. I didn't fall asleep, though."

"Hello, Matthew," Grace said with a smile. She ran her hands over the sleeping child, checking for injuries. "I'm Grace. This is my friend Katie. Your mother sent us to bring you and Lenny home. Are you ready to go?"

"I'm still tired," he said, watching from his seat on the damp ground.

"It's okay," said Katie. "We brought horses. Are you hungry? Or thirsty, maybe?"

Matthew scrambled to his feet. "I've never ridden on a horse."

"No?" Katie lifted Lenny, who was still asleep. When Grace was back in the saddle, Katie passed the small boy up. "Huh, are you sure? Oh, I know! I bet you're a camel jockey."

"I've never ridden on a camel!" Matthew laughed. The exhaustion immediately disappeared from his face, leaving only dirt smears behind and what might have been the downward trek of a tear.

Katie settled him on a rock, explaining she and Duncan would come up alongside the rock to get him. "You know, it's one of those cowboy things. The hero stands on the rock, then steps over into the saddle. Your legs are a little short, though, so I'll hold on to you."

"Okay." It was hard to discern if he was excited or unsure.

Matthew did exactly as she directed, and in two minutes, they were ready to follow Grace. He sat in front of Katie, watching the way from between Duncan's ears. Lenny, who had finally woken up, rode facing Grace, his arms around her in a death grip.

Matthew fluttered his legs against Duncan's shoulders, and Katie, one arm on either side of him, laid her hand on his knee.

"I know that's how you make camels go, honey, but Duncan thinks you're kicking him."

"Oh. Sorry, Duncan." Matthew leaned forward slightly to pat the horse.

Grace and Red Man disappeared over the edge of the steep grade. Katie drew a shaky breath. *Oh god*, she thought, *what if I drop him?* She shook off the visual of Duncan rolling over with her and Matthew underneath. As calmly as she could, she started talking again.

"So, about the camels, or did you say elephants?"

"No." Matthew smiled at her, unaware Duncan was about to go down the embankment.

"Give him his head," Grace called back.

Katie eased up on the reins. With an arm on either side of the boy, she grasped the saddle horn.

"I've never had a ride on a camel or an elephant," said Matthew. "But I did get to ride with my dad on a dirt bike last fall."

"Wow," Katie said. "That's great."

Duncan started down, sitting back slightly on his haunches and leveling himself out as he did. Katie leaned back, too, gently pulling Matthew's weight with her. In half a blink, Duncan was safely at the bottom, shaking his rear quarters to throw off the clinging mud. Matthew was still telling Katie about riding the dirt bike. Ahead, Grace had one arm wrapped around Lenny, her cheek on top of his head. Though the little boy wasn't crying, his eyes were huge with fear. Red Man was half quarter horse and half workhorse. Tall, but broad and strong. Grace continued to talk softly to the child, quieting his fears.

When they were all down off the rocky area, Katie changed the conversation.

"I know you used to live in the city, Matthew," she said. "Out here, in Parentville, it's different. You can't just walk out of your yard and go off by yourself. Even more important, you need to stay away from the brook. It's dangerous. You might be a big boy, but Lenny, he's still really little, you know?"

"I know," Matthew said sadly. He leaned back for the first time, letting Katie support him. His voice sounded teary now. "We were looking for our dad. He's building houses for other kids. I heard hammering and thought he was right on the other side of the trees. Then we couldn't find our house. We were going to look again after Lenny woke up."

"Well," said Katie, giving the small boy a hug, "you two certainly did walk a ways. Your mom and dad are going to be so happy to see you."

After they passed the site of the Small Farm, Grace and Katie turned their horses away from the brook, angling to the side of O'Neil Road, and onto Shelburne Road which ran in front of several housing developments. Grace remarked it might be the fastest way to find someone from the rescue squad. Her words proved true.

A pickup drove towards them, and Katie and Matthew flagged it down. The fireman took both of the boys into the cab of his truck and turned around. By the time Katie and Grace reached the end of Haystack Lane, the boys had been reunited with their parents. Sheriff Lewis and Chief Brown from the volunteer fire department rushed up to Katie and Grace, offering thanks. Right behind them was the boys' father. They could see the mother kneeling on the ground, arms locked around her children. When Duncan's back end twitched nervously, Katie gave a light tug on the reins, guiding him away from the crowd. She listened at a safe distance as Todd Welks tearfully thanked Grace, reaching up and grasping her hand. Big Man held, but his ears twisted back and forth. Finally, Todd rushed back the way he'd come.

"I have to admit," said Chief Brown, as Katie and Duncan returned, "that was the last place I expected to find those boys. How do you feel? Great job."

"They made it further than I would have thought," said Grace.

"I'm really glad they're safe, and I'm sure their mom is going to keep a better eye on them now. But my butt hurts," said Katie. "I'm thinking about getting off and walking Duncan home."

After saying their goodbyes, she and Grace left, both astride, before the shadows got any deeper. As they rode up the driveway to Katie's house, Grace said, "Good job out there, Katie."

"What? You're the one that spied Lenny's jacket."

"Yeah, there's that. But you didn't fall off of Duncan. Soak in a hot tub with Epsom salts so you don't end up with saddle sores."

"Yeah, I can feel those coming on." Katie laughed as she gently rose from the saddle and dismounted.

They were still talking and laughing when Ruth hobbled out to the front porch. Initially, she looked fearful, but smiled in relief when Grace and Katie told her the good news. Together, they helped the older woman back inside.

Chapter Four

At work the next day, a lot of people made a fuss over Katie. She was really clear to everyone that Grace, not she, had spotted Lenny's blue jacket. "I just helped tote the boys home," she said.

Davidson asked questions about how she and Grace chose their route. When he learned it had been assigned, he asked why.

"Maybe because that property abuts my farm," said Katie, bagging a customer's seed order. "Somebody probably thought I had some idea about the terrain or something."

"Do you?" Once again, Davidson's words reminded Katie that even though he was from nearby, he was still new to Parentville.

"Heck, no." She grinned. "I haven't been over there in fifteen years, and even way back then, I wasn't memorizing landmarks."

Arlo, Eugenie's husband, who was picking up fertilizer along with his brother-in-law Jake, said, "But that used to be family land, right? Didn't the Small Farm belong to your granddad?"

Words from Katie's past ran through her mind like a soaring rocket. "Yeah, it did. That was before I was even born. I think my mother wasn't even born when that section was pared off."

"Why was that?" Davidson asked.

Though Arlo's ears seemed to prick off at Davidson's continued questioning, Katie knew the young man was still trying to fit in.

"Part of the farm was ten acres or so on the other side of the river. Good for nothing except raising goats, my grandfather said. Too rocky. He had a cousin who came back from Korea. Guy had taken a shell shot, I think." She paused, trying to remember. The story seemed vague, like a book she had read long ago.

Arlo cut in. "His name was Larsen, Everett Larsen. I didn't know he was Fred's cousin, but I knew he was family. He suffered a head injury in the war and was pretty messed up. He lived at a little house on that side until he passed. There was some kind of stink, because his wife sold it off without offering the property back to Fred and Irma."

Katie and Davidson waited for Arlo to finish, but he shrugged. "That's all I know. That, and the fact people still talk about the weird cattle he raised."

Katie absolutely knew about those. "The Scotch Highlanders! There were three, all reddish gold and having a bad hair day."

The rest of the day flew by. Parentville, a small rural town that had come into its own as a bedroom community for Burlington in 1976, only a few years prior, had its own manner of getting news around. Gossip and the last of the party-line telephones kept everyone abreast of any doings. Today, there was a steady stream of folks coming into the hardware store, running their errands, but also wanting to stop and hear about Katie's major rescue. The fire chief had stopped in early on, telling Katie both boys were doing fine.

"It wasn't me," she insisted. "Grace Dean did it all. I just went with her and hoped not to fall off my horse. I'm glad the little guys are good."

Unfortunately, Katie had been involved in a couple of different incidents not long before, uncovering her grandmother's murderer and then helping exonerate Ruth from the death of her husband. People weren't believing her words. Because Grace worked from home making goat cheese and soap, she wasn't easily accessible. Katie was right there in the middle of town, where the public could find her. The other two employees on the sales floor had asked their questions first thing, as had the guys in the feed sheds. When Stan stepped out of his office to see what all the hubbub was, everyone took off. Only Davidson, who worked beside her all day, was left.

"For someone who always acts so low-key," Davidson joked, "you're pretty popular today, Katie. Everyone wants to be in your line."

"I'm going to go check the stockroom." Katie's brows drew together. "I need a break."

Stan agreed she should move out of sight and passed over the inventory sheets. He'd watch the backup register, and she could let her rising star fall over the horizon.

Chapter Five

At home, the well diggers had pulled out the previous day, leaving a muddy mess Rick and Katie would have to rake out and deal with. But there was a holiday excitement in the house as they ran water through all the faucets until the interior pipes ran clear of sediment. It was the golden moment of a dark experience.

Katie started laundry the next morning before driving to work. The joy of pushing the start button on the washer put a smile on her face and added to her heavy foot. She was inside the feed store and punching the clock in no time. The glow lasted until she had her cash register open and ready to go.

A few minutes later, the radio announcer cut in, destroying Davidson's rant about the choice of radio stations and Johnny Cash's latest declaration of woe. Once again, ears throughout the store perked up to listen.

"In breaking news, a report has just been received by the Vermont Sheriff's office about a body discovered in a wooded area outside of Parentville. The remains appeared to have been there for several days. Details are currently limited. The remains were found by local herdsman, Amos Surette. Details to follow at five..."

Most of the feed store customers hardly seemed to notice the interruption, their attention quickly returning to their own pursuits.

But Katie, standing beneath a speaker, stood with her mouth open, her earlier glow forgotten. The Surettes were the current owners of the Small Farm. Amos was the herdsman over two lousy cows. If he had been out with them and found the remains, then he had to have been close to where she and Grace had found the Welks boys. Gooseflesh ran up her arms.

She remembered seeing him walking across the pastureland, but neither Guernsey had been visible. How near to the spot where he had found the remains had she and Duncan been? Or those little boys? What if they had stumbled on the body?

Her thoughts were creeping her out. Automatically Katie rang another customer through while considering what she knew about the odd couple in the little old house.

He was tall, stoop-shouldered, and extremely long-waisted, with an oversized shaggy head, forever acne, and bad teeth. Every time Katie encountered him, she considered the fact he looked like an upright, two-legged reptile. His equally tall wife, Monique, also had shaggy hair. Hers was sandy blond. The woman's waist sat right below her breasts, and she never wore a bra. She walked with her hands perpetually curled like long, thick-knuckled talons. But when Monique looked up, beneath the badly trimmed bangs, you could see her small round face, smoky gray eyes, and welcoming smile. They were a couple of oddities. Katie had heard Amos was an ostracized member of the Mennonite community from over in Richmond. Rumor had it Monique's family lived in South Burlington. People there probably thought squirrels were vicious wild animals. The type of folks who would never understand the allure of two brown Guernseys with their soulful eyes.

Katie had never seen the Surettes in Saint Jude's church, but they did frequent the thrift shop. No matter the weather, the couple could be seen walking along the side of the road, hand in hand. Katie had been surprised to learn they were in their early thirties, slightly older than she was, and not the elderly couple their appearance had led her to believe.

* * *

At the end of the workday, Katie burst through the front door of the farmhouse. "Ruth!" she called, startling the older woman lying on the sofa. The cats on Ruth's lap took flight.

"You aren't going to believe what I heard on the radio," Katie said, breathless. Ruth waved an arm in a short, cutting motion, which had Katie swallowing the rest of her words.

"Katie, a woman's body was found in the Gypsy Copse." Ruth's words came out in a rush. "The police are investigating, and Sheriff Lewis wants to talk to you."

Katie and Sheriff Lewis had shared a love-hate relationship since her return. The only thing it was lacking was the love part.

"Me?" Katie blinked in surprise. "Why would he want to talk to me? I was at work."

"Because," said Sheriff Lewis, stepping out of the kitchen, cup in hand, "it happened on your land."

Twisting to see if she'd missed the sheriff's cruiser parked out front, Katie spun back, frowning. "How did you get in here?"

"I've been here a bit, sharing a cup of tea with Ruth. I parked on the side, near the chicken coop, to make sure there would be plenty of room for you to pull in."

Rick bumped into Katie as he came through the door behind her. He reached out to catch Katie's shoulders as she stumbled ahead. "What the heck?"

Without looking, Katie knew the cruiser wasn't parked next to the chicken coop for her convenience, but behind it, out of sight from where she'd pulled into the dooryard. Seeing the way Ruth was wringing her hands, she could tell the visit had been less than welcomed. She yanked loose of Rick's grip and immediately felt contrite. It wasn't Rick's fault the mere mention of Lewis pushed all her buttons. She continued toward the kitchen, swinging out her lunch pail as she walked in a way that made Lewis take a half-step back. It was a petty move, but it didn't make her feel bad.

Solomon, Rick's gangling young dog who'd been one of Katie's rescues, had spent the day riding with Rick. He wasn't interested in their guest. Instead, he skittered around her towards his supper dish, sending Lewis another step back. The few cats willing to be near a stranger responded to Katie's anger and ran for cover.

"Like I said." Katie dropped the lunch pail and thermos heavily on the metal washboard, then stood there for a moment, leaning on the cold steel and exhaling the bad feeling in her belly. "I didn't know anything about a body being found until the radio broadcast. *And* I don't own that piece of land."

"Actually, you do," said Lewis, smirk in place.

Behind him, Rick's face pinched up. Before he could say a word, Ruth, hobbling painfully on crutches, came into the kitchen.

"If we're going to talk about this, then everyone should sit down. I've got coffee on. We could all do with a cup." She gratefully sank into a chair at the table. Rick got down a couple of mugs and poured coffee.

Sheriff Lewis dropped his curled-brim Stratton hat on the table and pulled out a seat. Rick sat across the table next to Ruth. They were both looking at Lewis in a manner that dared the sheriff to send them away. This might be Katie's house, but they were as close to family as she had.

Before anyone else could speak and probably start an argument, Rick said, "When the property was cut out for the Small Farm, Fred specifically walked the line with the surveyor from Charlotte. He wanted to make sure he kept custody of the Gypsy Copse." Rick focused on Katie. "He was worried his relatives would drive the Gypsies away, and he didn't want that to happen. I know because I was out there with them. It was the end of the summer. I remember the LaPlatte was running low. Some beavers were out there trying to dam up the works. We'd been over there three times trying to get rid of the damn little buggers. I was all for shooting them, but your heart-of-Jello granddad said no."

"Okay." Katie stopped to take a sip of coffee. The word came out as a croak. "Then I own it. So, what, Sheriff, you need my permission to check it out? You've got it. Okay? Are we done?"

Over time, several people had cautioned Katie not to antagonize the sheriff. And periodically, the two almost came to a truce. But not enough time had passed yet for Katie to forget Sheriff Martin Lewis had dropped the ball on her grandmother's murder, allowing the case to be treated as death by natural causes. Then, too, Lewis had been related, though not closely, to George Beauregard, abuser and considered stabbed to death by his wife,

Ruth.

"When was the last time any of you were over there?" Sheriff Lewis looked at all three of them in turn. Rick and Katie made eye contact, but Ruth sat catty-corner to the table, massaging her bum knee.

"Seventeen, eighteen years ago, anyway," said Katie.

"When I walked the line with Fred," Rick said.

"Never," Ruth muttered.

Lewis laid a Polaroid Instamatic picture showing a mostly bundled-up set of remains lying on the ground. "You know this woman?"

Katie and Ruth took a look, and Ruth quickly turned away, shaking her head. She stayed that way with her eyes closed. Katie reached out, taking her elderly friend's hand.

"How can you tell it's a woman?" Rick asked. He had also taken a quick look, then pushed back from the four-square inches of photo paper.

"It was pretty clear when I was standing right beside it. Katie, you were just out there two days ago." It wasn't a question.

"I was on a horse, looking for two small children along the brook and in the upper scrub. We didn't even get close enough to see the copse. Ask Grace," Katie said.

"I guess I'll have to do that." Picking up his hat, Sheriff Lewis walked out the kitchen door.

"Well, there's a waste of good coffee," said Ruth as Katie dumped the contents of his cup down the sink.

Katie and Rick had taken over Ruth's work with the cats. As Katie mixed special diets and Rick cleaned out cat boxes, she asked Ruth, "How well do you know those people at the Small Farm?"

"I don't, really," said Ruth.

"I've heard the guy, Amos, is an expert on old buildings," Rick said. "Specifically, barn restoration."

"Really?" Katie said. If Lewis was going to start coming around, checking her comings and goings again, maybe she should do some of her own investigating. After all, he had proven to not do so well at it. Besides, she had an old barn. It needed restoration. And she had questions. "I wonder if he does estimates."

Chapter Six

For almost a week, Katie fought the urge to go over to the copse and look around herself. The photograph hadn't shown much, and her memories of inside the copse were vague. How had someone gotten in there? Why pick that spot? What else might be lying around among the trees, offering a hint of the answers, but not being shared by Lewis?

People coming into the feed store had moved from gossiping about the Welks boys to the identity of the body. Not many came directly to Katie, but she could hear customers talking in the aisle. She'd sneak down the next one, holding her breath while she listened. When Stan caught her eavesdropping for the second time, he banished her to assembling displays in the stockroom. It was beginning to feel like the stockroom was going to be her regular work area.

A tiny article in the Burlington Free Press, way back on page eight, said no progress had been made on identifying the remains *thought to be female*.

Phfft, Katie thought, sure that it was Lewis who was giving the reporters their information. *So, he's not even telling them what he told us.*

Finally, she couldn't fight her curiosity any longer and went looking for Rick, telling him she was going to take a hike over.

"If there had been a pool on how long it would take you to stick your nose in this, I would have lost," Rick said, lacing on his tall boots. "I thought you'd have been out there first thing the next morning."

"Where are you two going?" Ruth asked. Each grunting step hurt as much as the last one, slowing her ability to follow the other two.

"Steven Dean says squirrels are messing up where he strung a bucket line for next year's sap collecting," Rick said. "I've got a hankering for squirrel meat. We'll be back in a while." He picked up his twenty-two rifle and strode off. Katie ran to catch up, shoving her arms into her jacket as she went.

"What about church?" Ruth called out. She was dressed and ready to go.

"Maybe next week," Rick yelled over his shoulder. His stride lengthened, and he and Katie were into Lovers' Lane before Ruth could respond.

Avoiding the open area of the meadow, they followed the same route the Gypsy women had when they'd come for milk. Until that day, Katie hadn't realized how long a walk it was. To get to the copse, they needed to cross the LaPlatte. On the near shore, she looked across and saw the thick growth of cedars and white oaks. Here the brook had eroded the banks and, though the water ran fast, it was shallow over the gravel and sand banks. Rick held out his hand to help her.

"Walk soft and careful. Keep your feet apart and shuffle along on the bottom," he said.

She held on to the older man, not only for her safety, but to hold him steady as well. At the deepest point, the water sloshed against the top of her knee-high barn boots. Once on the far bank, the perimeter was less than a minute away, still marked by the orange ribbons the sheriff's department had tied to trees. Katie followed Rick around the perimeter of the area that had been marked out. Though the shifting of new leaves in the breeze interrupted their lines of sight, those same leaves were still small enough to let the sun shine through. Once they had completed a circuit around the exterior, Rick stepped into the trampled area, motioning Katie to stay on the paths the investigators had left.

"Wow, the forensic guys sure made a mess of the ground in here, didn't they?" Rick asked.

"Actually, Corrine, who investigated the remains on the ridge last season, told me that the ground gets all soupy as the body decomposes. Even after the remains are removed, the ground is kind of, you know, messy."

"Probably what draws the carnivores in to dig and roll," said Rick.

"Yeah. I asked her how come when they came out from inside the tape, they removed their rubber boots and put them in plastic bags. She said it was because the ground was wet, and evidence might be stuck to the soles."

"Glad I'm not leaving here and going to lunch," said Rick

They continued walking around, on the side closest to the Shelbourne Road and right off the dirt track loftily labeled O'Neil Road, they found car tracks with bits of plaster splatter left from making molds. The same white splash was visible near boot marks. Near the white splatter, and the slightly deeper impressions where the tires had rested, Katie found a messy pile of mud which hadn't been flattened by snow over the winter. She squatted for a better look.

"Sedan or pickup?" she asked Rick.

"Can't tell," he said.

"The investigators must have dug all this up." She waved her arm over the dirty slush and mud pile. Suddenly teetering, she put out a hand to settle herself and rustled a few leaves out of the way. Beneath them was another track of sorts. "Rick, what do you think made this?"

The print was a round hole, smaller than a dime, drilled half an inch into the soil. Two inches away was a narrow, triangular piece barely pressed into the ground.

"Some kind of tripod would be my guess," he answered.

They searched for other markings of the same, but found none. They both stood over it for a few seconds, contemplating what it was.

"Odd, ain't it, that no one made a mold of this?" Rick asked.

Katie nodded in agreement. Unwilling to leave the print to the ravages of nature, Rick made a covering of branches and leaves, marking the top with three small stones.

"I should have brought a camera," he said. "Let's see how close we are to the house on the Small Farm."

"I don't know why I didn't realize Poppa had held onto this bit of acreage," Katie said.

"It's only 'bout a half-acre square, like a finger stuck into what he sold. The eastern boundary is this road, such as it is."

They crossed directly over the rutted track and up onto a raised bank. Not twenty feet away was a barbed wire fence with a stretch of new wire filling in a gap. Rick walked up and ran his fingers between two sets of barbs.

"Something came through this fence. A bear or a moose. The Guernsey bossies wandered out, and Surette followed them."

Across the pasture, the roof ridge of the barn was visible.

"Why would the cows eat cedar if all this new grass was right here?" Katie asked.

Rick just scratched his chin, looking back at the Small Farm. "My thoughts exactly."

* * *

Just after lunch, the wind came up. In the living room, Rick and Ruth were listening to the Channel 3 weather report as Katie put the finishing touches on Sunday dinner. Charlie, the Vietnam veteran who drove the town dump truck, and was currently squatting in the backroom of the firehouse, was already there and washing up in the bathroom. The hundred-and-twenty-year-old three-story wood structure that had stood on upper main street and served as a boarding house since day one had burned to the ground in one of the most spectacular fires Parentville village had seen in years. Charlie was prone to alcohol, though trying to amend, and not given to regular bathing, a slight which he seemed to ignore. The three at the farmhouse believed this was the primo reason Charlie was having a problem finding housing.

As he came back out into the kitchen, he said, "Weather doesn't sound good, does it? After lunch, I think I'll drive out to the town garage and make sure there's sand in the back of my truck, and the spreader is all hooked up. I'd bet dollars to donuts I'll be out sanding roads early tomorrow morning."

The locals were fed up with winter for that season. The advent of more snow brought out the worst in people, or depression in others, Katie being one. A small pinch of pain had settled between her brows, a quarter inch up. It took away all thought of the copse, even the idea any evidence left would be destroyed. Late snow was often referred to as farmers fertilizer, to Katie it was a pain in the derriere. She was tired of slipping and sliding, shoveling and clearing.

Lunch talk circled around the probability of a hard frost and Katie ignored it, considering a slice of pie and a nap until the telephone rang.

Chapter Seven

Katie had to drive all through town and into Saint George, to get to the neighborhood of higher-end homes on the backside of the Pine River Golf Course, which was part of her area as animal control officer. It had been Gram's job. Gram was gone. The town had needed a volunteer, the job came with a per diem payment, and so Katie had stepped up.

The houses here were big with brick and fancy board trim. Professional lawn architects had selected, grouped, and planted trees, shrubs, and what would, in a few weeks' time, be flowering beds. The front door opened. A sturdy-looking woman of about fifty, wearing creased wool trousers and a chenille sweater, smiled at Katie. There were enough gray strands in the woman's hair to have turned the red encircling her face to a sandy coral.

"Mrs. Ross? I'm Katelyn Took."

"Perfect!" said Mrs. Ross. "Please come in."

The homeowner guided Katie down the hall to a set of French doors on the left. Katie found herself facing a living room that took up half of the house's first floor. At either end of the room, two wide, eighteen-pane windows offered passage to a flood of bright sunlight. She blinked hard, trying to clear the overwhelming glare reflected off the gilded ribbon wallpaper and furnishings of bright yellow, harvest bronze, and gold sheen. Directly across the room was a large fieldstone fireplace with a thick slate mantel. The apron of its raised hearth stretched deep into Rice-a-Roni-like shag carpeting.

Mrs. Ross continued into the room, but Katie hesitated.

"Mrs. Ross, I need to take off my boots before I go further into your house," said Katie. "Maybe we should step outside and check out your nuisance animal problem."

"Don't worry about your boots, Katelyn." The smile on Mrs. Ross's face dimmed as she motioned her forward. "The animal problem is in here. Can you smell that kind of funky odor?"

Katie sniffed, took a couple of steps into the room, and sniffed again.

What is that? She thought, then said, "It kind of smells like a chicken coop."

Katie almost bit her tongue when she realized she had spoken aloud. Mrs. Ross went back into the hall and returned holding the collar of a pretty golden retriever. The dog's coat shone from a recent brushing and the animal wore a wide collar resplendent with rhinestones. Even though the dog looked adoringly up at its mistress, it strained ahead. When the woman released the dog, it went straight to the fireplace, where it stopped at the edge of the slate apron and stared into the empty brick opening, finally sitting down, but remaining at attention.

Mrs. Ross picked up the metal fireplace tongs and reached up into the chimney to tap on the flue plate. From where she stood, Katie heard scurrying sounds. The dog surged forward, tail wagging, focused on the chimney.

"Raccoons," said Katie. "You've got a nest of them on the flue."

"That's what my husband said." Mrs. Ross replaced the tongs. "The question is, how to get rid of them?"

"Well, this time of year, it's probably a nesting female with new kits," Katie said. "Getting her out is one thing; getting them all out is another. I'm not sure if they'd be big enough yet to climb all that way." Katie studied the chimney. The fireplace was big, but according to Mrs. Ross, there was no other access besides the top, two and a half stories up.

"Is there a clean-out on the outside of the chimney?" Katie asked.

Mrs. Ross wasn't sure, but the two women left the house and walked outside to look.

"See here," Katie pointed to a metal plate near ground level. "This is a clean-out. It's used to help clear ash from the chimney and is below the burn level, or fireplace level, in masonry chimneys. It's always sealed with that tight fitting plate so no air or animals can get in." Katie looked around the yard. "We're going to need a plan."

With Mrs. Ross's help, Katie moved a picnic table near the outside of the chimney and set her largest live trap. "Raccoons won't come out until after dark," she said. "Here's a can of mackerel. Sometime after supper, put half the can as far back in the trap as you can. It really stinks, and it might draw the 'coon in. No matter what you catch, don't open the crate, okay? Call me, and I'll come right over."

"You think a raccoon is going to come out in this weather for fish?" Mrs. Ross looked dubious.

"Actually, no. Not right away." Katie set the trap. "What I think is, you're going to catch a few cats, and I don't know what else. But that she-coon has babies to feed. She might be your first catch, but if she's not, she isn't going to want to be sharing easy food with other animals. In the meantime, you need to get hold of a chimney cleaner and have him on standby. You'll need a cap on top to keep the animals out, and I don't clean chimneys. When was the last time you had a fire in there?"

"Maybe three years ago," said Mrs. Ross.

Katie almost laughed out loud. "That nest might be older than just this year. It's going to be a god-awful mess. You can try to clean it yourself, but if your stomach isn't rock solid, you're not going to like it."

Mrs. Ross's nose was already scrunched up. "Are you sure this is going to work?"

"Yes, ma'am."

Mrs. Ross had a questioning look, and Katie remembered that people not familiar with rural living often didn't understand that those who were, had lived through experiences that didn't include contacting an extermination team. Then too, Mrs. Ross might not consider raccoons as just common pests.

"I tell you what," said Katie. "It's already pretty late right now, so I'm going to set and bait this trap. You watch while I set it, so you'll know how this works. It's really easy. Later on, come out and stand right at the corner of the house. You should be able to shine a flashlight right into the trap. If you see anything, give me a call."

"What if the raccoon is rabid?"

"Wrong time of year for rabies, but so that you'll know in the future, a rabid animal isn't going to den up. Rabies screws up the wiring in a critter's brain, causing it to pace or prowl continually. It loses fear, would be after a person or dog outside, and might even be trying to get into your house. You know, ripping at screens or scratching the heck out of your door."

Mrs. Ross backed further away from the trap. "Is there anything else?"

"If nothing comes tonight, we'll add a little fresh bait tomorrow evening. In about half an hour, take those metal tongs and bang on the flue plate until you hear the raccoon moving around. If you hear it hissing, don't worry. It can't get in unless you open the plate, which the nest is probably holding closed. But hissing means the raccoon is going to be mad enough to crawl up the chimney. Keep the dog inside, and the door to the living room closed just to be on the safe side. The fish stinks. If the raccoon sticks its nose out of the chimney and smells the mackerel, it's going to want to investigate. And if it's got kits, it's going to need to eat. Check the trap with a flashlight before you go to bed and in the morning. Like I said, call me anytime. If I don't hear from you, I'll come back tomorrow night and reset the trap if you have trouble with it, okay?"

Chapter Eight

"My girlfriend and I were talking about the woman's body being found on Shelbourne Road. I told her if she was going anyplace, even if it was local, she better not go alone," said Davidson.

Stan Baldwin, the owner, had pulled the young man aside and told Davidson his training period was over. From now on, he would be expected to stock shelves, run the register, assist customers, and, when needed, help out in the feed sheds. Katie had hidden a secret smile at the pleased blush and puffed-out chest, her co-worker had sported for another thirty minutes. Since his arrival, she'd considered him a bit of a dweep, then for a half hour, he had sounded like every other young male she'd ever run into. Now, he was backsliding into dweepdon. She was not pleased with his dragging up the issue at the copse, already a week old and being replaced by other gossip.

During a lull in customers, he was straightening out the perpetual mess on the impulse rack while Katie read over the upcoming sale flyer. It wasn't unusual to find typos, and the only way not to get stuck selling a $99.99 item for $9.99 was to have notices already posted around the store that a printing error had been made.

"Wait!" Katie grinned, interrupting his tirade. "You have a girlfriend?"

As Davidson sputtered, Stan stuck his head out of his office.

"Katie, did you take an animal call on Tudor Lane last night? Lady on the phone says there's a wild animal screeching in the trap."

The Wrights on Tudor Lane had been her second call of the evening. She had pulled into her parking space as Rick was coming down the front steps.

Loading a second trap, she'd gone out to meet with a homeowner who had a varmint making regular dinner stops in her trash cans. Katie had helped the woman fix the trash can lid to keep anything smaller than a bear out, but knew the varmint would return to a known food source.

"Got it," Katie said. "Tell her I'll come over at lunch and pick it up. I'm sorry she called here, Stan." Her boss had been very understanding when she'd accepted the responsibility of her grandmother's former animal control job with the village. But this time of year, there was too much happening at the store for her to take off at the ringing of the phone. Instead, she got up early, spent her lunches in the car, and made pickups on her way home.

When Stan's head disappeared, she said to Davidson, "You don't mind if I take first lunch, do you? Since the critter's screeching and all?"

"What kind of animal is it?" Her colleague looked a little spooked. He was a village boy, rural but not farm-raised.

"If it's making a lot of noise; probably a raccoon." Katie rubbed her face. "If it's a male, I'll relocate him off in the woods. But if there's a chance it's a female, this time of year with babies in the den, I'll take her a little way down the road and let her go. If I don't, the youngsters will die. She'll find her way back to them if I don't go too far. I know that's not what I'm supposed to do, but I can't get around it." When she looked at Davidson, she found a pair of sad gray eyes looking back at her and the tiniest of tremors in his bottom lip. "That's our secret, Davidson. I don't want Sheriff Lewis ordering me to do anything different, like taking them off to the bog or exterminating them. You know, because of the babies?"

Davidson stiffened up. "No, I mean, yes. It'll be our secret. It's the right thing to do."

"So anyway, about your girlfriend…" Katie moved to a safer subject, one that might cause Davidson to forget she had said she was going to let the raccoon return to its home.

"Well, you know they found that woman over in Shelbourne, dead in the woods?"

"Davidson," Katie said patiently, "It was on the O'Neil Road, and that's in Parentville."

"Whatever, anyway, Laurie, that's my girlfriend, works in Williston and drives to work alone every day." Davidson puffed up with importance. "That's why I warned her. You can't be too careful."

Katie nodded, amazed at the way his brain worked. She let him prattle on until the big Hood's Dairy clock ticked eleven and punched out for lunch on the road. It was safer for him to be talking about his problems, than asking her about hers.

Later, driving out to Tudor Lane, a development of two-tone split-level houses near the high school, she considered it a blessing Mrs. Ross hadn't called. She would have had to be on two different sides of town at the same time. Shunting away from that, she thought about Davidson and Laurie. In her mind, he was a kid, but yet, here he was, all worried about something she and other adults had sitting on their minds.

She had known having Sheriff Lewis show up at her house wasn't going to be good. Grace Dean had called late last evening. Lewis had gone down to their farm, asking questions. Specifically, about how close she and Katie had gotten to the body site. It was clear Grace was wondering as well.

"Just who was the woman found in the Gypsy Copse?" Katie asked herself aloud. "And how did she get there?"

Katie wanted an answer even more than she figured Lewis did. She decided her first step should be Amos Surette.

* * *

The raccoon was indeed a big, fat sow. She was angry at being snared, growling, and snarling. With her heavy winter coat, she filled the live trap, which bounced around on the ground every time the animal moved.

"I first heard her about eight this morning," Mrs. Wright said. "I didn't call because it was so early."

Katie nodded politely. Early for her would have been around 4:00 a.m.

"Do you think she's diseased? Maybe tetanus?" The woman stayed several steps away, craning her neck to look at the crate. She stepped further back every time the metal contraption shuddered.

"Don't think so." Katie threw a piece of tarp over the trap to calm the animal. "Raccoons don't get tetanus." *But her babies are alone in the woods, and she's not happy about that.*

After getting Mrs. Wright to sign the collection chit for the town and telling her to call the house if she had another issue, Katie drove a quarter of a mile up Tudor Lane. There were no houses nearby, and the woods grew right up to the edge of the road. Katie pulled over. With the trap placed on the ground, she removed the tarp and sprang the release, then immediately vaulted back into her truck. The fat mama backed out of the wire enclosure, snorting and wuffing, before waddling back into the woods in the general direction of where she had been caught and probably where her kits were stashed.

"I'll probably see you again," Katie said as the sow disappeared.

* * *

She arrived back at Baldwins Feed and Hardware fifteen minutes late. Rushing up to the register, she relieved her boss, who was covering while Davidson was at lunch. Quickly offering an apology, Katie didn't get into the details with Stan about the animal issue. Fortunately, he understood that she was drowning financially and had accepted the fact her second job might take her away at times. There was always plenty for her to do to make up lost hours, especially during inclement weather. He wasn't a big fan of after-closing mopping.

When Davidson returned, Katie gave a whispered account of the raccoon event. He seemed relieved with her actions, and totally onboard with what she'd done by releasing the mama to return to her kits.

"As long as the trashcans are kept locked down tight, the critters won't be able to get in and spew a mess around the yard," Katie explained.

"Ix-nay," Davidson whispered. "Here comes Stan."

Their boss stopped right in front of the registers. Giving first Davidson, whose shoulders were bowed in guilt, then Katie, a hard look, he asked suspiciously, "What's going on?"

Katie rolled her eyes. "Late blooming testosterone."

* * *

Katie and Rick's evening was busier than usual. First, because she was handling Ruth's duties in the cattery, and second, because somehow, they had succeeded in depleting the supply of wood in the box next to the kitchen stove and also the stack outside near the kitchen door. Across the driveway were a couple of long rows of split wood covered by old sheets of tin weighted down by tires. She filled the wheelbarrow and hauled it across the drive, dumping out piles for Rick to stack or haul inside. The Tarn furnace in the basement was fed by a second row of stacks outside the bulkhead.

The cold snap Charlie had groused about hadn't abated. Katie's fingers and nose were chilled and red. Rick told her to go inside but leaving him to finish alone didn't feel right. She continued doggedly until he declared them done and all set for the next several days. When they were through, she took the truck out to Mrs. Ross's house to bait and reset the live trap.

"I can't believe nothing has gotten into the trap yet," Katie said to the homeowner when she was ready to leave.

"I've been keeping the dog on a leash and banging on the flue like you said," Mrs. Ross replied. "And heavens, you were right about the hissing. Even Roly took a step back."

Katie drove home, the heater making mechanical snaps, crackles, and pops, but emitting only cold wind.

"Good thing I took time to double up on socks," Katie muttered, hunching even further into her jacket.

Chapter Nine

The next morning was Katie's day off. After Rick left for work, she followed Ruth's instructions on the older woman's daily chores. She also needed to make a trip to Williston. Beauregard's General Store in town was good for a quick pick up, but full-scale shopping there was too expensive. Katie arrived at the larger Grand Union Grocery to find the aisles packed with women and preschoolers. Every way she turned, she encountered knots of bigs and littles whining, pleading, and sometimes threatening. If the families weren't bad enough, there were the socializers leaning on their carts and casually blocking the way.

"Who would have thought that doing nothing on your day off would be more exhausting than working all day?" she grumbled to Ruth when she got home. She was almost glad the next day, she would be back at work. As she stacked dry goods on the shelves in the pantry, she found herself drawn back to the window more than once. In the daylight, she could see across the still frozen landscape to the tall pines she believed marked the outer ring of the copse. She couldn't see any of the buildings at the Small Farm at all and wondered for the first time if lights at night would be visible.

I could drive around, she thought, *shouldn't take longer than an hour.*

She tapped her foot. Behind her, she could hear Ruth struggling in the kitchen and trying to be silent, but her canes rapped against the table.

"Get back on the couch. You're never going to heal," Katie called out.

No, there was too much to do here to just wander off on a fool's errand for an hour or so. But that didn't stop her from returning to the window though out the day.

At least the turkey vultures are gone, she thought, scanning the sky in the late afternoon.

* * *

Katie returned the next day from the feed store tired, but less stressed than from the previous day's journey to the devil's dungeon others called grocery shopping. She would have liked a quiet evening, but on Wednesdays, the knitting club met at the library. Its members were also the contingent of ladies that made up the Feral Cat Society board. When Katie had first taken Ruth to knitting club, she had sat quietly reading in the stacks until the meeting was finished and then brought Ruth home. Eventually, though, she had taken to wandering over to the church and helping Dorothea in the basement thrift store. The octogenarian who ran the church shop was a fountain of gossip. Katie was anxious to tap into what the crusty old woman had gleamed about the Surettes and the doings at the copse.

It was both a surprise and a relief when Ruth declared she did not feel comfortable attending. Then, at six o'clock, the kitchen barely cleared from their evening meal, and a knock sounded at the door. It was the first of several knitters. Apparently, the meeting had been moved to her own living room.

"Did you know the ladies would be coming over?" Katie asked, aghast that she had nothing prepared for the dessert and coffee offering.

"No." Ruth shook her head. Like Katie, she was unprepared, her gnarled fingers working the buttons to her robe closed beneath her chin.

"I told you I'd be dropping by," said Ellen, Dorothea's grandniece.

There was another knock, and the question of when she had been planning to come was never asked.

Arriving members brought snacks and casseroles for the family to enjoy later on. One bustling woman shooed Katie out of the kitchen, saying she was on the tea committee and had brought all they would need. Rick hightailed it down to the basement and his wood-building projects, leaving Katie to gather cats and put them to bed. Only Peanut, who slept with Ruth nightly, and elderly, gentle Sasha were left to wander among the guests.

Katie used the excuse she'd promised to help Dorothea that evening to leave before she was handed knitting needles and given a how-to lesson.

Once in the village, she drove down Route 116 in the glow of the six street lights on the southern end of the main street. Daylight was inching towards lasting until eight in the evening. She knew that by this time, Father Metevier would have crossed the parking lot to his home, finished his supper, and be enjoying a glass of wine with the radio tuned to a classical station, his fat house cat curled in his lap. He would never know she had been there or that he'd once again missed his chance to question her reluctance to join his flock.

A single sixty-watt bulb burned above the side door of the church, a circular metal shield above reflecting light downward. The glow didn't extend to where Katie had parked ten feet away. As she walked along the Saint Jude's outside wall, she looked up at the dark windows of the nave. The jewel-toned stained windowpanes lining the main floor didn't offer any luster in the dark. Without light shining through, the depictions of the Stations of the Cross were invisible. All that was offered was a more sinister message. Katie was relieved to see the warm yellow patches from the basement lights as she approached the entrance.

Her gloveless fingers adhered slightly to the frosty metal handle. She pulled them free with a little shiver before clattering down the steep staircase, heedless of the sign cautioning visitors to watch their step. Beyond the lower door, the space was chilly, with a heavy odor of damp walls and old clothing. Dorothea stood at the far end of the room behind the worktable, concentrating on a heaping pile of fabric.

"Evening, Dorothea!" Katie called out.

"You can't be any danged louder?" the octogenarian asked without looking up. She was a snarky, bitter soul who rarely had a kind word for anyone.

Where others found a hard, often sarcastic attitude, Katie had unearthed someone she didn't have to pretend to. Even if she didn't share her secrets, Dorothea took her as she came.

The door behind Katie opened again, and a woman came in, followed by a teenage boy of fifteen or so and two younger girls.

"Good evening," the woman said.

Katie hesitated at the look of the timid, washed-out appearance of beaten-down poverty. None of them were dressed for the weather. All looked like they could stand a hearty meal and a hot bath. Katie walked around a rack so she could observe them from the back without being seen herself. The woman and both girls wore cotton dresses, with the girls having on sagging tights and felt-lined snowmobile boots. The woman had neither stockings nor boots. Dirty orthopedic shoes and a black cloth coat were all that protected her from the icy drafts and slippery walking. Instead of jeans, the boy was wearing a pair of corduroy pants so old the wale had disappeared. The pant legs ended an inch above his lace-less sneakers, and instead of a coat, he had on a lined flannel shirt. He was the only one who appeared self-conscious. The woman was too exhausted, the girls excited and touching everything.

Dorothea looked them over. "Bags to your right, all you can get in, fifty cents a pound." After her spiel, she went back to sorting her pile. It was the same line she fed to all arrivals, regardless of the number of times they had come down the steps. Then, surprising Katie, she added, "One free coat. One free pair of shoes or boots each."

The woman pushed the boy towards the rack of button-down shirts and trousers. Clothing for smaller children was folded on a makeshift table with placards separating the areas by Girl or Boy and size number. The boy quickly gathered what he wanted, passed it off to the woman, and disappeared up the stairs.

Katie picked through the W, MED, 8-12 rack, looking for pants and a sweater warm enough to stave off the ongoing chill of Vermont spring. She always looked for things she could use before she settled down to helping Dorothea sort, label, and fold. Other customers came in, chatting among themselves, and went on their way with their purchases. It looked like it might be a busy evening, and Katie would rather question the elderly woman without curious ears standing nearby.

The shrill ring of the phone made Katie and everyone left in the room jump.

Dorothea answered it. "What?" she demanded without preamble. "Oh. Katie Took, it's for you." The old woman dropped the receiver on the wooden worktable, a move meant to alert the caller she wasn't happy with the interruption.

Father Metevier was calling from upstairs. Katie looked up at the ceiling. She had thought he would have no idea what was happening beyond his walls, but obviously, she was wrong.

A few weeks earlier, he had spoken to Katie about a young parishioner and a problem the boy had brought to him. Unsure how best to handle the situation, the Father had reached out to her. Katie's initial response had been no. She didn't want to be a member of the church and had enough problems. She was no counselor. Unfortunately, Ruth had been within hearing distance and volunteered Katie's assistance.

"It might be," Ruth had said later to Katie, "this young boy is having a problem someone as old as Father Metevier can't relate to. Think about what you went through when you were gone. The temptations, the…drugs, and all. Please, Katie, just listen, maybe help the Father out a little bit."

"Yes, Father?" she said with a defeated sigh.

"The young man is willing to sit down with you, Katie. I understand you are in the building. Would this be a good time?" Father Metevier asked.

You watched out your windows, you sly old fox. You knew I'd be here on knitting club night. "Okay, I'm on my way up."

A very few minutes later, Katie found herself seated midway down the length of the small church. The only other person there was the boy Father Metevier called Isaac. She wondered if his mother, who was still pawing through items in the thrift shop, knew where he was. Katie sat in the middle of the pew, against the center rib. The boy hung off the further edge of the same pew, trying to look cool, but with the appearance of an animal ready to flee.

At first, the only sound was the creaking of the old building. The sullen boy stared off, frowning at some distant point down the aisle. Katie watched his Adam's apple jerk up and down a couple of times. It would be up to her to start the conversation.

"Hello, my name is Katie. I'm a member absentee of this church." She waited a moment. That always worked at AA. Still no response. She decided to be more direct. "Let's start with the easy stuff. You brought your problem to Father Metevier. He doesn't usually ask for help, but I guess he thought this was beyond his scope, so I'm here as a sounding board if you want to unload. I won't offer advice unless you ask for it." She waited a few moments, but Isaac remained silent. "I understand this is strictly confidential. Believe me, I can do that. If you've changed your mind and you'd rather not talk to me, you can absolutely get up and walk away right now."

Isaac shuffled around in his seat. Katie thought he was about to run like a rabbit. Instead, he made a fist and brought it up to his chest, holding tight to something only he knew was there.

"It's not my problem," he said. "There was this thing I heard and kind of saw. I can't get rid of it because, I don't know, it's bad. Okay. It's just bad, and I know it is, and it's…" He stopped talking, fist pressing harder against his chest.

"And this thing is eating you up on the inside," Katie finished for him. "Maybe you're worried about your mother or your little sisters?"

His head snapped up. For the first time since he'd sat down, he looked at Katie.

"Hey, I don't know you," she said. "And you don't know me. But I've seen you in the thrift shop." She paused, and he leaned further away. "I lived on the run for almost nine years. When you do that, you learn to see everything and remember details. If you don't, you're as good as a dead junkie in a roadside ditch." She let that sink in, then added, "The ball is in your court. Tell me or don't. It's up to you."

"Isaac," he said.

Katie's eyes narrowed for a split second. She didn't tell him she already knew his name.

"We live over on the other side of Mechanicsville. My mom used to work at this place a little further on. Maybe actually in Richmond. It's a fat farm."

Katie's eyebrows went up. "Around here?" Even though she'd only been back in the area a short time, it seemed like she would have heard about the presence of any type of spa.

"Yeah, it's off the main road. If you turn onto Gil Anthony Ridge, you come to a set of stone gateposts. There's a sign for Corrapell Retreat. It's a place where rich people go to lose weight or get straight. My mom worked in the kitchen there. A lot of days when I didn't go to school, I'd go with her. I'd hang out, maybe help out a little, but I mostly poked around."

"Wait." Katie held up her hand. "Why didn't you go to school?"

"I've already been to over nine different ones," Isaac said. "I've never spent an entire year at one school. There doesn't seem to be any sense in going."

Katie hesitated. This kid was almost half her age, and yet, from the sound of it, even when she was still safe in Gram's house, he'd been tossed about like a windblown paper bag.

"Okay, so you just went to work with your mother, and nobody said anything?" She watched him closely, looking for a tell that would say he was fabricating. "Where were your sisters?"

"They go to school, then Connie, from next door, watches then till Mom and I get home. We don't have a car. We walked through the woods to get to the retreat. Mrs. Frances, she was the chef, she told me I should be in school, but she was also worried about my mother tramping through the woods alone, especially in the winter."

Katie wavered again. She wanted to ask how far they walked through the woods, and exactly how come there was no one else available to help them out.

"Anyway, we moved here over a year ago. Mom got hired right quick. She worked in the kitchen. The place was busy, full up. There was plenty to do. I didn't really work there. Sometimes, I just pitched in, and Mrs. Francis lets me have lunch as payment. Then Doctor Reveck came back full-time. He's a weird guy. Mom said there were some rumors about him, but I don't know what. Anyway, they weren't so busy anymore with the fat people. That's because they started taking in rehabs." Isaac shook his head. "Like, serious whack jobs."

Katie said nothing. She was breathing through her mouth, high in her chest. Her stomach felt crampy. Keeping her face calm was taking an effort.

"The wackos didn't stay long, either. A couple of them ran off and got busted. There weren't any guards or anything. So, there weren't a lot of patients, and Doctor and Mrs. Reveck started firing people. Well, like the regular people, then they had folks working when they were needed. My mom said they were from some agency. You never knew who was going to be there. Mrs. Frances left, and my mom got to have her job and be the head cook. I was still hanging around, but when the doctor and his wife were there, I had to hide out. Doctor Reveck made it real clear only authorized personnel were supposed to be in the building. I got really good at finding hiding places."

So far, Isaac's tale of woe hadn't hinted at anything hinky. Katie was starting to believe the boy, just like herself, was unhappy and frustrated, unable to find his place or maybe even dig out of poverty. And he certainly didn't want to go back to school. Katie was ready to stand up and brush her butt off to leave. She tried one last time to discover why Father Metevier wanted her to sit down with Isaac. Her time to question Dorothea this evening would soon be over. She needed to get back downstairs.

"You said your mother lost her job, so the owners must have fired her too," she said. "This sounds like a resort going the way of the dodo. It happens to a lot of places like that, I think."

"No!" Isaac said loudly, his frustration evident. "This isn't about the resort, or the workers, or even about my mom. It's about the people who are still there." Before Katie could speak, Isaac rushed on. "One of the best places to hide was in the patients' rooms. First, I was in the empty ones, but then they started locking the doors, so I had to go into the rooms where there were still people. It was okay because the people slept all the time. *All* the time. Well, except for breakfast and supper. They wake up; they go back to sleep. It's like they're dead."

Katie nodded but had no idea what he was talking about.

"Anyway, a little while ago, something happened to this woman. She had a fit or something. They locked the door. No one could go in for, like, two days. Then poof, she didn't need a dinner tray because she was gone. I didn't see her leave, and I was there every day."

Katie caught herself holding her breath. Her brain was clicking. She was connecting dots. Did Sheriff Lewis know about this place? Or the woman Isaac was talking about?

"And you think something bad happened to her?" Katie finally asked.

"Yeah. Like wicked bad. The same thing happened back after Valentine's Day. I remember because Mom had made cherry cupcakes for us to have as a treat. Only that time, the person who disappeared was this really fat dude. And he had bucks. I used to hide under his bed. One time, his arm was hanging down, and I spent all afternoon looking at this big fancy watch. His breathing got all funky. I went out into the hall and Wade was just coming in, he works there, taking care of the fatties. I told him the guy was, like, choking or something, and Wade went right down to the guy's room. I could hear Mrs. Reveck talking, so I went looking for a different hiding place. The next day, the guy was gone. I asked Wade what happened, and he told me to shut up. To forget it.

"Instead, I went down to the kitchen and told my mother. Mrs. Reveck came in while we were talking and sent me out of the building. I hid in the garage, waiting for Mom to get done for the day. She was all teary when she came out because they told her if I showed up there again or ran my mouth, she'd get fired. She can't get another job because we live too far out of town, and we don't have money to move. It didn't matter that I stayed away from the place. A week later, she got fired, anyway." Isaac stood up, pacing near the pew. Suddenly, he took off. Katie called out to him, but he hit the panic bar on the vestibule door and disappeared.

Katie sat there, thinking. She needed to talk to Isaac again. He was just a kid, and it was obvious he was hurting. She'd seen kids like Isaac while living in Illinois. They fell through the cracks of society. Not in school, from dysfunctional or failing families, sometimes like Isaac, too young to be the head of the household, but forced there because both parents were gone, or the only one left was too busy to guide their offspring. Too many times, she had seen teenage suicide. Just the thought made her heart pound hard in her chest.

I can't stand the thought he won't find somebody who'll listen and, I don't know, give up, she thought.

She spent a few more minutes trying to analyze the situation before realizing that when he'd run out, he could have gone anywhere. If the boy thought she, too, had failed him, bad things could happen. Was that why Father Metevier had drawn her into it? Because he was afraid for Isaac?

The kid nailed down the date of one disappearance as mid-February, but what about the woman? Katie thought as she hurried out the door and around to the entrance to the thrift shop.

Oh, Father Metevier, why didn't you ask somebody else? But in the next instant, she was thinking that if Isaac's mother had been warned to keep quiet about what Isaac saw, was either he or she in danger? And by extension, the two small girls. Looking around the parking lot for the boy, her thoughts took a twist. Maybe this is one time she should be talking to Sheriff Lewis.

* * *

When Katie got back downstairs to the thrift shop, Isaac was standing beside his mother. As Katie moved around the shop, the boy stayed the length of the floor away from her. Even though Katie wanted to talk with him or set up a time when she could, there was no way of knowing how much he had told his mother. It was a can of worms, and Katie wasn't ready to pry open. For his part, Isaac had no intention of approaching her and didn't make eye contact. For the next twenty minutes, he stuck close to his mother as she helped the little girls try on boots. Then, a car horn sounded outside.

"Ma," he said, "Mrs. Whitney is here. She's going to give us a ride home, remember?"

His mother stood in front of Dorothea's tin cash box, counting out her change to pay for the three bags of children's clothing. While she did so, Dorothea filled another bag with mittens, hats, scarves, a set of B-16 thermal underwear, and, lastly, a long W-L sweater.

"God knows," she said, shoving the bag at the boy. "We've got enough of this dang extra shit left over from the winter to line the road to Montpelier and back."

The entire family filed out, with everyone toting a bag and the girls already wearing their new, gently used jackets and boots. Katie put a bag of raggedy blankets she could use for the cats on the scales and laid her dollar down.

"I didn't hear you offering the special giveaway spiel to everybody, Dorothea. Or offering me a free jacket, either."

Dorothea threw Katie's money in the cash box, slamming the lid shut.

"I don't have a foggy danged clue what giveaway you're talking about," she said. "And it looks like you got a new coat for Christmas. Don't 'cha think it's about time to hang it up for the danged season?"

Katie smiled, running her hands down the three-quarter length of her quilted jacket. It was a definite step up from Gram's worn canvas barn coat. Without asking, she moved around the work table to assist Dorothea in the sorting. Ruth's friends would be out at the farmhouse for a while longer, working on their knitting projects and coming up with new ways to raise funds for the feral cat clinic.

Dorothea's grandniece, Ellen, was part of Ruth's group of friends and would be picking her elderly aunt up on the way home. Even though Katie was willing to discard her jacket, after a short time, she missed the knitted palm gloves she wore in the feed store. Even in the hottest part of the summer, the church basement was cool. Now with April showers melting snowbanks, it was damp as well as cold. Behind Katie and Dorothea was a small storage closet, filled to bursting with items to be sorted, boxes labeled for mending, buttons, zippers, and rags. They were never caught up.

"Dorothea," said Katie, "what do you know about the Surettes?" Direct was the best way to approach the old lady.

"Them people that live out of town? He's a Mennonite, but she ain't. Ugly as sin, both of them, so it's probably good they got no kids. I hear he's smart with a hammer and a saw, and a good worker, too. That's about all I got."

"Mm," Katie had been hoping for more. She remained silent, hoping the juices would run in Dorothea's memory and she'd add more. Time was passing.

"I'm going to take the box of clothing that needs buttons and the button box home," said Katie. "Ruth has to stay off her feet. Maybe she could get through some of it. Working would keep her busy and off her bad leg."

Dorothea huffed a large trash bag out of the closet, shrugging off Katie's help until heaving it up onto the table. The bag landed with a splat, the plastic splitting in multiple places.

"Look at these pants, will ya?" Dorothea said. "Fifty-four-inch waist and only a twenty-nine-inch inseam. That owner had to be one short and round fellow. Good quality clothes, but oh, my goodness. What a belly!"

Katie picked up the wool trousers, checking the insides. Dorothea was right. The wide inner waistband was lined and triple-stitched. The pockets were full and tacked down. And it looked as if the whole table now held clothing that belonged to the same individual. Two suits, several long-sleeve shirts, ties. Even a half-dozen pairs of boxers so big Katie could have fit into them twice over.

"Looks like the guy's entire wardrobe," she said.

"Danged old pisser probably kicked the bucket." Dorothea blew on her fingers. "I don't know about you, but I'm danged near frozen stiffer than a corpse in January."

"Well, it is April and raining," said Katie, a little abashed that an eighty-two-year-old would talk freely about corpses.

Outside, a car horn bleated two shorts and a long.

"That's Ellen. She's a little early, must be the driving is getting bad." Dorothea started gathering her own bags as Katie pulled on her coat. "Probably had to cut short the cats-in-a-crate meeting. Don't forget that box for Ruth. And don't worry about the open sign. Ellen will grab it when she comes in to help me lug all my danged shit out."

The avocado green phone hanging right behind Dorothea shrilled again.

"Dang near scared me to death! Twice in one night," the old woman barked into the handset without bothering to say hello or wait for the caller to identify themselves. Just as abruptly, she slammed the receiver back in place. "Father Metevier wants to see you before you go off." She waved Katie away.

Katie walked across the parking lot toward the rectory, the gravel beneath her feet rolling against itself. Dorothea had been right. There was already a light coating of ice. Father Metevier stood in the doorway, waiting with his cat, Boots, held firmly in his arms to keep the feline from escaping to the outdoors.

"Katie," the cleric said without preamble. "The young man you spoke with, he and his family are new to the congregation. I'm worried about their means."

Katie rolled back on her heels. She and the priest were of a height. His old gray eyes, surrounded by sagging pouches, were still bright and watchful. Father Metevier had been trying to get her to church on a regular basis since she'd returned. It wasn't working well for him. Still, the two were friends. He was gentle and witty. He made her laugh, but sometimes he got under her skin and made her care too much.

"What do you want me to do?" she asked, head tilted back, eyes half-closed.

"Now, that's no way to be thinking about it," Father Metevier chastised her. "The boy came to me troubled. I didn't know how to help him. You're such a smart girl, Katie. It's me that is asking what I can do to help him. You're closer to his age, and you've been out there in the world. He's like an old soul, and I don't believe it's right."

Standing in the old-fashioned kitchen with the man whose skin was as white as his cassock was black, she knew the meeting tonight wasn't a one-time deal. He was sucking her in, and even though she'd be angry with herself later, she was going to let him do it.

"Okay," she said with a sigh. "You might consider helping his mother find work. And maybe a food basket for the family? If you're thinking, a dime-a-dip or a fundraiser, you might want to run it by her before you talk to anyone else. I think they have a lot of pride. Other than that, let me think on it, see what I come up with, okay?"

"And you'll be sure to remember his story will be held in confidence?"

Right then, Katie knew Isaac hadn't told Father Metevier everything.

"You're asking a lot," she said with a smile. "You know, Sheriff Lewis and I are at odds. I don't need any more trouble with him." She turned to leave, hand on the knob, and paused. "This is a one-time deal, Father. I'm not looking to be your permanent confidante."

She left the rectory with Father Metevier grinning at his good fortune while Boots struggled to escape his tight grip.

Ellen and Dorothea were already gone. Katie sat in the dark, cranking the ignition on her truck. Once it had gone from sputtering to a rough idle, she made herself small, trying to stay warm until she knew the old Ford wouldn't stall. Eventually, she was confident the truck would continue to run and drove away.

Chapter Ten

Katie drove down Main Street, already chilled to the bone and not caring that if it had been warmer and people had their bedroom windows open, several would have complained about a careless hot rodder revving as she jumped from first gear to third. For Katie, it was a necessity. Second gear wouldn't be available until Rick and his mechanic friend Philip located second-hand parts.

Right about the time Katie decided to put both hands in the same mitten, she came up on Fire Lane 61, the last stretch to home. The Parentville/Charlotte Road wound off to the left, but Katie depressed the clutch, eased up on the gas, and shot the switchback turn. There was no way to make the curl back into the fire lane without downshifting to first.

By now, the fine, sleeting drizzle had picked up to heavier rainfall. Already the hill was glazed, and the back end of the pickup swayed from side to side up the grade. She was confident with what the truck could do, but there were other things that worried her. The knitters and cat ladies were making their way home, as were Isaac and his family. Would it be warm there? Was there enough food in the cupboards to fill their bellies?

It was a depressing thought, but she didn't take a moment to sink into that black mire. Her worries about the small family were connected directly to the woman in the copse. Who else would know? And what would Sheriff Lewis say if he heard she had started asking questions?

* * *

With a slam that could have broken the rusty hinges off the door, Katie exited the truck, catching herself against the fender as her foot slipped out from beneath her.

"Please tell me you got parts for the truck today," she asked Rick as she came through the front door and into the living room, unwinding her scarf as she went.

"Phil and I didn't find what we needed at the junkyard in Hardwick," he said, picking up his teacup and following her into the kitchen. "The owner called Barre. There's a small place there, so we drove over. 'Course, we had to pull the parts out of a junk truck ourselves. That took time."

Rick had a slow, comfortable way of speaking that drew the listener in. Ruth wasn't immune to it, and the older woman's head swiveled in his direction as she turned down the volume on Laverne and Shirley to listen while he spoke.

"Phil got parts for your Subaru, Katie, and a couple of other cars that he's got down at the garage. He'll be doing those first, though, and Irma's pickup after that. He said that once he's got your Illinois Subaru back on the road, he's got a buyer in the wings. After that, he'll let you know when to drop your truck off. If you get an animal call while your pickup is in the garage, you'll have to use mine. Any hoot, we were listening to the news, and the weather came on. There's another late and hard cold front coming in." He put the last bite of brownie in his mouth.

"Great," said Katie, surveying the empty dessert dish. She could use some chocolate right now.

Laverne's snorting laugh filled the room as the volume on the television went back up.

From the days of community style room sharing, the retired stagecoach hotel had large rooms with high ceilings and tall windows that rattled in the wind. The only heat was the wood-burning cookstove and the Tarn wood furnace Rick and his friends installed in the basement in the fall. Heat coming up the four-foot square grate kept the living room at about sixty-five degrees, if the grates to the second level stayed shut.

"There's already ice. We'll probably lose power. So, if it looks like it's going to be bad for a few days, maybe we should consider closing up the upstairs again," Rick said.

It was late. Katie didn't relish the idea of dismantling beds and bringing them downstairs, but if the power went off in the night, the blower on the furnace would stop.

"Okay," she said with a tired sigh. "I guess we better have at it."

"Hold on," said Rick, a grin on his face. "Phil and I stopped at the Army-Navy store, and I bought a couple of GI fold-up cots. Instead of bringing the beds down, we'll use these, temporary like. After the parts, I only had cash for two, but Ruth is probably going to be bunking on the sofa for at least a few more days."

Katie gave Rick an arched look. "You know, sleeping downstairs means you're going to end up sleeping with a cat."

"Yeah." He sighed. "It was a good run, keeping the bedroom door shut and most of the hairballs out. I'll hold out upstairs unless the power goes, then I guess I'll just have to man up."

He hung his head in dejection. Ruth giggled. Before she and Rick had started cohabiting, she never closed her bedroom door all the way, and if the felines didn't show up fast enough, she'd call them until they did. Now, any space not covered by knitting on the couch was a bedding spot for a feline. Even then, sometimes, it was shared.

Rick had suffered every time he had to sleep downstairs during the coldest parts of the winter. He just wasn't a cat person. It was one thing to have them in the house, another in his bedroom. But he was stoic and perceptive, and he loved Ruth enough to suffer this for her. Once he'd moved into the farmhouse full-time, it hadn't taken him long to realize what a job it was to hold down the amount of fur floating around the big rooms. That realization and the rising and falling numbers of the feline community had directed his Christmas shopping the prior year. In self-defense, he'd purchased two gifts tagged to be shared by both Katie and Ruth: an Electrolux vacuum cleaner and a case of baking soda. Both women had thought the high-tech and expensive Electrolux was an amazing gift. And the baking soda to be mixed with kitty litter, very practical.

As soon as Ruth uncoiled the vac cord every morning, all the cats except Peanut headed for the cattery. At nine months old, Peanut was almost full-sized, but his mannerisms were still those of a kitten. Katie had sewn a large pocket onto Ruth's apron because Peanut was forever trying to crawl inside the smaller one. Having suffered abuse as a baby, he was slower on the uptake than the other felines, and Ruth was his stanch protector.

Vacuuming and cleaning cat boxes weren't Ruth's only chores of the day. After a good wash, she would trudge down the slope to the Dean farm, assisting Grace with her goat cheese-and-soap cottage industry. The ladies lunched together, which made both Katie and Rick breathe easier. Ruth had been known to mess up her medication. Later, Ruth headed home to catch a quick nap. With no real income of her own except the minimal spousal beneficiary payout from social security, which she refused to let the government take from her, Ruth's time with Grace covered all of their dairy product costs and added a bit of jingle to the older woman's pocket. Now, because of Ruth's sprained knee, Katie and Rick handled her home chores, and Grace worked alone.

Sleet and hail tapped against the window glass. Katie stood at the door, barely able to make out their vehicles. By eleven, the small night light in the kitchen blinked out. There would be no going down the hill the next morning.

As they lay spread out around the living room, Katie told Ruth and Rick about her conversation with Dorothea and the funny-shaped clothes, but nothing about Isaac.

"You should have seen the shine on those leather wingtips," she said.

"That's odd, I don't remember anyone around town who was shaped like an inflatable clown punching bag and dressed like a Rockefeller," Rick said. "Ruth, do you know anyone like that from the village who passed away lately?"

"Be quiet," the drowsy response came back.

Wrapped in her cocoon of blankets with LG tucked in beside her and Old Tom lying on her hip, Katie smiled to herself.

And to think, I gave up being semi-homeless for this.

Twice in the night, she was awakened when Rick rose to fill the cookstove and again when he trotted down to the basement's depths to check that fill box as well. The dogs thumped their tails, but they also stayed in the warm bed they shared.

I should get up and help, she thought. But by the time Rick crawled back under the covers on his cot, she was asleep again.

Chapter Eleven

The sun shone brightly enough from the eastern horizon the next morning to make Katie squint as she looked off over the low meadow towards the village. But the wind was stiff and cold. Glancing over her shoulder, she saw Rick approaching with his work coat buttoned up to his neck and his ball cap pulled down to his eyes. Then she laughed.

"What's with the scarf?"

Rick had one of Ruth's hand-knitted scarves wrapped around his face from nose to neck. The long tassels blew out in the wind behind him.

"This kind of wind blows right through my skin and down to my toes," he said. "One time, I grew a beard to stave it off, but then I spent all my time picking food out in the summer and snot in the winter."

Katie made a face, but Raymond, who had pulled up on the John Deere with the snowplow attached, roared. "Same thing," he said. "I did the exact same thing."

"Double yuck," Katie said.

By noon time, Rick and his rebuilt Massey-Ferguson dinosaur tractor had sanded the drive around the house and down the hill. Robert Dean had shown up to help. With one man at the tractor controls and the other standing inside the bucket with a shovel, they got the job done in record time, allowing Katie to drive out to Baldwin's and report to work.

"I was a little late getting in this morning," Stan said, "and barely ahead of the customers. Good thing we still had half a pallet of rock salt left. But it's gone now, if anyone asks."

Davidson was a no-show, as were some of the other guys, but none of Baldwin's delivery trucks were going out. There was plenty of work for all who showed up. At one point in the afternoon, Katie left Stan at the register and went out to help in the feed shed. The man, Walt, was new to the job, which had been Katie's when she was a fresh hire.

"Come on, let's see if we can get you knowing where to find everything before Rick comes back to work tomorrow," she said.

"The old guy couldn't make it in?"

"Nah, it's his day off. Stan didn't call, so he didn't show."

She listened to Walt's rather pompous conversation for a while, knowing Rick would set him in place as soon as the guy opened his mouth around him for the first time. Even though Rick drove the local delivery truck now, the shed guys still looked at him as their supervisor. If Nate, who had lost his job to Rick after a DWI, had been able to get in from Saint George, he would have told the new guy to shut his yammer. Nate had learned his lesson, though. Word had it, he was a regular at the Sunday morning AA meetings at Woodman Hall, which, among other things, was used by the grange and the Masons.

After work, Katie drove out to the farm with heavy ice still sparkling along the way. She was grateful the days were getting longer, but sorrowful for the number of young trees that had bowed and broken during the storm.

Her first winter back in Vermont hadn't passed without raising issues she had never considered. She'd hoped to move Gram's cats along, get Ruth out living on her own, and leave the state in the dust. Instead, she still had nine of the original cats, one new permanent extra, and Ruth. She had also acquired Rick and Charlie, who worked for the town but were there for supper every other night, and Solomon. Walker, a wandering basset hound whose owner, Ida Jacobs, had passed gracefully in her sleep, moved in when no one else stepped forward. Then there was the cattery loan she was still just paying the interest on: a pig, chickens, geese, and friends she hadn't planned on. Just thinking about her complicated new life made her brain swirl.

Chapter Twelve

Over the next four days, the trap at the Ross house caught two cats, one twice. Neither was a feral, so Katie had to release them both and hope they would stay away. Mrs. Ross had graciously taken over baiting the trap, so Katie only needed to drive out when the trap needed to be emptied. Then, at two-forty-five in the morning, Mrs. Ross called again.

"Sorry to wake you, Katie. I don't know what's in the trap, but it's mad," the woman said. Her voice was shrill. The dog barked wildly in the background. Katie heard a man she presumed was Mr. Ross yell at the dog.

"I'll be right there," Katie said.

When she came downstairs after getting dressed, Rick was waiting, his heavy boots and jacket already on.

"Heard the phone," was all he said.

They rolled into the Ross' driveway about the same time the heater in his truck started working. Katie may have been still half-asleep, but when she saw the trap rolling around by itself on the frozen ground, she snapped awake.

"I hung a bell on it so we wouldn't be leaving an animal out in the freezing cold for hours or babies alone. As soon as we heard the bell start ringing, the trap rolled off the picnic table," said Mr. Ross. "That's one vicious raccoon."

"Yup," said Katie. She shined her flashlight along the ground toward the chimney. No fresh tracks showed in the small patch of snow at the base. That made her nervous. "You all should go in the house."

Mrs. Ross turned right away, but her husband hesitated.

"Really," said Katie. "We've got this. It would be better if you weren't right here."

After he left, she turned to Rick. "So, what do you think?"

"I think you should be glad I'm here." He went to the truck and returned a few minutes later. In his hand was his twenty-two-caliber pistol. "Let's have a little looksie."

The trap had rolled into one of the few remaining big snowdrifts. After using a couple of stout sticks to drag it into the driveway, they were able to see the snarling, fighting animal. The trap space was filled with dark brown fur and long, dangerous-looking claws hooked out of the metal mesh. A god-awful scream meant to scare them away did exactly that for Katie.

"Oh, crap," said Rick. "It's a fisher."

"Really?" Katie moved closer. The cage rocked, one end lifting off the ground.

"Get back." Rick grabbed her arm. "If that thing gets loose, it's going to come after you like no tomorrow. Fisher cats aren't afraid of people."

"How are we going to get it out?" Katie asked.

"I don't know, but we aren't doing it here. Go up to the house, tell the Ross family what's in the trap. We'll have to take it with us and bleach it out before any other animal will go near it again."

Dutifully, Katie went around to the kitchen door to inform the Rosses. Mr. Ross met her at the door, but his wife was across the room, a firm grip on the sparkling collar of her pet.

"I'll bring another trap out tomorrow," she said. "If that animal had ever got hold of your dog, you would have lost her."

Suddenly, in the still night, she heard the sharp snap of the twenty-two. Her back went rigid, but neither of the Rosses reacted, though Mr. Ross blinked hard a couple of times. By the time she ran around to the front of the house, the crate was in the truck bed, and Rick was sliding into the driver's seat.

Katie yanked open the passenger door. "What the heck?" she demanded.

"It was busting out," said Rick.

Sure enough, when they hauled the trap into the barn and pulled the forty-two-inch fisher out of the trap, the shut plate was partially detached on one side. The fisher was a magnificent-looking animal, the shape and color of a mink, but it also resembled in size a cat with small, rounded ears and a long, heavy tail. Fishers had a reputation of having no fear, not even of humans. They weren't a good match for a neighborhood with small children and pets.

"This one is really big," said Rick. "Look at those teeth and claws."

Katie nodded. The sight of those weapons would stop her from sleeping again that night. She didn't favor destroying any animal, but she wasn't about to let one rip her to shreds either.

Rick put the carcass in his wild animal freezer. "I'll drop this trap at Philip's tomorrow. He can weld the piece back into place."

Back at the house, once Rick was lying on his cot again, Katie silently made tea. Then she sat at the kitchen table, waiting for it to be time to go to work. *What next? A bear?* She wondered.

* * *

Rick scrambled eggs while Katie got ready for work. She was already dressed and had changed from tea to coffee.

"Ruth, when Gram had the animal control job, did she ever come up against anything dangerous?" asked Katie. "I was expecting cats, a few dogs, maybe a skunk or two. Not an animal so vicious it could rip me apart."

Rick handed Ruth a cup of coffee. She thanked him, and after a good, long sip, she said, "Well, there was the bobcat-in-the-cellar problem once. Critter squeezed in through a broken window where this old couple lived, but it couldn't get back out that way."

"That doesn't sound too bad," Katie said.

"It wouldn't have been, if there had been another way out other than the kitchen," Ruth said calmly.

Rick roared with laughter, and the fisher case was closed.

Chapter Thirteen

"It's bizarre," Katie told Dorothea when she joined the elderly woman after work in the basement of Saint Jude's. "Here I was all worried about heat costs and getting caught up on all of Gram's bills, and to be honest, the weather feels like the deal breaker."

Every time the door opened, Katie looked up, hoping to see Isaac and his family. She had come down to the thrift shop specifically for that reason. Dorothea was starting to look at her funny.

Dorothea dropped another stack of ironing at Katie's elbow. "I'm thinking if I were danged near to frozen and couldn't cook supper, things would get pretty ugly."

Katie pulled the long-sleeved blouse off the ironing board and reached for a hanger. Dorothea might be eighty-plus years old, but she was the final voice at the St. Jude's thrift, and she had declared the place wasn't a junk shop. Everything offered to those in need had to be clean, mended, and, if called for, pressed.

Having at one time mentioned ironing was therapeutic, Katie found herself facing the ironing board more often than she liked. She would never confess that besides spending time with the sour-faced woman she could be honest with, she felt more useful being able to work in the basement instead of stuck in a pew upstairs while services droned on. Ruth was just happy Katie was in the church building. Katie's explanation about being fine with all the kneeling and standing, but not with the general ritual she questioned the validity of, hadn't cut her any slack.

"So, what else has got your hair tied up in a knot?" Dorothea interrupted

Katie's silent pondering.

Katie laughed. "Well, I think the roughest part is the cats. I never had any until I came here. Some of them, like Old Tom, take a lot of work, and I didn't understand the rules."

The hours she spent sitting on the pipe railing surrounding the family boneyard and the time spent talking to the spirits hovering there weren't the concern of anybody else.

"Good thing you had Ruth to spell all them cat rules out for you."

"Actually, Ruth never said a word." Katie snapped a man's blue-checked shirt onto the ironing board. "Doctor Veronica, the veterinarian, stopped in a couple of weeks after Christmas to check on the puppies and kittens that needed shots and spaying or neutering before going up for adoption. She had a list of people looking for puppies, which was cool, and she also gave us a few bags of donated cat food that had been dropped off at the clinic. Since the bags were opened, the clinic can't use them. Anyway, before talking to Doctor Ronnie, I was down in the cellar with a spray bottle of bleach wash and a box of baking soda cleaning up after Old Tom. A lot."

"Isn't that danged old sod potty trained?"

"Yeah, but he's an old guy with outdoor habits, so he snuck down to scent-mark. Rick had a blooming fit. Old Tom is responsible for the house rule that no cats get below stairs."

"So, that was the important message the vet dropped on you? Keep the cats out?" Dorothea cackled at her own joke.

"No, I hadn't been using the crates in the cattery. I just let them roam. The vet explained the cats should be housed there and let out on a schedule. Cats nap for hours and don't really notice if they're doing their business shut in a crate, I guess." Katie pursed her lips. "I know it sounds weird, but it keeps them more houseable when they're out."

Just then, the sound of footsteps echoed down through the ceiling. Mass was over. In a few minutes, people would be downstairs looking for items they needed or treasures they hadn't expected to find.

"Keep an eye on that jewelry," said Dorothea. "There's been some light-fingered Lulu helping herself lately."

Reba and Jesse Holland, friends of Dorothea's and known gossips, arrived to help out, so Katie kept plugging away at the ironing. To her delight, one customer selected two house dresses from the unpressed stack.

There were always a few people who were not seen at Mass, but still came in to shop in the thrift store. A little girl giggled, and Katie looked up to see Isaac's mother and two small daughters headed toward the children's section. Dorothea whispered the woman's name was Helen O'Brien. Katie could see the church chit in the bigger girl's hand. The paper receipts were passed out to town residents in times of hardship. If Mrs. O'Brien had one, then she had been to talk to the town clerk about assistance.

Though Isaac had been with them before, today, he was nowhere to be seen. The three of them looked frozen solid. Though it was a sunny spring day, it was still cold and raw. One of the little girls didn't have on her new gently used boots. Katie watched them for several minutes while she continued to iron. Then, in the guise of straightening out the display, sidled up to one of the children.

"Where are your boots, honey?" She folded a red sweater while smiling at the girl.

The child watched the garment become a neat, rectangular package. "I left them at school."

The mother was near the household items now, running her hand slowly over a quilted blanket. Katie took a chance and approached her.

"Hi," she said. "I've seen you here before." Katie smiled, feigning confusion. "You're Isaac's mother, right? Mrs…"

"O'Brien," The woman smiled. "Yes. How do you know Isaac?"

"I don't, really," Katie said. "I've seen him here a couple of times, that's all."

She chewed on her lip, unsure if she should admit to talking to him on his previous visit.

Mrs. O'Brien walked away from the bedding, her few purchases in hand. Suddenly, she seemed nervous. "He's a good boy," she whispered defensively over her shoulder, as though she were worried rumors might be following her son. "He's just at that confused age."

By this time, they were all standing across from Dorothea, and Katie mouthed over the woman's head, *Lost job*. Then she said aloud, "I heard you live out on the Richmond Road, and you've been having some car trouble. I'm headed out that way in about twenty minutes. Would you like a ride?"

Katie could tell Mrs. O'Brien was on the edge of saying no, but right on cue, Dorothea cut in.

"Well, that'll be danged convenient. I was just about to offer these little whips one of them big old teddy bears we can't get rid of. They'd never be able to lug 'em that far. You youngsters pick out one each, 'cause if not, they go for dogs to shred up." The old woman's eyes crinkled at the little girls' happy yips.

"Really, we couldn't," Mrs. O'Brien protested.

"Pshaw, you'd break an old lady's heart? Here, and I gotta go now to hang up posters 'cause Father Metevier has to find someone to come in twice a week or so and clean his danged house."

Mrs. O'Brien's head snapped up. She took a quick look over her shoulder in the direction of the rectory, then said, "All right. But that's all. No more freebies. I would gladly accept a ride. It's only about three miles, but it is really cold. Thank you. I have to stop over at the grocery store, if you don't mind?"

"I'll pick you up there in half an hour," said Katie.

The girls picked out their bears. Katie offered to put them in her car while Mrs. O'Brien and her girls went over to the grocery store. The three headed up the stairs, with Dorothea following right behind them to the bottom step. A moment later, the old woman came thumping back across the floor. "Dang. Dang. Dang."

Katie jumped back, out of the way. Alarm on her face.

Ripping the telephone receiver off the hook, Dorothea dialed, then yelled into the phone, "I quit! There's a woman coming to the door right now. Name's O'Brien. Hire her. No, listen to me. I'm telling you to do it." Then, she unceremoniously banged the receiver back onto the chrome hook.

"And?" asked Katie, eyebrow cocked.

"I've been cleaning his danged toilet since Ida Jacobs passed. I'm tired of it."

Katie's smile grew, but before she could utter a single word, Dorothea jumped to another subject. "Now that you've done your goody-two-shoes bit for today, what'cha going to do about the guy that found the stiff in your backyard?"

"That's a nasty way to speak of the dead, and it wasn't my backyard," Katie retorted. "I don't know anything about it other than it was a woman. And if you're talking about Amos Surette, he's not my problem. I don't even know him and have no reason to be involved."

"See? You know who he is." Dorothea snapped a sheet open, calmly refolding Katie's haphazard work.

Katie ignored Dorothea's subtle hint her work was sub-standard.

"I know *of* him, but I don't really know him."

Dorothea cackled again, then she leaned in, gossip sliding off her tongue.

"Did you know that your buddy, Sheriff Lewis, has questioned him three times about the stiff? Twice at the sheriff's office?" With a superior sniff, the old woman went back to standing on the grain bags behind the counter that kept her boot-clad feet off the cold floor.

Katie watched her go. Was this just idle gossip, or something Dorothea felt she should know? The thrift store director had said before she knew practically nothing about the Surettes. This sounded like somebody was talking. But who, or maybe, why?

* * *

An hour later, Katie dropped Mrs. O'Brien and Sophia and Marcie off in front of their trailer. As the younger girl turned away, Katie handed the child the bag Dorothea had filled with the quilted blanket.

"Shh," Katie said, waving Sophia away. "Mrs. O'Brien? If you decide to take Father Metevier's job offer, you can talk to the school bus driver. He might let you ride in with him on the days you go. The driver who goes by our road hauls Ruth sometimes."

Before the woman could answer or notice the large brown paper bag, Katie was in first gear, skipping over to third and roaring away. She had to get home to get the bread she had left, doing a slow rise in the unheated pantry into the oven. Instead of driving right home to put together the big Sunday dinner she, Ruth, Rick, and usually Charlie would sit down to at three, she turned right onto the Shelburne Road, and, four miles later, left into the narrow O'Neill Road.

She didn't go far, there was no need, after all this was her property. Out of the car, she went directly to the first fluttering piece of colored ribbon Sheriff Lewis had left. One sharp tug and the thin strip separated from the tree.

"It's time these came down," she said to any forest animal who might be listening. Or any ghost who hovered over the site. When all the pieces were collected and shoved into her back pocket, she pulled out a disposable Kodak camera. It would take twelve pictures. The first five were of the tripod track she and Rick had found. After making sure it was again covered safe from trampling hooves or paws, Katie used the rest of the film standing in different spots around the copse. Sometime in the next few days, she'd have to swing over and drop the camera off at the Rexall in Williston. They would send it out for developing.

I'll need two sets, Katie thought, walking back toward her truck.

Hand on the door handle, she paused, looking over the cow pasture that edged the copse. She could just make out the top corner of the Surettes' small barn. So close. She chewed the inside of her upper lip, knowing she was going to have a talk with Amos.

A car passed on the Shelburne Road and slowed down. Was it because of the corner, or had the driver wondered what she was doing there? Moving quickly, she backed out and headed toward US Route 116. Sheriff Lewis had a lot of friends. Once before, one of them had told him what she was up to, hopefully not today.

Chapter Fourteen

"I need some fresh air," Ruth said after bumping her beau out of the way with her walker. "I'm about to do injury to the two of you."

Not only had Rick and his buddies uncovered a plethora of canes, crutches, and walking sticks in Grandma Irma's yard sale hoard in the barn, but friends from the knitting group and Feral Cat Society had been dropping in and dumping more off. One item was a metal walker that allowed Ruth to stand and move around in a bump-and-thump manner. After the first few tails got pinned under the legs of the walker, both the cats and Solomon gave the elderly woman a wide berth. Outside, it was clear but crisp. Inside, the smell of freshly baked bread had Rick lingering in the kitchen.

Dutifully, Katie assisted her friend into the cab of the pickup and threw the walker into the back where it shared space with Katie's collection of live traps.

Their time in the general store was not taken up so much with shopping as with Ruth meandering the aisles and chatting with town folk. Katie trailed behind, eventually resorting to shushing Ruth up every few minutes. After her run-in with Christopher Beauregard the previous fall and then her accusation he had killed his brother, Ruth's husband, the store wasn't a place Katie wanted to linger. There was gossip new owners would be taking over, but currently employees were still smarting from the Christmas Eve arrest of Christopher. A trial date was still pending.

"You don't need to talk to everyone you run into," Katie whispered into the older woman's ear. Again.

Coming straight toward them, her own plastic shopping basket in hand, was Monique Surette. Katie was about to say hello when her eyes landed on the slightly rounded bump protruding from the other woman's belly. Her jaw dropped. Monique and Amos were not young people. At least Katie didn't think so, and she was sure there hadn't been any local gossip about a new baby coming to town.

Is she pregnant? Katie wondered. Before she could say a word, Monique spoke up.

"Ssh, don't say a word. It's bad luck." She blushed. "I've lost two before. I won't lose this one."

Ruth had just turned from saying hello to Eugenie, a store clerk. "Oh, my goodness. Look at you. Wait until you see all the adorable teeny things we have at the thrift store!"

"No," said Monique, backing slightly. "Don't raise the black luck."

"What bad luck?" Katie was thoroughly confused.

"Certain people," said Ruth quietly, so no one standing nearby could eavesdrop, "believe it's bad luck to, ah, identify certain physical changes a woman might go through. The procuring of, ah, goods or accessories, also should be avoided." She looked at Monique. "Am I pretty close, Monique?"

"Yes." The woman immediately relaxed. "I've been avoiding going out, but Amos is working afar this weekend, and we need a few things."

Amos and Monique's only vehicle was a faded blue Dodge pickup truck. If Amos was working out of town, chances were that's where the truck was.

"So, you walked all the way into town? That must be three miles one way. Are you almost done shopping? We'll give you a ride home. Won't we, Katie?" said Ruth.

"That's okay. I'm really fine," Monique protested.

"Nonsense, we're practically going right past the Small Farm. It will be our pleasure. Let's move along, Katie."

Katie, who had been trying to hustle Ruth out of the store only moments before, gave her a bemused smile. "Yes, ma'am."

There was no way, unless they drove through the LaPlatte Brook, that the Small Farm was on their way home. And though Katie tried to avoid mixing with people from the village. It was chilly outside, and even if Monique had cut across the farmlands, that was quite a hike for a pregnant woman.

A few minutes later, they pulled up close to the back steps of the farmhouse. "Would you care to come in for tea?" Monique asked.

It was time for dinner, and Katie was about to say no thank you, but Ruth, seated on the outside where there was more room for her Ace-bandage-wrapped knee, spoke louder. "That would be lovely."

Both Katie and Ruth sniffed appreciatively when Monique put the teapot on the table. "I blend it myself," she said.

Katie narrowed her eyes suspiciously, bringing a laugh from their hostess.

"Relax. It's rose hips and herbs, no weed. Amos won't abide anything stronger than bark beer."

Katie felt herself blush at the thought Monique had read her mind. She reached for a meringue hoping her thought that the Surettes might be doping hippies wasn't as easily discernible to her hostess. The tea was actually quite good, as were the meringue swirls that Monique served on a piece of Impressionware glass.

"Isn't it pretty?" she asked. "Amos found it at the dump in Williston. He brought back several boxes. I guess somebody must have been cleaning out an old house and didn't want the stuff."

She went on to explain Amos was a master carpenter specializing in the restoration of old buildings and barns.

"He always says there are so many going to wreck and ruin because no one wants to take on the work," said Monique. "His family wanted him to do things their way, building their houses, making furniture, but his dream was to wander the land like Johnny Appleseed, making what was wrong right. You know what I mean? But instead of planting apple trees, he wants to fix all those beautiful old barns." Flushed with pride, she offered the plate of meringues again.

Katie gazed around the room over the rim of her China teacup. Monique would have gotten along just fine with Irma. The house was practically barren of furniture, but filled cardboard boxes lined the walls.

Ruth chatted about outstanding dump finds with her budding new friend. At a break in the conversation, Monique, who had been nervously twisting the hem of her skirt, said, "I want to thank you ladies for being so nice." The tip of her nose and cheekbones pinked up. "Since Amos found that poor woman in the woods, people have been kind of standoffish toward us. I understand, I really do. But Amos has been working over near Rutland, so his days away from home are long. Every time he comes home, it seems Sheriff Lewis has more questions to ask."

"You must be lonely," Ruth said quietly.

"A little. The worst thing is Amos was just starting to come back to his family, you know? That's probably best left to the side of the road now."

"He doesn't get on with his kin?" Ruth asked.

Katie wanted to kick her. It was none of Ruth's business what was happening in the Surrettes' private life. She didn't want to get tangled in it, but Ruth seemed to be ready to.

"No. He wanted to go to this special school upstate to train with a vintage architectural refurbisher. His family wanted him to do it the old way, among his people. They're Mennonites. But Amos refused. Then there's me. For a long time, they didn't recognize us at all. That's the way it is with them. Once you're shunned, you just don't exist. Something changed when his mom got sick. Now it's like we are people they know vaguely, but not family. Amos is willing to accept that for now." Monique's voice faded off.

"You wait and see. When they catch the person responsible, and Lewis has to apologize to Amos, his people will be just fine." Ruth patted the young woman's hand.

Katie wanted to shove Ruth's arms in her coat and drag her out the door, but at the same time she heard the lonely need in Monique's voice and felt herself going soft.

* * *

"Well, you made quite an impression on Monique being chummy and all," Katie said as they drove back up the O'Neil Road, through the village, and along the other side of the LaPlatte Brook to Fire Lane 61 toward home.

"Poor woman." Ruth shook her head. "That was a long way to walk for three items. And having lost babies before, she should have been sitting in her living room with a book and her feet up."

Katie agreed. She had heard the gossip swirling around the breakroom about Amos being a person of interest, and she knew Lewis. If he believed for even a moment he had the guilty person, he'd stop looking and put everything into building his case. It was a discouraging thought. Unbidden bits of what she'd heard gathered in her head, weighing against each other, with the irrelevant ones filtering out. When she realized what she was doing, Katie shook her head, trying to dislodge it all.

As she made the right turn onto Fire Lane 61, she looked off over Ruth's head to the old one-room schoolhouse. Her poppa had gone to school there. The building sat on the lower corner of the family farm. Abandoned since the old man's death, it had become overgrown with sumac and maple saplings. Irma had applied for a grant through a state-run historical group for repairs, and now the small building had a new roof, and the twelve-pane windows were whole. Rick and his cohorts had done the work and cut out the brush. For weeks, Ruth had sorted, tagged, and moved Irma's collection of dump finds and yard sale giveaways down the hill. Newly constructed sandwich signs Rick had knocked together with scraps from the dump leaned against the front, ready to line the road and beckon in customers for the occasional weekend sale.

Ruth sighed. She was also looking toward the building. "Well, I guess the grand opening next Saturday will have to be put off. Such a shame. We hung out so many notices all over the county."

"I'm sorry, Ruth," Katie said. "But there's no electricity, no plumbing, and you can't walk down here. It will have to wait."

"I know." Ruth sighed again. "I sure wouldn't be able to do it alone."

There was something in Ruth's tone—not sorrow, maybe speculation— that had Katie turning to look again at the other woman's silhouette. She couldn't be sure, but there was a pensive gleam in Ruth's eyes like she was speculating on a new ending. Then they were over the hill, and it was time to feed the cats and make supper. Charlie was already there and waiting at the door.

Chapter Fifteen

Early in the morning, before Katie and Rick pulled on their coats to leave for Baldwins, the telephone rang. Katie picked up the receiver, expecting the inevitable call to a wild critter invasion of coveted human space. Instead, she spoke to Father Metevier. It seemed Mrs. O'Brien had come to clean the previous afternoon, bringing her brood at the kindly cleric's invitation for a chili fest.

"The boy was here, Katie." Father Metevier sounded sad and greatly concerned. "He is still deeply troubled. It's all written on his face. Mrs. O'Brien confessed she didn't know what was ailing him. She's afraid he's involved in drugs. Perhaps you should have another word with him?"

"If I can get him alone, I'll see what I can do," Katie said. Her and Isaac's paths would be unlikely to cross under normal circumstances. But that didn't mean she wasn't affected by Father Metevier's concerns. He was a good man, and she liked him. She also knew this was his way of getting her involved with the rest of the people in his congregation, something he believed she needed.

During a weak moment somewhere in the last year and a half, she had confessed to him that her time away from Parentville had not been a glorious, sun-filled vacation. There had been black places, but she had survived. Now, he called forth the memories of evils she had crucified to stop Isaac from going down the same path.

* * *

Not once during the early part of her shift did Katie offer a smile to anyone, not even to her customers. Isaac's secret lit her personal paranoia. It was a niggly little worm infesting her every moment. Because it was foremost in her thoughts, she felt as if there were a glowing neon light on her forehead, telling others she was delving into something that wasn't her business.

Then, without warning, or a conscious thought on her part, her morose jumped the tracks landing in front of a different roaring engine.

Katie hadn't made any secret about not wanting to stay in Parentville. She'd left once, returned after Gram's death, ready to liquidate the property and leave again. When faced with the injustice of her grandmother's murder, she stayed. But had erected walls around herself.

She had become an expert in closing the shutters in her mind and to see the customers as two-dimensional paper dolls. It had been like that when she was stoned or drunk, others had moved in her peripheral like shadows, with no substance. Now, it was a habit. The picture of Isaac, angry and afraid, hugging the end of the church pew, was different. He was a kid in a small town. His experiences were limited as hers had been. There was a gnawing tempest deep in her gut that made her worry he would end up sleeping on anybody's sofa, trading whatever he had for his addiction. In the end, either failing to survive or, as she had, stumbling on one person willing to reach out and pull him out of the mire. But would he recognize the chance to grasp the gold ring?

She'd gotten cynical after her pre-Christmas overnight stay in the hoosegow. That time, she got in Christopher Beauregard's face, an established businessman and solid member of the community. He'd fought back, then convinced the cops he was the victim. Sheriff Lewis had hauled her away in cuffs.

She felt her entire body flush.

"I'll be right back," she told Davidson, headed toward the restroom. Instead, she stepped outside and stood in the shade beyond the loading platform, head against the dusty clapboards, pressing vomit back down.

For god's sake, she thought. *It isn't like you never spent nights in the drunk tank in Illinois once in a while, and one time over a weekend.*

Though disgusting, the stays were forgotten shortly after she'd been sprung. This last time, here in Vermont, had been different. Though she had gone home to the comfort of her makeshift family, by New Year's, the glow of that homecoming was gone. People looked at her differently. There were days she could suppress the hard edge of shame. This wasn't one of them.

Things—no, people—around her had changed. This deal with Isaac brought it all back to the forefront. Once again, she felt herself suspect, maybe even alienated in a place where before she had been invisible. It had been stupid to ask questions about the Beauregard family business and to confront Christopher. Even though she was right, and Ruth was proven innocent of killing her husband, George Beauregard, the old woman didn't move on with Rick to their happily ever after. Ruth accepted Rick's ring with its sparkly little diamond and his pledge of forever more. Then, time had stopped. No date was set. They hadn't moved on.

Would it be like that with Isaac? She'd go charging in like Joan of Arc, and in the aftermath, she would not be remembered as a helping hand, but as a snoopy outsider.

Katie headed back into the store. She'd been outside a long time. Stan was running her register, an eyebrow cocked at her mumbled apology. Davidson was oblivious to anything but what was right in front of him.

Her fragile ego took another dip at the question in Stan's look. He was one of the people who knew too much about what was inside of her, and more than Father Metevier, Stan was privy to the physical world problems she faced.

Offering a paper smile, Katie motioned the next customer forward. Work was her salvation right now. If she was busy enough, everything else got locked up tight, out of her mind and head. But not today. Even as words floated back and forth between Katie and her customer, a part of her brain checked off all the other crap that kept her stomach roiling.

When Stan left the main building for a conversation with one of the guys in the feed shed, Katie darted into his office and dialed the phone.

"Yes," said Father Metevier, "Mrs. O'Brien is here. But not Isaac, nor the wee ones. It's a school day."

Katie agreed and raced back to her spot, startling both Davidson and the next customer when her voice shrilled. "Step over. I'm right here to help you."

Stan may not have noticed as he walked in, but the customer dropped his purchases on the counter and took a careful step backward.

On her lunch break, she drove out to the derelict trailer park hidden in the woods where the O'Briens rented a rusty mobile home. It looked bleak and dismal from the car and not much better when she stood on the soft, rotting wooden steps. No one answered her knock. She dared turn the knob and found the door locked.

"Where are you, Isaac?" she asked herself on the return trip, which took her right by CVS, the high school.

If she pulled into the lot and asked at the desk, Katie knew no one would answer her questions. Isaac said he didn't often go to school. But it was cold. He wasn't at home, and he wasn't with his mother. Where else would he be? Who would know?

* * *

Katie slid into place right on time. Davidson grinned at her.

"Ha! The way you peeled out of the driveway, I figured you were gone on an animal call and would've bet you weren't back on time," he said.

Katie laughed. "Well, you would have lost that bet!"

Davidson had been neatening up the counter when she came in. He was kind of finicky about that, having everything right where it went. Katie was more casual. She watched him, long fingers making straight lines of all the impulse items, narrow shoulders up around his ears while he concentrated. He was so young.

"Davidson." Katie took to mimicking what the young man was doing, going so far as to round the front of the counter so that she was facing him. "You've only been out of high school for a couple of years, right? What do all you young guys do around here? You know? Where do you hang out?"

She took a quick peek. He was still shuffling mousetraps, not staring at her suspiciously.

"Well, I don't really live in Parentville," he said. "We're in Richmond."

Katie nodded, not interrupting.

"If you're a jock, the high school gym, I guess." He lifted his head, looking out through the big plate-glass windows. "If you have a car and access to booze, there's a place on the Mechanicsville Road behind the cemetery." He shot her a quick look, face slightly blushed. "I mean, I've never been there, but I've heard of it."

"But if you don't have a car?" Katie's voice was soft.

"At your friend's house, I suspect." He looked uncomfortable and picked up an empty box. "Storeroom," he mumbled and was gone.

Katie realized Davidson couldn't answer her question because, like Isaac, he hadn't had friends. No wonder he tried so hard to fit in here. Suddenly sorrowful, she realized she'd just reminded the tall, gangly youth of something he was probably trying to forget.

"Damn, my big mouth," she cussed under her breath.

When Davidson returned, the laughing mannerisms she had seen earlier were gone. He was friendly, but not open. She knew to give him time and hoped he'd forgive her.

Chapter Sixteen

"Must have been a slow weekend for news."

Stan dropped the local section of the Burlington Free Press on the counter in front of Katie. Just below the fold was a black-and-white photo of a familiar stand of trees and a caption leading into a tale of how the hunt for two lost little boys had culminated with the discovery of the remains of a mysterious woman. There was no sly hint of nefarious acts or outlandish speculation. What had been available as facts at the time of the event was all that was known.

Katie rolled her eyes. Looking up, she saw impatience in her next customer. The article, lost on page five, was just a reminder of what had happened, a filler for an empty space, but not something everyone would notice. If she allowed Stan's words to chigger under her skin and fester, it was going to be a long day.

When business slowed down, Katie drifted into the break area. The newspaper was lying on the table. She flipped the pages until she came to page five and read the story again. This time, she got as far as the second paragraph where the report stated Sheriff Lewis had commented the unknown female victim was five foot eight inches tall, Caucasian, with light brown hair and brown eyes. No sketch was available. Katie knew why, she'd seen the photo with the scavenger damage. The report posted a telephone number for anyone who had information. It was not the four eight two exchange of Parentville.

Probably some central office for the sheriff's department, Katie mused.

She searched the bulletin board for notices of lost cats or dogs that might come her way. There was a faded notice by the management of Gibson, Inc., owners of Corrapell Retreat, seeking part-time employees. That was where Mrs. O'Brien had been working and, according to Isaac, where he had seen something bad go down. She read the notice a second time. The message told job seekers that applications and return envelopes were available at the local library. As she returned to her register, she considered that if she showed up with an application in her hand, she'd at least get to see the inside of this place she hadn't even known existed. Maybe she could even get a tour. It wasn't a lot, but it might help her understand where Isaac was coming from.

Outside the window, Katie saw Davidson leaning against his car, eating a sandwich, his head bobbing to the car's radio. He didn't have a care in the world. Exactly the way it should be for a young man just getting started in life. Again, the picture stamped on her retina came up. Isaac, also ready to venture forth, and yet, unable to release his grip on the end of a church pew. A half-grown boy who had seen something frightening enough to take him to Father Metevier.

* * *

On her lunch break, Katie took a little ride. At the junction of Tudor Lane and Richmond Road, where she checked the trap in Mrs. Wright's yard, she hesitated for a moment, then took a left. Fifteen minutes later, she drove past the Welcome to Richmond sign. She knew she had driven too far and turned around, driving slower and searching. A small street sign indicated Gil Anthony Ridge Road and, on the left of the narrow byway, the first of a small group of mobile homes. These were the same trailers where Isaac and his family resided. Katie was slightly vexed with herself as she hadn't noticed the street sign when she'd brought the O'Brien's home.

"Well, knowing that would have saved me ten minutes," she growled to herself.

Further up, she came to a well-tended drive with brick gateposts on either side. There was no gate to be seen, but a neat white sign identified the property as Corrapell Retreat.

When Katie turned onto the long, snaking drive for Corrapell, she let the car idle to a stop. From here, she could see the main building and one long wing. On the other side, only the tip of another wing was visible. She realized the building had a central heart, with four arms stretching out like directional arms on a compass.

Interesting, she thought, and drove away. It was time to get back to work. She wondered if she was the only one who didn't know this sprawling structure was hidden back in the woods.

* * *

Ruth was putting supper on the table when Katie got home that evening. There was leftover corn chowder with sandwiches of fried venison and grilled onions.

"Where'd you get hung up?" Rick asked.

"I had to stop at the library and fill out an application," Katie said.

Rick and Ruth both looked at her expectantly.

"There was a notice on the corkboard at work. The spa, over near the Richmond line, is hiring. I stopped in, and Charlene told me to call the lady to see if they were still looking."

"You have a job," said Rick, setting his spoon down carefully on the table. "You also have an agreement with Stan."

"Relax," said Katie. "They are only hiring part-time, overnight." Before she lost her nerve, she added. "I'm going to work Monday and Saturday nights. I have the following day off from the feed store, and this is temporary."

"But why are you doing this?" asked Rick.

"First, I could use the money," said Katie, nodding to the bill box sitting on top of the refrigerator and the collection of labeled envelopes taped to the side. "And secondly, I'm not doing anything else right now. Things are slowing down with the town. I'm looking at only a few weeks, maybe. But believe me, if it gets to be a strain, I am so out of there."

Ruth made a disparaging noise. Before she could speak up, Katie asked,

"What do you know about this place? It's like a spa gone fat farm."

"I've never even heard of it," Ruth admitted.

"Been there a while." Rick took another bite. "They don't mix much. Out-of-town owners, out-of-state clientele." He shrugged. "That's about all I've got."

Katie took a few bites before the conversation resumed.

"You're sure this is only for a few weeks?" Ruth asked.

"Yeah, if that. I mean, if I walk in and somebody hands me a dirty bedpan, I'm turning around and walking right back out."

Rick nodded, seemingly appeased, for which Katie was grateful. It wasn't his decision, but if he'd made a stink, Ruth would have been on it in a gnat's blink, and the two of them wouldn't have given Katie a second to breathe.

"When do you start?" he asked.

"Tonight, at ten," said Katie, getting up. Her appetite had dwindled. After scraping the remainder of her corn chowder into the chicken bucket, she placed her bowl in the sink.

Both Rick and Ruth just stared, open-mouthed.

"Well," Ruth snapped, her earlier disapproval returning, "you had better have a lay-down now. I'll pack you a lunch to take with you before I go to bed."

The theory of just lying down and falling asleep was easier said than done. When Katie's alarm went off, she had only slept for an hour and a half. She got dressed, already wondering what she had gotten herself into with this new job.

Chapter Seventeen

atie's training at Corrapell lasted twenty minutes.

"The rules are simple," said Mrs. Reveck. "No one comes in, no one goes out, and other than what is on this chart, no one gets anything other than black coffee, tea, or water to drink."

"Seems kind of rigid," said Katie.

"These people are food addicts." Mrs. Reveck's shoulders tightened. In her pleated wool skirt, cardigan, and laced-to-the-knee high-heel boots, she seemed to rise taller over Katie. Her wide shoulders filled the room. "They are paying good money for us to help them overcome their eating addiction. Each one has a licensed doctor and therapist monitoring their individually structured program. It is your job to guard them from their own selves over the nighttime hours."

Katie wanted to salute.

After Mrs. Reveck left, Katie paced the corridor. Her wing consisted of ten rooms, six of which were occupied. She read the notes left regarding the disbursement of the two-ounce bottles of orange juice and individually wrapped salt-free crackers supposedly stored in the refrigerator and cupboards. However, everything within the kitchenette was locked. She hadn't been offered a key. On the counter at the end of the corridor nearest the lobby door was a hot plate with a pot of water, Sanka, teabags, and a pitcher of room-temperature water. Tired of pacing, she plopped down in the desk chair. Piped in soft music provided by WDOT lulled Katie's senses.

"I'm not going to make it all night," she muttered.

"Hi," said a decidedly male voice behind her.

Startled, Katie spun around. A second door next to the beverage table was open. A man of about her age lounged against the door frame.

"Are you trying to wear the carpeting out, new girl?" he asked. Before she could answer, he straightened up. About five-ten, solidly built but not fat, the man looked a little rough but had a friendly smile that made Katie forget his worn look. "I'm Wade, keeper of the guys in the underwear section."

"Katie," she said. "What does that mean, underwear section?"

Wade ducked back through the door, returning with a desk chair similar to the one on Katie's side. "Have you seen any of the inmates on your wing? To keep them from running, they get to wear cotton pajamas all the time. So maybe not actual underwear, but in this weather, nothing they want to be outdoors in."

Katie still stood in place. Wade motioned her closer.

"Come on over and sit down," he said. "I'm not going to bite you. This," he indicated the area beyond the door with his thumb, "is the guy wing where I work. I can't go far because I have to make sure the residents stay put, but lately, the overnight meds have been working better. The door key for your wing unlocks this door, too."

The clock on the wall said eleven-thirty. Knowing Wade was right, it was going to be a long night. Katie got her chair. She placed it on the other side of the door from Wade and at an angle where she could watch the hall. Over the next few hours, they talked, and Wade explained how things worked at Corrapell.

She tried not to smile at her luck. This guy was a gold mine of information, plus he liked to talk. All she had to do was keep her mouth shut, and he kept right on telling her all the rules, even the foolish ones, and all the gossip.

"It's usually a full house here," he said, "but lately, it's slowed down. I work four nights, pays good, work is easy."

"If you can stay awake," said Katie.

"Yeah, it helps if you bring coffee and food." Wade laughed.

"I brought lunch," said Katie. "Mrs. Reveck told me to put it back in my car."

Wade disappeared and returned moments later with a small green and white Coleman cooler and a gallon thermos. "That's because the fatties will be trying to get it away from you. Either they'll offer you money, or attack like a hoard of zombies. The trick is to wait until after everyone is sleeping and Reveck leaves, then bring your gear in." He opened the cooler and handed Katie a ham sandwich on homemade bread. "Then make sure you have any evidence back out of here before six in the morning." He poured coffee into two of the plastic mugs from the counter.

"I'm not supposed to leave my wing."

Wade sighed. "Not a lot of cars in the lot, are there?" He spoke like he was explaining to a child. "Residents aren't allowed to park near the building. Most of them don't drive their own cars, anyway. There's a fenced-in area out back that's kept locked. The idea is to keep the residents here, not running out for snacks. The nearest house is a mobile home a quarter of a mile away with a big, barking dog. When the chunksters get hungry, they represent a flight risk. If they're sleeping, they don't."

"There's a file on the desk listing what each patient can have for snacks." Katie retrieved the file to show Wade.

He kept chewing his sandwich and munching chips until she opened the file. The single sheet listed all six women on her floor. First name, nothing else. Some names were followed by the notation *Water only*. A lucky few were allowed two ounces of orange juice or a single saltine, not to exceed three over eight hours. But all that was kept locked away from all, Katie included. Dazed by the notes, Katie bit into her sandwich. A jolt of spicy mustard made her sit up straighter.

"Whoa," she said.

"My own blend. My girlfriend bakes the bread. Good, huh?"

"What if one of the patients walks out of their room and catches us with all this food?" Katie was nervous. This whole place felt like the late, late show on Saturday night. A horror movie that would make her want to turn on all the lights.

"Used to be, they might," said Wade, wadding up his wax paper and shoving it back in the cooler. "There were a couple of big-time runners a while back. Now everyone gets a vitamin before they go to bed that keeps them there until breakfast is served. Do you play cards? Got any change in your pocket?"

Even with someone to talk to, the overnight shift lasted forever. Katie was numb with exhaustion. By six o'clock, Wade was gone back to his section of the building. The door between them was locked again, and Katie had lost every cent she'd had in her pocket. She spent the last half-hour checking out all the rooms on her wing. Isaac had been right. The only doors that weren't locked were the ones with an actual person sleeping in the twin-sized bed. Bored and trying to stay awake, Katie had riffled through the desk. There wasn't much there, but way in the back of the center drawer was a single key on a piece of string. It turned out the key unlocked the resident bedrooms.

Well, that would have been good to know in advance if somebody locked themselves in.

She stepped into each of the occupied rooms, taking a close look at the residents, praying they were still breathing. Once assured she didn't need to call for rescue, she scoped out the closets. While walking back up the hallway she caught the glint of metal on the sill above the shower room door and found a small piece of brass wire with a round loop. It proved to be a trip key.

Her relief came, and Katie left. The ladies were still snoring as she walked out to her truck, passing Wade's vehicle as he backed out. He waved and was gone.

Chapter Eighteen

When Katie got home, there was a car in the driveway she didn't recognize. Walking past it, Katie peeked in the driver's window, hoping for a clue. All she saw was a flowered eyeglass case on the dash and a box of tissues in the middle of the bench seat.

Stepping inside, eyes adjusting to the dim light, Katie saw Ruth wrestling with an unknown person on the far side of the room. Taking two giant steps toward her friend, Katie was caught up short when Ruth, squealing happily, turned and blurted out, "Look who's here, Katie!"

There, with her arms wrapped around the older woman, was Marlie. Though Marlie was Katie's age, her top-heavy figure fit perfectly with Ruth's, whose ample buttocks resembled the *I Dream of Jeannie* bottle. The two women were of the same height and disappeared from view as Katie, four inches taller, enveloped both in a hug.

"Oh, my god! Why didn't you say you were coming, Marlie? What's going on? How long will you be here?" Tears of joy trickled down Katie's cheeks. It was difficult for her to take a step backwards. But Ruth didn't know that Katie was gay, or Marlie either. And that they were more than just close friends.

"Whew." Marlie laughed. "Give me a second to catch my breath."

"You'd better hurry up because I hear Rick pulling in out front," said Ruth. "Maybe you should wait and tell us all at once."

With Rick and Ruth seated at the table, cups of tea in hand, and Marlie laying out silverware, Katie whipped up Bisquick biscuits to go with the pasta and tomato casserole. Ruth told Marlie to lay out a fifth setting, explaining Charlie would be coming along in a few minutes.

While they waited, Marlie explained how her plan to come up from Pennsylvania for a visit to Vermont had come about quickly.

"Three days ago, I realized I was going to have to come up earlier than I expected. Instead of trying to work it out with everybody, I called my grandmother and told her I'd be on the bus after my shift at the prison. I slept on the way up and got off in Bennington. She picked me up the night before last."

Ruth's hand thrust out, grabbing the young woman's arm. "Is she all right, your grandmother?"

Marlie patted the slim fingers. "Yes, she's as good as it gets. I had an appointment that got moved up because somebody canceled, so I needed to get up here."

"For a doctor?" Ruth asked.

Marlie hesitated briefly. "Something like that."

Katie held her breath. Had she been the only one to catch that oh-so-brief pause? She looked at the others. From the expression on Rick's face, he had noticed it as well.

"Am I late?" Charlie came blustering in. His new buddy, Walker, rushed forward with a baritone woofing that drowned out everything else.

As they ate, Marlie told them the car belonged to her grandmother. She would be in Vermont for two more days before returning to Pennsylvania. While the others related all the gossip, only briefly addressing the body found in the copse and peppering Marlie with questions as to how she was handling the differences in her job after going from being a Vermont sheriff's deputy to a prison guard at the Pennsylvania Women's Correctional Facility, Katie was mostly silent. The things she had to say couldn't be told in front of the others, no matter how close. She would have to wait for a chance to wrap her arms around her love. Marlie looked up. There was a glitter in her hazel eyes that said she was happy to be back and had things of her own to say, bringing to mind her reference to an appointment. Marlie's announcement had Katie's guts in a nervous twist. Both women went silent, then Rick cleared his throat.

"So," he said, dishing out more of the casserole. "Tell us about working at the prison."

Katie realized she and Marlie had been staring at each other. Ducking her head, she shoveled a big forkful of macaroni into her mouth. Across the table, Marlie blushed, then spoke.

"Life in the WCF is different than I expected in lots of ways. Where I thought I would be wrestling hardened criminals off the walls as they tried to escape, I am finding broken women, mostly from Appalachia. I get to read their cases and listen to them talk. There are some who steal for the thrill, but most have children, elders, people living in the worst poverty. These women were driven beyond endurance to provide for them. The loss of men to the military and black lung is right in my face. Families barely scrape by.

"In the middle of this are little glints of hope, like sparkling Christmas tree lights. Two Amish women, Agnes and Beda, come twice a week. They're teaching inmates to read and write. All the inmates are skinny. These Amish ladies are also thin, but there is a difference. They don't preach, though they do say a little prayer offering thanks for being allowed to help. They bring these winter-coat-button-sized ginger cookies, and parse them out, one per person, student or not. Many of the inmates watch for these ladies."

Marlie paused, sipping milk, eyes on her plate.

"The Amish ladies give me hope as well that small actions will bring changes. Every month, when the Sheriff's Gazette comes in the mail, and I turn to the want ads first." She laughed self-consciously. "Does that sound stupid?"

Katie was choked up, but Rick reached over to cuff the back of Marlie's head.

"Smart girl, to keep your eye open. Maybe Ruth's knitting group could pack you up a box of mittens and hats."

While the three of them planned transport for the donation, and Charlie went for a third helping, Katie fought the tight feeling in her chest. She didn't want Marlie to be in this place of destitution, but it was beyond her abilities to rescue her. Marlie had been clear, she'd stay in law enforcement one way or the other.

The meal ended, and the dishes were in the sink, but no one was leaving except Charlie. Katie couldn't keep her eyes open a moment longer. She didn't want to go, but she needed some sleep. Nowhere in her original idea had she considered that staying awake all night meant more than a casual nap during the day. She slept through lunch, waking in mid-afternoon to find Marlie and Ruth back at the kitchen table, going over Ruth's records for the Feral Cat Society, which had been one of Irma's initiatives. Now, Katie working for the town of Parentville in the capacity of Animal Control Officer, would go out and trap not only nuisance animals, but feral cats. Doctor Veronica, the veterinarian in Charlotte, gave them a discounted rate for spaying and neutering, but even with the help of their patron, Mrs. Phyllis Ash, they were always slightly in the red. Ruth and her groupies from the Knitting Club banded together, making up the center of the FCS. They held bake sales and fundraisers. As a group of bossy elders, they did well and kept the initiative afloat.

* * *

*M*A*S*H* was on Channel 3-TV. Ruth and Rick were totally involved in the shenanigans of Corporal Radar O'Reilly. Charlie was outside tussling around with Walker and Solomon, and Katie bent over the sink up to her elbows in soapsuds. Marlie cootchie-cooed every cat that came within tickling range. LG stayed away, but several of the older felines, pleased to find someone who wanted to pet and cuddle, were very happy to queue up.

The volume of canned laughter rose as Charlie and Walker came in the front door, and Rick twisted the television dial. Katie took the chance.

"I know you've got some sneaky little thing going on with this visit, and so does Rick," she said to Marlie, taking a peek over her shoulder. "You can tell me right now, or I'll sic him on you."

"You think you're such a smarty-pants!" Marlie rolled Peanut over, tickling his belly. "I got a call for an interview, that's all."

Katie squealed, whipping around and sending soap suds flying. "Talk fast.

Where?"

"A larger than normal percentage of new-hire recruits quit from the sheriff's department. There are several open spaces." Marlie chewed on her lower lip. "Instead of just filling the spaces, the sheriff's department is re-evaluating the jobs, which will require a new contract. The applicant recruits in the wings have been offered a guaranteed spot if they will come on board as open assignments, working where they are needed until the new contract is ratified."

Katie opened her mouth, but Marlie held up her hand.

"Katie, I left my deputy job to save my reputation. No one within the department knew what was going on and I waited a while before going to a rep. There are going to be a lot of sheriffs who consider me damaged goods, or worse than that, not reliable. This chance is a bolt out of the blue, and I'm really nervous. There are so many open slots right now that I have been offered an interview. If I am accepted, I will join those ranks and eventually be assigned a slot. That's what's going to happen. But since we're being assigned, I don't know where my home office will be."

"How long before you'd start?"

Both Katie and Marlie swung around to see Rick, empty teacup in hand, standing in the doorway. Instantly, Katie remembered they needed to be aware every moment or someone might pick up on even a small clue and guess their secret. In a small rural farming community, being labeled gay would carry the same stigma as the whisper of being a witch two hundred years prior.

"If, and you need to remember, it's still an if," Marlie said, lowering her voice, "I can convince the board tomorrow that I'm a viable candidate, and they accept me, I have to give notice in PA. So, maybe as soon as two weeks."

Katie blinked. She wanted to sing out but feared being too hopeful. "That's pretty fast."

Checking to verify that Ruth and Charlie were still engrossed in the half-hour sitcoms, Rick asked, "How is this all going to work?"

"I don't really know," Marlie said with a sigh. "I was upfront with my boss at the prison about what I was doing. He was understanding, or so he said.

I'll drive into Montpelier for the interview, then head back to Grams. The next morning, I have to be on the bus at five to be back at work on time."

"But you'll let us know, right, honey?" Rick asked.

Katie was glad Rick was asking the questions she wanted because she was afraid there would be happy tears if she opened her mouth.

"Right, wrong, or indifferent, I promise to let you know whatever I find out," said Marlie.

A short time later, Rick threw Charlie out and told Ruth to go to bed. Katie was grateful for the time she and Marlie would have alone together. They held onto each other, loath to let go, each hoping Marlie would be back in Vermont soon. As they parted, Katie considered once again that Rick might know what they weren't saying.

Climbing the stairs to her room, she smiled at the memory of the last time Ruth had tried to fix Katie up with an eligible village boy. Rick had gently told his favorite lady to leave Katie to her own devices.

"No one forced me down your throat," he'd said with a laugh. "Though if I'd aknown you weren't going to pick me way back when, I'd have been a lot pushier."

Giggling shyly, Ruth had turned away. She might not have done exactly what Rick wanted when they were young, but times had changed.

Chapter Nineteen

Sunday morning when Rick and Ruth left for church, Rick had dragged Charlie with them. Ruth had expected the other two women to follow, not knowing Katie had already begged the day off with Dorothea. For three hours, she and Marlie had time for each other. They were well into Sunday dinner preparations when the others returned.

While Katie was making stuffing for the roast chicken, Marlie whipped up a pan of raspberry muffins. They wouldn't need to be frosted, and though it was the end of the frozen raspberries, they would be a treat.

"You demanded to know what I was keeping back," Marlie said as she measured out oil and water. "Now tell me what's got you all dark around the edges."

Exasperated that she'd been so easy to read, Katie told Marlie about Father Metevier's concerns.

"He went all word of god on me," she said.

"You don't mind, right?" Marlie asked tentatively.

"Not really. I like him. I know what he's trying to do for Isaac and his family." Katie gave Marlie a quick smile between the chops of her big knife through the onions. "He's just so transparent."

"And what else?" Marlie asked.

"Near the end of February, I got all cleaned up and dressed like I was going to church and drove over to the Charlotte town office. I had a meeting with Meara Myers, the tax collector. I was all pumped up to be hand-delivering the final payment for the back tax lien against the Mosher property. You know, the part of the farm that was Gram's dowry. She left so many bills, it was going to take a while to pay all of them back."

She added melted butter to the breadcrumbs and started pinching in herbs.

"She even owed money to Baldwin's, but Stan said as long as I worked for him, he'd wait. He warned me the tax bills could cost me everything. Janice, the tax collector here in the village, set up a payment plan, but she pointed toward the town of Charlotte, telling me they'd sell the note to get the money faster. The new holder would charge an interest rate so high; I'd never get caught up and lose the property."

"But Cindy was helping you, right? She was the one who figured out about selling gravel from the pit," said Marlie.

Cindy Baldwin was a stay-at-home mom who helped her husband with the feed store's books, but she was also a college grad with a degree in land management. She and Katie had walked the property, avoiding gopher holes and grass snakes. Marlie knew all the money Katie eked out of the land went toward the taxes.

Katie started talking again, but a lump rose in her throat, and she had to stop. Marlie waited while Katie rinsed out the chicken, then she handed her love a cup of tea and pointed to a chair.

"Spill," she said. "Take no prisoners. Tell me everything."

"I don't know if you've met Meara," said Katie. "She's our age, all gushing with apple dumpling cheeks. Then she dropped the bomb. It seems I wasn't caught up because our agreement didn't include last year's taxes, because, like, we were in the middle of last year at that time. I was so blown away that I couldn't even argue. I just took my receipt and left."

Marlie reached over, rubbing Katie's back. In a hushed voice, Katie continued.

"I wanted to pay Rick back for all he's done and Stan. I had it all planned out. I was so excited, and she just kicked the legs out from under me. By the time I got home, I was foaming at the mouth. And there's damn Rick telling me not to worry about it. That we'd figure it out."

"Then what happened, honey?" Marlie asked.

Katie released a choking laugh, wet with tears.

"The fool drops to his knees, dragging himself across the floor, miming he's dying of thirst. He had all twelve cats running in different directions. Solomon grabbed at his cuffs, and he took to wrestling around on the floor with the dog. You couldn't help but laugh out loud."

"And working at Corrapell is only short-term?"

"Yeah. It's not the place I'd ever want to work. But I have to tell you, just walking in the door you can feel that it's wrong. I don't know how, but kind of not honest." Katie dumped the onions into the seasoned breadcrumbs.

Marlie elbowed her as she passed. "You're on recon! You sly girl."

Then, before she could stop herself, Katie was smiling.

"Shove that bird in the oven, and let's go for a walk," Marlie said. "You can give me another dumb nature lesson."

They bundled up and walked until they barely had the strength to get back. Ruth and Rick were home, and the house was filled with the delicious aroma of roast chicken.

Chapter Twenty

With Marlie already gone the next morning, Katie went to work at Baldwin's with a lighter heart. She had called Father Metevier the previous evening, instructing him to call her when he saw Isaac, but not to tell the boy. There wouldn't be any snooping around about Corrapell until her next scheduled shift, but she was too excited at Marlie's news to care.

She was in luck. There was a full house at work that day. Every time somebody came in for a break, she'd ask what they knew about a spa over near Richmond. For the most part, the answers were that they didn't even know it was there. Even Davidson replied, "Not much."

One of the guys told Katie she didn't need a spa; she was fine just the way she was. When he came back from the breakroom, she was as far up the dog food aisle as she could get and hiding among the stacks. The last thing she needed was for this cowboy to ask her out.

The only one who had any real information was Stan.

"Yes, I know the place," he said. "We've made a couple of deliveries up there."

"For feed?" Katie asked. She hadn't seen any evidence of farm animals.

"No, they order from Fonda Paper, like we do. By having it delivered here, they save on shipping, and we get a bigger discount because our order is larger on a regular basis." Stan was filling out a stock order for hand tools. Katie followed him over to the display.

"What do you know about them, Stan?" she asked.

"Why the sudden interest?" he countered.

"I never knew they existed before last Friday. I'd think some high-price place like that would be knee-deep in gossip," she answered.

Stan shrugged. "Some doctor with money built the place. I don't know him. He's from away. Then, too, most of their clients probably run in circles; I don't. If I needed to lose weight, I'd just put down the fork."

"So, there aren't any locals there?"

"Probably just the hired help. Nobody I know, but I'm sure they don't pay enough for people to drive far to work there." He pulled all the gloves off one rack, stacking them by size on a nearby shelf.

"Then, too, I heard they'd fallen on hard times. Inflation maybe. Fancy spas in nicer places, I bet." He looked up, and it took Katie a second to realize he was looking at her. "You on a break?" he asked.

On the way home, she stopped at the post office, and the postmaster said, "My rural driver doesn't go that far out. The trailer park and that fancy place are served by Richmond."

Katie reported for her second shift at Corrapell that evening. It was more of the same, except that Wade had the evening off, and whoever was guarding the men in underwear didn't unlock the door.

It came as a surprise to her that the last time she'd checked the clock, it was twelve-twenty-seven, and the rattling of the door at five-forty-five jarred her awake. She'd fallen asleep, head on the desk.

"Way to get fired before you even get started," she mumbled as she gathered her things to leave.

* * *

Katie only got to sleep until noon because that was the time Grace dropped Ruth off. The women had spent the morning making goat soap, and the pleasurable scent of herbs enveloped Ruth like a warm jacket.

"KATIE!" Ruth yelled from the bottom of the stairs. "Grace sent chowder, and I've got a mess of boxes of marked goods to lug down to the farm stand. Can you help me?"

Dragging herself out of bed, dressing with her eyes still closed, Katie hurried to comply. Ruth's request wasn't unreasonable. After all, even though Rick was working today, it was Katie's day off. Except she was wasting time sleeping it away.

"How's this working for you?" The older woman asked when the chowder was gone.

She leaned on her crutches while Katie lugged the heavy cartons of resale items out to the truck for the short ride down the hill. The speculation in Ruth's eyes was not a question Katie wanted to answer. After unloading the truck, Katie started a fire in the schoolhouse chunk stove to take off the chill, made sure the two sandwich signs and flag were out announcing Ruth was open for business, and then, tired of Ruth bossing her around, spoke out. "I'm going down to help Dorothea for a couple of hours. Either Rick or I will pick you up later."

Confident Ruth was settled with a thermos of tea, a Tupperware container of snacks, and enough firewood close at hand, she left for the relative safety of the thrift shop.

Late in the afternoon while she and the elderly shop manager were busy sorting, folding, and pressing, another load of goods arrived. This time a donation from the Salvation Army.

"Katie," said to Jesse, another volunteer. "Can you put this bag of donations in the back room?"

After peeking inside, Katie detoured to where Dorothea guarded the cash box. "These are blankets," she said as Dorothea's customer walked away.

After a quick inspection, Dorothea pulled out a few price tags to attach. Blankets were always in high demand.

A hand reached out and plucked one off the counter. "I'll take this one."

"Hi, Monique." Katie grinned. "You didn't walk into town this late, did you?"

"No, Amos needed some stuff from the store, so while he's there, I ran over." The pregnant woman stroked the light blue blanket. She smiled. "I'm hoping blue is going to be my favorite color."

"Well, I hope so, too." Katie laid her hand on Monique's arm and gave a little squeeze.

Watching Monique try not to look at the baby section, Katie decided to update Ruth that Monique seemed to be softening her stance on not talking about the baby or gathering items for after the child's birth. Ruth would be pleased as punch to begin putting together a layette.

"Dorothea," Katie whispered across the table. "Do you think we should put aside some of the baby things for, you know, later on?"

"Mind your own business, Katie," the old woman snapped. Then her voice brightened, and she spoke louder. "Speaking of which, do you remember that nice woman who went to work for Father Metevier? Well, she's doing such a fine job cleaning the rectory top to bottom. He's got her working four days a week!"

Katie turned around and Monique was standing behind her.

"Look at the nice sweater I found," Monique said. "Plenty big enough for now, and it even has pockets!"

Katie agreed, thankful Dorothea had been watching her back and Monique hadn't overheard her inquiry.

* * *

Katie's prediction that Ruth would want to be gathering things for Monique was right on. The next afternoon, Rick brought Ruth into the village during his lunch so she could work with Dorothea for a few hours. Now that she only needed one cane, Ruth could slowly make her way down the stairs to the basement. To sweeten the deal of dumping Ruth for the afternoon, Rick carried a thermos of tea and a half tin of chocolate cherry brownies.

So, it was a surprise to Katie when one of the feed store's customers picked up their bird feed bags and rakes and moved out of line, and the next person was Dorothea.

"How did you get here?" Katie asked. The octogenarian didn't drive, and her grandniece was a day nurse at Mary Fletcher Hospital in Burlington.

"I've got my ways," Dorothea said with a wink and a cackle. She had coerced Davidson to lug a box of pint canning jars up to the counter for her. "With Ruth at the shop to help today, I figured I'd take a quick run over. I need another two boxes of pint jars and maybe three boxes of lids."

"Little early for canning, isn't it, Dorothea?" asked Stan.

With the boss eyeing him for being away from what he'd been assigned, Davidson looked like he wanted to bolt.

"Ellen ordered a bunch of that Paris Farmer's frozen food," Dorothea said. "Ain't no room in the freezer for it right now. I've been storing it out on the porch, but it's getting too warm. I'm going to can some up. I got plenty of quart jars, but that's too much for us to use up at a time. How about it? You got some hidden away, Stan?"

Katie knew there were a couple of pallets of boxes in cold storage. Ordered the previous fall for the next growing season, the cases of glass had arrived right after the first of the year. Stan directed Davidson to move the bird feeder endcap away from the front doors.

"We'll set up a display there," the feed store owner said. "There are probably others who will want jars."

"Yeah, me," said Katie, who had already decided to take two cases of pints. Their collection of empty mason jars was small and consisted mostly of quart jars. She made a mental note to have Stan add the jars and lids to her account. If they were going to sell out before the canning season, she needed to be ready.

While she waited, Dorothea jawed with a few other customers.

Katie accepted a half-sheet of poster board and a black magic marker from Stan. "Your handwriting is better than mine, so you make up a sign," he directed as he yanked on his coat. Working with Davidson and one of the cold barn employees, they'd get the boxes of canning jars inside in short order. Katie tapped her fingers on the paper, considering what to write.

"Is it true you're working up at the fat farm?" Dorothea asked. "You got extra time? I could use more help at the thrift store."

"Sorry, Dorothea. I don't mind helping out, but I'm a little strapped for cash right now, what with the well and all." Katie took the sign and a detachable sign frame over to the end cap. When she got back, Dorothea was still standing in place with the same accusing look on her face.

Katie sighed. "Okay. I tell you what, Ruth got all the buttons sewn on that box of stuff. I'll get it all pressed while I'm watching the clients sleep and get it back to you, okay? Then we'll get Ruth to pick out the broken zippers or cut rags or whatever and wear down that second box. Just have her take it home with her. How's that? Make you happy?"

Cackling with glee, the old woman moved toward the door. Mr. Fortin, Dorothea's ride, and Davidson hauling her boxes of jars, followed her out.

Nasty little old lady. Katie rolled her eyes.

Stan stopped on his way past. "Why do I have the feeling Dorothea just got the best of you on something? She's good at that, you know, getting what she wants."

Katie did know, which didn't mean she liked it, but what was a girl to do?

"I heard Marlie was in town," Stan said. "Is she going to get the deputy job in Parentville?"

"There's a job open here?" Katie asked, surprised to hear it from Stan and not from Marlie.

"I heard Martin Lewis complaining Brad was looking to transfer to the state police, and Angus isn't cutting the mustard. So, yeah, I think there's going to be an open spot."

"Hmm." There was a bit of information to put into her next letter to Marlie. Marlie's schedule was sometimes erratic. Calling her rent-by-the-week motel room didn't guarantee an answer, and there was a chance a nosy desk clerk would listen in on their conversation. Katie gathered local gossip and dutifully sent the news via the US mail.

* * *

Katie stopped at the Dean farm on the way home for goat's milk and cheese. The rich, fresh milk just begged her to make a custard. Grace gave her two bars of lavender-scented goat soap, which Ruth left on the side of the tub.

"It seems weird, you know," she said to Ruth, cracking eggs. "All this goat's milk and cheese, and we're still buying cow milk to drink."

"I told you; Grace doesn't have time to pasteurize more than the goat's milk used to make cheese. Even she buys whole milk for the boys." Ruth was folding laundry and working around Sasha and Peanut, who had curled up amid the clothing. "Oh, by the way, you got a letter." She nodded toward the small occasional table just inside the front door.

The stationery envelope was a dusky pink. The inside was decorated with flowers silhouetted in bright pastels against black. The return address was Bennington, Vermont, and the cancellation was the day before. But it was the two pages tucked inside that had Katie holding her breath. There were always two pages. One for Katie to share and another for her alone. Marlie's drop-in visit had been both surprising and exciting, but too brief. A letter was something more tangible to be read now, and again later, and maybe one more time. This letter and the ones that had come before it, all stored in the back of a dresser drawer, were tangible evidence that there was something Katie wanted besides the farm. Every time she held them in her hands, releasing the ribbon to add one more, she knew there was a chance she could have love in her life, but there would be a cost.

Katie sat in the broken-down Bennington chair in the living room and after a furtive glance to make sure Ruth wasn't watching, slit the envelope with her thumbnail. Separating the shorter letter with only her name in the greeting, she slid it into her pants pocket. She bit down on the inside of her lower lip to control the urge to run upstairs and read that page first. Instead, she read through both sides of the stationery page, smiling and hearing Marlie's voice in the words. When she was done, she went into the kitchen to share the news with Rick and Ruth for the first time.

"Listen to this," she said, reading the short letter.

Marlie was pleased with her interview, saying it went well.

The Commissioner kind of knows what happened. He was there and quite friendly. I'm hoping for the best, Marlie wrote.

Behind her, Ruth picked up the letter after Katie laid it on the table. "I can't believe you lot, didn't tell me what was going on."

"Sometimes," Katie said with a sigh, "you're just too enthusiastic."

While supper heated, Katie sat in the bathroom, door locked, and read the short note Marlie had sent for her only. Every word was about missing Katie and apologizing for the mess she had made in both their lives. The note was short. Katie read through it again. Among the words of anguish, she felt the love. These thoughts, shared on paper, were the ones they could not speak of when they were together. The glow was already fading from Marlie's short visit, but the pink paper in her hand gave her a feeling that made her want to crush it to her chest.

"How long you gonna be in there?" Rick asked with a knock on the door.

Katie put on her game face, tucked the note deep in her pocket, and yanked the door open.

"No privacy in this house," she growled, pushing past him to where a pan of biscuits waited to be popped into the oven.

With most of their canned goods used up, and the summer crops not even in the ground yet, they found themselves eating a lot of stews and casseroles. Tonight, was shepherd's pie made with venison hamburg, mashed potatoes, and lima bean and creamed corn succotash. Privately, Katie had already decided that this year they would not be planting lima beans or canning succotash.

She pulled the casserole out of the wood-burning kitchen stove and slid the custard in. There was also a plate stacked with thick slices of bread cut from the loaves she made every Sunday.

"Where's Charlie?" Ruth asked as she filled glasses with milk.

As if on cue, the kitchen door opened and the short, round man came waltzing in. His eyes sparkled and his cheeks were redder than usual. Ruth gave him the hairy eyeball as he struggled out of his coat. She closed in when it became clear he was having more difficulty than normal.

"Have you been drinking?"

Her shrill demand caused Charlie to falter, taking a step back.

"No," he said, shrinking as much as possible with his fat belly. "I didn't mean to be late, but we was working clearing a deadfall over by the Paris Farmers Union today." With his coat and one boot off, he hefted a five-gallon brass tin onto the table. We went in there to warm up. Look at this. There was stuff left after the frozen fruit order that people didn't come for. I bought a tin for us. You know, something special. It all had to go before it thawed out."

All four of them crowded around the tin. The Paris Farmers Union store in Richmond offered a deal once a year where residents in the surrounding area could order frozen vegetables and fruit. Katie, Ruth, and Rick had ordered three, one each of mixed vegetables, blueberries, and strawberries. There were over two dozen choices, but price was a factor. The ones they had selected offered a chance to get multiple items and not have to sell the family car to do so. The orders went in, and six weeks later, a freezer truck showed up. Rick had taken the money they'd set aside and gone down for the collection. It was a one-day deal. Obviously, if there were goods left afterwards, then some people who had ordered hadn't shown up.

"Peaches," Katie said with a sigh, reading the label.

Supper was forgotten. Rick pried off the lid of the tin. Inside were golden slices of peaches with the red core center like small, ruby-lipped smiles, filling the tin to the top. Katie flicked off a frozen bit of fruit and popped it into her mouth.

"Oh, that is so good," she groaned.

Rick tapped the lid back on. "After supper, we'll dish out enough for a pie and get the rest into the freezer before it thaws and we lose it. Good job, Charlie."

The little man glowed with pride.

Ruth, who was dancing around swinging her crutches out, dangerously near everyone else, grabbed the little man and gave him a big hug that had his face turning an even darker shade of red. "Pie. No, cobbler! Right, Katie? Cobbler?"

Katie smiled in agreement.

Later, just before bed, the four enjoyed a scoop of piping hot cobbler fresh out of the oven. The custard cooled and was put away for a different day. Ruth had moved back to her bed upstairs when Marlie had visited, so it was decided Charlie would camp out on the sofa that night. Since the burn-out of Charlie's apartment building the previous fall, he had lived in the back of the fire station and recently moved to a dingy little rooming house on the other side of the creamery.

When Katie went upstairs, she paused in front of the door to the back bedroom. When she had lived in the farmhouse with her grandparents, this door had been without a knob, therefore barring people from entry. After she'd left and Gram started collecting stray cats, the old woman had moved most of the household furniture into this room, and the door was closed again. It was one of the few places Katie hadn't tackled since her return. Reaching out to touch the flaking paint, she had a different idea. Before she had a moment to think about it and lose her courage, she went pounding back down the staircase. Flinging open the door at the bottom and startling everyone, she headed right over to Charlie.

"How does it work, Charlie, where you live at the boardinghouse? Is it nice? Are you happy?"

"I don't know what you mean," he said, more than slightly taken aback. "I pay thirty-five dollars a week and share a room with another guy. I get to take two baths a week and get supper every night. I pay extra if I eat breakfast." He paused, went pale, and then reddened. He studied his hands. "I can't drink or smoke. I have to go to the AA meetings at the Woodman Hall."

As usual, Charlie had the strong smell of male sweat and unwashed clothing, but that didn't stop Katie from getting closer.

"Rick and I are going to empty the back bedroom," she said.

"We are?" Rick asked, but Katie ignored him.

"Some of the stuff will come down here. The rest will go out in the barn. I'm hoping there might even be a bed in that room. Would you be interested in boarding here?" She talked fast, shutting down anything the others had to say. "Same rent, breakfast and supper. You're here almost every night, anyway. Lunch is optional, bath whenever it's called for, and use of the washer and dryer, but you have to do your own."

Charlie's eyes popped. Both Ruth and Rick's jaws dropped.

"However." Katie wasn't done yet. "Drinking and chew are out, as is smoking anywhere near the house or the barn. As far as AA, I'll know if you're going, because I'm going to go too." With that, she turned on her heel and headed back up to her room. Her face felt aflame with excitement, and she was shocked by her audacity.

* * *

The next day, Katie was late coming down the stairs. Both men had left for work. Ruth was just headed in to clean the cattery, but she hobbled back toward the table and sat down.

"Well, that was quite a bomb you dropped last night, Katie. Why didn't you just let him have your old room?"

Katie hesitated. Rick's things were still in there, but it was more than that. She just wasn't ready to turn it over to anyone else.

Sitting in a kitchen chair, she pulled on her boots. Solomon had his butt parked by the back door. Though there was no chance she'd take him with her to work, he was doing his best to entice her. She gave him a pat and a smooch, apologizing for leaving him behind.

"I don't know, Ruth. Maybe we'll let Marlie stay in there if she comes to visit again." She blew out a breath. "It just still feels like it's my room. I feel bad about Charlie's situation. It's depressing. And I understand his problem with alcohol and what happens when it's mixed with bad feelings." She stared at her bootlaces, unwilling to look at Ruth. "I guess you never get over the feeling it's an escape route, and maybe you should use it." She shrugged. "You both like Charlie, so I knew you'd be okay with him being here for a while."

Ruth turned to the stove, hiding a little smirk. She knew inside Katie's walls there was a warm heart, even if Katie hadn't realized it yet.

Rising from her seat, Katie taped a new envelope on the side of the refrigerator below the ones that said things like ELECTRIC, TAXES, TELEPHONE, and the most evil of all, LOAN. This new one said WELL DRILLING. Every back bill left from Gram had an envelope. Incoming money was divided up, a predetermined percentage marked on each one. There was always a certain amount of revelry when an envelope was no longer needed and could be taken down, ripped into tiny pieces, and cast into the stove. It hadn't happened as often as she had hoped, what with minor emergencies popping up all the time.

"This will be where Charlie's money goes for the loan payments," she said. Rick had made a similarly titled list, for items like chair cushions, bed pillows, maybe even real drapes instead of the thin plastic ones. Little luxuries they might get if there were a few extra dollars and a sale running at Gaynes or Forest Hills. Something else that didn't happen often.

Chapter Twenty-One

fter Katie left for work, Ruth finished up in the cattery. Grace would be coming to pick her up soon. It wasn't a long walk down to the neighboring farm, but if she fell with the crutch, she'd be on the ground for a while. However, there was something she wanted to check out before she left. Pulling a screwdriver out of the junk drawer, she headed upstairs. One twisting crank and the knobless door opened.

The big room was exactly how she remembered it from when she and Irma had moved all the contents upstairs. The door swung inwards to reveal a jumble of furniture and cardboard boxes stacked to the ceiling. Even though Katie and Rick had previously removed the big farmer's table and chairs for the kitchen, she could barely see an open space. Light came in from unseen windows, backlighting a solid mass of boxes she would not be able to walk through.

Crap, she thought. *We aren't going to get this done in a day.*

Ruth poked around, filling cardboard boxes and grocery bags with small items, until Grace arrived and called to her from downstairs. After telling Grace they were planning to take in a boarder, her friend agreed it would solve Charlie's problem and one of Katie's as well. Grace offered to have her sons, Davey and Billy, come over after school and hike up and down the stairs with whatever they could carry to the barn.

It was a marvelous idea. With the offer of date bars and hot chocolate to follow, Ruth's plan worked well at first. The bottom door had to be left open, as was the door to the dormitory backroom, allowing the fur babies into a hitherto unknown area. The boys worked fast with what was available.

After the first few trips' downstairs, the cats remained in the living room investigating what had been hauled down with Ruth and Monique, who had been invited for supper. Solomon followed the boys until his young legs were exhausted.

Rick rumbled into the yard at the end of the day in the Baldwin truck, loaded and ready for the next morning's early deliveries. Business was ramping up with the seasonal demand for seed, fertilizer, and lime. Katie was right behind him. Both stood in the kitchen doorway, inhaling the delicious odor of roasting chicken.

"Oh, hi." Monique closed the oven door on the freshly basted fowl. "Shh, Ruth is taking a nap on the couch."

"Monique," Katie protested. "We invited you for supper. You weren't supposed to bring it."

"Well, I feel grateful you would have me while Amos has to stay down in Brattleboro on the job site for a couple of days. It's not a big chicken, and they've kind of stopped laying. I got here early this afternoon because Mr. Dean let me ride back with him. He bought our two Guernseys. When Mrs. Dean's baby goats are older, we're taking two does and a buck. Kind of trade and pay. Anyhow, I have browning potatoes and parsnips." The young woman blushed with pride.

While Rick went off to wash, Katie pulled out a chair for Monique to sit and rest. Then she sat beside her.

"Monique," Katie said softly. "I don't mean to interrupt your life. I'm sure you're really busy, and Amos, as well. But since we've been talking, I've heard you mention the old barns several times."

Monique nodded, taking a sip of her tea.

Katie licked her lips. She wanted to be done with this before Rick came out of the bathroom.

"Anyway. You may have noticed my barn is collapsing on the slope end. I don't want to lose it. I thought about calling a contractor, but they build houses, you know? Amos has experience with barns. He'd know if it was worth saving. Maybe give me some advice on who to call. Do you think he'd come over and have a look?" When Monique paused, Katie hurriedly added, "I'd pay him for the consult."

"He wouldn't take your money, Katie. You've been so kind. I'm sure he'll come."

She spoke softly, reaching out to touch Katie's arm as if consoling her. Suddenly, Katie saw Monique in a different light, not as some aging back-to-the-land hippie, but as a sensitive woman with simple needs.

The bathroom door opened, and Rick came blustering out. "I am starved! When do we eat?"

His noise roused Ruth. As she limped into the kitchen, Katie filled the cat's dinner bowls, leading the parade into the cattery. When she came out, Monique passed her the bowl of parsnips.

Not being a big fan of the springtime root vegetable, Katie pressed her lips together before saying, "Rick will be thrilled. He loves these. Why are you giving up the cows and going with goats?"

While they put supper on the table and Rick fed the dogs, Monique explained that their farmland was just too rough right now for big stock.

"It's been gone to seed for a long time. Mrs. Dean says goats will eat anything. I'm hoping so. When they get bigger, I want to make yogurt and soap. I don't much care for goat cheese."

"For the next few months," said Ruth, coming in and settling in her chair, "Monique is going to come over and help with putting in the garden and down at the schoolhouse yard sale. I told her she could put her treasures in there and keep all the money if she'd work while I'm still kind of crippled up."

Katie raised her eyebrows. Ruth kept saying how she was pretty much all healed, and here she was playing the sympathy card. Ruth ignored her look.

"How are you going to get over here, Monique?" Katie asked. "It's too far for you to walk right now, and should you be doing a lot of lifting?"

"That's the part we're still trying to work out," Monique said with a sigh.

Katie started to speak, then pulled herself up short. She knew a half-grown boy who might be able to help with the lifting and hauling. She looked around for Rick and considered again that it was probably time to tell him what she was up to.

"Not to worry tonight, because I'll take you home in Katie's truck. Oh, look, parsnips! Yum." Freshly washed and combed, Rick sat down with a smile on his face. Katie gladly passed the bowl of mashed vegetables.

As usual, Charlie rushed in at the last minute. Between the two men, the parsnips didn't stand a chance.

* * *

Walking out the pig door later, across the space where the sties had been located when she was a girl, Katie couldn't help but acknowledge the heavy place in her chest. It felt like twenty pounds of lead curved just below her breasts. Once past the short passage through the orchard and up to the pipe fencing around the family cemetery, Katie started talking.

"When I first came back, I was out here all the time, and lately, I just haven't gotten this far." She plodded along through semi-frozen mud, eyes on the ground, but seeing nothing. "I'm lost inside myself. I don't know what I want to do. The other day, I walked into the store looking to buy a fifth. If I hadn't run into Monique, I would have been sloshed in no time. There's nobody here for me to talk to, not really. I feel so hollow inside." She entered the tiny plot and perched on the pipe fencing, still talking to her grandparents, who shared one stone in the corner of the fenced area. "I want to make this right for you, I really do, but sometimes I want to run away as well. How can one person be as useless as that?"

The setting sun warmed her back as a swooping chick-a-dee landed on the pipe, listening attentively while she talked. Her thoughts weren't centered on the tax bill or the barn or the schoolhouse, but more on her emotional confusion.

"Sometimes I get this powerful urge to just drive over to I-89 and head south. If I just showed up, Marlie wouldn't send me away, would she?"

When no answer came, Katie ended with the bit of exciting news Rick had brought to the table and then had Ruth grinning like a banshee.

"I rescued some kittens last fall at this electrician's house. You know, over in one of the new developments across the brook," Katie said. "Rick stopped by to see the guy. He said he'd come over and assess the situation at the schoolhouse. We'd need a pole and a meter. If you buried a three-pound coffee can of money, this would be a good time to let me find it."

Behind her, a scree and a few excited barks let Katie know Bonnie and Solomon had followed her scent through the orchard and discovered her. Time to go. As she entered the first row of gnarled trees, all past their fruit-bearing lives, the woofing pig and bounding dog converged. Both were thrilled to have found her and wanted pats, scratches, and love.

Chapter Twenty-Two

It was a surprise to Katie when she got home from work at Baldwin's the next day and found not only Amos and Monique's truck parked in the drive, but Amos sitting in one of Ruth's rockers on the porch.

"I thought you were working out of town," Katie said as she walked up the steps.

"I am, actually."

Amos rose up from the chair. A step above Katie and at six-feet tall it felt like he towered above her. He looked uncomfortable and sad. A lump jumped into Katie's throat, as she immediately believed it had something to do with Monique and her unborn child. She was close to right.

"Monique had to go into Burlington today for an ultrasound test. It's not something normally done, but because she's had difficulties in the past, the doctor wanted the test."

Katie didn't mention that she knew what the difficulties had been.

"She told me that you wanted an opinion on your barn. I been down and took a look," Amos said.

"Well, let's have a seat. Would you like tea or coffee?" Katie asked.

She wasn't sure what time Rick would be coming, and if Ruth was lying on the sofa, she might not have known Amos was outside. He declined but sat back down. They spent twenty minutes discussing the barn repairs. Amos offered to ask the man who had trained him to have a look.

"He'd know right off what was what," Amos said. "But the building is actually in very good shape. If the bank hadn't washed away, there wouldn't have been any problem at all."

Right about the time he finished his narrative regarding the old wooden structure, Katie was trying how best to ask him about what he'd found in the copse. She opened her mouth, but he was already there.

"I'd like to thank you for all you've done for Monique," he said. "She'd been pretty down, and now she's doing fine. If you don't mind, I've got something I'd like to get off my chest about the copse and that mess in it."

At her nod, he continued to speak.

"Deer or something ripped through my barbed wire, and I went out to fix it before one of the cows wandered off. While I was there, I saw the buzzards circling overhead, coming down lower, and then darting into the trees. I'm basically nosy, so I went for a look. Let me tell you, the stink was God awful, and the sight of it was worse than that."

"I bet," Katie said.

"I called the sheriff's office and got to talk to Lewis. He came right out, and he's been back several times since." Amos paused to look up the lane. "I know he's got a bee in his bonnet about me knowing how that got there. But honestly, Katie, I don't. I keep telling him. He keeps coming around. It's not a good thing."

"I know," said Katie. "I've had to deal with him myself, and he can be a jerk."

"Mm," Amos agreed. "I don't have anything to add. I just happen to be the poor sap that stumbled on it. My point in talking to you about it is that I'm sure there's gossip running amuck in town. This is a hard time for Monique. Please don't let what others have to say cause you to turn aside from her."

There was pain in his eyes and his voice.

Katie took the easy way out. "Funny guy, you are. You just don't want me to have to teach her how to feed those baby goats."

Amos understood what she had to say about other people's attitudes, and after giving her the name of the restoration company, she left.

She went inside to find the fire burned down to practically nothing, Ruth sound asleep on the sofa, and supper still waiting to be cooked.

"What's the matter with you guys," she asked the assembled cats. "None of you knows how to make a meatloaf?"

Chapter Twenty-Three

On Katie's next night shift at Corrapell, she was in a better mindset, and among the items in her lunch pail was a flashlight. Like Wade had said, the residents were all sound asleep when she got there, with no movement beyond the rise and fall of their chests as they snored. Following his recommendation, she waited until after eight and brought her lunch pail in. Coming back, Katie took a silent, and very fast, tour of the building. Looking out the dining room window at the back, she could see lights in the darkness.

"What's back there?" she asked Wade as he dealt out the cards.

"A double-wide. That's where the Revecks live, though it used to be only her. I'm not sure what happened to bring him back full-time. There used to be a cook here, Mrs. Frances, and she told me after he got back, there were some big arguments between the doctor and his wife. Right after that, they changed the type of clientele staying here."

"Really, how so? All the women sleeping in here look pretty heavy." Katie threw her useless hand down on the table.

Wade shrugged before dealing out a new round. "This was always a fat farm retreat. Reveck seemed to think he could make more money if they took in people suffering from other addictions. I don't think he thought it through, though, because those people needed a lot more than we had to offer."

Katie waited, studying her cards. She paused long enough for him to start talking again, then threw down two for a couple of new cards.

"They were housed in the other wings on the far side. And I'm telling you, they ruined the place. Tore out the fixtures, punched holes in the wall, puked everywhere. It's going to take a bundle to fix it. Back then, the place was full all the time. Mrs. Francis and Mrs. O'Brien had three young women working for them."

"Hm," said Katie, eyes on her cards. "Didn't Mrs. O'Brien's son work here?" She took a quick peek at Wade, but he was still studying his own cards.

"Isaac? No. He's just a kid. A good kid, but with a good imagination. He was around, but never worked here. There were a couple of times I had to tell him to watch his mouth because he said some off-the-wall things. There were plenty of aides, but no guards which were needed here when the substance addicts started arriving. For a while, it was under control. Then, a couple of them ran out the doors and into the woods. They found the first one pretty fast, but one guy was gone for a couple of days. When they finally found him, he was almost dead. The state came in to investigate. Corrapell wasn't licensed for that kind of rehab. The case is still in the courts. Until it's settled, no new clients. I gotta tell you, there's a whole lot of weirdness around this place sometimes. And the new nighttime vitamins are the least of it."

Katie wanted to ask more about Isaac but didn't want the boy's name tied to the other questions she had. Isaac said Wade told him to shut up. Wade's version was more like he'd been counseling the boy on what was appropriate to say. Who was giving her straight information?

"There's gossip in town that a guy disappeared from here around Valentine's Day. Like poof, and he was gone. A really big guy. Dead or something." She threw another nickel into the pot.

Wade laughed. "You gotta love gossip. I was working here then. I remember the guy leaving." He laid down two pairs and scooped up the pile of change. "People sign up for the fat farm because they're all alone. They've got nobody. They come here thinking they'll take a little two-week vacation and walk out a whole new person." He dealt a new hand. "Usually, they leave disappointed. If we're thinking of the same guy, I remember him. Mr. Dion. He was here for a couple of months. He had enough bucks in his pocket, so both the Revecks were really nice to him. Then, one day, he decided he'd gotten skinny enough, and it was time to go. Walked in through the door looking like Santa Claus in a three-piece suit, walked out looking quite dapper."

"Dapper?" Katie frowned at her hand. She hadn't gotten a good deal. *Is he stacking the deck?* She wondered.

"His words. I helped him pack his stuff the night before he went home. He was having it shipped. We had to use regular boxes instead of suitcases."

"Well, there are some people here who think he just upped and disappeared. That it was suspicious, you know? Like, not a good thing." She laid down three cards to be replaced and still had nothing in her hand.

"That's all hogwash." Wade stared down the hallway behind him. Every door was locked. There was no noise, nothing to see. "He had an odd first name. Not Edward or Everett, but something similar. But I'm telling you straight, he decided he was ready to leave, and he meant right now. Like I said, I helped pack his stuff. Dr. Reveck had to drive him to the bus station at about 1:00 A.M. The good doctor was not pleased, but the old guy had a ticket for an early bus."

"You're sure he left with the doctor, Wade? That he went to the bus station? Montpelier or Burlington?"

Wade stared at Katie with narrowed eyes. "I told you what I know. Why are you asking all these questions?"

Katie bit her lip. "Actually, I'm curious about what happened with all his fat clothes. Or any of the fat people's clothes. The thrift shop is always looking." She felt a sudden prickle of sweat on her back. Had she said too much?

This brought a guffaw from Wade. "You'd have to eat a lot of cake and shrink by six inches to fit them. As far as I know, they're still in boxes around here somewhere." He was still chuckling as he adjusted the cards in his hand.

But Katie knew better. Somebody had anonymously dumped trash bags, not boxes of the fat man's clothing at the thrift shop. Everything Wade was saying led her to believe the good quality merchandise had come from here. It was on the tip of her tongue to ask if Wade knew who the shipper would have been, but he still seemed a little tense.

"All in all, I think it's a good thing when somebody walks away happy, don't you?" Katie asked, trying to diffuse him.

At Wade's nod, she took a chance and asked, "Is that what happened to the woman who left a few weeks ago, too? She got skinnied down and left?"

Wade frowned. "I don't remember a woman. Flush." His fanned-out hand took the last of Katie's cash.

"You sure are lucky," Katie said. "I think I need a little air. That was my last fifty cents."

"Go ahead. Step outside, I'll cover for you. Just don't get lost." Wade pulled out a paperback book and put his feet up in her seat.

Once outside, Katie moved fast. The layout in the front of the building was already a known factor. Trotting around the women's wing took her to the far backside. The road continued until she had passed the end of the men's wing and then a loading dock outside the kitchen area. There was a split in the dirt road she assumed led to the Revecks' home. Just as Wade had said, there was an area encircled by a chain link fence. A padlock held the gate closed. Her flashlight glow lit up three, maybe four, cars. Continuing in the same direction, she came to the small lawn that separated the empty wings of the retreat from the woods. On this side, the grass was overgrown, and the wild bushes were hedging in. Up against the building, flowerbeds looked tall and reedy with old growth.

Well, if they can't use these rooms, maybe they aren't bothering with the landscaping, she reasoned.

Once back inside, Katie found Wade yawning and rubbing at his eyes. He had told her earlier he worked a full-time day job as a laborer.

"You must be exhausted," she said. "Why don't you find a place to sack out and catch some z's?"

"There's a sofa in the lounge." He yawned again. "If you're sure about that, maybe I could take a twenty-minute nap."

"Sure," she said. "Just show me where you'll be, and I'll wake you up in twenty minutes."

Wade was almost snoring before Katie walked out of the lounge. She came back through the kitchen, silently walking around the room, opening any of the doors that weren't locked, looking into cupboards, searching for anything that appeared out of place. In the dining room, she ran her fingers along the edge of the table, guiding herself, and realized her fingers were covered with dust.

If people are eating here every day, how come it's so filthy?

She opened each of the empty rooms on the far end of her wing. Each room was totally devoid of anything beyond the long cotton curtains. She slipped down to the end of Wade's corridor. Knowing she was about to ruin it, she used her only credit card to open the locked doors because her key didn't work. The rooms were the same as the other wing.

After a careful search into the closets for any boxes filled with men's clothing, perhaps already taped closed and ready for shipment, Katie had to wonder if Wade had been mistaken. There was nothing there. Not a single shoe or tie.

It could have been shipped out when Wade wasn't here. He works nights and wouldn't know what was going on during the day, right? Chewing her lip, Katie considered the options besides the one that said those trash bags dumped so unceremoniously on Dorothea's table were originally in boxes Wade had packed.

They were all the same size, an entire wardrobe, for crying out loud.

She was sure she was right, but short of asking Wade exactly where he had left the boxes, there was nothing she could do. Making him more suspicious wasn't a good answer. If there was something hinky going on, and he was part of the group setting it up, she didn't want him to be passing out her name.

Once again, she swept her light around the last room, then decidedly clicked it off. There was no more to see here. Outside the single window, Katie caught the glow of another flashlight. When she realized it was moving towards her, down the road leading from the Revecks' home, she knew someone had seen her own light as she conducted the room-by-room search. She thundered down the hallway. It was time to wake up Wade, fast.

* * *

Katie slid behind the desk on her wing, sucking in a deep breath and holding it to calm her racing heart. A key turned, opening the door leading into the lobby/common room area. She jumped up, feigning alarm. In the doorway was Mrs. Reveck, still completely dressed at 3:00 A.M., right down to her high-heeled boots.

"Holy crap!" Katie yelped. "You scared me to death!"

"I'm sorry, Katie," said Mrs. Reveck, sounding anything but. "I thought I'd come out and check on how you were doing, being new and all."

Without bothering to ask why her new employer hadn't checked on her the first night she'd worked, Katie told her she was doing fine. "I haven't seen or heard a peep. Not even a field mouse has moved in here," she said.

"Did I tell you there is a flashlight in the kitchen if the power goes out?" asked Mrs. Reveck, crossing the corridor and non-nonchalantly trying the door. The lock held.

"That's good to know," said Katie before pointing out, "but I don't have a key."

"Hmm," said her employer. Unlocking the connecting doors, the woman walked through. As the door closed, Katie heard Wade greet their boss.

Katie spent the rest of her shift berating herself for being clumsy and planning a little visit with Isaac. He had said he'd been everywhere in this place. It might be safer to see what he remembered than blunder along by herself.

* * *

At the end of her spa shift, a woman old enough to have been in the same grade in grammar school as Dorothea relieved her. Katie dawdled, getting her things together. Without a word or even a glance in Katie's direction, the woman dumped her tote on the desk, poured coffee from a thermos, and opened a wax-paper package of cold toast and peanut butter. After plunking her butt in the seat, she pulled out her knitting and, for all accounts and purposes, seemed oblivious to the rest of the world.

"Phfft," Katie muttered, heading toward the lobby. "There's a personality I don't need to know."

Mrs. Reveck was seated in her office, bent over paperwork. As quietly as possible, Katie scooted across the room and into the dining room. In the kitchen, a woman of considerable girth worked at the stove while a fresh-faced young woman laid trays out on the counter.

"Can I help you?" the cook asked.

"Hi, I'm Katie. I work here. My truck was acting a little rough last evening, so I'm waiting for my uncle. Are you Mrs. Frances?"

"No, I'm Edna. Mrs. Frances is no longer with us." Edna stopped stirring and peered at Katie. "What did you say your name was?"

"Uh, Katie." Suddenly, this didn't seem like such a good idea. "Oh, listen, there's my uncle. Have a good day." At almost a run, she crossed the lobby. Wade's car was gone, but several new vehicles filled the front row of parking.

Chapter Twenty-Four

It was after noontime before Katie woke up groggy and ill-tempered. Being Tuesday, Rick was gone to work, and a note on the table told her Grace had taken Ruth home with her. Seated at the table with toast and reheated coffee, Katie was arguing with Walker about custody of the crusts when she remembered her plan to contact Isaac. Looking at the clock, she realized the afternoon was well advanced. There was a piece of notepaper tacked on the wall with telephone numbers, but Saint Jude's wasn't on the list. Climbing over the dogs, she darted to the junk drawer, looking for the directory.

"Saint Jude Rectory," A woman answered the phone.

"Hi, Mrs. O'Brien. This is Katie Took. What a nice surprise to hear your voice!"

"Hello, Katie." There was a blush in the older woman's voice. She was obviously pleased that someone would know it was her. "Father isn't here right now."

"That's okay. I'll catch him later. Did you and Isaac have a problem getting into town today?"

"Oh, Isaac is at home. But I took your advice and asked the bus driver for a lift. He's so nice, Mr. Eliot."

As soon as the words regarding Isaac were out of his mother's mouth, Katie threw a notebook, pen, and Tupperware container of date bars into a tote. Still yanking her boots on, she raced out the door, headed back toward the Richmond town line to have a face-to-face in-depth conversation with Isaac.

* * *

"You want me to draw a map?" Isaac asked.

"I want you to help me plot out the layout inside the building and maybe the outbuildings," said Katie. The open container of date bars was between them, and she'd put the teapot on. Isaac didn't know she was working at Corrapell, and she wasn't ready to tell him. "Then I want you to tell me everything you can remember about the employees, starting with Edna and Wade."

"I don't know anything about Wade, except he's kind of a good guy. He works at night. The people who work during the day are all pretty old. Mostly, they just kind of sit around. Mom used to complain that they never got a lot done. Edna is older and a lousy cook. There's a girl with brown hair and crooked teeth named Holly. She helps take care of the patients and does housekeeping. My mom told me Holly knows more than Mrs. Reveck because she is a real nurse. She used to work at the hospital in Burlington but got burned up."

"Burned out," Katie corrected.

"Whatever. Everybody else that comes in works for some agency, so they're always different. There used to be aides that helped get the residents up, showered, dressed, all that kind of stuff. None of them work there anymore. I remember Mom saying it was a lousy job and not worth the money. I don't know who works there now. Besides maybe Holly. Mrs. Reveck is always in the building. I mean, always. She's as weird as her husband. I can draw you a really good map. Do you want to know about the connecting doors?"

Now, there was an interesting tidbit: connecting doors. She nodded as she poured water into two mugs, the teabags floating to the top.

While they filled the notebook with diagrams, Katie asked about the staff that had been let go, like his mother. Isaac said Holly had been there the entire time that he and his mother had. His information about Dr. Reveck was limited.

"What about the man, the patient that disappeared? Or the woman. Can you describe her?"

"Yeah, she was real heavy, blond hair, older than my mother. The guy was about the same age, and when he first came, he was like, HUGE. I noticed when I was hiding that his watch just dangled on his wrist, so eating only lime Jello must have worked. But to be honest, I didn't want to look at him much because a lot of those people were like zombies."

"So, you saw them when they were in the common room or the dining room?"

"No, Katie, I told you. They didn't come out of their rooms. Once the whackos started arriving, everyone ate in their room."

"What room was the blond lady in?" Katie asked.

"Two-oh-eight."

"Can you remember if the man's last name was Dion?"

"Yeah, Dion, like dying. Like zombies." Isaac gave a self-conscious laugh.

They talked for a short time longer, but Katie wanted to be gone before the school bus showed up. She took a chance and said, "Isaac, right now, our talking together is like you're speaking to Father Metevier. Between you and me, okay?"

"Yeah," he said.

He was a kid, but he was also acting twitchy. Katie was worried if he had told someone else what he had said to Father Metevier or herself, he would go back and tell that unknown person about Katie. It made her nervous and reminded her to sit down with Rick.

"Isaac, I don't want to take a chance by coming here again. If I need to talk to you, I'll look for you at school." She left him believing that she stopped by there on a regular basis, even though she knew he didn't.

She met the school bus on the road ten minutes later. Mrs. O'Brien was seated right behind Mr. Eliot, with her back to the other traffic lane. Katie could only hope Isaac picked up the Tupperware container she had forgotten. Once in town, she kept straight on Main Street until she got to the sheriff's office. Stick-up-his-butt Deputy Brad was working. Gabardine pants creased; shoes shined.

"I'm here to see Martin. Sheriff Lewis," Katie corrected.

Brad took a long look down his nose at her before asking if the sheriff was expecting her.

"No, but tell him I want to talk about the da-da-da-dum, body." She gave her best Vincent Price impersonation.

She was shown right into the inner office. Sheriff Lewis leaned back in his seat, not offering her one. But she picked the chair she liked best and sat down.

"I want to see the crime scene pictures from where the body was left on my property," she said.

"Nope."

"Then I need a description of the remains. Or a name, if you have it."

"Nope."

For a moment, she sat there sucking on the inside of her lower lip. Then she leaned forward and asked, "Do you want some help, maybe some intel, or not?"

Lewis copied her movements. "You can tell me what you know, or you can go to jail."

"I don't know anything. I'm just surmising." She sat back. He was trying her patience, and all she wanted was a quick answer.

"I don't believe you, Katelyn Took." Lewis's eyes were flat. He wasn't giving anything away.

"Mm. Let's play a game. I'm going to give you three bits of information. You tell me how many I have right. Okay? Middle-aged, overweight, blonde." She waited, forcing herself to breathe.

Lewis leaned back in his seat again. For just a moment, Katie thought she'd hit the trifecta. Then he let out a loud, rough laugh, and she knew she'd failed all the way around. Without another word, she stood up and walked out.

The last newspaper article she had seen told her the remains were female, and there was some question about the death. Even though she'd been watching closely and listening to the news, she hadn't learned any more than that. There was a lot of gossip swirling among the locals, but she had no way to sift the facts out from the fiction. Sheriff Lewis had just proven no info would be coming from him. At least not to her.

Maybe Rick knows somebody Lewis gossips with. She revved the truck's engine and squealed out of the driveway before considering that move could get her arrested. Again.

***

It was after supper, while Ruth was sorting through the box of unsalvageable clothing Dorothea had sent to be torn into rags, that Katie pulled Rick aside.

"You got a minute?" she asked.

Rick looked over her shoulder. "From the look on your face, this sounds like something that should happen far away from Ruth."

He led the way down to the cellar. While he filled the firebox of the Tarn furnace, Katie told him about her first meeting with Isaac and what she'd been up to since.

"Why am I not surprised?" he asked.

Katie was relieved his first words weren't for her to drop the whole mess.

"Rick, over all this time, whenever I think about the Gypsy Copse, it reminds me of Poppa, and it's a good feeling. Now, it's blighted somehow. I don't want that. I want it to be good again. I know Sheriff Lewis knows more than he'll share. Not just with me, but with the staties as well. I don't know what the deal is with Edward Richardson from the Montpelier Forensics. He might be talking to the state police, but he's not going to talk to me either."

"Point there," Rick said.

"I'm not asking you to do anything, I just want you to know what I'm doing."

"How come you aren't telling Father Metevier?" Rick asked.

Katie laughed. "Hysteria."

Rick looked up toward the kitchen door. "You know, it does seem odd there isn't more information in the paper. If you've got to do this, keep me in the loop. If you don't, I'm going to tell Ruth."

"Deal," Katie said and followed him upstairs.

While she put Jacob Cattle beans on to soak overnight for her weekly baked beans, Rick pulled out the telephone directory. It wasn't until he started talking that she realized what he was doing.

"Is this the news desk? I've gotta question," he said into the receiver. "I live in Parentville. This deal with the remains found here in town has got a lot of us really nervous. The local sheriff refuses to give us any information, like a description of the woman that was found dead."

He listened for a few moments.

"No, I don't want to give you my name. But you should know that we rely on the Burlington Free Press to keep us informed about the doings, and right now, we feel like everyone is letting us down."

Rick listened again, with the occasional ah-huh, yup. Finally, he said thank you, hung up the phone and went into the living room. The theme music for *Mork and Mindy* was playing.

Chapter Twenty-Five

A meetings were held on Sunday mornings from seven until eight, finishing before Mass. The day was overcast, with the forecast for a late-season frost. Ruth said her arthritis agreed, but most locals declared it wouldn't be rainy until later in the afternoon, with the possibility of a few slick places on the roads in the early evening.

Katie pulled into the Woodman lot and found six other vehicles parked in the back. She slowed down, considering making a U-turn and leaving, but the grill on the front of a big Ford filled her rearview mirror. Two other cars had pulled in behind the truck.

Inside the building, there were open seats at the back. She headed for one that looked inconspicuous. The room held more people than cars in the lot, probably because some had lost their right to drive. She saw the back of a familiar head. Nate had lost his delivery driver job to Rick because of a DWI conviction after a holiday party. AA was a stipulation of his work-release program.

Just as she prepared to sit, Charlie popped up. He was seated near the front and waved enthusiastically for her to join him, indicating he had saved her a seat.

No, I don't want to, Katie whined to herself.

Charlie waved again, this time mouthing her name. Shoving her fists deep into the pockets of her jacket, Katie skulked up the aisle. Shoulders up to her ears and face beet-red, she dropped onto the cold seat of the folding chair, whispering a terse thank you as the meeting director started speaking. Charlie beamed, happy to have helped her out, making Katie smile even though she didn't want to. Forty-five minutes later, after listening to words of wisdom and a few attendees willing to tell their stories, Katie bypassed the coffee and cookie table and, with a pat on Charlie's back, headed out the door.

There was time for her to go home before Mass started at ten o'clock, but she didn't want to face Ruth and Rick's hopeful smiles. They both knew where she had gone and though not one word had been said, she knew they were hoping she might find some inner peace. All she wanted was some control of her life, enough to replenish her willpower and give her the strength to say no to people like Father Metevier and Ruth, who were trying to direct her life.

Katie knew from experience stability wouldn't happen after one meeting. It had taken several gatherings, almost one a day, in church basements all over Chicago, for her to quit drinking.

I just have to start somewhere, she reminded herself.

Instead, she pulled into the church parking lot and found a hidden spot behind the dumpster to wait. It was cold sitting in the truck and she was worried Father Metevier would look out the window and see her. She could almost visualize him dashing across the gravel and puddles to usher her into church for Mass. After twenty minutes; she went over and tried the thrift store door. It swung open. Dorothea was already on the job. Gathering the ironing she had promised to get done for Dorothea from where it lay on the seat of the truck, she headed down the stairs.

As the electric heaters started snapping and popping, tiny fans came on, pushing wispy sighs of heat into the church's basement.

"How about you work the sewing machine today?" Dorothea said.

"You're the boss," Katie said, dumping the first bag of mending her elderly friend had stacked up at the end of the table. There were elbows to replace. Sheets ripped for pillowcases and towels with holes. There was also half a trash bag of little-kid pants with the knees worn clean through.

"Just cut the legs off, hem 'em for shorts," said Dorothea.

Katie rubbed the soft and worn corduroy between her fingers. It seemed a shame. Her eyes ran around the room, landing in the infant area. In the stacks, she found a receiving blanket that had monkeys stamped into the pattern. Back at the sewing machine, she laid the tiny blanket on a torn towel and cut out a two-layered monkey patch. Some of the pants had snaps running up the inside of the legs. She started with them, laying the fabric flat and zig-zag stitching the patch into place and back and forth. She was silently congratulating herself on finishing her first piece when a man spoke behind her.

"That's cute."

Katie almost jumped out of her seat. "Cripe," she said, embarrassed by her reaction. "You scared the bejeebers out of me!"

"Sorry," Father Metevier said, equally embarrassed. "Didn't mean to. I saw you working over here when I came in. I just thought I'd say hello." There was an awkward silence. "Charlie told me this morning after the meeting, you were probably headed over here to work for a while."

"Charlie said… Wait. You were at the meeting?" If there had been a rock handy, Katie would have crawled beneath it.

"Yeah, I usually stop in and check to see what's going on. I had him run out and pick up the boy so he could help out down here for a while." When Father Metevier stepped aside, Isaac stood behind him, scowling with fists jammed deep in his pockets.

There was a good chance Father Metevier and Mrs. O'Brien had strong-armed the lad down into the thrift shop. Katie knew from her own life experience that wasn't the way to get him to open up. The priest looked at her hopefully, but Katie pressed her lips together, refusing to say a word.

"What are you people yammering about?" Dorothea asked, coming out of the back room with an armful of clothes hangers. "There's work to be done."

The priest laughed and walked off. Katie held up the small pair of bib overalls. "What do you think?"

Reaching out gnarled fingers to snatch the buttercup yellow pants, Dorothea smiled. "Look at that. I'll be danged. They look like they came from the maker all decorated. Too bad you can't do the bigger ones. Some of them are lined. They'd be nice and warm for the little snorters."

"Actually, I think I can." Katie explained that by slitting the side seam, she'd be able to reach the torn place and put on a neat patch. "Then I can double stitch the seam back in. One row of straight stitch and an inside row of zig-zag. I may have to use up another receiving blanket, though."

"There's a cute one that's got fat little bumblebees on it." Dorothea handed the overalls back and headed toward the cash box and a waiting customer.

Through the morning, the cranky thrift store custodian kept Isaac hopping. She knew where he was every moment, leaving Katie with no time for a private conversation. Later, Dorothea gave Isaac and Katie sliced ham sandwiches and tea for lunch. The ham was a little dry, and the mustard was too thick, but the sentiment was good. Katie knew it was hard for Dorothea to express gratitude, and this was her way. After the elderly lady turned to her own lunch, Katie watched the boy inhale his sandwich.

Laying hers, still wrapped in wax paper, to the side, she whispered, "Someday, I'm going to tell her not to bring me one. My family waits to have Sunday dinner with me when I get home." Lifting a seam ripper, she attacked the French seam, holding the small pants together.

"You're not going to eat that?" Isaac asked.

"If I do, then I have to tell Ruth no at home. That wouldn't be good," Katie said innocently. "How about you? Do you think you have room for another?" She didn't look up, but slowed her work enough so she could hear his movements.

"Thank you." Then, both Isaac and the sandwich were gone.

Dorothea sidled over. "I brought him a second sandwich. Do you think he'd be offended if I offered it?"

Surprised that bossy Dorothea would ask her opinion, Katie looked up.

"Give him a few minutes to digest the first one, then just give it to him," she said, turning away to laugh silently. *His belly is going to be too full for his hands to work.*

Chapter Twenty-Six

"It's going to take days," Rick complained when he and Ruth got home from church, and his fiancée told him to get upstairs and start hauling boxes down.

"Quiet down, you big baby." Ruth laid her crutches aside and parked her butt on the sofa. "Davey and Billy hauled down a bunch of boxes, so there's some already done. And Katie is going to make them brownies as a thank you, right Katie?"

Dutifully, Katie headed toward the kitchen. She needed to get the cooking done so she could have a lie-down, as she'd missed her nap that morning to go to the AA meeting. Several cats ran along beside her, hoping she'd pour a little milk in their saucepan.

Charlie had followed them home, and after a good Sunday dinner of leftover roasted chicken and mac and cheese, which Katie made by the blue galvanized roaster full so it would cover more than one meal, the men started bringing down heavier items and furniture. This time a few cats made it all the way into the back bedroom and stayed there a while, running amuck among Gram's hoarded mess.

The final decision was to get everything downstairs and put it in the empty parlor, a room usually kept closed, until all could be sorted out. Katie hauled boxes and bags until it was time for her to rest, as she would be working at Corrapell that night. She had told Mrs. Reveck she'd come in early for a few extra hours that evening. When Ruth complained that she thought the resort manager was taking advantage, Katie didn't mention her hope to be there when the residents were awake and possibly willing to talk.

Katie walked away, laughing to herself as Charlie moaned and groaned. His belly was full, and he wanted to take a nap first. But Ruth got out her notebook and shoe box of handmade price tags, then she sent him upstairs. Opening the first box, she and LG and Peanut peeked inside.

It was well past suppertime before Ruth called a halt to the tramping up and down the stairwell. Katie hadn't lasted an hour after cleaning up from Sunday dinner. Wrapped in her quilts and trying to sleep, she had long before realized the speed of the men's trips had fallen off severely. Through the open heat grate in the floor, she could hear Ruth, ever the little general, still giving orders.

"That pile over there is pure junk. You can take it to the dump tomorrow," Ruth told Rick. "This stuff I got tagged and ready for the yard sale, we can haul straight down to the schoolhouse. There's a bit already over there to go out to the barn. We'll leave the rest here in the parlor while we decide what to do with it. That way, the cats can't get at it. Watch it; don't let more of them in."

Katie gave a soft chuckle. Even before she'd come upstairs, the pile she was sure Ruth was referring to as ready to haul down to the schoolhouse was definitely the lion's share. She finally dozed off, missing the rest of the conversation.

"My back already hurts," Rick said. Though he didn't say a word, Charlie nodded in agreement.

Then Rick added, "The upside is, there appears to be a bunk bed that came out of the hired help trailer up there. Probably needs to be cleaned up, but it can stay. And the old maple dresser."

"We can take the mattress off Katie's old twin bed for the bunk," said Ruth.

"There's one on it. You can look at it later. I've had enough for tonight. My muscles are fried." Rick slumped in a corner of the sofa, barely noticing when Charlie said good night and left.

"It's okay," said Ruth. "I'm only going to work for a couple of hours in the morning with Grace. Then I can start cleaning up in that room before we move anything else in or around. Getting this stuff out of the way will just have to wait. With the big things you guys have to haul down to the schoolhouse, there won't be a lot more room." She paused, running her hand over the free-standing kitchen cupboard. It was a beautiful piece, but there was no room in their kitchen for it.

"What was it Father Metevier wanted when he collared you after Mass?" she asked.

"He's got some youngster he wants to let follow me around and learn about real work," said Rick, kicking off his boots. "I don't know if I'm up to that."

Chapter Twenty-Seven

Katie walked into Corrapell, tote bag in hand. There were just enough people wandering around so she could sneak her supper inside. She was acutely aware, however, how many day workers left with tote bags and even personal coolers.

"Phfft," she muttered, "I guess there's a heck of a difference between working days and nights."

The tote was barely hidden beneath the desk when Mrs. Reveck showed up at her elbow.

"Things work a little differently during the early evening than when you normally come in at eleven," said Mrs. Reveck. "Our residents will be winding down their afternoon activities, preparing for dinner. You will be expected to assist them in getting in and out of the bathroom if needed, get meal trays passed around, and later, perhaps help a few prepare for bed. Nothing strenuous. But we have to make sure everyone is safe." Mrs. Reveck smiled, showing lots of teeth, but no happy glow in her eyes.

"You know I'm not trained for anything like this, right?" Katie asked. "Shouldn't there be a nurse or an aide here?"

Mrs. Reveck leaned forward, suddenly a buddy. "Normally, dear, there is. Unfortunately, tonight, our regular girl isn't available. You understand, don't you?"

"Sure." Katie found herself leaning back. Once Mrs. Reveck turned away, she righted herself. "I'll go check on everyone."

"Oh, this is their quiet time. Perhaps you should give them a little privacy."

As her employer unlocked the joining door, Katie obediently took her seat behind the desk. Nothing appeared different from when she had been here during the nights. The small table held paper cups, a pot of water on the warmer, teabags, and Sanka. There were no crackers or fruit set out. As soon as the door lock clicked back into place, Katie was up, checking the door on the kitchenette. Still locked. She listened at the connecting door and, when she didn't hear voices, dared to tiptoe to the first resident's room.

Beyond it, and every other door she opened, guests were moving around, but they seemed to be slightly lethargic or in the first stages of waking. On the west side, the rooms were stifling hot. The air was almost unbreathable. Katie walked up to the first woman and saw beads of sweat on her face and upper arms.

"Oh, my goodness," Katie said, alarmed at the deep red flush of the woman's face. "Stay there for just a second."

Katie opened the window as far as it would go, before rushing into the bathroom and returning with a cool cloth and a glass of water.

"Do you feel better? I'm Katie; I'll be here for the next few hours."

The woman offered a weak smile. "I'm Cecile."

When Katie was sure Cecile was going to be okay, she went on to the next room. All along the west side of the corridor, she found similar situations. After making sure each resident was okay, she hurried on to the next. On her way out of each room, she left the door open to allow the heat to escape.

"The last thing I need is for someone to go into heat stroke while I'm here," she muttered to herself as she walked back up the hall. She had every intention of telling Mrs. Reveck that the person attending that wing during the afternoon had not checked on her charges or had not bothered to make sure they were safe.

For the next hour, Katie kept checking on the women, bringing them warm washcloths and making sure they got into the bathroom safely. One woman wanted a shower, so Katie walked with her down the hall. Then she went back to where Cecile had finished changing her clothes. The woman was seated in the armchair in front of her window.

"All set, Cecile?" Katie asked. "Are you ready to go down to the dining room or maybe just the social hall?"

"We aren't allowed to go down to the dining room or the lobby anymore." Cecile had a soft voice with a faint southern drawl. "Since the bad people tore it all up, we've eaten in our rooms and just stayed here. Missus Reveck says it's safer that way."

"So, you just stay in here all day, alone?" Katie thought she might have heard wrong. Each room held only one resident. There was a small television, but out here, only Channel 3 could be depended on. At the far end of the hall was an open place with a sofa, a table and chairs, and a stack of puzzles. If the ladies didn't want to go out to the main reception area and gathering place, they could still visit each other in their own wing. Before Katie could ask why the women didn't go down there, a bell rang across the intercom.

"Fifteen minutes until supper," Cecile said.

Excusing herself, Katie ran out. From room to room, she went along, helping those who were not quite ready before their evening meal arrived. She was just finishing up with the woman who had showered when she heard her name called.

The young woman, whose name tag identified her as Gail, and who had been helping Edna days earlier, stood in the doorway with a tiered cart of trays.

"Here you go," Gail said. "Make sure you pick up all the trays before you bring the rack back."

Katie's jaw dropped. "How do I know who gets what?"

"Funny girl. Except for how many leaves of lettuce they get, the trays are all the same." Gail walked out into the reception hall, shutting the door behind her.

"Okay…" Picking up the first tray, Katie went into the nearest room. The resident was seated in her chair, a small table pulled up in front of her, and a look of anticipation on her face.

"Turkey day," the woman said.

After placing the tray on the table, Katie lifted the plate cover and stopped short. The plate contained two thin slices of white meat turkey loaf, half a cup of green peas, and a small bowl of lettuce with a slice of tomato and two onion rings. A ceramic monkey bowl held half a canned pear. There was a glass of water and a cup of see-thru tea. The woman reached eagerly for her silverware. Katie left for the next tray, considering how she put more food in a single sandwich than these women got in a complete meal.

By the time she had delivered Cecile's meal, the first woman was finished and had pushed the table away. It was time to collect trays.

"Are you all through, Cecile? Would you like to go down and sit in the lounge?"

"I don't think so, honey. I'll have a wash-up. Mrs. Reveck will be around at seven to make sure we're all gone to bed."

Out in the corridor, women made their way toward the shower room. Both stalls were busy, and women waited in chairs lining the wall. By the time Katie got back to the kitchen to drop off the rack, the cook and her assistant were gone. The atmosphere in the big room felt tense. A young man was emptying trays, loading the dishwasher, and scrubbing out pots. He very clearly did not want to speak to Katie, and she wondered if he had been told not to gossip. The reception area was fully lit up. It looked welcoming, for a place no one was allowed to enter, and though she skirted around it, she could tell Mrs. Reveck was still in her office.

The shower occupants had changed. There was a bit of lively conversation happening among the residents, making Katie smile.

I guess they just needed to wake up a little, and now they're fine.

The door opened behind her. Everyone looked up. It was like someone had thrown a light switch. The easy movement up and down the hall had changed to a scuttling race as the women rushed toward the sanctity of their own rooms. Even the last women still seated, waiting to take a shower, gave up and hurried away.

"What just happened?" Katie wondered aloud.

"It's time for night meds," said Mrs. Reveck. "Seeing that you have no medical training, I will be dispensing this evening."

Though not invited, Katie followed her employer. Mrs. Reveck carried a single bottle of pills, a pitcher of water, and a small stack of paper cups. Signaling Katie to stay in the hall, she went into each room, gave the occupant two pills and a glass of water, and waited until the medication had been swallowed. Katie watched the first resident lumber to her bed and make herself comfortable immediately after Mrs. Reveck left. It was the same in the next room.

What kind of vitamins is she giving them, exactly?

There had been an incident a while before where a local man, Geofrey Ash, had been using medication on his wife, making her appear mentally incompetent. Katie had interrupted his plan to have her institutionalized and gain control of her fortune. She felt a touch of déjà vu. This couldn't be the same thing, could it? Suspicious, she dogged Mrs. Reveck's steps.

Coming out of Cecile's room, Mrs. Reveck said, "You can return to your desk, Katie. I can do this by myself. Thank you."

As the other woman kept walking, Katie wondered if her questioning thoughts had been easily read on her face. Still standing in the doorway, she turned just in time to see Cecile shove two fingers down her throat and gag up the white tablets. With them in her hand, the obese woman headed toward the bathroom.

"Stop, Cecile!" Katie darted into the room, grabbing the woman's hand as it traveled toward her mouth. "No. Give them to me. It's okay. Go lie down. I'll be back in a little while."

In the bathroom, she wrapped the slightly dissolved tablets in a paper towel, then rinsed her hands thoroughly. With the folded paper towel in her pocket, Katie returned to Cecile's room. Mrs. Reveck was nowhere in sight.

"I'm pretty new here, Cecile. To be honest, this isn't my regular job. But there was a young guy who was kind of around here a lot. He and I were talking, and he has some far-fetched ideas about what's going on. I'm trying to make sure everything is on the up-and-up, you know?" Katie said. "How about if you and I have an honest conversation."

"Why would you be helping some young kid? Is he your brother? One of the dope people?" Cecile asked.

"No. He's a neighborhood kid, and he's confused. Before he runs his mouth and gets into any trouble doing it, I'm checking around a little bit." Katie leaned against the door frame, offering a shrug and a small smile.

Cecile pulled the covers up to her chin, her cornflower blue eyes brimming over. "I'm so sorry. I know I should be grateful, but those tablets Mrs. Reveck is passing around scare me terribly."

Katie had left the door open behind her, stepping backwards into the hall, she could see that all the doors were closed. No lights shone beneath them. Katie was sure this was how come the other residents slept so soundly until morning. Staying right there, in full view of Cecile, but in a position to keep watch for Mrs. Reveck, she spoke softly. "I want to help my friend and I want to help you too. Please tell me your story."

Cecile sighed. "My husband threw me aside because I had grown to be such a fat pig. His words exactly. He got rich on the job my daddy had given him, then he just turned me out. His new slim and sexy wife moved in. My mama said I was an embarrassment, so they shipped me here. I didn't have a lot of choice. It's not a bad place, really. Though it used to be nicer, back when there was someone to talk to, maybe play cards."

"How long have you been here?"

"About a year."

Katie gaped.

"It was different when I first came here." Cecile moved around in the bed, an uncomfortable look on her face. "The Revecks had just expanded to helping people who had other issues besides eating disorders, you know, like drugs. But then that didn't work out the way they wanted. Anyway, to keep us safe, we were asked to stay in our rooms and not talk to people on the outside about the changes here. We were told it was for the privacy of all the residents."

Katie closed her mouth.

"There was some grousing and complaining. I think that's what led to us all being given the nighttime vitamins that are actually sleeping pills. I know what they are. I suffer from bouts of insomnia. Some nights, I can't sleep without taking those pills." Her eyes flicked to the door. "I haven't spoken with all the other women here, and I don't think even those who realize what's happening care. At least one other remarked that if she was sleeping, she wasn't eating, so that was a good thing."

"You're sure she knew what you were saying? If you know what the pills are, and they're going to let you sleep, why are you afraid?" Katie had been moving around, getting closer and trying to see Cecile's face, maybe tell if she was lying. Cecile turned, looking directly at Katie.

"Because I'm afraid. I easily get addicted. That's how I got this huge. First, it was cigarettes. Then it was wine coolers, then bacon cheeseburgers." Cecile teared up. "I just want to get down to a weight where my mama will leave me alone, and maybe by the grace of God and a good psychologist, I will be able to get myself straightened out. I know I can't do it alone, but I refuse to take those pills."

Katie was now inside the room, and nervous Mrs. Reveck or someone else would come along and find her and Cecile talking. She thought for a moment, scratching her forehead before she spoke.

"Okay, Cecile. How about a cup of tea? You and I can talk about this a little more. And, to be truthful, I have a few questions."

"Where are we going to get tea? There's nothing here after supper." Cecile frowned at Katie, obviously thinking the idea was absurd.

"Actually, there are tea bags and hot water up by my desk. We'll go down to the sitting area and watch the sunset."

"What if Mrs. Reveck sees us?" Cecile asked. The edge of the blanket crept a little higher on her face.

"If we shut off the light in here, it'll look like everyone is sleeping. Mrs. Reveck doesn't usually bother checking before she goes. With the lights in the sitting room off and only the ones in the hall on, we won't be visible from outside. We'll be sitting in the dark, and I'll keep watch."

They sat on the sofa for a long while, watching the sun dip behind the trees and talking about the things Cecile had seen since her arrival. Katie wasn't sure if she should just jump in with her questions about the missing residents. Her interrogation skills were limited. One thing she did remember was how her lawyer had gotten her to open up about what she'd been doing to discover how her gram had died. With that in mind, she decided to come clean about how she, too, had suffered from addiction and used AA to keep a grip on her life. Once she got started, she wasn't been able to stop talking.

"Back in Illinois, there were days I went to more than one meeting a day. Since I got back here, I've been holding my own so far, but I can tell it's time for maintenance meetings. There have to be meetings for people with food addictions, too. If not, then maybe you just have to woman up and go to AA. It's for addicts. Alcohol, drugs, tobacco, why not cheeseburgers? I bet you'd pull the rug off and uncover a bunch of people with the same issues."

"I know you're right, Katie, I do. But I have to get out of here first." Cecile sighed.

"Well, you're free and over twenty-one. You can sign yourself out of here anytime. The big issue, I guess, is how you'd live once you were out."

"You mean like money?" Cecile laughed. "Oh, honey, I've got lots of money. The judge made my Hank pay up big time, every month until one of us kicks off. And my grandmother, bless her soul, left me a small inheritance. I just don't have anywhere to go."

"I bet you do, if you really think about it," said Katie, she had other questions, but this didn't seem to be the right moment. She stood up, it was time to check on the other women. "I'll bring you stationery and stamps. You should write letters to your bank or lawyer, and to your friends. Be honest, and somebody will be there for you."

Cecile went back to her room, and Katie checked Mrs. Reveck's office. The lights were off and the door was shut. It made Katie edgy. She hadn't seen Mrs. Reveck walk around the end of the building, but she could have gone through the kitchen to leave. That led Katie to wonder if there were more exits, she didn't know about.

Chapter Twenty-Eight

Even though Katie had been relieved of her duties at midnight and was able to catch a couple of hours of sleep in her own bed, she still lacked energy at the feed store the next day. Cindy Baldwin had shown up early. She had convinced her husband to expand the line of lawn ornaments, an item he thought useless, but one she approved of. To that end, Katie was assigned the boring task of helping to flip through catalogs so Cindy could place her orders.

"We're late this year," Cindy explained. "This should have been done at the end of last summer, so we'll have to go with whatever is left in stock. No mailing this order in. It's going to be me on the telephone for a while."

She stood beside Katie, ticking items off the order sheet and calculating how many she wanted. "Who would order a gross of the exact same fifteen-inch gnome? Wouldn't a mixed lot be better?"

"No idea," Katie said. With the line of customers in front of her gone and the catalogues finished, she moved to the area where winter hats had been stacked on the shelves. She pulled items off, searching behind them for more pieces that had been pushed back and forgotten.

"What have you got planned for this weekend?" Cindy asked.

"Well, there's work here, work at the farm, or I can go down and help out Dorothea." Katie tried to inch away. She didn't want to explain to Cindy about Corrapell.

"Don't you do anything fun?" Cindy asked.

"Is there a dollar in it?"

"Phfft." Her friend laughed.

"Then, no."

When she was done searching the shelves, Katie made a quick circuit of the store, passing the office where Cindy was diligently phoning in her orders.

"I'm going into the stockroom to check," she told Davidson.

She listed SKUs, original prices, calculated sale percentages off, created new tags, and moved the items to the space she had cleared for the final sale. It was mind-numbingly boring work, but today, she totally welcomed it because it stopped the merry-go-round of other thoughts swirling in her mind. She had tucked the pills she had taken from Cecile in the glove compartment of the truck. Her friend Corinne worked in the forensics lab; she'd be able to tell Katie what the pills were. But calling Corinne was a long-distance call, not something she could do from work.

She turned to leave and found Cindy standing in the doorway. Very casually, Cindy said, "I hear you took on another job. And you're going to start going to AA."

Katie went still, wondering how Cindy had heard and, worse than that, who else in the village, like Sheriff Lewis, knew. Cindy's remark was made worse because Katie had just been thinking about Corrapell.

"Temporary second job," she said. "The well bill was pretty steep. It's nice having adequate water again and knowing it won't be an issue in the future. AA is, like, once every two weeks."

"Not usually. I hear they meet every Sunday morning," Cindy said softly.

This time, Katie turned. Her friend's eyes were sad.

"I told you before, Cindy. I left here in trouble, and I kept in it for a long time. I'm not a good person." When Cindy opened her mouth, Katie held up her hand to stop her. "I left here looking for something I didn't think I had. A family. My uncle and aunt took my two brothers, but not me. I was angry and couldn't see that they had two boys of a similar age. They were all in school. They're professionals, lawyers with big practices, and didn't want to take on a toddler. They'd only seen me twice in my whole life, and both times I was sick. Not a great introduction. Gram and Poppa loved me unconditionally, but he let me do whatever I wanted, and she sat on top of me like a big old rock. It left me confused. Sometimes, I don't know how I made it this far and am still alive."

"It's because you're smart and careful." The order blank in Cindy's hand was forgotten.

"No. I didn't live carefully. I was damn lucky. Now, I'm back here, and I hate to say it, but there are a lot of days I consider being somewhere else. Lately, the cravings have grown. Smokes, booze, maybe something stronger." She looked away, north and west, toward the farm. "The day will come when I run again. I know it. I can feel it growing inside me. I just won't be able to stop myself."

The silence between her and Cindy felt like heavy, choking humidity.

Finally, her friend smiled. "Well, when you get ready to run, Katie, you call me. Really. I'll drive you to the bus station, the airport, the state line, wherever you want to go."

"Thanks, buddy." Katie smiled back as she walked past.

"Oh, no problemo." Cindy held the rest of her words in silence. *And after I talk you out of it, I'll drive you right back.*

Chapter Twenty-Nine

Knowing she was facing another overnight at Corrapell turned Katie's fingers cold as ice with dread. She was so tired. Even lying down after supper would give her only a few hours of sleep.

I'm not going to make it all night, she thought, barely able to keep herself on track to finish the cat chores and make supper. At one point, she had to steel herself against barking at Ruth as her old friend hobbled along beside her, chatting. She burned her fingers on the woodstove, and when an animal call came in, all she could do was stand and stare as the telephone rang. She didn't think she had it in her to go out that evening to face a homeowner and set up live traps.

Rick took the call and wrote down the address. "I'll do this call after supper," he told Katie. "You need to lie down. You're overdoing it lately. How long before you fall asleep driving or worse?"

"Thank you," she mumbled.

Then clearing her throat, she said it again. This time Rick looked up. There was a message in his eyes, she couldn't quite read, but she was starting to see the wisdom in his words. Then the telephone rang again and Ruth answered, she could hear a woman talking fast on the other end. The volume was such that the elderly woman held the receiver half an inch away.

"Yes. Of course. Don't worry." Ruth didn't seem to be getting many words into the conversation. "Okay. As soon as I can. Bye."

Ruth returned to her seat at the table just as Rick and Charlie came in from loading traps in Rick's truck. Katie turned from the stove, meatloaf in hand. "S'up?" she asked.

"That was Monique," Ruth said with a sigh. "You know how she feels about getting anything for the baby before it's born? Well, her folks brought all this stuff they've been saving, dumped it on her, and left. She tried to stop them. Amos came home and found her in a panic. He told her as long as she didn't actually touch it, she would be okay."

"Really?" Katie asked. "That's how that works?"

"No." Ruth passed the platter of meat to Charlie. "She won't go in the living room, and Amos is already gone back to the job in Windsor for the week. He had to go because he's riding with someone else, so she has the truck to use. I said I'd come over and move it all out of the way for her."

Rick frowned. "That's ridiculous."

"Rick, the woman has lost babies. Her doctor told her this is her last chance." Ruth pushed her plate back. "She's terrified, and she's there all alone."

Chewing thoughtfully, Rick tapped his fingers against the table. "Eat your supper. I'll drop you off while I go out on the animal call and pick you up when I'm done. You can make her a plate and take it. Charlie can help Katie clean up before he leaves."

"There's about one serving of cobbler left. I can take that too." Ruth pulled her Blue Willow plate back and dug in.

"Don't worry, Charlie," Katie whispered. "I can handle the cleanup."

After Ruth and Rick had departed. Charlie loaded the rest of the already price-tagged treasures into his pickup to drop off at the schoolhouse. He was ready to go about the same time Katie finished.

"You want me to help you lug some more down from upstairs?" he asked after he'd taken the last box out to his truck.

"Let's go see what's up there," Katie said. Her pre-work nap would just have to wait.

Rick had salvaged a beautiful crystal doorknob at the dump, and the door swung open easily. It was a big room, as large as Katie's, on the front of the house. The bunk bed left from the hired hand trailer was a homemade affair of two-by-fours, with a metal spring nailed in place. The maple dresser needed a coat of paint and the floor lamp, a new shade. But there was a comfortable-looking rocker by the window alongside a small table. Bedding was stacked, folded, and waiting on the chair.

Katie, who had been too busy during the last day to pay attention to the work that had been happening here at home, blinked in surprise. "Actually, Charlie, it looks like everything is about done, including the washing and cleaning. I'm thinking you can give notice at the boarding house and move in at the end of the month." There was a slightly mildewy smell when she stood next to the bed. *Probably the mattress*, she thought.

The town-employed truck driver was wiggling like an excited puppy as he left.

Chapter Thirty

"Hey, Katie!"

Cindy walked in the front door of the feed store, a little girl perched on her hip, while her two sons dashed ahead, looking for their father. Katie stood behind the register, lost in her own thoughts. The morning was slow, as had been the night before. She hadn't learned anything new. Nor had she had an opportunity to call Corinne. It might be for nothing, and then, she considered, there could be legal reasons Corinne would not be able to help her identify the pills. Wade had been absent the night before, and not knowing the man on the other side of the door, Katie hadn't turned the key in the lock to speak with him. She had done as she had promised and given Cecile paper, envelopes, and stamps. To her surprise, before the night was over, Cecile had brought back three envelopes to be mailed. One was heavy enough to require two postage stamps.

"My lawyer," the heavy woman had confessed.

Katie had been quite impressed. Cindy's greeting had called her back to her place under the fluorescent lights, surrounded by bird seed, small tools, and farming paraphernalia.

"Hey." Katie smiled. She loved watching Stan and Cindy's three small children race around, even though they brought a little havoc into the store.

Though she'd had other plans, her day off had been spent mostly sleeping and getting through the bare minimum. Rested and refreshed, she was happy to see her friend. The toddler was just so doggone cute, the spitting image of her mother in miniature and covered with sticky, red Tootsie Roll lollipop.

"S'up?"

"We're getting ready to move my mom into the apartment we converted out of the garage, and tomorrow, I'm driving to Winooski for a new mattress and box spring. Forest Hills Factory Outlet is having a truckload of furniture sale."

Katie's ears came up. The memory of the mildew-stinky mattress rushed her senses. "Really?" Here was a chance to step outside of her daily routine, get something done, and have fun at the same time. She almost squeaked with excitement.

"Yeah, I know you're supposed to work tomorrow, but I need an extra pair of hands and Phyllis said she'd come in to work to cover your shift if you wanted to go with me. Would you like to go? I'll buy lunch." Cindy waved the tantalizing treat in front of Katie like a worm calling a fish to the hook.

"At McDonald's?" Katie waggled her eyebrows. Cindy had made her promise not to tell the kids they had gone there before, and the French fries were out of this world.

"Nah, there's an ad in the paper that the Main Street Bar and Grill has an all-you-can-eat sandwich board. I thought we could try it out."

They consolidated their plan, and Cindy went off to retrieve her boys. Katie sighed. An extra day off sounded heavenly.

* * *

By nine the next morning, Katie and Cindy were rolling down US Route 116 in Stan's new three-quarter-ton Chevrolet pickup. Katie wanted to keep the windows rolled up so she could immerse herself in the new car smell, but the day was already heating up.

"How is it that after doing all that building and getting this truck, you can afford new furniture?" she asked while cranking down the window.

"You're so funny," Cindy said with a wide smile. "I can't afford squat. But Forest Hills Factory Outlet is offering a mixed lot mattress sale. You know, a truckload sale. Mom has been sleeping on a pullout sofa, and we decided it was time to give up the two toddler beds and crib." The young mother shrugged. "We bought all the beds used, but there's something yucky about old mattresses. Besides, we saved a bundle because the guy who did the renovation work, you know, from garage to mother-in-law apartment, had a helper we didn't have to pay."

"Was the helper his kid brother, or a neighborhood kid?"

Earlier, Katie had gone through the newspaper until she'd found the mattress ad. Siphoning a small amount of money out of a couple of the bill envelopes, she hoped to find a mattress for at least Charlie's bed. Cindy had interrupted that thought. For a second, Katie was excited at the idea Isaac had found something to do instead of sitting around all day dwelling on his problems.

"Nope. State-reimbursed. It's a young guy that's part of the CETA work training program, the deal to keep dropouts in school. He lives in Mechanicsville, near the contractor, Todd."

Katie stayed quiet, her disappointment palatable.

Cindy continued to chatter away, but finally realized it was a one-person conversation. "Earth to Katie. Did you fall asleep?"

Unwilling to tell Cindy, she had had a moment's excitement that something good was happening for Isaac, and then worrying about what he was doing, Katie looked out the side window and spoke. "No, actually, I was thinking about the mattresses."

"How so?"

"Funny story." She gave a dry laugh before she continued. "Deep in the middle of a cold, cold winter's night," Katie began in a deep voice, "while the lady of the house was fast asleep, dust elves were hard at work. They were nasty little vipers with a penchant for bad practical jokes. Beneath her bed, the elves cut the bailing twine that in the far distant past had held the bedsprings together. Then, just before the last strand frayed, the little buggers scampered out into the hall, giggling behind their hands. Imagine the woman's surprise when she was jerked awake as the springs twanged apart and the skinny old mattress sank to the floor. She was sandwiched like a hot dog in a soft bun, unable to extradite herself. Yelling out her need for assistance, she stayed squeezed together, hoping not to smother before the two elderly people who shared her home heard her cries."

Cindy laughed, banging on the steering wheel with her palm.

"You're kidding, right?" she finally gasped out. "Your bedspring fell apart during the night?"

"Nope. True story." Katie looked out the side window. They passed the airport, and a jet soared upwards.

"Are you sleeping on the floor?" Cindy asked when she could breathe.

"Nah. I was on the couch for a bit, but Rick found a couple of bedsprings at the dump. People who upgraded to box springs, probably. Ruth and I have a pair of antique metal double beds. They have a lot of character. I'd like to keep them. But the mattresses are so old that with the windows closed, you can smell the mildew. I thought I'd check some prices, and if we have room in the truck, maybe I could get at least one."

Cindy nodded. Katie didn't bother to mention that the mattress on Charlie's bed was the worst and there was no spring beneath, just a few wooden planks lying side by side.

* * *

Forest Hills Factory Outlet was an old mill building squeezed in between the granite banks of the Winooski River and West Canal Street. The main floor ran up three stories, the top two vacant. Deep inside the store, a ramp led to the side and down a level, and beyond that, a second ramp did the same. The lowest level, which held reduced-price groceries, had a secondary entrance. Out in the lower lot, an over-the-road trailer was parked on the far side. The back doors were wide open as two brawny men unloaded mattresses and box springs for the shoppers' inspection. A third, pot-bellied older man was doing sales and collecting money.

Katie followed as Cindy checked the offerings. There were very few matched sets, and each of those was marked as a second. Cindy whispered the prices were even lower than she expected.

"Bad stitching. Possible loss of stability," the man said when asked for an explanation.

Faced with the size of the actual pieces, Cindy turned a critical eye to Stan's truck. "I may have to make a couple of trips, and I'm not local," she told the guy.

"I'm only here until the truck empties out, lady," he said. "And they're going fast." He turned away to help a different customer.

"It'll take two trips," Cindy said to Katie. "I need to find a pay phone."

Katie felt the weight of the cash in her pocket. If there was only one trip made, she wasn't going to get even one mattress, but two meant she had a better chance. This trip had been for Cindy's benefit, Katie couldn't ask her friend to give up space for her. "What are you going to do?"

"First, I'm going to make sure I can get all the pieces I want out of here today," Cindy said. "Then I'll haggle for a lesser price. Even though this is technically a sale, if I take four sets, I want a break."

Katie lagged behind as she followed Cindy into the front entrance of the store, where they found a pay phone. She kept looking back over her shoulder at the mattresses. Common sense told her no, but the chance to score something everyone on the farm needed screamed for her attention.

"Listen, Cindy." She laid her hand on her friend's arm, stopping her from dropping a dime into the top of the phone. "Instead of making Stan leave the store, Rick is working in the feed shed today. He could leave early and drive out in his truck. He'll come if I ask. So maybe you could negotiate for your four sets and then three mattresses for me as part of the deal. I have cash."

"That's eleven pieces. We'll have to pack creatively," Cindy said with a sly grin.

Katie held a handful of change, ready for the operator to tell her how much the call would cost. "I'll have him bring rope and maybe Philip." *And the money in the electric company envelope.*

Chapter Thirty-One

While they waited for Rick, the women walked over to the Main Street Bar and Grill. The sandwich bar was pretty popular, and seating was by the buddy system at long tables with complete strangers. Cindy opted for a short glass of draft, but Katie drew a deep breath and declined.

"Sorry," she told the waitress, whose name tag read Ann. "Can't do it. No control once I get started."

"You're not alone on that," Ann said. "Soft drink? Coffee?"

Katie settled for Pepsi and lime juice. While they built their sandwiches at the long table, which held all the fixings, and waited for Ann to bring back an order of fries, Katie looked over the crowd. There were a lot of people inside wearing medical scrubs.

"Is this where all the local doctor's office employees come for their lunch?" she asked as Ann put down a large plate of crispy brown, hand-cut fries.

"That's funny," said Ann. "No, the hospitals have staged shift changes. So, there are people without alcohol who are eating before their shifts. The others are on their way home. We get a lot of personnel because both of the hospitals in Burlington are within a mile and a half of here, and we're on the bus route."

"Yeah," said the young woman on Katie's other side. She wore a name badge that said "Sarah." "No one can afford to live in Burlington because all four colleges are in the hospital district. It's the same in Essex, about ten miles that way. Fanny Allen Hospital and Saint Michael's College. It's cheaper to live here, and it's actually close enough to bike or walk."

"If that big hill doesn't kill you," Ann said with a laugh.

Sarah added, "Besides these mill buildings, there are three more four blocks up where East Allen Street and East Spring Street meet at Hood Street crossing. They're being renovated into one-and two-bedroom apartments and are pretty reasonable, rent-wise. A lot of us live there."

"So, you work at one of the hospitals, right? Is it Mary Fletcher?" Katie asked, a French fry hanging out of her mouth like a crushed cigarette. Isaac had told her Holly had been a nurse. What were the chances she had worked in a hospital or even with one of these people? If she didn't ask, she'd never know.

Sarah pointed to the logo stitched on her scrubs. "Ah, yeah."

"I met a nurse who works there," said Katie. "Her name is Holly Guptill."

Shaking her head, Sarah said she didn't recognize the name, but asked the woman on her other side.

"Yeah, I know her," said the new voice. "But I don't think she was a nurse. Maybe an aide? You remember, Sarah, she was living with Dwayne."

"Oh, yeah." Sarah turned back to Katie; her cheeks flushed with embarrassment. "I guess I do know who she is. She doesn't live around here anymore, and I hate to say it, but she got canned at the hospital. Gossip was she helped herself to patient meds."

Katie chewed on her fry, listening to the others talk. If Holly had been fired for stealing meds, how come that didn't show up in her references? Didn't Corrapell bother checking them? Mrs. Reveck told Katie that she was dispensing the meds in a way that sounded like that wasn't how it usually worked. There were enough people housed at Corrapell so there might be other meds prescribed and issued. Then what about when the drug addicts had been there? Surely, their medical needs would have been expansive. She looked again at Sarah. The seating was close enough, so that if she asked a question, others would hear. She couldn't believe her luck when she heard the friendly group were nurses who worked at Mary Fletcher, but she needed to try fishing for more information. With Sarah, she'd landed a whopper. Keeping her face neutral was an effort, but she tried again.

"Oh, wow," said Katie. "It's not like we're friends. I just met her."

"You know," said a woman wearing mauve scrubs who sat across from Sarah, "that girl Holly had a friend she was really chummy with. She was a nurse, but she's gone, too."

"From around here?" Katie asked.

"No, out in the boondocks." The woman finished her coffee before adding, "Like in Richmond or Parentville. Her name is Faye Pigeon."

"Bus in five minutes!" somebody called. All the scrub wearers who had been sipping cokes, including Sarah, ran out the door and across Main Street to the bus stop.

After an enjoyable half hour with their new friends, Katie and Cindy went back over to Forest Hills, where Cindy put on her best hard-ass face and worked out a price with the pot-bellied guy. Their bedding was stacked off to the side. The man told them, they had half an hour for Rick to show up with the envelope, then their selection became fair game. Both women stayed right by the pile, guarding it and warning other shoppers off as the trailer pickings got slim. Rick showed up with Charlie just as the mattress muscle men were headed back in Katie and Cindy's direction.

While the men loaded the trucks, Katie and Cindy ran back inside the factory outlet, where a big display of pillows and sheets was set up just beyond the cash registers. Katie bought four pillows, but Cindy had pillows, sheets, blankets, and, as she admitted on the way home, an empty checking account.

"Either head out the Williston Road or keep your speed down on the highway," Rick warned, tying the last knot. Cindy and Katie led the way, with Rick and Charlie following.

When they were finally home lugging the new mattresses in and the old ones out, Katie was flying high. She'd gotten all the mattresses she'd wanted and some information as well.

"How is it," she huffed, holding her end of the mattress up as she and Rick came down the stairs, "the old ones are heavier than the new ones?"

"Because they're full of dust, old skin, and sweat," Rick said from his position on the high side.

"You are disgusting." Katie jerked her head away from the mattress, fumbling to get her grip back.

"Nevertheless, it's the truth," Rick said.

Ruth inspected the new pieces as they came off the truck to make sure they hadn't gotten wet on the ride from the city. When she was sure each one was dry, she started making beds. Rick and Charlie loaded the old mattresses into Rick's pickup. Solomon and Bonnie were in the mix. The pig kept poking at Charlie. He had a can of chewing tobacco in his back pocket, and she was drawn by the smell.

"Git," he said.

"Woof," she grunted.

Katie laughed as the two squared off, both approximately the same weight as Bonnie had started filling out since returning home from wintering in the Dean family barn.

"Spanish Rice for supper, Charlie. Are you going to be back in time?"

"Biscuits?" he asked, dodging Bonnie to catch the rope Rick had thrown over the load.

"And date bars," Katie called as she headed back inside.

Given the go-ahead to move in, Charlie hadn't waited until the end of the month, but showed up the next evening with his first month's rent in hand, as well as an old cardboard suitcase of clothes and an army duffle of winter outerwear. As soon as he'd entered the house with all his worldly possessions, the odor of long-unwashed laundry had permeated the first floor.

"Phew." Ruth's nose practically retreated into her face. "No wonder your landlady was willing to let you leave right off. Dump that stuff right there in front of the washer. It's going to take a couple of runs through and days of airing out on the line to get rid of that stink."

Charlie blushed all the way to his toes. "Katie told me I had to wash my own."

"Yeah? Well, Katie can pee up a rope if she thinks I'm going to let you mess with my washer or foul up all the air in this house."

With her cane leaning on Katie's hidden chair, Ruth stuffed the washer with the first load. Solomon slunk in, tail between his legs, sniffing at the duffle.

"Out!" Ruth ordered the dog and Old Tom, who had also followed the smell in. "Not you, Charlie," she said as he headed away. "You're in the bathroom. Lots of hot water and use the Lava soap, not my lavender bars."

While Ruth was sorting Charlie's laundry, Katie and Rick sat down in the living room. Without any preamble, Katie told him about the pills she had taken from Cecile and had hidden in her truck.

Rick cut in. "Are you sure these are legitimate medications?"

"According to Cecile, these are the same prescription sleeping aids her doctor gave her back home. The only way I'm going to know for sure is to get someone like Corinne to look at them," Katie said.

"Or," said Rick. "A doctor. Ruth has a follow-up appointment with Doctor Gillian tomorrow afternoon. Grace was going to take her, but I'm thinking I might instead. You go out, put them pills in my glove compartment. I'll see if she'll take a look at them."

"How are you going to explain them?" Katie asked.

"Working on that thought right now," said Rick, tapping his forefinger against the side of his head. "Now, let me tell you that Sheriff Lewis has not forgotten about that whole mess. He doesn't care if the state police are involved or not. Chet told me he stopped in at the town hall and heard Lewis on the phone ripping someone a new butthole because he hadn't gotten some forensic report he'd asked for."

"Edward Richardson," Katie said, referring to the forensic pathologist based in Montpelier.

"Probably," Rick agreed. "Monique told Ruth; the sheriff is still out there harassing Amos on a regular basis even though he asked Lewis not to come to the house. It's keeping Monique's blood pressure up."

"That would be bad for the baby," Katie said.

"Like Lewis would have a clue," Rick said with a nod. "And he's gonna be real ugly after he sees the paper today because there's an article from an interview with one of the state police corporals."

Rick dropped the paper on the sofa next to Katie and walked off. It had been folded so the article was right on top. In it, Vermont State Police

Corporal Derrick provided a description of the remains found in Parentville. Though no artist's rendition was attached, he asked for any information the public might have on someone who was missing and fit the description.

Katie's jaw dropped.

Just then Charlie came out of the bathroom, the first load was in the second spin, his winter coats had been sprayed with Lysol and were hanging out on the line, and he was as red as a boiled Maine lobster. Katie refrained from asking if that was due to embarrassment or hot water or excessive scrubbing. Probably all three.

Chapter Thirty-Two

The telephone book on Stan's desk didn't have all the information Katie needed the next morning. But dialing 1-555-1212 for directory assistance got her the address she needed for her unscheduled visit after work.

The light blue cape home had a first-year lawn and a detached two-car garage. Unlike the road, the driveway was paved. Once into the turn, Katie could see why. Set in the peak of the garage was a four-foot square of plywood painted white and sporting a rusted basketball hoop. A woman and a pair of young teenage boys were shooting hoops. All action stopped at Katie's arrival, their eyes watching to see if she would advance. Katie braked, backed out into the road, and left her car there.

As she walked up the drive, the boy holding the ball dribbled it toward the woman.

"Hi, I'm Katie Took," she said with a big smile.

"Faye Pigeon." The woman bounced the ball once. "Wade told me you might be around."

Without being asked, both youngsters walked up onto the small deck and into the house. Faye bounced the ball again.

"You've been asking a lot of questions, what is it you want to know?" she asked. Her tone was inquisitive, but her knuckles were white against the dirty orange basketball.

Katie stood on the opposite side of the basketball hoop, facing the house. One of the boys popped up in the window, then disappeared. It was a warm day. Birds were singing, and from somewhere, the smell of newly cut grass hung wet and sweet in the air. The last thing Katie wanted to do was cause this woman angst. Pressing her lips together, she considered her next words.

"The priest from a local church came to me because a member of his congregation told him about a troubling event. Right around that same time, the remains of a woman were found on my grandparents' property." She hadn't planned on telling Faye so much, but now, face-to-face, there didn't seem to be another way. "It could be two separate issues. However, I've had a visitor who told me a patient disappeared from the Corrapell Retreat right about the time the remains were found at the Small Farm. He also told me that once before, someone sort of disappeared, but the sheriff doesn't seem inclined to believe it might be connected. I've been checking around, and most of the employees who worked there three or four months ago have left. Wade only works nights and has limited information. He suggested I talk to you. I'd like to talk to your friend Holly. She's not working at Corrapell. Do you know where I can find her?"

Faye bounced the ball twice, then sent it up and through the hoop. It came down to bounce at Katie's feet. Automatically, she reached out and grabbed it. Fifteen feet away, Faye was studying the grayed tar surface. Katie hooked toward the hoop and hit the rim, deflecting the ball. Faye responded, catching the ball and sending it back up for two points. Katie passed the ball back.

With the ball against her hip, Faye said, "I worked days since the boys are in school, not directly for Corrapell, but through the Knight Employment Agency. I'm a CNA. I've known Holly since college. She and I worked together at Mary Fletcher Hospital in Burlington. Then, she had a bad breakup with her boyfriend and walked away with nothing. Barely the clothing on her back. She didn't have a car and needed a place to stay where her ex couldn't find her until he got hooked up with some other poor girl.

"I offered to let her stay here, but because I have kids, she didn't want to. She was terrified Dwayne would come around. They have mutual friends. She wasn't sure who she could trust, and she didn't want to go home to Maine. Anyway, she took to hiding in one of the empty wings at the retreat. Once all the rehab patients were cleared out, the trashed wings were locked down. No one ever went in there. Holly said she was safe. I'd bring her clean clothes, food, whatever she needed. Her plan was to work there and collect her pay until she had enough to find a place in Burlington and a different job. She was pretty close to being ready to do that. I even took her to a couple of interviews, and my husband said he'd help her find a used car."

Katie could see Faye biting her lip. After a glance toward the house where her children were, she dribbled and shot. Another two points.

"I don't always get sent to Corrapell. I did a private duty for a week. When I showed up at Corrapell, I found out that the day after I had worked last, Holly failed to show."

Katie had caught the basketball and jump shot, once again missing by a fraction. Faye grabbed it and held the ball against her middle.

"I didn't get it, you know? She didn't call me or anything. She just split." Faye's expression flashed angry, then sad. "I thought we were friends. Then I started listening to the news, and I got scared, so I asked Wade what he knew. I'm probably upset about nothing. If she had a lick of sense, she went home to her family."

"Did you check the room where Holly was hiding?" Katie asked.

"How was I supposed to get in there? Holly had a key she'd pinched from Mrs. Reveck's desk. I can't take a chance doing something like that. I need this job."

"I get that," Katie said.

"Did the police give you any information about the remains, other than it was female?"

"Not really." Katie sighed. Sheriff Lewis was playing his cards close to his chest. Every newspaper article repeated the same tired information. "Wade seems to think it's the female patient that disappeared from the retreat."

Faye gave a harsh laugh. She ran the basket, tossed the shot, then snatched the ball away before Katie had a chance.

"Lillian, right? I heard some wild rumor about her being flushed down the toilet. Just kidding. I was there the day she checked out. Her parents came to pick her up. It seems her mother figured out her little darling wasn't eating kosher. Not only that, but there was another way to know for sure it wasn't her."

"What's that?" Katie asked.

"She literally weighed four hundred pounds. They would have needed a derrick."

"You're kidding, right?" Katie asked.

"Nope. Scout's honor, as my little guys say." Faye bounced the ball once, then held it against her middle again. "She was there for almost two months and lost the same two pounds every week. Somebody was feeding her goodies."

"Thank you for your time," Katie said, walking away.

Katie sat for a minute in the car, considering what Faye had said. If Holly were still in the building, someone would have found her by this time. Either seen her or realized someone was stealing food. If the boyfriend, Dwayne, had figured out where she was, either she was back with him or had run away. She started to open the car door to go back and ask Faye but changed her mind. The two boys had returned. Under the hoop, Faye was demonstrating the advance move for a hook shot.

* * *

Katie drove back through the village and headed home, considering the different story versions she had heard regarding the patients—or residents, as Mrs. Reveck referred to them—at Corrapell, as well as the mystery of Holly Guptill. Was she a good person in a bad place? Why was Faye's story so different from Sarah's? Faye never said Holly had been fired from the hospital for stealing a patient's meds. Had Holly fallen off the rails, or had speculation put her there?

It was a cinch she was gone, yet neither the sheriff's department nor the state police had concluded she might be the poor soul left in the Gypsy Copse. Katie had started driving away, then set her foot down hard on the brake.

Is it possible no one has questioned the Reveck's?

She knew instantly it was entirely possible. Corrapell was all the way on the other side of the town, close to Richmond. There hadn't been anything in the paper, and no gossip that sounded like the woman lost was anything but a normal citizen.

Except maybe the rumor floating around that the phrase "not natural causes" meant drug-related. I don't know, she thought. I think I'd vote first for a mugging gone bad. But why aren't we hearing that? Could it be Lewis isn't sharing that information with anybody. Maybe not even the staties.

It wasn't a good thought. Even more frightening, there didn't appear to be any family raising the alarm that one of their beloveds was missing. All the way home, Katie's back itched, and her butt wasn't comfortable in the seat. It seemed the realization she was the only one considering Holly's safety, and her own laissez-faire attitude thus far, made her twitchy to do something. She just wasn't sure what.

Katie pulled into the yard, still feeling guilty and helpless. Ruth was outside where the sun shone on her, and the temperature was tolerable. For a few moments, Katie sat in the truck watching her friend. With her recent thoughts of Holly still fresh, Katie considered what might have happened to Ruth out here all alone if she hadn't stayed in Parentville for so long.

She could have been stranded here over the winter. Would she have been found come the spring, dead on the floor, left alone and forgotten? A shiver ran down Katie's back.

Katie stepped out of the truck and started to walk past the old woman. There were words in her heart she wanted to share, but her throat was closed down. Instead, Katie pulled the other rocker up, synchronized their motion, and ever so casually, allowed the side of her hand to graze Ruth's.

Porch sitting was still a little chilly, but with the addition of a heavy cable-knit sweater, a cup of tea, and a cat lying on her feet, Ruth found it tolerable. Bonnie took advantage of a dry spot on the lawn and the lingering rays of the sun. She happily woofed and rolled, making three tries before she hefted her increasing bulk over. Once on her back, she got in one wiggling scratch before she tumbled to the other side. From her perch on Katie's toes, LG watched her porky friend. Since spending the winter in the Dean barn, the pig was now well over a hundred and seventy-five pounds. The ten-pound cat was severely outclassed. Though still willing to follow, the feline was no longer interested in a possible wrestling match.

* * *

Ruth sat in the rocker, clad similarly to Katie, but up by one more cat. Katie's chair was close enough to hers, so their fingers brushed against each other's as they rocked. Though she was a little nervous about getting the tips of her fingers pinched between the wooden armrests, she was enjoying the fleeting contact. It made her think of Irma, and how much she had loved the child, but never having been a truly demonstrative woman, hadn't seemed to be able to connect with her. Even now, Katie wasn't much of a hugger.

"These came out nice, didn't they?" Ruth said, running her fingers along the smooth, freshly painted edge of the seat.

"Are you fishing for a compliment?" Katie asked with a laugh.

"No," murmured Ruth, but her slight blush said otherwise.

The three chairs had been unearthed in the jumbled chaos in the barn. Ruth had cut away the straw seats, then mixed small amounts of paint until she had enough to cover the chairs, one mango, another lavender, and the last a light bluish green. Her frustration at not being able to find someone to re-cane the seats for a reasonable fee had evaporated when Donna Fontana, Cindy's mother, offered to do the work.

"You should be pretty proud of yourself," said Katie, breaking into her thoughts.

Ruth, who had been staring into her teacup, raised her head. "Why?"

"Well, you had a need. You found someone who could fill it. Then, you and Grace convinced her to hold a class in Woodman Hall. She earned a little money, got her name out there, and, according to Cindy, has a fledgling business going now."

"Seriously? A business?" Ruth quirked an eyebrow. She was surprised as she saw Donna on a fairly regular basis, and her new friend hadn't said a word.

"I'm not messing with you, Ruth. It's been a month since the class, and Donna has taken in three chairs for new seats. Cindy says she's happy as a pig in poop." Katie got to her feet. "Speaking of pigs, it's time to take ours down to the barn for the night." She made a soft woofing sound, and Bonnie sprang to her feet, ears, and tail at attention. Katie moved around the corner of the house with the pig-keeping step, the same way Solomon had followed Rick.

Ruth watched them go, fingers still curled around the empty mug, all growing colder by the second. But they, like the chilly space between the top of her ankle socks and the hem of her coat, weren't foremost in her thoughts. Twisting in her seat, she looked down the road where it dipped to pass the Dean farm and continued to the intersection with the Parentville/Charlotte Road. Tucked into the corner, a half-mile away, was the small, one-room schoolhouse where Katie's Poppa, Peter Moore, had been educated. He'd kept it standing when no one else even remembered it was there. Then Katie had found it among the sumac and saplings. Now it waited again ready to be open on the occasional Saturday. Ruth wanted more.

She thought about asking Donna Fontana if she'd like to hang a poster, maybe offer a caning class at the schoolhouse. Or maybe even man the Schoolhouse Thrift Shop on an afternoon. Heaving to her feet, her crutches scattering cats, Ruth turned toward the front door. In the kitchen, a small fire burned in the old cook stove, taking the chill out of the house that was even older than she was.

"One day," she said to Peanut, "that little schoolhouse will make a fine thrift shop. It just needs electricity, water, paint, and I don't know what else. Lord knows we've got all the product we need. But let me tell you this." She scooped the petite cat up, burying her nose in his fur, "Ain't any way I'm giving up on it."

Chapter Thirty-Three

The next evening, Katie and Rick stood outside the house, leaning on his truck. It wasn't often they both got to leave Baldwin's at the same time, but tonight was one.

"I stopped in to see Dr. Gillian this afternoon when I was out on deliveries," said Rick. "She told me they were Zarall, a type of benzodiazepine. Your friend was right; they're highly addictive."

"A prescription drug? So, a doctor would have to have written an order out, right?" Katie's brow furrowed.

"Yeah. Think about it. That place has an in-house quack." Rick levered off the truck, but Katie stopped him.

"There's a missing woman up at Corrapell. I went out yesterday and talked to a friend of hers."

"Are you thinking this might be from there?" He nodded across the acreage toward the Gypsy Copse. When she remained silent, he spoke again. "Time, Girl, for you to be speaking to the sheriff."

He headed inside, and she followed, so they came through the kitchen door together. Warm light and the smell of supper cooking welcomed them.

Ruth stood by the table holding out two sandwiches wrapped in waxed paper, her crutches leaning on the chair next to her. "I saw you out there dawdling. Another minute and I'd a'had to go out. Katie, you got a call, and I think this is going to take both of you."

Scarfing down the sandwich as she changed into an old pair of canvas pants and Gram's barn coat, Katie sighed as the dream of a peaceful evening ran over the hill and away on furry feet.

"I put the two biggest crates in the back of the truck with some grain bags." Rick had the truck keys in hand. He knew the way, so he'd be driving.

The call had come directly from a farmer. A pack of loose dogs were running deer behind his barn and had gotten into the holding yard for his dairy herd. Once spooked, the cows had done a number on some of the dogs.

"According to Ruth," Rick said, shifting into reverse and backing out onto Fire Lane 61, "two are dead, and two more are injured. Aaron Barclay has got those two locked in a tool shed." He shifted into drive. "He's saying they're half-grown but nasty as all get out."

"So, we don't know if these are pets just running loose, or dogs that have been turned out and on their own for a while? Perfect." Katie chewed on her lip. She didn't like handling dog calls. It was bad enough in broad daylight. Now it was already getting dark.

A blistering cold wind assaulted them as they got out of the pickup at the farm. Aaron directed them down to the tool shed but added as he opened the gate to the holding yard. "The dead dogs are trampled into the manure muck. You might want to pick them up first. If this wind keeps up, everything's going to freeze solid real fast."

Katie nodded miserably. The downed dogs needed to be collected and turned in for rabies testing. There was no telling how long it would take to corral two injured dogs. Her job was to catch and transport them all. She was glad Rick walked beside her because if first aid was needed, she would be woefully inadequate.

There was no outside light, and the overheads from inside the barn didn't shine through the big double door as far as the dog carcasses. Between them, Rick and Katie had two flashlights, grain bags, and a spade. As they approached the trampled remains, Katie's heart swelled and bled tears within her chest.

People are so stupid, she thought. *These poor babies didn't know. Why were they running free?*

Behind her, Rick was talking.

"Did you recognize the dogs?" he asked the farmer.

"Nah," Aaron said. "It was already dark. I was just getting ready to let the cows in for milking when there was this thundering, squealing noise. When I opened the door, the first few cows bolted inside, almost ran me down. I wouldn't have known about the deer, except one came running in with the cattle. I've got it trapped in a free stall. I don't see any damage, but I'll leave it there till you say to let it go."

"Okay," said Rick. "As soon as we're out of the way, I'm sure it'll hot-foot to the doors and out."

"Yeah, that's what I figure, too," said the farmer. "I ran out thinking something was attacking a cow, but what I found were these two dogs squashed into the muck, and them young ones cringing down nearby. My boys and me chased them into the shed. We couldn't get close enough to lay a hand on them."

"Are any of your cattle hurt?" Katie asked.

Aaron said no and continued speaking, but Katie wasn't listening. She blew out a deep breath and squatted near the closest dog. It was clear the animal was long dead. Without realizing it, she slipped down onto her knees in the churned-up manure. Her throat filled with bile as she reached out a hand. Her flashlight lit up the dark fur, and she aimed it toward the animal's head, unwilling to survey the wreckage. She had a moment's relief it wasn't a dog, but a coyote. Then, the pain returned as her imagination flashed. She could feel the animal's excitement the moment it turned to terror. From the size, this was a last season pup, end of the winter hungry and probably terrified when the deer chase turned into a foray into a forest of kicking hooves and bawling cattle.

Katie stayed on her hands and knees, fighting the urge to weep. Behind her, the two men were unaware of her reaction. Then Rick stepped closer.

"What are you doing, getting all wet?" he asked. "You're going to catch pneumonia."

"It's not a dog." Katie stopped, spitting out the stomach acid that had risen in her throat. "It's a coyote."

Both flashlights turned away from her to the second carcass.

"So is this one," said Rick. "A full-size female and not all stomped to bits like that one."

He sounded relieved they wouldn't be bagging somebody's pet.

It's wrong to feel like this is better, her heart screamed. *It's the law of nature,* her mind said calmly.

With Aaron's help, they got the two carcasses into grain bags and into the back of the pickup. But when it came to corralling the pups who had blindly followed their mother, the farmer left Katie and Rick on their own. The two of them closed themselves in the tool shed with snare poles and nets, facing off against two half-grown but very angry wild animals. By the time Rick had the first pup trapped with the snare, they were both sweating. Fortunately, the second pup sunk into shock, and it was easier for Katie, who had to work alone, to snare.

With the two critters safely stowed and the crates wrapped in a canvas tarp to keep the wind off, Rick aimed the truck toward Richmond. Because these were wild animals, they couldn't go to the vet's office in Charlotte. They had to be taken to the wild animal compound. In the event there had been any bites with the threat of rabies, Aaron would need to have a look at his herd. His wife called ahead to Richmond so someone would meet them. Soaked to the thighs, Katie shivered. Her chattering teeth were loud enough for Rick to hear. He gave her a sideways glance.

"There's a couple of extra grain bags behind the seat. Wrap them around you to hold in the heat."

A mile into Richmond at the crossroads, they came across a small Mom-and-Pop store. Rick ran in and came back with candy bars and a cup of coffee that had been brewed five hours earlier.

"It'll taste like the manure you got all over you," Rick said, "but it'll heat up your innards."

By the time they got to the compound, Katie was huddled on the edge of the seat, wrapped around the pitiful heater vent. The coffee hadn't done much to warm her up. She felt hollow on the inside and sick from the chocolate and overcooked caffeine. Rick left the truck running and got out at the compound to speak with the rehabilitator. The exchange took close to an hour. Katie wanted to get out and listen. This was the first time she'd done something like this. The next time, she might be on her own, and it would be good to have some experience. Instead, she huddled against the door and had a single-person argument as she fought tears and told herself she was going to quit this job. While she waited, immersed in her pity party, Katie dozed off. The slamming of the driver's door woke her up.

"Okay," said Rick. "Let's get you home. I called Ruth. She'll have a hot bath ready for you."

As he ran the truck along the dark back roads toward Parentville, Rick told her one of the pups had a broken leg, but the other seemed merely terrified. "They'll send samples out for a rabies test on the other two," he said. "After Chad took what he needed, he let me keep the hide off the big coyote." Like Katie, he rode hunched over. "We're going to have to invest in a couple of bigger crates, though. A big coyote wouldn't have fit in either of those." He kept the running dialogue going.

Katie tried to respond, but she was so tired she couldn't say a single word. She didn't realize he kept taking peeks at her, as if finding her sleeping had frightened him. The back end of the pickup slipped on an ice patch. Rick slowed down, but not a lot.

Katie got her hot bath, but wasn't able to eat supper, and once wrapped tight in two quilts on the army cot set up near the heat radiator in the living room, fell right to sleep.

"What happened?" whispered Ruth. "No one got bit, right?"

She drew a chair up to Katie's cot and sat down with her knee propped up on a hassock and her knitting in her lap.

"No, no bites. I don't know about the cattle." Rick came closer and stood over both Katie and Ruth, cup of coffee in hand. "She just took it bad." It was his turn for a bath, but he stayed there wondering, just as Katie had, if it was time for her to give up working for the town.

* * *

Katie woke early the next morning to find herself weighted down by felines and groggy. The cringing lasted until the percolator spit the first droplets of

173

coffee. Ruth found her sitting at the table, filling out a chit to bill the town for picking up the four coyotes.

"That's my job," said Ruth, yawning widely.

Right from the first, Ruth's high school education in secretarial filing and typing had kept the records for the in-house cats, the Feral Cat Society, and Katie's animal control job. More than once, Katie had admitted it was only Ruth's efforts that kept everything straight.

"Have at it," Katie said, pushing the form and pen across the table. She got up and poured two more cups of coffee. Rick was already moving around in the sitting room. They could hear him grousing at the cats.

"It's sausage gravy and biscuit day," he said with a smile, relieved to see Katie had recovered from the previous evening's excursion. Charlie bustled in, rubbing his hands together. He also liked Rick's sausage and gravy.

She smiled back watching as her elderly friend pulled out the iron skillet and the cold biscuits from the refrigerator. Initially she didn't think she'd be able to handle breakfast, but the smell of the sausage Rick was frying, and the creamy milk gravy he poured over the grilled biscuit halves, had her mouth watering. She gave him a thumbs up letting him know she was good, and all three relaxed and enjoyed their breakfast.

Chapter Thirty-Four

It was after midnight and the door hadn't opened from Wade's side. She knew it was because Mrs. Reveck was still in her office. At eleven, Katie had finished writing a letter to Marlie and tried to sneak out for her thermos and lunch. As she'd tiptoed across the lobby, a big yellow rectangle of light shone across the wall-to-wall carpet. The boss was still at her desk. Katie had retreated. An hour later, she decided to try again. Listening at the door for Wade, she heard two voices. She couldn't make out the words, but one voice was female. It had to be Mrs. Reveck. It was too late for anyone else to be in the building.

Instead of going into the lobby, Katie slipped into the first patient room on the backside of the building. Standing in the shadow of the heavy drape, with a resident sleeping in the twin bed behind her, Katie watched until the flashlight glow through the window indicated Mrs. Reveck was walking toward her home. When she was sure the director couldn't get back fast enough to catch her, Katie ran out to her truck.

Fortified by two cups of coffee and a cold grilled cheese sandwich, she considered her options. There was a tap on the door.

"Psst, Katie, are you in there?" Wade whispered through the small opening.

"I'm right here. Nobody else except the sleeping bunnies. What's up?"

"I don't know." The young man sounded edgy. "Mrs. R. has been in here three times this evening asking questions about some of the other people who used to work here. I'm betting it's not good for somebody."

Katie considered that the boss hadn't been in to talk with her at all. But that could be because she was the new kid on the block and only worked intermittently, whereas Wade had been here for months and worked four nights a week.

Or Faye could have come in asking questions and dropped my name in the mix.

"Wade," whispered Katie. "Did she mention me?"

"No. Mostly she wants to know about the people that came in from the agency, you know, like have they been asking questions or poking around."

Katie swallowed hard. She was sure now that Sheriff Lewis had never come out and asked questions. Wade would have said something if he knew. Right now, she was the one talking and sticking her nose in places it shouldn't be. Somebody had noticed. She didn't want to involve Wade, and he apparently hadn't ratted her out, but he was getting nervous, and she still didn't know anything.

She heard her co-worker moving around a little. When he next spoke, he sounded further away.

"I don't think I should open the door tonight," he said. "But if I sit over here, I can see if she comes back up the road."

"Wade, listen!" Katie hissed. "I need to go check something out. I'll be as fast as I can. If you see Mrs. R. coming back and she gets inside while I'm gone, you need to stall her, okay?"

"Where are you going?" he asked.

"Better that you don't know." She pulled the door closed until she heard the lock catch.

Once in the lobby, Katie sprinted across it, through the dining room, and over to the two doors leading into the closed wings. Ignoring the door to the wing at the back of the building, she shoved her damaged credit card between the door and the frame. The card broke into two pieces. Shoving them both into her pocket, she moved quickly down the length of the hall. She didn't believe Holly was still in the building, but she hoped to find some trace she had been there.

It's not like I'm going to find a note tacked on the wall saying she was moving back to Maine, Katie thought sarcastically. She inched down the corridor, one light step at a time. *If I were going to hide in here, I'd pick a room that wasn't on the same side as the double-wide. And not the first or the last one, either.*

On the back of the retreat, where the sun was least likely to shine in, the rooms were an unorganized mess of furniture and boxes of dishes and linens. Several wooden pieces had been haphazardly thrown in through the door. Katie squatted beside them, flashlight in hand. Broken pieces of bedsteads, small tables, and dresser drawers. She leaned closer and picked up a whiff of well-aged offal.

Eww. This had to be the stuff the addicts had busted up, Katie realized. Wade had said several of those people had been out of control, strung out on drugs, and barely coherent. Katie had seen addicts living on the streets while she was in Illinois. People like herself who had nothing, or worse, unable to take care of themselves. The day she'd ducked into a post office to get warm and found an old woman defecating on the floor, she'd realized it was time to pull herself together.

The Puerto Rican woman who ran the corner mom-and-pop convenience store had recognized Katie's futile attempts at righting herself, and let her fill shelves and mop up. She also made her go to AA meetings, sometimes three a week. Eventually, the woman sent Katie away so that she could take on another lost soul. The experience had been enough to keep Katie sober and allow her to see where hard drugs were taking others she knew. She didn't want to be found dead in an alley, chewed by rats, and covered in needle tracks.

Shielding her flashlight beam, Katie got to her feet and looked around at the destruction. There seemed to be a path off to the right, along the wall. She crept ahead to investigate. The pile of broken refuse was higher near the back corner of the room, but Katie was tall. Standing on tiptoe, shining the light from her outstretched arm, she saw what was definitely a nest of blankets. Pulling a wooden chair out of the way caused the tower to tremble, and she stepped back. There were other rooms to search, and her time was short, but this was probably what she was looking for. She'd take a quick look and come back.

Four rooms in total held an assortment of items. Inside one, she found a broken-down stack of cardboard boxes. Each box was labeled DION and included an address in Queens printed in black marker on the brown exterior. These were the boxes Wade had packed. Katie was sure now the size fifty-four suit had come from here. Taken out of the boxes so no one would know.

The last room was the same as all the others, except a blanket had been hung over the curtain rod to screen it from the outside. Katie detected a pungent odor she recognized.

Lifting the corner of the blanket, she found a window that faced the end of the other wing where the bushes grew up to the glass. This end was out of view of Reveck's double-wide mobile home. Taking a chance, she turned her light toward the outside, revealing a flower garden. The stems and stalks were all brown and withered from the winter, but a few leaves had dried out and pressed against the window. The five pointy leaves were curled up and dead, but still easy to identify.

Marijuana.

The lingering smell had to be from plants drying in the room. The stink couldn't have come in through the glass. Katie searched around, finally opening the closet.

"Bingo."

But the plant's stalks hanging from the hanging rod weren't all she found. Three dirty needles lay on the floor, along with a tarnished and burnt spoon, a candle, and a Bic lighter. More than she'd expected. Katie left behind the drug paraphernalia, rushing back to the swirl of blankets. There were some empty food containers, dirty cups, and a t-shirt. Her fingers reached for the shirt, then stopped. Marijuana was one thing, but the drug kit on the floor put this out of her league. She needed a cop, preferably not Sheriff Lewis, maybe a state cop.

One slow, backward step led to another. In the tangle of furniture, Katie tripped, falling backwards onto a soft backpack. Her fingers curled around the handle as she jumped to her feet; startled and wanting to get away, she rushed out the door. With fear as her copilot, Katie made it all the way out into the hall before she realized she had touched doorknobs and, further back, a wooden chair. Her fingerprints would have Sheriff Lewis chasing her down again. Katie retraced her steps and wasted precious minutes wiping down everything she could have touched.

A sudden chill ran up her arms. A signal to get out now if she'd ever felt one.

Grabbing the backpack, she ran down the corridor. The dining room was in darkness. Before she was all the way across, Katie heard a key turn in the lock to the kitchen door. Mrs. Reveck was less than a minute behind her.

As she slid into her wing, she banged on the door unthinking that Mrs. Reveck might hear her.

"Coming at you, Wade, from the other side!" she called in a hoarse whisper, barely getting the pack shoved under the desk and her butt in the seat before her own door opened.

"Katie?" said Mrs. Reveck. "Did I just hear one of your residents yelling?"

"For crying out loud, you've got to quit scaring me like this, or I'm going to drop dead on the spot!" She almost bit her tongue when she realized what she'd said, but ignored the remark about voices her employer might have heard.

Mrs. Reveck laughed. "In these heels, you can hear me coming from a mile away. I just wanted to ask if you'd be available tomorrow evening as well. It seems we're going to be a little short-staffed."

The director went on to explain she would need Katie from three in the afternoon until eleven, but had the overnight covered.

Katie agreed, and Mrs. Reveck left through Wade's door.

Ruth isn't going to be happy when I tell her, Katie thought.

A little later, there was a tap, and Wade's head appeared in the door opening. "Where did you go?"

Katie wanted to tell him, but she wasn't sure how far he could be trusted. She didn't know him well enough. He had said Holly was just someone who had been served up some bad knocks. If the personal drug lab she'd found belonged to Holly, there was more there than bad luck.

* * *

Katie had set out two live traps at Mrs. Wright's house. The traps needed to be collected on the way home. Both contained a very angry raccoon that hissed and complained inside the metal box. Pulling in at the base of Mechanicville's Hillside cemetery, Katie released her two hitchhikers and returned to the truck. She couldn't help eyeballing the backpack. The pull to look was so strong, her fingers were already reaching before she could stop herself.

Instead, Katie drove home, waiting until Rick was gone to work and Grace had picked up Ruth to bring the backpack into the house. Once in her bedroom, with the contents spread on the threadbare area rug, she was glad she had waited so she would have time to carefully examine the contents. Besides one change of clothes, the bag was stuffed with the small, and very personal effects, of a woman Katie believed she would never know. A small photo album, a few knickknacks, a cloth bag of jewelry, and a packet of letters with envelopes identifying the recipient as Holly Guptill, all addressed to "My darling daughter" and ended with "Love always, Mom." The nurse, Sarah, had said Holly was from Maine, and the return address was Bowdoin, ME. Katie sat back, feeling deflated. Holly did have family. These letters, all dated in the last two years, were from Holly's mother, telling her daughter she could come home anytime and that she was missed and loved. A brown knee sock held a roll of currency and a half sheet of notepaper. There were five numbers on the paper, one labeled "FP."

Katie knew these items—this whole world in a bag—belonged to Holly. And now she had an eyewitness to the release and retreat of Lillian, Katie knew where Holly had ended up. The question was how she got there.

Chapter Thirty-Five

"Hi, Janice." Katie walked up to the town clerk's counter and laid her stack of animal collection chits down. While she'd been standing in line, she'd stood over by the adjoining door, trying to decide if she should walk in and hand the sheriff the backpack. Belatedly, she'd realized she shouldn't have removed it from Corrapell. She was feeling guilty for the act, but not for cheating Sheriff Lewis from being the first to examine the contents.

The older woman, who had been a school chum of Katie's mother and a friend to Gram, left her desk, bringing with her a file from the top drawer. It was common practice for Janice to go through the chits, verifying that every "t" was crossed before Katie left. There would be a tally, the chits stapled to the top copy of a receipt, and Katie would pocket the carbon copy.

"Wow. Busy week, huh?" Janice said, handing Katie the envelope with her payment for the prior week.

"It's that time of year," said Katie. "All the wild critters are out and moving around. The feral cats and loose dogs are a nuisance, but at least none are for Walker." Katie had taken on Walker, the wandering Basset when his elderly owner had passed. Prior to this, Walker had been her most frequent call. Now, he and Charlie were great chums.

"How's he doing, the poor old fella?" Janice laughed.

"He settled right in. I wasn't expecting to ever have a dog. Now I have two. I'm going to need to change the address on his license information."

"I'll take care of that for you. Two, three, four..."

Katie edged back toward the sheriff's door while she waited until Janice was done counting chits. But again, before she walked in and announced herself, she turned away. "Janice, do you know anything about the state wanting to shut down that fat farm over near Richmond? They call it a retreat." Even though Katie knew the part that had been closed wasn't the weight loss section, she didn't want to appear to be knowledgeable about the whole operation. There was always the chance Janice had heard the gossip about her working there, but maybe not.

"Nope, not my problem. Though word is the people running the place crossed the line with what they could and couldn't do there, according to their license. Probably because they're from New Jersey or something, and the laws are different there. But I don't really know."

Looking up from her receipt, Katie saw Janice's sharp eyes were on her. "Why are you asking, Katie?"

Damn knitting club, this will get straight back to Ruth. No way of getting around it except for some version of the truth. "I'm working up there overnight twice a week. I heard some gossip about the place getting ready to shut down and was wondering if I should start looking for another part-time job."

"How many part-time and full-time jobs do you need, Katie Took?" Janice asked. She gave Katie the same look Gram would every time she caught Katie doing something she didn't approve of.

Katie felt the shuffle of someone coming up behind her. "My last lottery ticket wasn't a winner. I'm hoping if I buy a fistful, I'll score."

She laughed and moved out of line, allowing the next person to address Janice. Instead of leaving through the front door, she walked through the connecting door to the sheriff's office. Amos, with his Coke-bottle glasses perched on the tip of his nose, manned the desk. Katie sighed. If it had been Marlie, she could have gotten some answers. Amos squinted in her direction, already closing down. She decided to give it a shot, anyway.

"Any news on the remains found out at the farm, Amos?" Katie asked.

"Restricted information." The words came out with a mist of spit.

"Yes or no, Amos."

"No, to you and everybody else."

Katie hadn't stopped walking throughout their short conversation. With a flip of her hand that could have been a wave or something not as friendly, she stepped out the exterior door. There were two other good places for local information within walking distance. But Charlene at the library had nothing, and Dorothea at the thrift shop didn't either.

"Are you staying to help for a bit?" Dorothea asked.

"Can't today. Have to get some sleep because I'm working again tonight." Katie yawned hugely.

Dorothea's yakking followed her across the parking lot. Father Metevier invited her in for tea, but when he told her only Mrs. O'Brien was there, Katie left. She'd been by the trailer several times. No one ever seemed to be inside. Where was Isaac hiding, and other than asking his mother, how was she going to figure it out?

Chapter Thirty-Six

Katie's short shift at Corrapell was a disappointment. Wade wouldn't be there until she was leaving. Most of the residents stayed in their rooms, but Cecile had a restless evening, which stopped Katie from wandering far. By eleven o'clock, Katie's eyes were drooping, and it took an effort to keep both open for the ride home.

Stan gave her a look when she walked into the feed store the next morning that let her know he didn't think her night job was a good idea. Then Katie's brain began to whirl, and by the time lunchtime rolled around, she had a plan. Sort of. She also had unanswered questions.

Katie left the feed store, telling Stan she might be a few minutes late returning. He assumed she was going to handle animal calls. She didn't correct his thinking.

"Sorry, Stan," she said to herself as she drove away. "I'll make it up to you."

At Corrapell, she drove around to the kitchen.

"Hi, Edna," she said as she walked in.

"What brings you in here this time of day?" asked the cook.

"I thought I lost my purse." Katie gave a little laugh. "But then I remembered I put it in my locker."

She held up the offending handbag for Edna to see, but the cook was too busy preparing lunch plates to notice.

Katie stood on the other side of the work table, looking over the trays the cook was assembling. "Kind of skimpy lunch, isn't it?"

"Well, I hate to say it, but these people are paying us to protect them from themselves." Edna sighed.

Her words sounded remarkably familiar to what Katie had heard Mrs. Reveck say on multiple occasions.

Katie twisted as Edna darted around her, never looking up. The woman focused on the plates lining the worktable, each with a resident's meal plan sticking out from beneath, mumbling about what needed to be added or left off. The portion weights were listed in ounces in red. Tiny beads of sweat glistened just beneath the edge of the cook's hairnet. On the other side of the table, Gail, who would serve up, waited nervously. Her fingernails kept creeping upwards to the overbite, waiting to rip and tear.

It was clear Katie was in the way. She decided to move before the cook either ran her over or threw her out. Katie had come in the back door, hoping to avoid running into Mrs. Reveck. The retreat director wasn't the person she wanted to talk to. During a long-ago conversation with Isaac, and more recently with Wade, she'd heard about Trinity, but dismissed her as irrelevant until she realized that someone, who's title included programs and activities might be worth talking to.

Ducking into the women's wing, Katie checked down the hallway. It was already filled with dour-looking residents. Each pair of eyes focused hopefully on the swinging door she had just walked through. They didn't care who she was, only that she was not carrying a plate, no matter how skimpy the fare. A few, like Edna's assistant back in the kitchen, gnawed on their cuticles. Katie didn't waste time chatting but moved quickly through to the reception area.

A young girl with a messy ponytail centered on the top of her head and a tie-dye t-shirt over dance leotards sat at the reception desk. Her back was to Katie as she giggled into the phone. This had to be Trinity Saint Pierre, the exercise program woman Wade had mentioned.

"If Mrs. Reveck catches you chatting with your boyfriend on the company telephone or with your feet up on the desk, you can say goodbye to your job," said Katie.

The telephone receiver slammed down at the exact same moment Trinity's feet hit the floor.

"May I help you?" Trinity squeaked. Her blue eyes were the size of dinner plates. They had never met, and Katie could be someone important.

"Is Mrs. Reveck here?" asked Katie, leaning her hip casually against the desk.

"Both Mrs. Reveck and the doctor are away at this time," said Trinity. "But I could take a message."

Katie smiled, friendly and inviting. "You know what?" she said. "I bet it's you I actually want to talk to."

Confusion pulled Trinity's plucked brows together. She didn't move as Katie drew up a chair, settling beside her and pulling a package of Juicy Fruit gum out of her pocket. She offered Trinity the first pick of a slice. When the younger woman had made her selection and was busy removing the yellow paper sleeve and foil, Katie continued.

"I'm not surprised you're not dining with the residents after seeing the meal selection," Katie said.

Trinity folded the gum into a single wad and popped it into her mouth. "I usually wait until Edna leaves. Then I raid the fridge," she said around the semi-solid glob.

Katie nodded. "Yeah, I would, too." She waited until Trinity relaxed slightly. "I'm Katie Took. I work overnight in the women's wing."

Trinity nodded. Katie wasn't sure if that meant she already knew or if it was just an acknowledgment.

"Anyway, one of the other caretakers told me you were the physical therapy and program director. I have a couple of questions, so you may be able to help me."

A slight blush crept up Trinity's neck to her cheeks. The small praise had gone far.

"I'm actually not the director," she said.

"You coordinate the program, though, right?" asked Katie. "Anyway, lately some of the residents have been getting up in the night. You know, kind of antsy. This one can't sleep; that one has a Charlie horse. Stuff like that."

Trinity chewed open-mouthed, snapped the gum, and waited. Katie sighed. The weight of the conversation would be on her.

"I thought you might have some stretches or something they could do to help relax," Katie said.

"I could check it out," said Trinity.

"Ah." *Girl has no clue*, Katie thought. "Great! Well, you could leave me a note at the desk."

Then Katie remembered what Wade had said. Mrs. Reveck had been asking questions. Katie considered her next move. If she offered to go to Mrs. Reveck for assistance, would Trinity jump on the horse, maybe not mention to the boss she was doing something worthwhile as an act of defiance? Trinity's attention seemed to wander. The girl's fingers tapped on the handset of the black desk phone. Obviously, she wanted to get back to her phone friend.

"Most of us working at night only work part-time," said Katie. "You're lucky to work full-time."

"I only work four days," Trinity said. "Monday, Tuesday, Thursday, and Friday. And let me tell you, this job can be bor-ring."

"Really?" Katie cocked her head. "How so?"

"Well, for the most part, these people don't do anything but lie around. I mean, I schedule activities, and nobody shows. Once a day, Mrs. Reveck drags them outside for a walk, like to stand in front of the door and get some fresh air. It doesn't matter how cold it is; they gotta go. When they get back inside, all they want to do is huddle in bed. I spend most of the day sitting here, waiting for the phone to ring. And staying out of the Revecks' way."

"That doesn't sound like fun." Katie frowned, commiserating with Trinity, who nodded back.

Leaning forward, Trinity spoke in a lower voice. "It didn't used to be like this. The people that came here when I first started were more fun. Hip, even. They talked about their friends, life in the city, cruises they were slimming down for, or some big trip. They would get all dolled up every day. I made a lot of extra money for, you know, illegals."

"Drugs?" Katie's eyebrows shot up.

"No." Trinity gave a horsey laugh. "The gardener has that covered, ha. I'd buy chocolate bars or chips in town and triple the price to make a profit. The rich people didn't care. As long as they got them, they just kept dropping the dough on me. They all had fancy cars. Some even came in limos."

"Why would anyone with money come to a hole in the wall like this?" Katie asked.

"Because no one knew they were here." Trinity sat back, a glint in her eye. "Sure, they went to the big spas where everyone else was going. But sometimes, they needed to get cleaned up or back in shape, and they didn't want all their buddies to know they were slipping. It was like a vacation from their realities, I guess. If you can believe they'd want to come to the sticks for that."

"And those people don't come here anymore?"

"No," said Trinity. "Suddenly, all we started getting were these stodgy, boring residents. Don't get me wrong, they all have money. It's just they aren't exactly party people. Most of them aren't really happy, I don't think." Trinity snapped her gum. "They're like fringe people, or something. And no more extra cash for me."

The door behind Katie opened, and Gail came through, pushing the tall, tiered rack of lunch trays. Stepping aside, Katie headed out the front door. As she approached it, she looked out the side light window. Mrs. Reveck was on the walk, headed toward her. With an abrupt about-face, Katie rushed toward the dining room door. Trinity was already on the telephone, eyes intent on her nails, and didn't notice. In the kitchen, Edna was also busy. But Gail was there, watching. Katie slowed her steps, giving a little smile and wave to the taciturn younger woman. Hopefully, Gail wouldn't wonder why Katie was headed out the backdoor. But her near miss with Mrs. Reveck, and then the tracking piggy-eyes of Gail had sweat gathering on the back of Katie's neck.

* * *

Katie was passing the driveway entrance to the high school. When she looked down the paved way, among the groups of teenagers, she saw a single boy walking alone. The size was right, the hoodie, bent shoulders, and hands deep in his pockets. She was ninety-eight percent sure it was Isaac. Even though he had told her he wasn't attending school, she couldn't figure out where else he would be. There was no time to stop, and with the proximity of other kids, she didn't want to be seen asking him questions.

Five hundred yards up the road, she circled back.

"Got a minute," she asked Isaac when she pulled up beside him.

He leaned on the passenger door, seemingly oblivious to the other teens hanging around him.

"S'up?" He asked.

"How come you're at school?" Katie asked.

"Lunch and heat." Isaac swung his head around, giving a cursory look at the crowd headed back inside.

Katie started to ask if he'd seen the newspaper article by Corporal Derrick and the description of the remains. Instead, she said, "Can you describe Holly for me? Like was she short, maybe five foot seven inches? What color was her hair? How about her eyes? Was she a little on the chubby side?"

Isaac screwed up his eyes. "She isn't short, taller than me. I don't remember her eyes, but her hair is the color of honey, and she isn't fat. Oh, she has a funny accent. I don't think she's from here."

He spoke about Holly like she was alive and well. When he asked Katie why she wanted to know, she replied she was looking for her.

"I feel a little awkward walking up to every woman I meet and saying, Hi, are you Holly?"

Isaac nodded in agreement. A shrill buzzer went off inside the school, and like everyone else still outside, he headed for the door.

Katie drove away, comparing Isaac's description to Corporal Derrick's. The state trooper had referred to the remains as female, five foot eight inches, slight build with light brown hair and brown eyes.

"Pretty close," Katie said to herself.

Chapter Thirty-Seven

atie rose early on Tuesday morning.

Well, it's not lunch yet, anyway, she thought. With only her left in the house, Solomon moved over to where she sat at the table, vying for space among the cats.

With coffee, oatmeal, and a writing tablet in front of her, Katie scratched a few critter heads, including Solomon's, before picking up her pen to finish her letter to Marlie.

I'm pretty excited about your chance at a new job. Rick and I both have our fingers crossed... She hadn't heard a word from Marlie about the possibility of an open slot in the sheriff's department, but Marlie hadn't known how long it would take for a decision to be made and probably didn't want to dwell on it while she waited. Katie continued to write, sending letters to the motel address in Pennsylvania, not mentioning her own heartbreak on their separation or the depression that washed over her so often of late. Instead, she passed along the local gossip, lighthearted stories, her offer to rent a room to Charlie and how fast he moved in, and only one quick sentence about her decision to go back to AA.

Ruth had left a note on the table for Katie, saying Grace had already picked her up and a reminder to order kitty litter and fifty-pound bags of cat chow from Stan, who gave her an employee discount. Shoving the note in her pocket, Katie headed out the door. She knew Ruth's continual little reminders weren't meant to demean her, but merely the way the old woman communicated her love and concern. This morning, however, Katie had her own errands to run.

The volunteer manning the front desk at Mary Fletcher Hospital provided directions. Upstairs, Katie explained three times that she wasn't looking for a patient or a job. Once to the receptionist, another time to the personnel clerk, and again to the department head. All she wanted was verification that Holly Guptill had at one time been employed by the hospital, and perhaps why she was no longer there.

She got the same answer each time. "I'm sorry. We realize that Holly Guptill is no longer an employee here, but the hospital maintains information security for all employees, current or previous. Unless you have a warrant?"

Katie politely said no and thank you, then left the office. From her spot next to the elevator, she watched the woman from personnel return to her inner office. The receptionist raised her head, making eye contact for a split second. Just long enough for Katie to wonder if she shouldn't find a place to wait and watch for the woman to go to lunch. Her final decision was no. There hadn't been even a tiny conspiratorial spark in the look, merely a dismissal as duty done.

Katie sat in the lot for several minutes as the truck idled. Several wings had been added to the big, red-brick hospital over the years. Another construction project was going up at the far end. There would be no way of finding an information source without knowing in which of those wings and on which floor or shift Holly had worked. She had one other choice. Shifting into gear, she drove down the sloping drive between the lawns and, at the light, turned toward Winooski.

It wasn't difficult to find the apartment buildings where Holly and Dwayne had lived. With no plan in place regarding what she would say, Katie walked into the manager's office, still working it out in her mind. The sign on the door introduced him as F. Heatley.

"Good morning, my name is Katelyn Took. I'm an employee with the town of Parentville. You know, small place, limited budget. We, and the sheriff's department, are in the middle of collecting information on an incident that occurred in our village. It's a rather sensitive issue right now, and not one where a lot of information is being shared with the public." She laughed self-consciously. "I had intended to send you a letter, but then found myself here in Winooski today and thought perhaps I'd save us both time and the nasty shock of a subpoena. This case involves Holly Guptill and, by extension, Dwayne Pena."

When the manager drew back, ready to exit the conversation, Katie played her last card.

"I know you don't know me from Adam," she said. "And I'm sure you have rules, legal and ethical, but hear me out for just a minute. This case is all the more personal to me, because I own the piece of property where a woman's remains were found a few weeks ago. The case seems to be already old news. Mostly, I think, because no one in our area is missing. Even though there have been alerts in the newspaper, and the police have asked for help, no one has stepped forward to report a woman gone. I don't know Holly, but a woman who is a friend does. She told me Holly just up and left. A fellow nurse from Mary Fletcher Hospital told me Holly used to live here. I'm hoping you can tell me something that will make the authorities look harder for her. Maybe discover where she actually went to."

"What do the police say about you sticking your nose in this?" asked Mr. Heatley.

"To mind my own business," said Katie truthfully. "But maybe if you remember Ms. Guptill, you could just describe her to me. That's kind of what I'm looking for. Was she twenty, thirty, forty? Blonde or brunette? Tall, heavy, what was her race? What bit of info can help me?"

Mr. Heatley leaned back in his squeaking desk chair, fingers rubbing his lips. Katie didn't move, knowing he was fighting an internal battle. The fact he was even willing to consider her request was more than she had received in the hospital personnel office. Finally, he grunted and rose to his feet. A large ring of keys hung from his belt. He came around the desk, unsnapping them.

"I don't know when the woman left."

He walked out of the office, motioning Katie to follow. They went deeper into the building, past a laundry room to a series of doors marked for maintenance: electric, water, and storage.

"Dwayne Pena gave up his apartment over two months ago. He didn't leave any forwarding address, so I don't know where he went. After residents move out, we go in and clean before new renters move in. Sometimes there are things left behind. By law, we are required to notify the exiting parties, or if they can't be located, to hold the items for three months before we dispose of them. I'm not sure how legal this is, but there are a couple of boxes of stuff down here from that apartment. I'll let you take a look, okay? That's it."

"Thank you," Katie said, disappointed she wouldn't be able to track down Dwayne.

Mr. Heatley hit the light switch and pointed to three boxes marked "PENA" stacked on one of the metal shelves. Katie lifted the first box down to the floor and knelt beside it.

"I'll be right back," Mr. Heatley said.

The box was filled with women's clothing. The second box held bathroom stuff and a few framed photographs. One showed a smiling, light-haired woman and a man of similar height embracing each other. It was clear these two were a couple, not just friends, but people who were bonded together. Looking over her shoulder, Katie pried the back off the frame and yanked the photograph out. Tucking it under her shirt, she opened the third box and found an odd assortment of kitchen utensils and knick-knacks. Mr. Heatley returned as she was placing the boxes back on the shelf.

"Thanks again," she said.

Concerned he'd see the guilt on her face, she walked down the hallway and out of the building as he locked up behind her.

There was a gas station just before the I-89 on-ramp at Exit 14. Pulling into the lot and behind the building, Katie finally dared remove the picture from beneath her shirt. She rubbed the place the paper had touched her; sure, the stolen photo had blistered her skin. With trembling fingers, she took a good look at Holly Guptill.

Chapter Thirty-Eight

Faye opened the door, and the welcoming smile on her face morphed into a sickly grimace.

"Hi, Faye. I'm Katie Took, remember me?"

"I know who you are." Faye glanced nervously behind her, then sidled ahead, forcing Katie backward and off the step. With the door firmly closed behind her, the dark-haired woman demanded to know what Katie wanted. There was no friendliness in her tone.

"I need some information about Holly Guptill," Katie said. "You seem to be the only one who really knows her."

Faye pressed her lips together until they turned white. Exhaling slowly, she motioned Katie away from the house until they stood near the truck.

"I-I don't know what else I can tell you." She stammered.

"That's just flat-out wrong." Katie leaned against the fender as if she had lots of time to waste. "Let's start with her losing her job in Burlington, then her split with Dwayne."

Faye stared at the ground. Katie didn't move. Finally, the woman looked up, pale and miserable.

"Okay. When I first met Holly, she was a different person. Not a saint, but more in control of her life. She drank, partied, smoked a little weed, but basically, she was cool.

"While she was working at Mary Fletcher Hospital, she met Dwayne. They started going together and rented a place in Winooski. He was so hot. Knew all the cool people, was into recreational drugs. It wasn't a problem for him. For Holly, it was different. It didn't take long for her to get hooked. I tried to get her straight. She said she was getting counseling. You know, working on it."

"Then what?" Katie asked.

"I heard Dwayne was roughing her up, telling her boss at the hospital lies about her," said Faye. "That was about the time I left to do private duty work so I could spend more time with my boys.

"She came to me—just showed up out of the blue here one day—and said Dwayne threw her out and got her fired. That was a couple of months before you arrived. The last time I saw her was, like, weeks before I met you. And it was at Corrapell. The place was a mess, so I went back to shift work at the hospital. I heard a different story there from what Holly said."

Katie waited while Faye got her thoughts straight.

"It seems Holly wasn't getting any help at all. Her addiction was out of control. Dwayne threw her out because she stole from him, blew the rent on dope. She got fired because security caught her red-handed, stealing patients' medications.

"The police were looking for her, which is probably why she was hiding out at Corrapell, and then she split. I know she was surprised to see me walk in there. I told her I wouldn't tell Dwayne where she was, but she still was all edgy. She looked terrible. She cried, and I folded. Tried to help her out."

"When did you see her last?" Katie asked.

"I was straight with you on that," Faye said. "I showed up for work expecting to see her and was ready to tell her I was going back to Mary Fletcher. She was just gone. No one knew anything."

"Do you know where she was hiding at the retreat?" asked Katie.

"Not really. She said there were a couple of places, not all of them in the building. Oh, wait. One time, she laughingly told me she was right under the Revecks' noses."

"Like in the empty wings?"

"I considered that, you know? She had a key she'd taken out of Mrs. Reveck's desk. But in the long term, I don't think so. Mrs. Francis said there was no heat on down there. She was complaining because there was a connecting door through the kitchen. Mrs. Francis was always complaining about a draft from under the door. This was after Christmas, but still in the winter."

Katie sat in her own thoughts for a minute or two. "So, you're sure you don't have any idea where she is now, or where she would go?"

Every time someone told her what was happening in Holly's life, she became more convinced the remains in the Gypsy Cove weren't a patient from Corrapell, but an employee. There had to be somebody Holly was friendly with, or who she thought was a friend, and then the relationship had gone south. But so far, not one person who would fall under that heading except Faye had surfaced. Katie watched the other woman closely, looking for a tiny hint Faye might be guilty of an unspeakable act. Unfortunately, Katie wasn't seeing one.

"No." Faye shook her head. "Her mother is in Maine; that's all I know. I'm worried, Katie. I have a real bad feeling about this."

"So do I." Katie pictured the leafless saplings and orange plastic ties Sheriff Lewis had used to mark off the restricted area in the Gypsy Copse.

There was no doubt in her mind that she should be sharing her theories. The issue was finding the right person to share what she knew with.

* * *

Tell Rick. Tell Wade. It was like a stupid song lyric stuck in her head. No matter what she tried, it wouldn't go away, but hung out in the shadows, waiting for a chance to jump out and dance around like a wild man, muddling her thoughts again.

It seemed logical, in Katie's mind, that she just walk up to the Revecks and ask about Holly. Mrs. Reveck, to be precise. Having only met the doctor one time, and less than impressed with his people skills, she believed Mrs. Reveck would be more open to the idea that Katie's questions came about innocently from a friend on the outside who had asked if it were possible Holly had met a bad end.

She's kind of a stiff-lipped pain in the ass, but once she hears the facts, she'll get it, Katie told herself as she drove to Corrapell.

She marched inside with her questions ready to spew over like beer suds from a quick pour in a cold glass. The door to the office was closed. Katie stopped short, her list of theories tumbling out of order. Trinity sat at the reception desk, loudly snapping her chewing gum, as usual.

"Hey, Trinity." Katie nodded toward the closed door. "How long will Mrs. Reveck be tied up?"

Trinity looked up, snorted, and went back to her magazine. "She ain't in there."

Katie waited. Trinity turned the page.

Trying not to sound either agitated or put-upon, Katie asked, "Where is she, Trinity?"

"I'm supposed to take messages." There was a small pause. "But actually, she went home."

"Okay, then." Katie turned toward the door.

"Are you gonna leave a message or come back?"

Katie looked back. Trinity had finally raised her head, a question on her brow.

"Neither, I guess. I wanted to talk to her, that's all." Katie hesitated just long enough for the look on Trinity's face to change to speculation.

"Are you quitting?"

"What? No. I, um, wanted to ask about, you know, job stuff."

Trinity was still looking at her suspiciously. Katie fought the urge to lick her lips. "Maybe I'll stick around a little while and wait for her." She pivoted toward the kitchen. "I'm getting a cup of coffee. Would you like one?"

"Are you kidding? That swill can't be called coffee. There's none left, anyway." Trinity returned to her copy of the *National Star.*

Katie continued through the dining room, across the kitchen, and out the back door to the loading ramp. Gail was nowhere in sight. Edna, busy at the stove, hadn't even raised her head.

Maybe it's better to have this conversation with Mrs. Reveck out of the building.

The ground was mushy underfoot. After one particularly squishy step, Katie started watching where she placed her sneaker-clad feet. She had found the blue plaid, slightly used shoes at the thrift store and willingly traded seventy-five cents for them, hoping they'd last the summer. Suddenly, mid-stride with left foot suspended in the air, she stopped short, sidestepping to catch herself from falling over. Before her was a short line of tracks, she was pretty sure she'd seen before: a circular dot topped off by a triangular imprint. She gulped air. There were four tracks in a row. Looking around, she realized there were several more going in both directions between the Corrapell building and the double-wide mobile home at the end of the drive.

Baffled, Katie squatted and reached out a tentative hand. "Footprints," she said aloud to the light wind. The lone print found in the Gypsy Copse had been unrecognizable, but here they were, plain as day. Raising her head, she could see the last few yards up the lane to the front steps of the double-wide. There was no way to know for certain, but with what she had seen of the Revecks, they probably didn't get a lot of guests. And she was willing to bet that only one of them wore high heels.

Mrs. Reveck stepped out the front door, fifty feet away. "Katie? Are you looking for me?" She started down the steps. "What are you doing?"

Katie rose slowly, feeling a thick place in the back of her throat. She was all alone out here. One of Mrs. Reveck's hands was out of sight behind her hip. Being busted and having to explain was one thing; having to run was another. Even though her mouth was dry, she swallowed hard, no longer sure she wanted to talk with her boss and unaware that regardless of the puddles, her blue plaid sneakers were moving backwards. Mrs. Reveck was still walking forward. Somewhere nearby, the purr of an engine drowned out the spring bird twitter.

"STOP HER!" Mrs. Reveck yelled.

Katie turned, ready to run, but the front fender of a shiny black BMW was barely five feet away. She leapt, tried to shift the angle of her escape, and was snagged by the long arm of Doctor Reveck as he jumped out of the driver's seat. Six feet tall, thin, but obviously strong, he spun her around with one arm wrapped around her chest, holding her arms down. His other big hand covered her mouth. His speed and dexterity proved to Katie that the man had perfected the move over years of dealing with addicts and others of a fragile mind.

"What the hell?" he demanded of his wife, who came running over.

Surprisingly fast in those high heels, Katie thought.

"She knows." Mrs. Reveck's voice was shrill. "She's been talking to patients, snooping around, and now she's here. Faye Pigeon stopped in to see me earlier. She was asking questions about Holly, like when did she get done? Did she leave a forwarding address for her last paycheck? Not only that, but when I dropped off more applications at the library, that nosy little peanut that works there was bragging about how Katie was instrumental in solving the murder of her grandmother and some old guy. I'm telling you, she's trouble."

Doctor Reveck, with Katie still secured and struggling, strode to the double-wide, up the steps, and inside. "If you keep kicking me," he said into her ear, "I'll give it right back to you."

Katie kept fighting. She felt a slight lessening of his grip when the door shut and locked behind them. She renewed her efforts, but the doctor still held her firm. The doctor removed his hand from her mouth to adjust his grip. "Get me some duct tape. Then move the car up," he instructed his wife.

Katie gulped for air. Instead of screaming, and regardless of the fact she now believed she was lying, she said, "Listen, I know you didn't kill Holly, either of you. She was a junkie, an addict, and took advantage of what she found. You don't have to worry. The sheriff will understand. Really. Just let me go, and we can talk this out."

Reveck's body went rigid. Katie knew instantly she would have been better off keeping her mouth shut. With his wife's help, he wrapped Katie's arms against her body and her legs together with wide gray tape. She tried one more time to reason with him before he shoved her jaw up and slapped a long piece over her lips. The tape edged her nostrils. Katie panicked, then realized she could still breathe. The doctor dumped her on the floor, then stood silently until Mrs. Reveck returned from moving the BMW from where he had left it in the driveway with the motor still running.

"Now what?" she asked, closing and locking the door behind her.

Doctor Reveck shook his head. "Go back to the clinic. Make sure everyone sees you working. Be careful but see who's around and might have seen this one."

Katie went rigid, immediately remembering Trinity. Would the airheaded exercise instructor remember her being there? Would she tell Mrs. Reveck? And worse than that, if she did, would the young woman be in danger as well?

After his wife left, the doctor made two trips out to his car, bringing in a briefcase, a duffle, and a few bags of groceries. While he was outside, Katie rolled back and forth, desperately looking for something she could use to slice through the duct tape. She found nothing, ending up near a small bookcase filled with dusty pamphlets. He'd barely made it in from the second trip when the phone rang. Katie could hear Mrs. Reveck talking on the other end.

"Trinity said Katie was looking for me and went to the kitchen, but Edna said nobody had been in there. I told Trinity I'd be working for the rest of the day and sent her home."

"I don't know if that was smart."

"I told her that tomorrow I'd get the patients up in groups of four to take a walk, but I needed to make sure it was all right with the insurance company for her to be in charge. Then, it would become her project because I wouldn't be doing it anymore. I'm sure she thinks she'll be getting more hours, because she was pretty gung-ho with the idea. A bigger problem is that Katie's truck is parked right out front."

"Darn." Doctor Reveck ran his hand through his hair.

Katie noticed he wore a gold ring with a large stone, like an elaborate high school ring, on his left hand. Not a wedding ring. She had seen Mrs. Reveck's wedding ring, a dull, dark-colored gold band. She didn't wear a diamond. Katie closed her eyes, exasperated at the untimely realization that Mrs. Reveck's ring announced her status, but his didn't.

Mrs. Reveck was still talking, but her husband had moved across the room. Katie could still hear the other woman talking but could no longer make out the words.

"Okay," he said. "Call me after Trinity leaves. How many other people are working?" There was a pause. "So, the only ones who might notice are the two in the kitchen?" Pause. "You'll have to keep them busy while I move her car."

The doctor came back into the living room and squatted next to Katie, riffling through her pockets for her keys. Once he'd grabbed them, he stood up and crossed the room to flip on the stereo, turning up the volume.

"There's nowhere for you to go, and I won't be long." He went out, closing the door with a solid thud.

Katie immediately began to squirm toward the kitchen. She had already discerned there was nothing in the living room that would help her. The furnishings were sparse, without even a glass ashtray she could break to saw apart her bonds. Maybe the kitchen would offer something more useful.

Her journey took several minutes. She rolled, wiggled, and finally laid on her side, using a weird, humping frog-leg motion to inch ahead. The bags of groceries were still on the table, but nothing else seemed readily available. From the floor, she couldn't see so much as a spoon on the counter. Humping over to the cabinets, she struggled to roll onto her back and then up into a sitting position. Using her heels, she pressed and slid her back up the cabinet until she stood precariously. Grasping a drawer handle, she quickly realized she'd fall over if the drawer opened. She leaned back against the cabinet until she was sure she was balanced.

Her heart was racing, and she felt the cold trickle of sweat from her armpits. With the thudding of her heart and the rasping wheeze of each breath, she was having trouble making out other sounds.

Get your act together, she berated herself. *That quack could march back in here any moment, and you wouldn't even hear him coming.*

She worked at slowing down her breathing, unaware she was making headway until she realized her vision had narrowed before, but now she could see more of what was in front of her. On the far edge of the counter, beyond the sink, she spotted a wooden knife rack holding a selection of seven blades.

Carefully, so she wouldn't topple over, Katie flexed her toes, then her heels. Each set of maneuvers moved her maybe an inch and a quarter. Every few moves, she had to stop and recenter herself.

Bathed in sweat, she stood with her back to the knife rack and started the process of making a full turn. Giving up the ability to lean on the counter increased her nervousness that she would fall. To compensate, she leaned further over the Formica. That was fine, because the only way she'd reach a knife was with her teeth. Grasping the handle of the closest knife, she tried to pull the blade free. Instead, the entire rack moved toward her. It wasn't until the block fell to the floor, taking all the other knives with it that one pulled free.

Katie panted, barely able to hold on to the black plastic handle between her teeth, unsure what to do next. In the living room, the front door opened. In a moment, Dr. Reveck stood in the archway between the living room and kitchen. He looked totally surprised to see what she had accomplished. Then he started laughing.

"Who would have thought?" he guffawed, calmly plucking the knife from her lips, then picking the knife block up off the floor and putting them out of her reach. "I think, this time my foolish wife might be right, you are trouble."

She tried to talk through the duct tape gag, but he paid no attention. Tears gathered in her eyes, bringing an immediate filling of her sinuses. Her muffled moaning was part pleading and partially the struggle to get a breath. Each flawed draw for oxygen raised her hysteria. Her choice was to fight against him, or somehow to regain enough control to be able to get air. She was still leaning precariously against the counter edge, but barely. Shaking her head, silently begging Doctor Reveck to let her go was a waste of her energy.

Placing his shoulder just above her waist, he had no difficulty flipping her over his shoulder before exiting the kitchen door. Beneath her narrowing vision, Katie made out the planks of a redwood deck, faded and splintery. Like the far end of the retreat building, facing the woods and out of sight, the rest of the backyard was overgrown. But she didn't have a chance to make a note of that. Once on the ground, he took a few steps away from the deck, staying close to the side of the mobile home. He didn't go far.

"I need to figure out what to do with you," he said thoughtfully, dropping her on the ground next to his home. "This appears to be the best place to leave you while I figure it out." He swiveled, looking around the yard. Other than the trees along the edges, there was nothing but shaggy grass and sprouting wildflower stems. "But before I go, I want to tell you that you were right about us not killing Holly, though we would have if we'd known what she was doing. She wouldn't have been the first to suffer an accidental ending. Pity we didn't have time to make her a patient before she died. It would have been neater, cleaner for all of us. But what happened to her, she did to herself. We were just trying to protect ourselves, really. Believe me."

He squatted beside her, close enough so that she felt the brush of his pants leg against her arm. Katie didn't believe him for a moment. His proximity made her muscles pull together, trying to make her small and invisible.

"Given a little more time, we would have had a new set of investors, made upgrades, gotten the rich and idle to return. Not just those old, fat slobs looking for a mystery cure to make them young again, but their sons and daughters, grandchildren. The ones that are tripping around in the psychedelic rainbow. I'll tell you a little secret, that's where the money is. Hiding them until they get sober, then going back and wringing more and more out of a generation that can't bear the shame."

He chuckled, and Katie heard the same fervor as the religious fanatics on the radio. There was no truth, but his. He wanted to be held above all others, and fear was his way. She felt that rivulet of terror creeping into her veins, traveling up and down her body, leaving ice in its wake. Now, there was nowhere for him to go. Because of Holly, and now Katie, his rise was finished in Parentville. He laid his hand on her head, offering a blessing in parting.

"You believe me, don't you?" He asked again, more softly this time. "Taking her off like we did, we were just trying to protect ourselves. We still are."

Katie shook her head, then realizing that if he thought she was a threat, he'd never let her go, began nodding vigorously, hoping he would remove the gag so they could talk things out. Even if he just left her lying here for a while, that was better than whatever he had in mind. She might be able to get free. The yard was probably full of forgotten things to be used to slice her bonds. If he'd just go.

That, however, didn't seem to be foremost in Doctor Reveck's mind. He continued speaking, and the sinking bottom of Katie's stomach dropped even lower.

"For now, I'm just going to put you under the house, hide your car, then figure out what we need to do. I'll probably have to dump Sheila as well. She really isn't the type of person I would want for a wife. Not for the long term. She's so boring, and so…needy."

He pulled free two pieces of the heavy plastic panels that encircled the bottom of the double-wide releasing the stink of mold and mildew, exposing a dimly lit expanse far more frightening than the basement of the farmhouse could ever be.

Katie turned her head, looking into the dark, dank hole. Yanking back around, she tried to edge closer the shins that barred her way, shaking her head even more vigorously. Now, her inability to draw a breath beyond the top third of her chest wasn't due to the snot dripping down the back of her throat, but to terror. Behind her lay a crypt, a place crawling with things she didn't want to encounter. Grabbing her by her bonds, he hefted her away from himself, closer to the opening he had made.

As if the heavens were agreeing that yes, she should be afraid, a cloud slid across the sun, and within the tight circle of trees and house, twilight fell. No longer intent on making him believe she was harmless, she fought against him. Doctor Reveck shoved her into the opening. As soon as his hands were off her, she tried to wriggle her way back out. Grunting, he shoved her deeper inside. The overwhelming smell of decomp, some small animal that hadn't lasted the winter, rolled over her.

Standing, Doctor Reveck pulled a wooden Adirondack chair off the deck. Then he rolled it onto its side and pushed it into the opening. Its wide paddle armrest scrapped the ground, and the steel I-beams three feet above. His grunting noise told her the chair was wedged tight, a secure fence to hold her away from the plastic panels that skirted the mobile home. Katie tried to fold her body, bend her knees, anything that would get her out of this cold and damp crawlspace. But she found herself effectively wedged in between a handle-less gas lawnmower that had been there so long she felt flakes of rust fall onto her arms and, on the other side, disintegrating cardboard boxes dumping their contents on the damp ground, and finally, at her feet, the chair. Her muffled cries went unheeded as the doctor worked the interlocking panels back into place.

Tears dripped off the side of Katie's face. Once again, crying curtailed her ability to breathe. She forced herself to shut off the waterworks. At least lying on her side kept her throat clear, and leaning against the lawnmower kept her in one place. With no space to draw back and get a good start and strapped together, every time she kicked her legs out, she unbalanced herself. The chair didn't even rock with her blows.

* * *

It seemed to Katie as though a long time had passed. Her thoughts were filled with Sheila Reveck's words. If she had been telling the truth and spoken to both Faye and Charlene, when Katie failed to show up, one of them would surely tell Rick, Stan, or Sheriff Lewis. Katie tried to concentrate and send out a message to either woman over the static airways. It wasn't that she believed it would work, but it kept her panic at bay.

A four-inch piece of Barminco piping ran in a slanting line from the bottom of the double-wide to a waste outlet. It cut off most of Katie's view beneath the unit.

Periodically, she heard the doctor walking around. He had shut off the stereo, opened closets, slammed drawers, and gone outside. Katie worried he might return to her, but she was also frightened he would drive away and no one would know where she was. To her relief, the car engine didn't start, but she heard another heavy slam that indicated the trunk lid had been closed.

She was startled to hear the tap-tap of Mrs. Reveck's high-heeled shoes overhead

"Gary?" her boss asked. "What are you doing?"

"I'm packing our things. We have to get out of here," Doctor Reveck said. "Where's the girl?"

"Out of sight, in case someone comes around."

The pair moved further into the house, away from the kitchen. Katie's eyes followed along the bottom of the house. She tried to remember the layout. Where they were.

"What are we going to say?" Mrs. Reveck asked.

"Nothing. We don't know she was here, right? She didn't see you in your office, did she? Nobody saw the two of you actually together, right?"

"No, but she might have told someone she was coming here. Trinity spoke to her. Where is she now?"

Katie groaned. She hadn't told anyone she was coming here. There was no note or clue left behind. What Trinity remembered would probably amount to Katie having come in and then left. She wanted to scream in frustration. Above her head, an inner door opened and closed. Katie stopped thinking and listened.

"Where is she, Gary?" Mrs. Reveck asked again.

"Never mind where she is. In the event the authorities ask, it'll be easier if you don't know. We won't have to worry about getting our story straight if only one of us knows."

There was silence above, not a single footstep. Katie could only hope Mrs. Reveck was reconsidering what they were doing.

Then the doctor spoke. "Come here, my love. It is you and I; always it has been you and I. I would never allow anyone to harm you. Listen to me closely; did that girl come into your office, into Corrapell, anytime in the last few days and see you?"

"No." Mrs. Reveck sounded hesitant. "But, please, where is she? You didn't, you know, get rid of her, did you?"

"Oh, for heaven's sake, Sheila. She's somewhere that somebody will find her after we're gone." Reveck had gone from being a loving husband to an irritated spouse. "We'll get our stuff together, jump into the car and drive away. If we wait until after shift change tonight, no one should notice until tomorrow. And then, maybe not for a while. That will give us a good head start. I've got more to do to get ready. Go back to work and keep your ears open. I'll call you when everything is all set."

The heavy sound of footsteps was coming closer, back toward the kitchen area, which, due to all the pipes running upward, Katie believed was above her head. After a few moments, the tap, tap, tap of high heels followed. The first set had been measured; these were faster, like a small dog afraid of being left behind trying to keep up. And just like that nervous pooch, there was a desperation in Mrs. Reveck's words.

"Gary, we can't leave. This place is all we have. We used all my money to buy it. What will we do?"

Hearing the other woman's trepidation clearly in her tone and words, Katie remembered what the doctor had said to her earlier about dumping Sheila. Would he tape his wife up and dump her on the side of the road, perhaps beyond the ability of hoping to be found?

Would that be a better place than this? Katie wondered. *No one is going to find me here until there's a really bad smell.*

Katie's heartbeat ramped up, and she closed her eyes. If she could empty her mind, maybe let her senses focus on something other than the specter of death, she'd stand a better chance. She knew it. She did. It was just so hard getting there.

In the mobile home, the conversation was continuing. Mrs. Reveck was also far from calm. The volume was rising.

"You promised we'd get married, have a good life. We've been here a long time. You told me this would be easy. Just collect the checks. Let the minions do the heavy lifting. In a dump like this area, they'd be glad for the jobs and not ask any questions. You said the locals would be beating down the doors for a chance at a steady paycheck. You never told me I'd be stuck out here in the woods for *months* while you were out schmoozing with investors. And don't try to deny that you've been sleeping around. I do your laundry, damn it. I'm not stupid!"

Doctor Reveck was walking away. If it was possible, his steps were heavier than before. There was no pause between the footsteps of the man and the woman this time. Her tapping heels followed him closely.

Mrs. Reveck spat out. "Believe me, it's been difficult, at least for me. You never did a damn thing to get your hands dirty until some rich dude caught you in the rack with his wife. And that, my dear, sweet husband, was when our entire lives made a turn for the worse." Her voice rose. "What are we going to do now? With no money. No place to go."

Heavy footsteps returned to where the tap, tap, tap had stopped.

"*Run!*" Katie gagged out from behind the duct tape.

Instead, she heard the low murmur of a deep voice and a few female sobs. She heard the doctor tell his wife that she was right. He had made a mess of things. But he had a plan, and amazingly, he had cooped a small amount of cash before the witch had beguiled him. He assured Sheila they would be safe.

Then Doctor Reveck said, "There you go, my beautiful, smart girl. Go ahead. Pack up what you need to take from your office. Act like nothing is different from yesterday. By the time you get back, I'll have everything ready to go."

The tap, tap, tap crossed over Katie's head. Somehow, Mrs. Reveck's steps sounded less certain. When the front door closed behind her, Katie knew she was in acute danger. All the time she had been considering the remains, and then Holly, and even that something hid in the corners of the retreat ominous enough to have brought all this bad into her backyard, her focus had flittered around Mrs. Reveck. Gooseflesh ran up her arms and onto her cheekbones. She might have been right on the small scale, but when Doctor Reveck had laid his hands on her head in benediction, an electric thought had run from him to her. He was silent danger. With his wife gone, there was no one to stop him from coming back outside and dragging Katie off into the woods, leaving her body for the wild animals to find.

Duct tape held her wrists together, and the rest of her body secured like a sausage. She was effectively gift-wrapped.

The double-wide wasn't set on a concrete pad, but on stacked cinder blocks. A cheap set-up, and, from Katie's view at this time, a disgusting one. Lying on the ground in a place where the sun hadn't shown for years was cold and damp. Unable to move, her muscles had started cramping. Even lying still, she had the sensation of sinking into the ground. It was worse when she struggled. She'd been in tough places before, but being angry and scared, but mobile was way better than this hot-dog-in-a-bun feeling that smelt like death.

Okay, she said to herself. *I know you're scared. This mess would scare anybody. But, hey, if you don't do something, you're going to have to answer to Rick eventually.*

Her bottom lip trembled. She swallowed a hard lump, refusing to dwell on that later might be the hereafter.

"STOP IT!" she moaned behind the duct tape gag. "FOCUS!"

It took an effort to look up at the bottom of the double-wide, studying the steel beams and flaking boards, looking for some bit that would help her, anything. What she saw was a labyrinth of spider webs and deserted insect cocoons. The boxes were soft moldering stacks of cardboard, old clothes, and many-legged creepy crawlers. She couldn't get beyond the Bermico pipe because the lawn mower chassis was in the way.

The feeble light around her was fading. The doctor had continued to go in and out, and at one time, she thought she'd heard a car start, but it was quickly shut off. The front door was open, and the doctor came into the kitchen. Shortly, Katie smelled coffee brewing. Her stomach called out for a cup, but even if she could have had one, her bladder said it wasn't a good idea.

"There you are, sweetheart."

Doctor Reveck's baritone drifted through the floor, rousing Katie. Immediately, she pulled her feet upward, looking beyond the Adirondack chair, expecting to see his face peering back at her. Then she realized the tap, tap, tap had returned.

"We're going to be driving for a while, so I made us coffee. Here, let me pour you a cup. Be careful, it's hot." He just kept talking. "Relax for a minute, then have a good look around and make sure I didn't miss anything we should take."

There was a whining murmur, which had to be Sheila Reveck. Katie strained to listen.

"No, we won't eat now," said the doctor. "These sandwiches will go in the cooler. I packed everything we could use for snacks. Once we're on the interstate, we can have a regular picnic in the car."

Katie heard a hiccupping sob.

"I know, sweetheart, this is rough. I've been thinking maybe we should go to that little place in New Hampshire for a bit, the one with the cute cottages. Do you remember?"

There was a solid thud as something weighty hit the floor, followed by a rolling of said heavy object across the floor in the direction of the front entrance.

Please let that be a really heavy suitcase, Katie prayed.

The noise went out the front door. Katie didn't hear anything else, except faint cursing, until the screeching of one rigid plastic panel against another indicated more of the ground-level paneling was being removed. Twisting her head, she could see behind her and off to the far side, where a square of semi-light sky grew larger as a second piece of the paneling surrounding the base of the double-wide disappeared.

The cursing continued, only louder. Doctor Reveck was stashing another cumbersome bundle beneath his house.

The pit of Katie's stomach fell out. There was no doubt in her mind that the long, floppy tube was Mrs. Reveck, bound as Katie was, but not conscious. Katie could tell the man was kneeling, intent on getting the bundle that was his wife shoved far enough beneath the mobile home so if she were still alive and possibly regained consciousness, she wouldn't be able to work her way out.

Suddenly, Katie realized that if he looked up, there was just enough light so that he would see her watching. Better he thought she had succumbed and was also unknowing. Throwing her head and shoulders down, she made contact with the corner of the mower plate, and it hurt enough for her to call out. For the first time, she was grateful for the gag, which muffled her outcry.

When the doctor had the bundle in place, he spoke to it, apologizing and saying goodbye. His words seemed to indicate his wife was alive, but there was no struggling, no muted cries for absolution. Katie couldn't tell for sure. She laid still, the devils on her shoulders arguing whether she should stay silent and forget or try to get the good doctor to remove her gag and listen to reason.

There's no thought of reason in him, only escape.

The panels were replaced. The car drove away. Night fell, bringing total darkness.

Chapter Thirty-Nine

Katie woke to hear something shuffling around near her. Initially, she hoped it was Mrs. Reveck, no longer bound, but the squealing, screeching sounds Katie heard as she jerked fully awake sent that wish out the window. She'd heard that angry noise from trapped raccoons before and could only hope these were not some of them coming after her with revenge in mind.

She was very cold. It had been several long hours since her last trip to a bathroom, and she was totally disgusted with her body's inability to contain itself. She listened hard. The animal noises had subsided. There was not so much as a whimper from Sheila Reveck. No sirens sounded. Sheriff Lewis wasn't calling her name, nor was a bloodhound howling in the distance.

Frustrated, she thunked her head backwards multiple times, finally crashing against the wheel of the lawnmower chassis. The place where she had smacked herself earlier was still a touch sore. She pictured the metal plate, solid and unforgiving.

Wait. The lawnmower. She thought, picturing the machine.

Her initial assessment when she had been being shoved into place was that the mower, less the handlebars, was old and broken. Maybe the motor froze up, a piece of junk. But maybe not. Even with the handles gone, or the motor not running, there was every chance the twin cutting blades were still attached on the bottom. Twitching around, she was able to get her shoulder under the cowl, lifting the side of the machine. But it was heavy and wouldn't stay up while she adjusted her position. Thrusting up against it, Katie hoped to flip it over without severing an artery on the blades beneath.

The lawnmower went up and came down twice. Running out of energy, she tried again. This time, when the machine rose up, Katie threw away her fear of getting sliced and pushed herself backwards, forcing the machine to rise up even further. Metal grated against metal as the mowing plate scraped one of the I-beams. She pushed against it again. The mower top moved less than an inch. When she pulled back to push harder, the mower stayed upright. It was stuck against the bottom of the I-beam.

That's okay, just stay there. She panted.

Twisting until she felt the edge of the blade, Katie worked, unable to see as she sawed her hands free. It was a tedious process as the blade periodically swiveled. When that happened, Katie had to adjust her position and, with the tip of her finger, force the blade back to where she needed it to make contact with the duct tape. The irony of her bare finger not getting sliced as she worked to sever the duct tape wasn't lost on her.

Concentrating on the blade and the duct tape didn't stop her from noticing dawn was growing. There were tiny vent holes in some of the panels, and she could see little dots of color as the sky lightened. From where she lay, she was unable to see the other bundle, which remained ominously silent.

The release of tension as the duct tape on her wrist snapped sent Katie rolling onto her belly, face in the dirt. Grunting, she rolled back onto her side. Her hands were free, but her arms weren't.

Doctor Reveck had put more tape on Katie's wrists than around her body. But to cut through those two bands would mean putting her spine near the blade. She moved a few inches deeper under the double-wide until she felt the edge of the blade above the pressure of the tape. Her chin was buried against her chest the back of her head pressed against the Bermico pipe. Katie didn't give a thought to how being against that filthy pipe would have disgusted her hours before. Carefully, she inched backwards, maneuvering to slide the blade beneath the tape. The cold metal sliced through her shirt, scraping her flesh. She stopped, unable to go further. Sweat was turning the dirt clinging to her to mud.

It's okay, she thought. *Remember? We've been all over this. Just a little bit more. You're doing a good job. Before you know it, you'll be free and out of here. I bet there's a nice hot shower up in the mobile home. You can stand there for hours. Okay? Okay! Relax. Take it slow. Try again.*

Slowly, she inched around, working by feel. Once sure the entire two strands were beneath the blade, she rocked gently back and forth, sawing and hoping she wasn't cutting too deeply into her skin. Her teeth held tight to the swollen inside of her inner lip. She worked with her eyes closed, visualizing what was happening behind her.

This time, when the tape gave, she laid still, fighting the rising hysteria, but it wasn't bad, more like morphing into excitement. She was almost free. She wanted to push herself out into the open, to hurry, but instead, she worked at getting the tape off her arms and wrists. As soon as one arm was free, she ripped the piece off her face, along with a long strip of flesh. None of that mattered. The bigger issue was her being wedged in a spot so cramped she couldn't effectively rip the layers wrapped around her knees. There was absolutely no way to reach her ankles.

She kicked out at the Adirondack chair again. It didn't move. Instead of wasting her flagging strength, Katie GI-crawled beneath the greasy Barminco waste pipe and toward the front of the double-wide. She crawled over gravel and clay-like mud, with bits that smelt like animal spoor and a depression that might have been a nesting place. To her right was Doctor Reveck's second bundle. She could see it, lying unmoving. It was scarier than any Halloween prank. She kept going.

At the front wall, she located a seam between panels and, shoving her fingers between the slight crevice, yanked one forward while pushing the other out. One fingernail ripped off. Cuticle skin ripped on several other fingers. Grunting with the strain, she kept up the pressure until one of the panels gave with an almost metallic screech.

She was out. The ground was dew-wet. Mosquitoes the size of cocker spaniels found her immediately. It didn't matter. She was free.

Katie was shivering on the ground. It was a bad combination of being physically wet, sweating, a little shocked, and fearful if she looked around, she'd see another danger waiting to attack. Once she caught her breath, she rolled onto her butt, pulling her knees to where she could unwind the duct tape. With nothing to use to cut through the strands, she was forced to pull and twist as the glued side of the tape held on. She was unbalanced and kept tumbling over.

"Come on. Come on."

It was taking too long; she was getting agitated again. Finally, the last bit ripped away, and she was forced to rest and catch her breath before she started on her ankles. This set of straps was the least secure, and it was almost with maniac glee Katie rolled the length of tape in a ball and pitched it away.

Believing the worst was past, she tried to stand. Her knees were weak, folding beneath her weight, and the muscles in her thighs shivered. Unable to stand alone, Katie hugged the side of the double-wide until she got to the section where she believed Mrs. Reveck had been dumped. Down on her knees, she again strained to pull panels apart. When the first one came away, Katie immediately saw high-heeled feet right in front of her. Unable to force herself back under the building, Katie grasped Mrs. Reveck by the ankles and pulled the woman out into the early light.

Mrs. Reveck had been bound in the same manner Katie had. Katie's fingers were so cold she couldn't tell if the woman was still alive, but when she ripped the tape off Mrs. Reveck's mouth, she heard a gasping breath.

"Mrs. Reveck? Sheila?" Katie gently shook the other woman's shoulder. There was no response.

Knowing Mrs. Reveck needed medical help, both of them did. Katie left Mrs. Reveck and semi-crawled back to the front door of the house and found it locked. There was a telephone inside. She just needed to get to it. She overturned flowerpots and looked under the railings but didn't find a key. By this time, she was sobbing. She was so close.

"Why?" she pleaded. "Why is this happening to me? For crying out loud, God, give me a break!"

Mrs. Reveck's car was right there. Katie stumbled to the driver's door, but that was also locked. She had no choice but to head back down the lane to Corrapell. From where she stood, the building looked miles away.

She walked as far as she could. When she stumbled, she crawled on all fours. Near the edge of the loading dock, she could hear a woman talking and tried to call out, but all she could raise was a croaking grunt. Finally, she made it to the loading dock steps and crawled up. She was on her knees, leaning on the kitchen door. The knob was slippery beneath her fingers. When it finally turned, she fell in. Startled, Edna and Gail, who were just starting the prep work for breakfast, spun around.

"Wade," Katie whispered before she passed out.

When Katie came to, Wade was kneeling on the floor beside her. He dabbed at her face with a wet dishtowel.

"Don't move," he said. "We've called Rescue, and they're on the way. I can't tell if you're hurt. Just stay still."

She reached up and grabbed his hand.

"Mrs. Reveck is on the ground behind her house, tied up. It's bad, Wade." The face above hers paled. "Is she dead?" he whispered.

"No, but not conscious. Please, help her." Katie closed her eyes, afraid she would pass out again herself.

She lay still, but felt Wade move away. A moment later, a roughened hand took hers. Katie knew it was Gail and felt grateful. When the work-worn fingers squeezed hers, she squeezed back, happy to be lying on the worn, dry linoleum. In the distance, a siren wailed.

"I know I smell bad," Katie whispered, "but I'm going to be okay."

"Yes, you are." Gail gave another little squeeze.

Chapter Forty

The first ambulance hauled Mrs. Reveck away. Wade told Katie that their employer had still not regained consciousness. While they waited for the second one, which had to come from Richmond, she told her story to State Police Corporal Derrick. He had been Wade's second call after the rescue unit. His patrol area included Parentville and the Richmond area and had been close enough to intercept the ambulance as it passed CVU High School, and lead the way to Corrapell. Sheriff Lewis had been demoted to last contact.

The residence of Martin Lewis was on the Monkton Road. Though he had been almost ready to leave for the sheriff's office when the emergency response call had come in, there was no direct route from where he was to Corrapell. His choice was either to drive all the way through Parentville village or back and forth on rutted and poor dirt roads. He arrived shortly after the state trooper had hurried toward the double-wide. Mrs. Reveck would need assistance before Katie. Lewis' harsh reaction to finding Katie once more involved in a near calamity made it difficult for her to explain what had happened.

"I should have known when Rick called last night saying you were missing, that you'd be up to your neck in trouble," he groused.

"Martin, please just listen for a minute." Katie's head hurt and she was feeling nauseous.

This wasn't the time for them to start ticking off all the reasons they couldn't get along. The sheriff paused. Katie took advantage of that moment.

"You need to find Doctor Reveck. He did this. The girl in the copse was

Holly. He did that, too."

"You're telling me you've been digging into this one as well? Messing up my case?" His voice was rising.

Katie squinted, focusing on the blurry face above her. She could tell from his tone that his nose was severely out of joint. If that wasn't enough, that same bulbous appendage was roiled up between his puffed-out cheekbones. To Katie, he looked surprisingly like her pet pig, Bonnie. The arrival of the second ambulance and the trooper were a godsend.

"Did you let Ruth and Rick know where I am?" she asked Lewis as the sirens went silent and she heard doors slamming outside.

"We'll get to that. Right now, we need to know what happened," he answered.

He was standing above her, bent slightly at the waist. Beyond him, Katie could see Matt and Edna hovering. She wanted to tell Edna the hash was burning but couldn't seem to find the energy.

"My family needs to know I'm not dead in a ditch someplace." Katie was irate.

Matt stepped forward, *accidentally* shouldering Sheriff Lewis back a half a step.

"It's okay, Katie," he said. "I called. Your uncle was here last night looking for you, so I have your telephone number."

Rose, the on-duty EMT, hustled in, shouldering Lewis out of the way. "Excuse me. Move over, okay? Let me check her vitals, see that she's stable."

Lewis moved, but he was still scowling.

"Phew, aren't you a mess?" Rose smiled down at Katie. "The last time I saw this much mud on somebody, we were pulling him out from under a tractor."

Lewis started to speak, but the EMT cut him off. "We're loading her up. You can meet us at the hospital. Cory, get that stretcher over here." Rose backed up, her square frame forcibly moving Lewis further out of the way.

While the sheriff sputtered in the background, Rose and Cory wrapped Katie in a thermal blanket and strapped her into place. The employees of Corrapell stepped forward, hands reaching out to help with the gurney, but

Rose and Cory were on it.

"Out of the way," the bossy EMT ordered. In one smooth move, the gurney was out on the dock where the ambulance had been backed in. Before Katie knew it, Rose was jumping inside. Cory slammed the door, smacked the side of the vehicle to let Rose know they were pulling out. Katie was finally able to release a long, sobbing breath. Rose squeezed her arm. "I've got you," she said.

Once they were underway, she told Katie that as they were loading, Sheriff Lewis was questioning Wade about what he'd found behind the double wide.

"They're walking back that way," Rose said. "You know Lewis has to see it for hisself, like he can't trust anybody else. Lewis is all complaining that the scene needs to be secured, blah, blah, blah." She gave a little giggle and another squeeze. "Oh, and that tall, cute statie is riding ahead of us. Lights and sirens roaring."

"Ruth? Rick?" Katie was parched, but Rose refused to give her anything to drink yet.

"Nope, chance of choking. I'm hooking you up to fluids, you can suck it in out of your veins." Even as she spoke, Katie felt the small pinch-prick of the IV needle sliding in.

"Cody is calling the house, notifying Ruth and Rick. Knowing how Rick will use any reason to speed, they should arrive at the hospital right after we do."

But Rick, having taken the call from Matt earlier and been told an ambulance was on the way, was waiting in the emergency room when they pulled in. Ruth was holding his arm, to keep him out of the EMTs' way.

"Let me just see her," he said loudly. "Just to make sure."

Katie heard the emergency room nurse tell him, 'Not now.' Katie was moved from the gurney to an ER cot with the plastic sheet that had been beneath her still in place. The nurse, whose name tag identified her as Alice B., cut Katie's clothing off, ignoring her protests.

"Every time I come here, I lose clothes," Katie said.

"That's okay, honey. We're going to give you some nice cotton jammies. The state police are taking all this as evidence. Your family can bring you clothes tomorrow."

"I'm not staying!"

"Yeah? You wanna put a ticket on that? I'm willing to bet you're here at least one night."

Alice dropped Katie's ruined clothing into a plastic bag and tied the top tight. That was when Katie considered that a person she didn't know was going to be handling her disgustingly filthy garments. She flushed with embarrassment.

When Alice turned back around, her nose was still wrinkled at the smell wafting off Katie's body. "How about I get a basin of warm water, and we wash you down?"

The rubber sheet was removed, folded in onto itself, and dropped in a different plastic bag. Then, the cleaning took four basins and lots of hot water. Somewhere out in the hall, Katie could hear Rick talking. From his tone, she expected him to burst through the cubicle curtain at any time.

Alice, brusque and professional, and whom Katie had already decided would not get her vote for Kind and Gentle Caregiver of the Year, returned. "The trooper wants to talk to you. Are you ready?" Before she could answer, the nurse twitched the curtain open enough to let the young man in.

"Your family wants to see you," he said. "But we need to talk about what happened first."

"They'll be good as long as they know I'm okay," Katie said. "If you let Ruth in here, you'll never get rid of her."

Corporal Derrick looked at the nurse.

"On it." Closing the curtain again, she walked away, calling out for the family of Katelyn Took.

"Should we wait for Sheriff Lewis?" Katie asked.

"Naw, it'll take forever. Heard they have forensics coming out from Montpelier to go over the scene," Derrick said. "He'll also oversee the transfer of patients from the retreat to somewhere else before the building is sealed. Let's go with what you've got."

"What about Doctor Reveck," Katie whispered.

Derrick's eyes changed. For just a moment, he went from cop-mode to caring and back again. "We have an APB out on him. Any law enforcement officer anywhere near a radio got the immediate all-points bulletin. Second level and public notice is being broadcasted on local channels. Don't worry, Katie, we'll find him. Now, tell me what happened."

Katie started at the beginning, the day after she and Grace had ridden out looking for the Welks' boys, making sure to tell him. Trinity said Holly had access to drugs through the gardener. The trooper listened, taking notes as she spoke. Occasionally, he cut in with questions until she got to the part about seeing the tracks on the lane behind the retreat.

"Crap," he said.

Leaving the cubicle, the trooper went to the desk. Katie heard him tell the nurse he needed an outside line. She heard him ask for dispatch and explain about the need for the second crime scene to be secured. Then, Katie heard the squelch of his two-way. A disembodied voice from far, far away, squeaked out that his message had been received. Derrick returned to the cubicle, looking relieved the tracks had been found and isolated until they could be photographed, and molds made of them.

"Okay," he said. "Where were we?"

"Where is Mrs. Reveck? Is she here? Is she okay? I mean like, you know, still alive?" Katie paused for breath. The moment she had pulled the panels apart and seen the other woman's high heels flashed into her mind. "Derrick, she was wearing those lace-up high-heeled shoes when she came in."

Derrick jumped up and ran out into the corridor, returning ten minutes later with Sheila's shoes in an evidence bag. While he was gone, Katie heard him on the phone again, issuing an order for someone on-site to enter the house and collect any and all the high-heeled shoes he found there. "…just in case she was wearing a different pair."

"Okay, I think we have that issue all covered." Derrick pulled out his notepad, looking expectantly at Katie.

As she described Doctor Reveck grabbing her and the events that led to her falling through the doorway in the Corrapell kitchen and waking to see Wade, Katie's body went ice cold. She shivered, teeth chattering together. The trooper called Alice, asking for a couple of blankets and maybe a hot water bottle. Katie hiccupped out the last of her tale, sinking further among the blankets. The nurse rang for the doctor.

The emergency room physician said, "We're moving her up to her room. She's suffering from shock. The IV fluids are helping, but she needs rest and some nourishment. Her family is upstairs waiting for her."

Katie was wheeled through the secret, personnel-only tunnels deep in the interior of the big hospital complex. She experienced a few minutes of fear while traveling through the dark, sour-smelling corridors, pushed along by the silent orderly. It was a journey akin to traveling with the devil as he hauled a person to Hades. When the elevator door opened and light flooded in, she turned her head into the pillow, unwilling to look at her surroundings in the event her comparison had been more right than wrong.

"Katie?" Ruth said softly.

With her eyes still closed, Katie disentangled the hand that was free of the IV and reached out. Ruth wrapped icy fingers around hers, and then Katie felt Rick's around both of theirs. She slept.

* * *

She awoke in the late afternoon. Ruth leaned on the bed, snoring lightly, but across the room, Rick was watching her. Dark half-circles lined his eyes, and he was unshaven. He held his finger to his lips, but to no avail. Sheriff Lewis was in the corridor, talking to the security guard outside the door. She knew he, too, was watching. She drew a deep breath and began coughing more filth from her lungs, waking Ruth. Everyone in the room rushed toward her. Over Ruth's shoulder, Katie could see Lewis. No one saw him step into the room.

Rick held a plastic cup with a straw so Katie could sip. A floor nurse bustled in, alerted by the monitoring system and did a quick check of Katie's vitals. When she retreated, her smile told them all was good. Ruth took her place. By this time, Lewis stood at the foot of the bed. No one challenged his being there.

"I have a few questions regarding Holly Guptill," he said. "Would you rather Ruth and Rick leave?'

All three shook their heads.

"Tell me how you found that druggie's nest."

If he was trying to sound conversational, he was failing. His tone, body language, and even the look in his eyes demanded. Katie was too wiped out at that moment to stand up to him.

"On the backside of the building, off from the kitchen, are two closed corridors. They're off-limits to anyone at the retreat. Even the employees don't have access," she began. The effort caused her to cough again. Ruth held out the plastic cup with its tall straw.

"How did you know to look there?" he asked.

"I didn't. I just knew she had been hiding in the building somewhere," said Katie. "Her friend told me she was down there, that she had stolen a key. No one else had any reason to go in there." Katie paused, looking towards the window. She remembered the feeling of isolation being down there. Safe, but not secure. And the confusion and mess. She turned back to Lewis. "That whole end has been left from when things went bad at the retreat. If Holly was using a lot of drugs, that jumbled-up deserted place probably felt like a maze no one would be able to find her in."

She continued to watch Sheriff Lewis. His eyes were flat, unreadable. Katie could hear the toe of his boot tapping on the floor. Tap, tap, tap. Like the sound of Mrs. Reveck above her. She gasped and started coughing again. Rick slid his arm behind her, raising her up off the pillow.

"Relax," the old man said.

"Maybe you should leave," Ruth told Lewis coldly.

But Katie held up her hand. She didn't want him to have a reason to come back. It was better he had his say now and went away.

"What else?" She finally rasped out.

"We found pieces of your broken credit card on the floor inside the inner corridor. It wouldn't surprise me if Reveck claims you were in on the doping deal and broke in to steal what Guptill left behind."

"I don't do drugs," said Katie, easing back down to the pillow.

"Your rap sheet says something different." Lewis' eyes were hooded, but there was no mistaking he didn't believe she had cleaned up her act.

"Step outside," said Rick, his voice low and demanding.

"I'm not done here," said Lewis, filling his chest with air and stretching taller.

"Yeah, you are. As soon as we saw your ugly face in the corridor, I put in a call for Costello. I'm thinking you should wait for him on the other side of the door."

Katie rolled her eyes. She was getting to be a regular client of Attorney Joseph Costello. The short, round, and very direct lawyer had come to her aid twice before when she'd stuck her nose in Lewis' business.

Maybe I'll get a friend and family discount, she thought.

After Lewis stomped out of the room and took a position next to the security guard. Rick closed the door, he turned to Katie. "I'm not accusing you of being involved, Katie, but did you know you were going to find drug paraphernalia when you were looking for Holly, or where she might have been hanging out?"

Katie hitched herself up higher on the bed. A tray of tea, applesauce, and a Hoodsie cup sat on the bedside table. She reached for the tiny container of ice cream.

"No, but what I heard from others was that Holly was an addict. I knew there would be stuff somewhere." She turned the Hoodsie cup upside down. "This is empty."

"It was melting," said Rick.

* * *

After her light meal and another full glass of water Ruth forced on her, Katie nodded off again. Ruth gently shook her awake when Joe Costello arrived. His visit was short. He had already seen Corporal Derrick's report, and his only comment was that the state trooper should take a typing class.

"You're not being charged with anything, Katie," he said. "Calling me in makes it look like you have something to hide."

"I made the call," Rick said. "Katie has a bad relationship with Sheriff

Lewis. He was out in the hall, pacing like an enraged bull. If the state police corporal had been here so that Lewis wasn't going to come bulling in here alone with his drawers in a kink, I would have held off. But I haven't seen Derrick yet."

"Well." Costello took the chair Rick offered and made himself comfortable. "Let's see if we can calm the sheriff's ruffled feathers."

Rick opened the door and waved Lewis in. Costello spoke first. "I'm only here on an overabundance of caution, Sheriff. Ask my client your questions, please."

Lewis proceeded to walk Katie through the events of her day, going back several times for details.

"Has Doctor Reveck been found yet?" Katie asked as soon as there was a break in the questions. "What is his wife saying? He tried to kill her, too."

"The search is ongoing for Doctor Reveck. I can't share with you any of what Mrs. Reveck is saying. What we're covering here is what happened to you. How you came to be left bound and gagged under the mobile home. What you remember about how Mrs. Reveck ended up underneath as well."

Even though Katie and Lewis had been having issues since she had uncovered that her grandmother had not died naturally, Lewis had dropped the ball on the investigation. It seemed as if, in the last few moments, he was less antagonistic.

Is it because Mr. Costello is here, or does he realize I'm not trying to steal his job? She wondered.

She reached out with an olive branch. "One thing I've come to realize is that I would never want to be in law enforcement. It's too dangerous."

"Then maybe you should consider taking a step back the next time instead of marching into something you don't know anything about." Lewis' snide answer snapped the willowy branch in half.

"If that lawn mower hadn't been there, *no one* would have found me until I was a stinking, rotting corpse. Or Sheila, either." Katie's temper flared.

Attorney Costello popped out of his seat, holding his hands up. Katie took a breath; she remembered the portly attorney cautioning her at another time that this reaction was exactly what the Sheriff wanted. If she got angry enough, she'd stop thinking about what she was. Before Lewis could get another verbal jab in, the lawyer spoke up.

"Have you," Costello asked, "spoken to Mrs. Reveck? I heard the attending physician had her stomach pumped."

"There was a chance she had been drugged," Lewis admitted.

Costello raised an eyebrow.

Katie, Ruth, and Rick waited for Lewis to say it was not a chance, but a definite.

"She is not yet conscious," was all the sheriff added.

Costello sat back in the chair, fingers steepled in front of his chest. "Hmm, well, if I were a betting man, I'd say Ms. Took has given you all she has for information. The rest will have to come from what you learn from Mrs. Reveck. And her husband, of course."

Sheriff Lewis was a rigid ramrod of muscle and bone, a tick flexed in his jawbone.

"You'll keep us apprised of developments, won't you, Sheriff Lewis?" Costello asked.

Ruth and Rick, standing on either side of Katie's bed, watched the match between the two men. Katie had turned to the window. Darkness was falling. She didn't want to see it and be reminded of lying beneath the double wide. Closing her eyes, chin drooped to her chest, she listened to Lewis' footsteps as he left the room. His boot steps echoed down the hall; a hard slamming heard over everything else.

"I'll go along now, too," said Costello, rising. "Get some rest, Katie. We'll talk again."

* * *

The doctor came and went. Every fifteen minutes, a nurse came in to check on Katie. Another bland meal arrived at five-thirty. Katie was quick to grab the Hoodsie cup out of Rick's reach.

As she pried the lid off the paper cup, she said, "Thanks, guys, but please go home. I'm going to sleep. You heard the doctor say I could be discharged tomorrow morning. I'm going to need clothes, okay?"

Ruth's grip tightened on her arm.

"I'm good now, really," Katie said. "The nurse is in here every time I turn my head. Just make sure you come back to get me." She smiled at the elderly couple and scooped ice cream out of the cup. The lump of cold sat on her tongue. Her throat would not open to swallow it.

Reluctantly, Ruth and Rick left. Once they were gone, Katie spat out the ice cream and pushed the tray aside, holding back only the cup of tea. The nurse wasn't happy when she arrived to pick up the tray.

"You need to eat if you want to go home," she said.

"I'm not really hungry. But do you think maybe I could get some toast?" Katie said.

"Grape or strawberry jelly?"

After the nurse went out, taking the untouched tray with her, Katie laid back, pressing herself into the pillow. She wanted to sleep, she really did, to be in a place where she couldn't think about what had happened over the last day and a half. Every time she raised her hand to her face, she smelt the foul, rotten dirt from beneath the double wide. She had been washed with soap and hot water, an antiseptic solution, and soap and water again. Yet, the stink, the clammy feel of cold clay sticking to her skin, even the smell from wetting her pants hung on to her.

Rubbing her feet against the sheets didn't warm them. Tucking her arms beneath the blankets didn't stop the cold chills from rising. For the first time, she wanted the nurse to come in and offer her a sleeping pill.

"Here you go," the nurse put a plate on the bedside table. Lifting the metal lid, she showed Katie four pieces of perfectly browned bread, all buttered and waiting for jelly.

"Wheat or white?" the woman offered; sure, this was the answer to the sorrow showing on Katie's face.

Chapter Forty-One

In the blue and white Chevy pickup traveling down the Williston Road toward Taft Corners, Katie's elderly friends were making their own plans.

"You pack her a bag," Rick said. "I'm going to get everything ready at the house. Charlie will be there with you, so keep everything locked up and stay inside. No one knows where that whack-job doctor went. The two of you will be safe if you're watchful."

"What about Katie?" Ruth asked fearfully. "Once the hospital closes down for the night, she'll be in that room alone."

"Once I get you settled, I'm going back. One way or another, I'll be sitting in that hallway, watching. Tomorrow, after I get her home, we'll figure out what to do next."

They pulled into the dooryard, where Charlie waited.

"They ain't found Katie's truck yet," he said. "Lots of people been calling. I tell 'em all, I don't know what's going on. What should we do?"

Rick explained his plan. As Ruth scurried around getting Katie's things together and tended to the cats, he made a couple of calls. If he couldn't be home tonight, he wanted people he trusted to know Doctor Reveck was still out there. He had heard Katie tell Sheriff Lewis she believed the man was off his nutter. If there was a chance Reveck was still in the area and would come looking for revenge, Rick wanted both Ruth and Katie to be protected.

It wasn't much later that Rick drove back through Saint George, headed toward Burlington and the Mary Fletcher Hospital. On Shepardson 3, he spoke with the floor supervisor and Katie's nurse.

"She doesn't need to know I'm here," he said after explaining about Doctor Reveck. "But Ruth and I need to know that someone has your security guard's back. I'm just going to sit quietly over here and watch."

The unarmed security guard who had just come on duty nodded his understanding and slid his chair directly in front of the door to Katie's room.

"She barely ate anything," said the nurse. "And she was adamant that the lights stay on. The doctor ordered a sleeping aid for her IV, and she went out like a light. She won't know anything for hours."

The supervisor, overhearing the conversation, directed an orderly to put a recliner in Katie's room.

"You don't need to stay out here in the hallway. You can stay in there with her. The nursing staff will monitor her through the night. If she wakes up, we'll try to get her to eat again."

Rick nodded his thanks and followed the Barcalounger into Katie's room.

Chapter Forty-Two

No one bothered Katie that night. Rick was exhausted. He knew he would eventually fall asleep, no matter his intentions, so he set up a booby trap. There was an observation window for Katie's room. He drew the drapes closest to the door shut. From outside, no one would be able to see that few square feet. Then he closed the door and pushed the Barcalounger close enough so that if an intruder larger than a size 2 tried to open it, the metal panel would hit his chair. It wasn't a perfect solution, but it would be enough, as tense as he was.

His anxiety regarding Ruth's safety back home had been appeased when Stan called to tell him he'd taken up residence on the farmhouse couch until morning. With both Charlie and Stan there, Rick knew his elderly love would be safe.

Hell, he thought with a smile, *she could probably beat off any criminal alone.*

It was five-forty-five before Katie's coughing alerted him that she was awake.

"So dry," she whispered.

Rick got her water and went to notify the nurse. When they got back, Katie was already up and had the bathroom door locked to protect her privacy.

"Well, you look a little shaky," the nurse said when Katie exited the bathroom. "But overall, I think you're looking much better. How about I order you up a breakfast tray? It's early, but if you can eat, I'll get it."

"Thanks," said Katie, selecting scrambled eggs instead of a bowl of Cream of Wheat. After the nurse left, Katie turned to Rick. "Have you heard anything more about Mrs. Reveck? Is she on this floor?"

"I don't know where she is." He watched Katie fidget for a few minutes, then said, "If you promise to stay right here and not wander around, I'll go see what I can find out."

"I won't even move," said Katie. "You have my word."

* * *

Rick came back to find Katie polishing off a plate of scrambled eggs and an order of toast, her left hand wrapped possessively around a cup of coffee. Only dregs remained inside a second cup on the edge of the rolling table.

"I bet that was for me," he said.

She shrugged. "It was getting cold."

At that moment, the doctor walked in, followed by a nurse and four medical students. Katie was skeptical about sharing her private information with a bunch of trainees, but her case description was quick and generic.

"Twenty-nine-year-old female held for observation following an assault." The doctor's monotone inflection changed only slightly when he addressed Katie directly. "How are you today, Ms. Took?"

Rick had been asked to leave. Katie stayed on the positive through her mostly verbal examination and was pronounced ready to go home. The doctor left, and Katie's nurse popped back through the door.

"It should take twenty minutes or so to get your paperwork processed," she said. "Let's get you unhooked and dressed before it gets so busy around here that you're stuck for hours."

The young woman's estimation of time was practically spot-on. Before Katie knew it, she was being wheeled out to the front door, Rick was pulling up in his pickup truck, and the smiling nurse was saying goodbye.

"Take it easy getting her into the truck," the young woman said as Rick fussed around, and she turned to leave.

He set the brakes on the wheelchair and turned his back on Katie long enough to open the door of the truck. Katie carefully stood up, inching away from where Rick was moving tools off the floor so she could step inside. He was still telling her about leaving Ruth and Charlie guarding the cats while Katie hustled back into the hospital. There were things she wanted to know, and no one would answer her questions. When the two guards were changing shifts earlier. She had heard one tell the other that after Katie left, he got to go home until five. Then, he would have to report to Mrs. Reveck's room. They had a good laugh at where the doctor's wife had been hidden. Katie knew exactly where to go.

When Rick swung back, the smile on his face faded. Katie had disappeared into the crowded lobby.

"What the hell?" he cussed.

Jumping behind the wheel, Rick pulled up further along the curb, away from the front doors, and chased after her.

Katie had been held up waiting for an elevator. When the door opened, she stepped in and pressed the button for Shepardson 4. She hadn't seen Rick chasing after her and knew he wouldn't be able to leave the truck parked right in front of the main entrance. He'd never find her. When she had what she wanted, she'd be back.

Better sometimes to ask forgiveness than permission, she thought.

A hand shot into the narrow space as the doors closed. She didn't need to look to know Rick was faster than she'd given him credit for being. She blew out her cheeks, ready to be ordered off the elevator and back into the truck. However, in some ways, Rick knew her better than she knew herself.

"You just can't leave it alone, can you?" he asked.

She hung her head. There was no rational reason for what she wanted to do, just her need to do it.

"Where are you going?" Rick asked.

"Up," she said, relieved he wasn't making her leave and also that she wouldn't be alone.

He stepped inside, and she pushed the button. Exiting on Shepardson 4, they faced a directional sign that indicated the maternity unit to their left and surgical patient rooms to the right. Halfway down the corridor, an intern leaned on the high counter of the nurse's station, chatting with a youngish redhead. Katie pushed Rick toward the other side of the wide corridor and motioned for him to go ahead. After a five beat, she strolled down the same side the elevator was on, peeking in open doorways as she went.

The intern lifted his head, elbows still on the counter, watching Rick's approach. Katie came to a closed door. There was a chart file in the holder, but no name showed.

Busy floor, closed door, file chart with no name on it. Hmm, I wonder who is hiding in here?

Taking a chance, she pushed on the door. At the desk behind her, Rick spoke up.

"I'm not sure if I'm on the right floor. I'm looking for my niece's room. She just had a baby."

While the nurse explained to a very thick-headed uncle that he was on the right floor, but had come down the wrong wing, Katie slid into the room and was rewarded by finding only one bed in the two-person room occupied. Sheila Reveck, connected to several tubes and buzzing, beeping pieces of hospital machinery, gazed out the window over the University of Vermont campus.

It hadn't occurred to Katie prior to this she might have found Mrs. Reveck still unconscious, or worse, in a coma. The drapes between the two beds were open, pushed back against the wall, but the drapes on the observation window were also open. Katie was faced with staying by the door or walking around the foot of the first bed and being exposed if someone looked in the window.

Mrs. Reveck turned when the door clicked shut behind Katie. One hand went to her throat. The other reached for the buzzer. If the look of fear on the face of her former employer hadn't been confusing enough, the quick revelation that it was Katie she was afraid of, almost undid the younger woman.

"Please, Mrs. Reveck, give me just a minute." Katie stopped. She was standing in full view of the window. She held up her hand, halting Mrs. Reveck's thumb from depressing the call bell. "I'm not here to hurt you. Really. You know your husband took off and left you—us—tied up beneath the house. We could have died there. Hypothermia, starvation, whatever. And you were drugged."

Slow down, her brain said, but Katie knew she didn't have time. She couldn't move any closer, and a quick peek had shown the nurse's station directly across the corridor.

"He isn't my husband," Sheila whispered. "I was a fool, and he sucked me dry. The money my folks left me, my pride, respectability. The sheriff told me I'm going to go to prison because I was stupid." Her eyes filled, and she fell back against the pillow, gasping for breath, her sallow skin pale.

Katie didn't feel any pity. She knew in her heart that no matter what Mrs. Reveck said, she was the keeper of her own council. She had abused all those patients. Her husband hadn't been there directing her. She had worked independently. Holly was dead. Even if Mrs. Reveck hadn't been responsible, she had been there when Holly's body had been dragged away and discarded like rubbish. For Katie, who tried hard to be a rough, tough individual no one would mess with, that behavior was unconscionable.

"He's going to get away if you don't help. Where would he go?" Katie asked.

"I don't know. He traveled often by himself. We haven't been anywhere together in years. Even when we did, we ended up in some dirty little hole in the wall. I have no idea where he'd go."

The light above the bed blinked. Mrs. Reveck had pushed the call button. Before Katie could turn, the door behind her opened. A nurse rushed in, cut in front of her, and yanked the curtain around Mrs. Reveck closed.

"What are you doing in here?" she demanded.

"Wrong room," Katie said, backing away.

Exiting, she was nose-to-nose with the intern. Repeating herself, she sidled off and then hurried toward the elevator. Jabbing the button didn't open the door, and she heard the hurried patter of footsteps coming her way. She was afraid to look up, in case it was a rent-a-cop. Suddenly, Rick was at her elbow, and they were in the stairwell.

"The truck is right outside the front entrance, so pick up your feet." He moved with her, supporting her as she tried to speed up to keep pace.

Chapter Forty-Three

Though everyone warned Katie to take it easy as she moved up the porch steps, she saw Ruth inside hobbling toward her. She ran up to the elderly woman, wrapping her in a hug while at the same time moving them both toward the sofa. Charlie and Stan had gone to work, but Grace had come to stay with Ruth. Using a powder blue Selectric typewriter, they were putting together a list of things Monique would have to know when she took the baby goats home, and another list for when her baby was born and that little one also came home.

"She's got the goats all named, and Amos is modifying a pen area in the barn for them," Ruth said once Katie had successfully turned the conversation from herself. "But she's still shying away from anything to do with her baby, and time is running out."

"There's been no word of Katie's truck yet?" Rick asked.

"Philip called a while ago," said Grace, referring to her brother, Philip, who ran the local auto mechanic shop. "He got a call-out to pick it up and tow it in. The forensic guys are going to meet him at the garage and go over it."

"Where did they find it?" Katie asked.

"There was a news bulletin on the radio asking the public to keep an eye open for it." Grace was packing up her papers and typewriter. "The woman who works down at the church called it in. Apparently, it was left in the trailer park where she lives. People there were wondering who owned it."

"That's Helen O'Brien," Katie said. "She's Father Metevier's housekeeper."

Grace nodded and headed toward the door. "If you decide to go down there, drop Ruth off at the house. I got a new yogurt machine for us to figure out."

Their neighbor was barely into her own driveway, when Katie decided she wanted to go down to the garage. She sat in the middle of the bench seat of Rick's truck until he had helped Ruth out and into Grace's kitchen. Katie could hear Ruth complaining the entire way.

"Let go of me," the elderly woman quipped. "I can take care of myself."

"So, I guess she's better," said Katie when Rick got back into the truck.

Rick grunted and shifted into drive.

The small dirt area in front of Phil's was chockablock full of vehicles. Closest to the road was Sheriff Lewis' cruiser.

"I can't win for losing," Katie said with a sigh.

While they were discussing the best way to approach the thick knot of cruisers and the big forensic van, Lewis walked up to Rick's truck and told them to move along.

"I'm concerned about the damage to my vehicle," Katie said.

Lewis all but laughed in her face before saying, "If you're going to stick around, pull out and park on the edge of the road. Then stay in this truck. If I see either of you out and around, I'll have you escorted out of here."

"When can I have my truck back?" Katie asked.

"Two or three days," Lewis called back over his shoulder.

Edward Richardson, the Chief Forensics Officer for the State of Vermont, whom Katie had met when human remains were found on Eagle Drop Ridge, saw her and waved. The person who crawled out from beneath the vehicle also looked up. Corinne Cox, Edward's assistant, was a friend and might be more forthcoming than Lewis with information. She nodded before returning to the job at hand.

Perfect, thought Katie.

She and Rick stayed parked on the edge of the road for a few minutes longer, speculating about what was happening with the case.

"Still early days," said Rick. "It's like being in Nam. Shit like this, you don't know how it's going to affect you until one day the boogeyman jumps out of the bushes."

"That's what the doctor said about getting caught unaware one day. I can tell you this, though: don't be surprised if I'm sleeping with a light on for a while. Even with the sleeping meds, I was having nightmares."

"If it makes you feel better, Ruth is willing to share a room with you until things calm down."

Laughing, Rick started the truck, and they drove across town to Baldwin's Feed and Hardware. Cindy stood behind the register. As soon as her eyes lit on Katie, she gave a squeal that had the teeth of every customer in the store grinding together and flew at her friend.

"Oh, my god!" she said. "Oh, my god."

"Take it easy." Katie laughed, accepting the hugs and kisses from her boss's wife. "We just stopped in to let Stan know we'd both be back at work tomorrow."

Stan came out of his office to see what the noise was about. "Are you absolutely sure that's the best?"

Katie reached out and gave him a hearty handshake. "This is where I want to be, Stan. Surrounded by birdseed, tools, and cow-stinking farmers." She didn't add that here, away from Ruth's watchful eyes, she'd be able to sort out everything else in her head.

Chapter Forty-Four

Katie got to pick up her truck sooner than expected. Other than Gary Reveck's fingerprints on the key and steering wheel, nothing was found. The man himself had disappeared into thin air.

Corporal Derrick stopped into the house to speak with Katie. He had Sheriff Lewis in tow. She had nothing to add to her story, and other than informing her the leads Mrs. Reveck had provided for locating the doctor had come up empty, there was no news from the law enforcement side, either.

"Sheila Reveck was arraigned while still in the hospital, charged with tampering with the scene of a crime, tampering with evidence, and mistreatment of a corpse, not murder. She's still at county. She never stopped saying she wasn't part of the decision to hold you hostage," Derrick said. "And to be truthful, my opinion is, the fact she ended up in the same boat is going to work in her favor. What's keeping her as a resident of the state is the situation we uncovered at the retreat. As the manager and part owner of Corrapell, she was in a position where she could have pulled the plug on the whole deal, but she didn't. She has no ties here and is a flight risk. To be honest, I think she feels safer there right now. Bail has been set, but there doesn't appear to be anyone working in her interest."

Katie opened her mouth, but Derrick held his hand up.

"It goes on from there. None of those people were being held hostage. They could have left at any time. Damn few of them are willing to file a complaint that they were treated inhumanely. You and Matt said the residents were given sleeping medicine, the residents said they were vitamins. We can't prove they were forced or coerced. The best we have to work with are those you gave Doctor Gillian, which included a saliva sample. That one patient may be the only one able to file a complaint."

"What about Holly?" Katie felt as dry as if she'd been working in a hayfield all day. *This can't be right*, she thought.

Derrick sighed, twisting his neck to relieve the tension. "All evidence at this time points to accidental death by overdose."

He sounded miserable, and Sheriff Lewis looked equally so.

"I don't understand," she said. "They hauled her body off. Dumped her in the woods. No one knew. Her family would never have known."

Katie was sure she had more questions, but Derrick's words were dinging around in her brain like the pinball wizard's game ball. From side to side, igniting lights of green, yellow, and blue, but never stopping long enough for her synapses to grab a thought. The men sipped their coffee. She watched them in silence until she thought about Cecile.

"What happened to all the people, the residents, who were staying at Corrapell? My friend Rose told me it was a nightmare."

Sheriff Lewis spoke up. "Well, maybe not as much a nightmare as a solid mess. While we were still investigating, somebody called the Department of Health and Welfare. They immediately sent out two representatives. One was a nurse. At their recommendation, we had everyone removed by ambulance, which kept both Parentville and Richmond hopping. Those folks were taken to Fanny Allen Hospital in Essex, evaluated, and either set up to return to their homes or moved to the convalescent center on the old National Guard base."

"I think only a couple ended up there," Derrick added. "Then Corrapell was sealed pending the state's investigation."

After the two officers left, Katie sat in stunned silence. She was home alone with only the dogs and cats. After the excitement of company, all the fur-balls found a place for a nap. Katie was left at the kitchen table with her thoughts and the realization that, as Rick had pointed out, Doctor Reveck was still loose, and he was the real danger. Rick had also told her to call Marlie before her friend heard the news from someone else.

"She probably won't see it on the five o'clock news way down there," Rick had pointed out. "But if she's in contact with someone else up here, waiting to find out about a job, she'll be pissed if that's the first time word of it comes up."

"I could write her a letter," Katie told Solomon as she dialed the phone.

Marlie answered, saying she'd just gotten in from her shift. She was bubbly and happy to hear Katie's voice. Instead of letting her prattle on and then not wanting to circle back to why she was calling, Katie cut to the chase.

"Look, Marlie. Remember, we were talking about how remains were found over in the Gypsy Copse? And I told you about the kid, Isaac O'Brien, who was telling Father Metevier about strange doings at the fat farm?"

"Yes," Marlie said slowly.

"Well, ah, I also mentioned I was working out there for a few nights, you know, looking for some extra money."

"Katie, you said that was only a short-term job."

"You'll be happy to know I'm all done working there," Katie said.

"That's good, right?" Marlie paused, then asked, suspicion in her words. "Why are you telling me this?"

"Here's the thing." Right then, Katie decided to go with the Reader's Digest version. "Before I left, I had a little altercation with the owner, Doctor Reveck."

"Ah-huh."

"Yeah, and somehow Sheriff Lewis got in on it."

"Katie!"

"No, it's fine. He's fine. But I might have had to go to the hospital for a couple of hours."

"What are you talking about?" Marlie demanded.

Katie didn't want to say anything more but was too deep into it to stop now.

"Doctor Reveck and I had a little tussle. I bumped my head. He's sorry. I'm okay."

"And now what?" Marlie asked.

It was hard to tell if she was disappointed in Katie's actions or concerned about the tussle and bump.

Katie gave a tired sigh. "That's really all there is. I just wanted to call and tell you instead of sending a letter, you know? That idea sounded so cold."

"You're okay, right? I don't need to worry? Ruth and Rick know?"

"Yes. Yes. And, yes."

"Alright, but if something changes, you'd better let me know," said Marlie. "I love you. I want you safe."

Katie thought she was going to cry. After professing her own love, and promising to write, she hung up and sat back, staring at the telephone, knowing she'd lied, and Marlie was going to be angry when she found out.

Instead of working on the letter that would amount to a confession and apology, Katie called the office of Attorney Costello, relieved he was there to take her call.

Joe Costello listened and empathized with Katie's concerns. But he had been a lawyer for a long time in the city of Burlington. His father had served before him, and later as a judge. There wasn't much information he couldn't get his hands on. Yet, as a professional, he was duty-bound to hold back anything that might jeopardize another lawyer's case.

Katie heard him clear his throat. "Often, in cases like this, the system is looking for the person highest up the ladder responsible for the crime. That's the meat of it, highest up the ladder. If you don't get much above ground level, or only so far up, you're going to be holding the person you can get your hands on as currently most responsible, but not necessarily for everything. As I see it here, Mrs. Reveck is sitting on that top rung right now. Then, too, Katie, the state's attorney, is only going to charge her with those crimes that there is enough evidence to support. They won't take a chance of losing the case trying to get a sentence on something they can't prove."

"It's not right," Katie said.

"It's the law, Katie. She's innocent until proven guilty, and she can be charged as an accessory to a crime if you can prove the crime happened and she knew about it," Costello said. "Just because you think what she did was criminal doesn't necessarily make it so."

Next, Katie called Helen O'Brien to say thank you for finding her truck. When Katie asked about Isaac, his mother said it was a funny thing, but for the last few days, the boy had insisted on going to school. Katie drove out to the high school but didn't spot him coming out of the building at the end of the day. She called Dorothea at the thrift store.

"I ain't seen him," the old woman said. "You coming back to work soon?"

"Yeah, soon," Katie said before hanging up. *Where would he go?*

Isaac had never mentioned anything about friends. Katie drove up the ridge behind Hillside Cemetery in Mechanicsville. She found the place where kids from the high school had been hanging out. Cigarette butts and beer cans were the biggest clue.

Meanwhile, Amos had taken to working closer to home for the time being. Either he or Eugenie, from the store, would drop the soon-to-be mother off at the Dean farm. It made everyone feel better that Monique wasn't home alone. While Ruth and Grace put the truck gardens in, Monique operated the yogurt machine, then spent a few hours on Fridays and Saturdays at the Schoolhouse Yard Sale. In the afternoons, if Amos worked late and didn't swing by to pick Monique up, she'd join them for supper. Talk was always about the baby goats or her plans for the Small Farm.

"I'm going to have a garden next year," Monique explained to Katie. "Mr. Dean is going to come over and plow and harrow later in the summer. Amos and I can fine-rake it and get it all set to over winter."

She was very excited, talking on and on about seedlings and starter plants. Currently, she had tomato plants in five-gallon buckets lining the porch. Katie knew Monique had pushed to have more this year, but there was still the over-hanging concern regarding her pregnancy. When she made it to the seventh month, Ruth and Katie secretly celebrated. Amos was worried that even bringing the three young goats to the Small Farm would be too much. But to Katie's eye, Monique seemed to be blossoming.

"I see Doctor Gillian now," Monique explained as Rick filled her plate with a big scoop of bacon-wrapped squirrel cooked in the crock of baked beans. "She has a midwife working with her. It's the funniest thing. The woman is a Mennonite and Amos's cousin. I wasn't sure how it would work out, you know? But she just gave me a big hug, and we were all good. Is this squirrel? Are you sure? They're so cute. Is this going to taste gamey?"

"That's why we cook it in the beans, like duck. Makes the wild dark meat more tender," said Rick.

Monique paused. "Oh." Then, she was right back to talking about the goats and planting green beans.

"But not lima beans," said Katie.

"Ew, no, I hate 'em."

Katie laughed. "Me, too."

* * *

At ten o'clock that evening, the phone rang.

"Not another raccoon," Katie whispered, reaching for the receiver. Rick had been helping out with the animal calls because she still wasn't sleeping well, but only a few days before, she had told him she was all set to get on with her part-time job as well.

"Hi, Katie! Is it too late for me to call?"

"Marlie! What's wrong? Are you okay?" Katie's voice rose.

Rick, who had one foot on the lowest step on his way to bed, turned and came back to the kitchen. *What?* he mouthed.

Katie shook her head, laughing and crying all at one time. On the other end of the line in Pennsylvania, Marlie was still talking.

"So, do you have that all straight? Saturday is my last shift at the Women's Correctional Facility. Sunday, I'll be on a bus back to Brattleboro. Gram is picking me up, and Tuesday is the swearing-in ceremony in Middlesex. I told her I'd take her. It'll be a long day, but she's excited. I could come down on Thursday, but Saturday, I have to drive up to Long Pond. That's where I'll be working."

"What about the job here?" Katie asked.

"There's no job there yet. Brad hasn't said he was leaving, officially. I have to go. Miss you." And the line went dead.

Katie turned to Rick. The look on his face said he had heard it all. "You should take Monday off," he said.

"Seriously, Rick? I'm surprised Stan hasn't already fired me."

From that point, everything else was forgotten as Katie pushed to get all the chores waiting caught up. She wanted to spend some time with Marlie and even considered crashing the swearing-in ceremony. But Marlie hadn't invited her, making it clear she was taking her grandmother. And then she'd need to take the elderly woman back home to Williamsburg. It *would* be a long day.

I can wait, Katie thought as she pushed the lawn mower down to the family boneyard.

Bonita and Solomon followed, both staying a respectful distance back from the noisy, oil-smoking contraption. Behind the two bigger animals came a small contingent of cats. This was a prime hunting area for grasshoppers and crickets. To have a path cleared for easy access was a bonus.

Katie mowed inside and around the small family plot, talking to her late grandparents as she worked.

"I got a letter the other day from Cecile. You wouldn't know her, but she was one of the people who had been at Corrapell. She and I struck up a friendship, sort of. Anyway, she'd sent some letters back to her home before all the hoopla up there, and when she had to leave, she went to stay with a friend. Now, she has her own place and is getting counseling. I don't really know her all that well, but I hope her new life works out for her. She sounded happy."

The lawnmower coughed out a last exhaust-filled puff of smoke.

"Marlie's stuff is still all in the parlor. Rick put the bed together so she could sleep in there while she visits. I mean, we just don't use that room for anything. I don't know how often she'll be able to come down. Then there's her grandmother. She'll want to visit, but overall, I'm pretty excited. Am I babbling? I feel like I am." Finally, she stopped, wiping her face with the bottom of her t-shirt. Now came the hard conversation. "I'm sure you know by now that I'm gay, Gram and Poppa. I don't know how that would strike you, whether you'd be disappointed and turn me away. I'd like to think not. I mean, Gram slammed the door on Julian when she and I drove over from Illinois all those years ago, but that could have been because of the bleached-blond buzz cut or all those tattoos and piercings. I don't know."

She swallowed and kept going. "I'd like a sign. Not like a coffee can of money. Maybe something more personal?"

A blue jay landed on the pipe across from Katie. It peered at her with his beady black eyes, eventually spreading his wings to show off his beautiful coat before taking wing.

"Was that it? The sign?"

She wasn't sure. The experience had been so fleeting. Suddenly, she got a sharp poke right behind the kneecap. A snorting skree told her Bonnie wanted to know what all the chattering was about. Right behind the pig, jumping up on both of them, was Solomon. Katie laughed away the tears in her eyes. This was her sign, a hug wrapped in bacon and drool. They took up her time, made her anxious, and gave her all the love they had. Just like Ruth and Rick. They were all new to each other, but old souls from the beginning of time.

Katie gave Bonnie a shove, and the pig dropped to the ground, exposing her belly to a scratch. As soon as Katie knelt down, Solomon rolled against her side, demanding the same.

"I've only got two hands." Katie laughed. "If the cats try to get in on this, too, we're in trouble."

"Katie!" Ruth was waving from up near the barn. "Raymond is here, looking for you."

Chapter Forty-Five

So," Raymond said, coffee in one hand and an oatmeal cookie in the other. "I know this isn't a town animal call, but I thought you might want in on it."

"Where did these people get so many animals?" Katie asked, her own coffee cooling at her elbow.

"From what I understand, they've been driving up to the cattle auction in Saint Albans once a month or so. They figured they had a two-car garage, and all those little baby critters were so cute."

Rick leaned back. "But now the babies are growing up, and they're a lot of work and mess."

"Exactly," said Raymond. "Then, too, the folks never considered zoning."

"How did you get involved in this?" Katie asked.

"One of the other people in the development said they were going to contact the SPCA and the cops. The property owner came across me driving the tractor up the Parentville/Charlotte Road over to where Steven is trying to reclaim old pastureland. The guy figured I was a farmer, so I'd want any farm animals I could get."

Everyone sitting around the table, including Billy, Raymond's youngest son, laughed.

"What is your new friend trying to rehome?" Katie asked.

"Two half-grown calves, a heifer and a bull, a doe goat, a ram, both of those are last seasons and a mess of chickens. I thought, seeing as you only have three hens, you might like some new laying stock. Right now, they're all pullets, but come September, they'll be paying their way."

"We don't have room for a mess of them," Katie said.

"We can put them in Bonnie's stall, leave her out in the pig yard," Rick said. "Charlie and I can knock together a bigger coop, maybe move it over to where the bunkhouse used to be."

"I've got some old lumber you can have for the taking," said Raymond.

"Then there's Chet at the dump putting stuff aside for you," Katie said. "I'll be feeding that old man till the day I die. When is this moving going to happen?"

"Boys and I are going over this afternoon," Raymond said. "We'll move the stock, go back for the poultry. I just need to know where you want them dropped off."

"Yeah, I'm real good at wrangling chickens." Billy's smile lifted his apple dumpling cheeks all the way to his eyes.

"Well, then," Katie said, leaning forward, "I'm probably going to have to pay you off in oatmeal cookies."

* * *

Katie left the chicken dormitory prep to Ruth and Rick. Right from the start, the chicken coop and three hens had been one of Ruth's absolutely favorite projects. But Katie was on automatic pilot, unable to concentrate on any nuance of her day that was not part of a familiar pattern. Her co-workers at the hardware store didn't notice. It was spring. The weather was clearing up, and everyone had their own distractions. Ruth put Katie's absent-mindedness down to her recent trauma. Once told Katie was doing fine, she'd never been informed about the ongoing nightmares.

Rick had stopped treating her with kid gloves, and Katie concluded he knew she was living and breathing for the return of Marlene Foster, a.k.a. Marlie.

The Thursday after Marlie's swearing-in arrived. Katie dressed neatly and went to work as usual. Long minutes ticked by on the forty-year-old Hood's Dairy clock on the wall behind her. Every time she turned to look at it, her mouth went dry.

She hadn't expected Marlie to arrive until close to suppertime, but just before her lunch break, the wide front door of Baldwin's swung inward, and Ruth entered. Right on her heels was Marlie. There was such a volume of squealing and chatter that Stan was roused from behind his desk and appeared out front to check on the commotion.

"Go to lunch and take that crowd with you," he ordered.

Their two days went quickly. It was exciting to have Marlie back home, even though the thought of the number of miles between Parentville and Long Pond was depressing. They only had a few moments to be really alone. Ruth, Rick, Charlie, and, to a certain extent, Monique seemed to be continually underfoot.

"I'll be living the same way in Long Pond that I did in Pennsylvania, at least for a while," Marlie said around mouthfuls of chicken and dumplings with Grace's homemade cranberry relish on the side. "There's a motel up there called the Grand View. I've been warned that it's old. Like, fifty years old."

Everyone smiled, but Katie felt a lump rise in her throat. Marlie sounded so happy, smiling at those seated around the table, and Katie was proud of her lover's strength and fortitude.

"So, if it's no trouble, I'd like to leave my stuff here for a while. Hopefully, I'll be able to find an apartment soon. I mean, there has to be something up there, right?"

"Moose," said Rick. "Black flies, mosquitoes, black flies, deer, black flies, poachers…"

"Yeah, I got it. Black flies." Marlie laughed. "I'm short. I'll hide in the bushes."

"Poison ivy," said Charlie.

"Ouch! You guys aren't helping at all."

That last night, Katie and Marlie sprayed on extra insect repellent and walked down into the orchard. All too soon, Marlie was gone.

* * *

Though she would never have thought it possible, Katie's mood swings worsened. One minute, she was fine, anticipating seeing Marlie in a couple of weeks when Marlie's scheduling got leveled out. The next, she was lying in the bottom of a coffin hole, looking up. She attended another AA meeting, this time explaining to Charlie in advance, she'd rather sit in the back. When she arrived on the Sunday morning after Marlie left, Charlie was holding down two seats in the last row.

She was in just such a low place, ready to leave work at the end of her Monday shift, when Stan stepped out of the office.

"Katie, Father Metevier is on the phone for you," he said.

"Well, it's been a while. I wonder what Boots has gotten into now?" She handed Stan her cash drawer and reached for the telephone receiver.

"Katie, can you stop here on your way home? Young Master O'Brien is sitting on the step. He'd like a word," the cleric said.

Isaac! Father Metevier's request left her sputtering. "Of course. I'll be right along. Make sure he waits, okay?"

She hurried to punch out, impatient with other drivers also making their way home at the end of their workday. So much had happened lately, the boy had been brushed from her thoughts. She felt guilty, and for some reason responsible.

Isaac hadn't moved by the time she arrived. However, thanks to the good cleric, he was enjoying a glass of lemonade and a ketchup and mustard sandwich.

"These are pretty good." He grinned and took another bite of the white Fassett bakery bread.

"Weird, aren't they? Father Metevier would eat them every day if the doctor would let him." Katie sat on the other end of the step. "So, what's up?"

Isaac fidgeted with the last few bites of his sandwich and laid it aside on the plate. "I've been looking for you at school. You know, so we could figure out what was going on over at Corrapell?"

"I was looking for you there as well." She didn't mention she'd only driven by a couple of times. Her guilty conscience pinched her, but she ignored it.

"Have you heard the gossip? Everything seems to be pretty well buttoned up at the retreat."

Isaac nodded. "I've been listening to the radio and checking the newspaper in the school library."

The boy's voice dropped to a whisper. Katie could see Father Metevier, camouflaged behind the heavy screen door, leaning closer as though he could barely hear the words.

"I'm not seeing any news about the cops finding Doctor Reveck. Then there's all this horse pucky about his wife saying she's innocent."

"Unfortunately, I'm in the same boat as you. That is, I believe there's a lie here. I'm just not sure what to do about it," said Katie. "Then too, the police have been clear I should butt out."

She caught a quick movement as the priest adjusted his position. For a moment, she thought he might be coming out to curtail her conversation with Isaac.

"I'm scared, Katie. He's mean. He'll come back for whoever he thinks turned him in. He's going to be looking for me and my mom."

"You don't know that, Isaac."

"Yeah, I do." The boy turned to look at her. His were not the eyes of a child. "He's a really bad man. I've seen him do terrible things to hurt people when they pissed him off. She's bad, but he's like, I don't know, evil."

"You've *seen* him do terrible things?" Katie was skeptical.

Everything she had heard since she'd been going to Corrapell indicated Doctor Reveck was rarely in Parentville. Or that he had only recently returned and didn't spend much time in the retreat itself. Isaac was telling her something different.

"Actually, I *heard* him." Isaac didn't hesitate or turn away as if he were lying. "Remember, I told you I used to hide in the building? I've heard him on the phone, calling people and telling them that so- and- so they just hired was a thief, or had physically hurt the patients. He was out there trying to get people fired, or not get a job at all. Just plain mean.

"Then, a couple of days before she got fired, Mrs. Francis came to see my mom. I heard them talking. Mrs. Francis was scared to death because

Gail told her that Reveck was complaining about the old lady talking bad about him. Mrs. Francis was sure he was talking about her. She said he was vindictive and cruel. She warned my mother he might do more than just talk bad about her. After that, my mom was scared. We live out in the middle of the woods in that crummy trailer park, and we can't move. When we got home that day, my mom went into the bathroom and stayed there for a long time. I could hear her crying."

Katie leaned back against the railing, looking at Isaac. She heard the flutter of Father Metevier's slippers as he moved away from the door. It was on the tip of her tongue to tell Isaac he had nothing to be worried about, but the boy had known Mrs. Francis. Katie had never met her. Some time ago, Isaac had said they'd come here at least a year before. He'd been hanging out, or hiding, around Corrapell for a while, listening to the gossip, maybe actually hearing the doctor. There was every possibility Isaac could be right.

"Isaac," she began. She wanted to know how long the doctor had been back.

But he cut her off. "Why can't they find him? Why don't they ask Mrs. Reveck where he is?"

"Mrs. Reveck gave the police a list of places to look for the doctor. You know he left us tied up under the double-wide, right?"

Isaac nodded. His eyes widened. She could see he was thinking, and fear was edging in. Katie tried to comfort him.

"Sheriff Lewis and Corporal Derrick were at my house the other day. They told me there were police all over the state looking for Reveck. They know what he's driving for a car. She said he doesn't have any money, so he's limited as to where he can go. He's not going to come after me or you. He's going to run and hide. When the police searched their home, they found his passport and a notebook that listed all the investors he was talking to."

"And they looked in all those places? Have they found him?" Isaac jerked up straight, excited at the thought.

"I don't know. Some of those people might not be real cooperative. They won't want to get involved." Katie wet her lips. "I don't want to make this sound like we shouldn't keep our eyes open, because we should. No one really knows what Reveck is thinking. Sheriff Lewis told me they confiscated all the files and business papers they could find in both the house and Corrapell and are looking for someone who might hide him."

Isaac sat on the step, his hands pressed together between his knees, and the last bite of his sandwich forgotten. Katie was tempted to inch closer, to offer to take him and his family home with her so they would be safer.

"Files?" Isaac lifted his head, brows furrowed as he thought. "You mean like patient files, or his business Rolodex, or her diaries?"

"I'm sure patient files, and if either one of them had a business Rolodex, that too, I guess. I didn't hear anything about a diary."

"It's right there, hidden in her office," said Isaac. "If the cops went all through the place, they should have found it."

It was Katie's turn to look perplexed.

When she didn't speak, Isaac added, "I was hiding in the closet. I saw her get it out of her hiding place, write some stuff, and put it back."

"How do you know it was a diary?"

"Phfft. My mom has one of those silly books. All she writes in it is stuff about us." His ears went red.

So, you've read it. If Mrs. Reveck had a private journal, then dollars to doughnuts there was more information there.

"Keep this close to your chest for right now, Isaac. I have to make a couple of phone calls." Katie stood up and dusted off her bottom. "C'mon, I'll give you a ride home."

"No thanks, I'm waiting for my mom. Some lady from welfare is over at the library talking to folks about food stamps and whatever. Father Metevier is going to give us a ride home."

* * *

Lewis's car was still in the sheriff's parking lot, so Katie went home. Later, when she was sure he would have left for the day, she made a phone call specifically looking for Angus, who she knew would be working the night shift. Isaac's fear had brought her own concerns back to the surface. She wanted to know if Lewis was still looking for a place Reveck would have gone to hide.

It didn't take her long to get Angus to admit their office was not sifting through all the documentation that had been confiscated from the Reveck properties. As deputy, he spent a lot of time listening to Lewis complain about Katie's big nose and took his lead from his boss. Angus did, however, voluntarily boast he had been pulled out from behind the desk to work at the Corrapell site.

"Yeah, I helped load all them boxes into the forensic van. They were some heavy, I tell you," Angus said.

Katie hung up and dialed Corinne Cox, the assistant to the Chief Forensics Officer.

"Yes," Corinne said. "Several boxes arrived at our building, but there's a task force working on that. What is it you want to know, Katie? You know I can't arbitrarily give out information."

Instead of beating around the bush, Katie explained about Mrs. Reveck's diary.

"You know," she said. "Not like office notes, but her private thoughts. The type of thing that might have been tucked into a cubby or stashed away."

If Corinne couldn't help her, Katie was going to have to go to Lewis.

No, scratch that, she thought, *Derrick.*

"Diary? Let me make a call." Corinne hung up, but she was back thirty minutes later. "I called a friend who's working with the task force. She couldn't say what they had, but seemed really surprised when I asked about diaries."

"Surprised like, oops, you caught me?" Katie asked.

"No," said Corinne. "More like, what are you talking about? She's probably going to go back to her boss and ask. This might jump up and bite you in the butt, Katie. Sheriff Lewis is not going to be happy."

Katie walked away from the phone, blowing out her cheeks. She needed to meet with Isaac again. The telephone was right in the middle of the kitchen. Rick had walked through while she was talking with Corinne, and she'd turned away, speaking softer. Out of the corner of her eye, she saw him hesitate, looking back at her. Though he had continued into the living room, she knew he was suspicious of what she was doing and would eventually ask. To cut him off, she opted to set up a smoke screen and called Marlie's motel room.

"I just got in," Marlie said. "I was going to call you tomorrow. I have to go to Norwich University in Northfield for two weeks of refresher training. My boss here is nice. He told me I can have next Saturday and Sunday off, because I have to report Monday morning to Norwich."

"Are you coming here?" Katie held her breath.

"I will if you understand that the second weekend I'm going to my grandmother's," Marlie answered coyly.

"That would be so cool!" Katie smiled so wide that she thought her cheeks would split. After she hung up, she rushed into the living room to share the news with Ruth and Rick.

"You should plan on doing something special on Sunday," he said, as excited as she was. "You know, not just hanging around here watching us work on the chicken coop."

"And the duck house," Ruth added.

"Duck house?" This was the first Katie had heard about ducks.

Rick rolled his eyes. "When we opened the boxes of chickens Billy caught, there were five ducks. Three Peking and two smaller ones that I think are young mallards. The two geese we got last year are sitting on half a dozen eggs and…"

"Splish and Splash," Ruth said proudly.

"…make such a mess in the chicken coop. I think all the waterfowl should be moved down to the duck pond."

"Will that be safe for them?" Katie asked.

"They'll be a pretty big group. And we already know the geese can be nasty to deal with. They'll keep everything short of a bear away." Rick rattled his newspaper at Ruth's muffled titter. The geese took pleasure in chasing Rick. "Anyway, think of something better to do than just hang around with us old folk."

* * *

During her lunch the following day, Katie took a ride over to the trailer park where Isaac and his family lived. When she pulled into the driveway, he sauntered from the stoop over to the truck, leaning in the passenger window. He looked a trifle smug.

"What did you find out?" he asked.

"No one knows anything about a diary," she said. "Where is it?" Her eyes swelled. "Do you have it here?"

He looked off, chewing on the inside of his lip. When he turned back, the smug expression had been replaced by something more feral.

"Nope, I don't have it, and I can't explain it to you. I'm gonna have to get it out myself."

"That's not going to happen. The place is locked up tight," she said.

She was looking at the boy, trying to act tough. Be a big guy. She'd seen that same look in the mirror. If she blew him off, he was going to go alone. Before she could come up with a plan, Isaac hinted he already knew what she was going to do. "So, you're going in during the night?"

Katie was about to deny it, but she could tell Isaac had already figured that out.

"End of the road," she said. "Tonight. Ten-thirty."

It occurred to her as she returned to the feed store that taking a juvenile to a nighttime B & E might get her more than a weekend in jail. Maybe she'd get to bunk with Mrs. Reveck in County. That would be one way to get some information out of her.

* * *

Katie slowed down as she approached Gil Anthony Ridge Road. Just as she made the turn, Isaac stepped out. He was dressed in all dark clothing. She hated to admit it, but he had startled her enough to put her heart in her throat. As they approached, her headlights picked up the reflective glow of the police tape crisscrossing the front door. She hadn't thought there would be a security guard left out here. Corporal Derrick and Sheriff Lewis had alluded to the building, having been searched at least twice. Their focus seemed to have been on where Doctor Reveck would have gone seeking asylum, or just hiding out.

"When we get up to the retreat, I'll park in the trees near the back, where no one will notice the truck," she explained as he got in. "Then we'll look for an open or unlocked window."

"Won't need to," Isaac said. "I know where there's a key."

And he did. Actually, a whole ring of keys, hidden beneath a piece of statuary in one of the flower gardens. Katie had followed him to the garden, looking back over her shoulder as she went. There was little light, even the moon seemed subdued. The windows, dark and empty, spoke to her soul of betrayal and abandonment.

"How did you know about those?" Katie whispered when he held up the jangling ring.

"Relax. I didn't steal them. Someone lost them a while ago out back. They were so rusty when I found them I figured no one was still missing them. I just put them under the statue where they would be safe."

It was kid logic, and she didn't question what he thought he was keeping them safe from.

Isaac unlocked the kitchen door. The power had been shut off, so even the emergency lighting wasn't working. The building was cold and still. There was a stale stink.

"They locked everything up and didn't empty the garbage or the refrigerators," Isaac said.

"How do you know that?" Katie asked, guessing he had already been inside.

His shoulders rose in a shrug. It was the last thing she saw of him before he stepped further into the interior shadows. The two of them left the kitchen and were halfway across the dining room when Katie heard a scratching, scuttling noise and a bump as something fairly small and heavy fell off a table on the other side of the room. Isaac's hand grabbed her arm. She felt it was safe now to turn on her flashlight.

CHAPTER FORTY-FIVE

"Are you okay?" he asked, but his voice cracked, hinting he was not.

"Probably a raccoon, or squirrel or something, moved inside," she whispered.

Still, the hair on the back of her neck had risen. She sincerely hoped that some woodland critter was what had caused the noise. They took a few more steps. There was more scuttling, tiny, sharp nails on the wooden floor. Now, she was certain she and Isaac were sending small animals away to safety.

"Mice," she whispered.

"Okay," Isaac whispered back.

In Mrs. Revek's office, Katie turned toward the desk, but Isaac reached over and took her flashlight. Keeping the beam of light pointed toward the floor, he moved toward a pair of four-drawer filing cabinets. Beside one of them was a wooden chair. Isaac moved the chair, ran his fingers along the wall, and peeled back a section of carpeting. Lifting a single piece of tile and the board attached below it, he reached inside and brought out three small diaries. Each was blue and had a flap with a tiny gold-tone lock.

The boy handed the books to Katie, and they knelt on the floor in the dead silence. She fingered the padded faux leather of the first diary. Just as she opened her mouth to speak, a loud howl rose from outside. A tree branch shifted in the wind and a beam of moonlight lit up a patch of the carpeting. Both Katie and Isaac ran back towards the kitchen, slamming into furniture and each other.

Safely back in the truck cab, they took a minute to catch their breath, then laughed at their own behavior.

"Do you think you'll find anything in those that will help figure out where Doctor Reveck is?" Isaac rubbed his hand along the side of his face. There was a sharp odor of sweat coming off both of them.

"I don't know. I guess the question is, why did Mrs. Reveck keep these diaries hidden here instead of in her home?" Katie's fingers itched to open the clasp and read the first pages. Instead, she started the truck.

"Katie?" said Isaac. "When you figure out what's in those, will you let me know?"

There was a tiny bit of hope in his words. He wanted to be safe. And his family as well.

"Yeah, I will. Promise." She drove him as close to his home as she dared and watched until she was sure he was inside.

In her room at the farmhouse, Katie opened the diaries. She found postcards stuffed inside the first one. Mementos of vacations taken. She was tired, her eyes wouldn't focus, but for a few moments at a time. Instead of trying to read the pages, she put the diaries in her backpack. This was something Lewis should have. She knew it.

"I'll get it to him first thing," she whispered to LG, then she slept.

Chapter Forty-Six

Katie spent the next day sneaking peeks at the diary pages whenever she wasn't working with customers. But by mid-afternoon hadn't discovered anything. Putting them away, she forced her thoughts to what Rick had said about doing something special when Marlie came for the weekend. But other than telling her about the diaries and maybe having her look at them, she drew a blank.

"Before the kids," Cindy said, "if Stan and I wanted a day off, we'd get in the car and just drive. Maybe take a lunch, stop at a fair or fishing spot we came across. Sometimes we flipped a coin at an intersection. Right or left, no matter where it took us. We found places we never knew existed. That might be something fun to do with your friend."

That sounded perfect to Katie.

Marlie wouldn't show up until after lunch, so Katie worked a half day and arrived home with just enough time for a bath before Marlie pulled in. Leaving her elderly housemates inside, Katie sat out on the porch, wanting to be the first thing Marlie saw. Then, too, there was the suspicion that even though Marlie had never mentioned the letter Katie had finally sent. There would eventually be a conversation.

The sound of the car's engine crested the rise. "Be calm," Katie said.

The top of the windshield. The hood. The wheels rolling closer with each rotation. Then Marlie was out of the car, wrapped in Katie's arms.

"I missed you so much." Katie wanted to say more, but the screen door banged open, and Ruth, Rick, Solomon, Walker, and a parade of cats came streaming out.

There was no getting away from Ruth, who, with the Schoolhouse Thrift open, wanted to share everything with Marlie. They spent the rest of the afternoon there. Katie painted the outhouse Rick and Phil had built. She had a little red and a small amount of blue, which she mixed together and ended up with a pleasing bluish shade of lavender. Marlie filled flowerpots with dirt and tiny wild violets. Both improvements offered eye appeal and drew people cruising into the store.

"At the rate, Ruth is selling stuff today, I'll have to haul more boxes down from the barn," Katie said.

"We can do that tomorrow while they're at church," Marlie answered.

"No. Tomorrow, after they leave, you and I are going to get in the truck and beat feet out of here."

"Where are we going?"

Katie dipped her brush into the paint can. "That's the million-dollar question."

It wasn't until hours later, with supper finished and the two of them seated at the kitchen table, tea in hand, that Marlie started asking questions.

"I have in my suitcase a letter you sent me a while ago that has to do with what you implied was a small misunderstanding."

"Okay," Katie said, focused on her cup.

"You lied to me, Katie."

"You were far away. I didn't want you to worry. I mean, I wanted you to know what happened so you wouldn't get the story from somebody else, but I didn't want you to freak out."

"I was sitting on the side of the road. I had to read the letter three times, and if there had been a payphone handy, I would have needed a pocketful of change."

"I'm sorry, Marlie."

"Is this a done deal that we'll never need to talk about again, or is there more?" Marlie asked.

Katie raised her eyes. "I guess it's a done deal until Doctor Reveck shows up, or Mrs. Reveck confesses. But there's other stuff."

"Go ahead."

"I'm still having nightmares. The other day, Isaac and I were talking. He's scared, too. His family lives out there in the woods, with no car, and I don't think they have a telephone."

"Are you afraid Doctor Reveck is going to be coming back here?" Marlie asked.

"I don't know. No, I don't think he will. I think part of my problem is that I'm just so angry that this is still haunting me. No one has seen a hair of him."

Marlie reached out, lying her hand on Katie's arm. "It's okay. You'll be fine, I know you will. It was a terrifying ordeal, but you'll get past it.

"There's more," Katie said, nervously playing with her teacup. "Every time I open my mouth about it, somebody starts boohooing about how I'm probably still in shock and that I need to take some time off from work, relax, and heal."

"That's not what you think?" Marlie asked.

"Heck, no!" Katie peeked around the corner to make sure Rick and Ruth were still listening to the news. "I don't care what everybody is saying. I can't relax. What I want is this triple-double-A-hole, to get knocked out of the sky."

"And?"

It was clear to Katie Marlie didn't think her anger was a good thing.

Blowing out a breath that felt like burning ashes, Katie said, "There's not a lot I can do, really." She explained to Marlie about the diaries, how she had gotten them, and the little she'd read. "I can give these to Sheriff Lewis, like I've given everything else to him. I'm just afraid he's waiting until I leave the building and dumping it all in the trash."

"Then he's a fool," said Marlie.

There was a moment's silence. They both burst out laughing. From the first time they'd met, they had shared a similar opinion about Lewis' abilities. Marlie's words had hit the nail square on the head.

When neither Rick nor Ruth called out, asking what the joke was, Katie pulled her file out from where it was hidden on the top shelf.

"Look at these notes I made from Mrs. Reveck's diary. I've only made it through the first two, but there's lots of good information."

Marlie flipped the small book open. When she did so, the postcards scattered across the table. As she read passages, Marlie listened with half an ear, waiting for Katie to wind down.

"You need to give that book to Lewis," she said.

"How am I going to explain where I got it without telling him about Isaac? He'll come down on that kid like a ton of bricks. And there's a lot of personal stuff in here about Mrs. Reveck's relationship with the doctor, and her fears as well. But nothing that says here's where you'll find him."

"Give it to the Trooper. Be honest. Tell him Lewis is blowing you off." Marlie fingered through the small cards that were Mrs. Reveck's memory lane. Each one denoted a vacation place the Revecks had visited. A small personal note about each was written in the message area. She came upon one that was more comical than the others and smiled.

"What?" asked Katie.

"I bet you haven't even looked at these cards? Look at this one. It's so funny. This is where we should go tomorrow."

Marlie held up a card that showed a short line of staggered cabins, quaint little buildings that looked like fairy tale cottages. The marquee on the bottom of the card read *The Seven Dwarfs Motor Court: Where Fantasy Sleeps.*

Katie stared at the card. Then, just as Marlie reclaimed it, Katie remembered her conversation with Sheila Reveck in the other woman's hospital room.

"She said they always ended up at some hole in the wall," Katie muttered. "Not the type of place an investor would go. I'll bet those are the people the cops are focusing on."

Chapter Forty-Seven

If it hadn't been for the tiny script on the back of the card, Katie and Marlie would never have found the place. Neither Ruth nor Rick had ever heard of the cottages. Marlie had told Katie to show them the card.

"If they see the picture, it might spark a memory," she had said.

"Or with it in their hand, they'd turn it over and see who wrote it." Katie shook her head. "Before I hand this over, I'm going to check it out. Let's go for a ride, you and I, and just see. I've never been in that area, have you? This would be something new for both of us."

Marlie had been hesitant. Katie should give the books to the authorities. She understood about Isaac, but this was still not the way the situation should be handled. In the end, however, Katie's enthusiasm about them spending the day together, some place where they didn't need to be looking over their shoulders, and her promise they would only look, then report, came out the winner.

A road map from Marlie's trunk pointed the way, and they left, headed across Vermont toward Twin Mountain, New Hampshire, and then up along Route 3 towards Jeffersonville. They set off right after breakfast.

The trip took four hours, with two stops for coffee and one to pee. The road from Twin Mountain east was long and winding. The terrain was mountainous, with the forest growing close to the road on either side. The two lanes were mostly empty of other vehicles. Marlie lolled back on the seat, demanding if they were there yet at five-minute intervals. Suddenly, Katie saw a five-by-eight sign on the right. Black lettering on dirty white, trimmed with a lurid Pepto-Bismol pink, declared they had arrived at *The Seven Dwarfs Motor Court*. A looping, single-lane dirt road led into the pines.

"There it is!" Katie tromped on the brake, sending an unprepared Marlie sliding off onto the floor mat. "Oops, sorry," Katie said.

"It's disgusting down here. Don't you ever clean this truck?" Marlie hauled herself back up onto the seat.

"Gram used to say the only thing that held her vehicles together was the dirt." Katie rolled to a stop at the edge of the road. "Should we check it out?"

"Do you think we came all this way so we could look at the sign, say yup, there it is, and drive home?" Marlie brushed rust off her hip-hugging capris. "Forward-ho."

The track wound behind a single row of lush pines. The seven cabins were lined up in two rows, with the office a slightly smaller version. Each had a crooked little sign over the door with the name of a specific dwarf. The structures were painted white with the same gagging-pink color as the highway sign trimming the windows, doors, and roofs. The front doors and window boxes were a sun-faded teal. They looked well-kept, but the small lawn area was choked with weeds.

"Well, they are adorable," Marlie gushed, pointing out the gingerbread trim and matching flower boxes.

But Katie was more interested in the shiny black BMW with Vermont plates among the other three vehicles parked beside the buildings. "What are the chances?" she mused.

Marlie had already popped out of the truck. With her small Instamatic camera in hand, she snapped pictures of the whimsical buildings and similarly themed yard ornaments.

"Smile, Katie!"

Before Marlie could focus and snap, Katie took a couple of running steps so the rear end of the Beamer's license plate was beside her. It would make for solid evidence. A man walked out of the office.

"Can I help you?" he asked.

Leaving Marlie to finish her roll of film, Katie smiled and walked to where the man waited.

"I'm sorry to bother you," she said. "My friend and I were in Bethlehem the other day, and she swallowed something wrong. There was this doctor there who helped us out. I'm ashamed to say that I let him get away without so much as a thank you, but one of the clerks in the store said he was staying here. We're on our way home, so, you know, I just wanted to tell him how appreciative we are."

The man didn't look convinced as Marlie ran past on her way to the truck for another roll of film.

"He had a funny name." This was Katie's last chance. "Something like Reveckia."

"There's no doctor here." The man grinned, showing chaw-darkened teeth. "They always sign in using DR, like maybe it'll get them a discount. I've got a Ramstad, but he's no doctor. This guy, he don't ever go anywhere, except down to the diner on 3."

"Too bad." Katie tried to make herself look disappointed. "Thanks anyway."

The man nodded and headed back into the office. Marlie waited by the truck. She hadn't realized at first what Katie was up to, but when she'd come up to her and the motel owner, her deputy's instincts kicked in, and she knew to keep walking and snapping off pictures.

Katie pulled the truck back out to the dirt track, then stopped when she had gone far enough so the feathery White Pines hid them from view. Both she and Marlie exited the truck, closing the doors, but not all the way. Staying close to the pines, they sneaked back to a place where they could see the black car but would be out of view if the manager looked out of his window. Once again, Marlie was taking pictures.

"I know it's the same car," Katie whispered. "I just wish there was something I could remember about it, you know, like a dent or a missing hubcap. Something that would tell me it was actually Reveck's."

A crow flew past, and she shaded her eyes to watch its flight upward. There was a radio playing in one of the other cabins, but no one was in sight.

"You mean like the owner opening the trunk?" Marlie nudged Katie's side with her elbow.

Sure enough, when Katie turned, she saw a tall man with skinny knees and pale blue and white striped shorts closing the trunk and walking back into his cabin.

"Well?" Marlie asked.

Katie grinned ear to ear. "And he's staying in Dopey. Can you believe it?"

* * *

Instead of continuing towards Jeffersonville, Katie backtracked toward Bethlehem, then on to Saint Johnsbury, Vermont. As they sped along, she explained to Marlie contacting the New Hampshire police—local, sheriff, or state—would only alert Doctor Reveck that he had been found.

Marlie tried to argue with her, but Katie wouldn't be deterred.

"If we get back to where we can make a call, like from home, and get hold of Corporal Derrick, we stand a chance of them catching Reveck before somebody walks up to him and asks for identification."

"We could use a payphone at a gas station, or maybe a restaurant," Marlie suggested.

"No, I have to get hold of Corporal Derrick!" Katie was adamant and picking up speed.

"So, Lewis is out," Marlie added.

"Absolutely." Katie gave a disgusted huff. "First, Lewis will call me a liar, then he'll call some like-minded Joe Blow in New Hampshire. They'll sit down, have a beer with the good doctor, and bingo. He'll go back to Dopey to pack his bags, promising to turn himself in before dark."

"Katie," Marlie said soothingly, holding on to the seat and the dashboard to keep from being thrown from side to side with Katie's erratic driving. "Honey, you need to slow down and think about what you're saying. It's like you've morphed into Lewis. Like suddenly, you're both thinking the same way and only trying to one up each other. This guy is a killer. If we keep racing along like this and die in a car accident, he's going to get away scot-free."

They were a mile outside of the Saint Johnsbury town line, just before

266

Fairbanks Scale Company. Katie slammed on the brakes again, sending the back end of the truck jittering toward the ditch.

"For crying out loud! What's with you stopping?" Marlie lashed out as she slid to the edge of the seat, barely catching herself before she ended up in the footwell again.

Instead of answering, Katie executed a jerking, rough, three-corner turn. Then, the truck leapt ahead two hundred feet to a driveway on the right. The sign read "Vermont State Police."

"You're right. I'm acting just like Sheriff Lewis. One of us needs to be an adult, and I don't think he can manage it."

Marlie followed as Katie jumped out of the cab and hurried toward the front entrance.

"What happened to calling Corporal Derrick?" Marlie asked when she caught up in the doorway.

"That's exactly what I'm going to do," Katie answered.

It took several minutes of tag-team arguing to get the officer in charge to make the first call. Even when Katie was finally speaking to Corporal Derrick, it took several uh-huhs, a couple of whats, and a you've-got-to-be-kidding before he understood. Derrick asked to speak to the OIC again. Lieutenant Weeks told Katie and Marlie to make themselves comfortable and he'd have someone step out and get them something to eat. They were just finishing up the KFC when Weeks re-joined them.

"Corporal Derrick and I just ended a conference call with our counterpart in New Hampshire," he said. "We will be commencing a strike as soon as all components are in place."

"What does that mean?" Katie asked. "What components?"

"What he's saying, Katie, is that there are certain members of law enforcement that want in on this grab," said Marlie.

The lieutenant nodded. "Corporal Derrick as well as the initial response first officer on scene are en route," he said.

"Are you talking about Sheriff Lewis?" Katie asked.

"Affirmative."

Katie started to boil. Instead of responding with the words that curdled on her tongue regarding including Sheriff Lewis, she sat back, exhaled, and asked, "Is it okay for us to go now?"

Marlie blinked. She was looking at Katie, whose face had taken on a dark flush. When Katie spoke, words came out, but her lips didn't move. Lieutenant Weeks didn't appear to notice. Marlie rose slowly, following Katie out of the barracks building.

"Katie?" Marlie began tentatively.

"Yes?" Katie's words were cold. She pulled up to the stop sign at the end of the parking lot and sat there staring straight ahead.

Marlie fumbled, trying to think of a way to ask what her friend was considering without raising Katie's anger. While Marlie ah'd, Katie put on her right directional and pulled out.

"You're going the wrong way, Katie," Marlie said.

"I don't think so."

"Okay." Marlie pressed herself into the corner, as close to the door as she could get. The tension in the truck cab was stifling.

They rode in silence until they arrived back at Twin Mountain, just east of Bethlehem. At the tiny post office that occupied half of someone's private living room, Katie pulled off the road.

"You can get out here, Marlie," she said. "I'm sure they'll let you use the telephone. I should have let you out in Saint Johnsbury, but I wasn't thinking." Marlie shook her head, but unable to face Katie, stared through the passenger window.

"Marlie." Katie reached out but stopped just short of touching the other woman. "If this goes south, it'll ruin you. Get out."

Marlie shook her head.

Then, right past where they were still parked, two Vermont state trooper cars roared by. Both ran without sirens, but the bubble lights on top of all the cruisers were lit. Katie didn't hesitate, but fell in behind them. She hadn't gotten a good look at the drivers, but in the second car, the passenger sported the same white Statton that Lewis normally wore. All the vehicles took a left on Route 3.

"Fall back, Katie," Marlie said. "Give the troopers space."

Katie did as she was directed. They crested the rise to see that the cruisers had arrived at the dirt track leading into The Seven Dwarfs Motor Court and joined two others already there. Katie pulled over so far that the truck practically wallowed in the ditch. She sat there waiting.

"This is as far as we're going, right Katie?" Marlie asked.

Katie continued to stare ahead silently. A tiny muscle near the base of her jaw jumped.

Marlie chewed her thumbnail.

"Katie?" Marlie tried again, then, frustrated said, "For crying out loud, I just got my darn job back."

"Maybe you should get out," Katie said quietly.

"Not happening," Marlie answered.

Further up the road, the four vehicles, strobe lights now extinguished, turned onto the road leading into the motor court. Katie shifted into first gear and pulled back onto the highway. They arrived at the dirt track as the last set of taillights disappeared. She pulled further ahead and eased the old pickup into the young, feathery growth of six-foot white pines where they hid before. This time, she continued forward until the front bumper split the trees, and she could see what was happening near the buildings.

One of the cruisers was parked in front of the manager's office. The man stepped out onto the door stoop and handed the trooper a small white card. Then he and the trooper moved so they were not in visual range of the Dopey cabin. The BMW was still parked out front.

At this time, the other three vehicles moved ahead to encircle Dopey. Officers stepped out but stayed behind their cars. Lieutenant Weeks, with Sheriff Lewis a step behind, approached the door. Katie leaned out the side window and heard Weeks order Reveck out of the building.

No response. Weeks called out again. Then, before anyone could react, Lewis kicked the door, and the sound of splitting wood filled the parking area. Both officers charged into the building.

Within minutes, Reveck was led out, hands behind him in cuffs.

"Holy cow!" Marlie whispered. "Did you see...Katie?"

But Katie was already out of the truck, pushing aside tree branches, hardly aware of what she was doing. Her vision had narrowed, darkening the same way the space beneath the double-wide had at the end of the day. Her feet moved faster, each breath a searing burn.

Lewis looked up. "Stop!" he shouted, holding up his hand.

But Katie was already airborne. She hit Reveck in the right collarbone, twisting him out of the sheriff's grasp and to the ground. Her fists were already pummeling his face before they landed, and her weight held him in place. Then she was screaming, accusing him of killing Holly, trying to kill her and his own wife. She was out of control, raging, weeping. It took two men to pull her off.

To Marlie, who had followed Katie out of the pickup and into the parking lot, it looked like Sheriff Lewis was holding Reveck down, and Corporal Derrick and Lieutenant Weeks were trying to remove Katie, but not very strenuously.

Katie's scream turned into a sob. She grabbed the front of Reveck's shirt with one hand and his hair with the other, shaking him. There was blood on his face. Lieutenant Weeks was behind her, holding her elbows and pulling her back. The second officer stepped in front of Katie, barring her way.

"You're a killer. You were starving all those people. It was your fault that needle was in Holly's arm." Katie's sobs started to drown out the words.

Reveck, initially silenced by the shock of her attack, took up his own defense.

"Stop!" he cried out, face turned toward the dirt. "I didn't kill her! We found her body in the locked hall. It was stinking, and when we opened the door, she was right there, sitting against the wall. All we did was try to keep her death from closing the retreat. KEEP HER AWAY FROM ME!"

Weeks pulled Katie further away, finally stopping near the manager's building. Marlie pushed the lieutenant aside and wrapped her arms around her love. Katie hid her face in the soft flannel of Marlie's shirt and wept.

Someone suggested calling an ambulance, but after a few minutes, Katie regained control. She and Marlie sat on a splintering bench near the office. With Marlie on one side and a New Hampshire trooper on the other, Katie watched as Doctor Reveck unwound. He might have remained stoic through the arrest, but Katie's attack had unnerved him.

At one point, Katie noticed Sheriff Lewis looking at her with a sly grin on his face, like he had gotten something he wanted. A gift dropped in his lap.

All but two of the cruisers pulled out. Reveck was in the back of the second one. While another officer interviewed the motor court manager, Weeks issued Katie a written warning and released her into Marlie's care.

The two of them drove away with Marlie at the wheel, both knowing that, if Reveck pressed charges, Katie would be in trouble. She had left the relative safety of Parentville, crossed a state line, and accosted a man.

Marlie's driving was slower than Katie's. While they traveled back to Vermont and towards home, the deputy kept up an ongoing monologue about what they had done that day and all the reasons they shouldn't have done it. When she got to the end of what she had to say, Marlie took a deep breath and started again. On the other side of the bench seat, Katie feigned sleep. She didn't want to listen to what Marlie was saying, but she knew her friend was exactly right. Then there was that look on Sheriff Lewis' face.

I know what he was thinking, Katie mused. *He looked as pleased as a pig in a bakery. It's more evidence I'm a nut job. Another stone he can throw at me at any time.*

* * *

"What were you thinking?" Rick demanded.

It hurt Katie terribly to see the disappointment her actions had put in his eyes. Instead of answering, she went into the bathroom, locking the door behind her.

Ruth laid her hand on his arm. "Doctor Gillian said there might come a time when all the bad stuff that happened to her that night would boil over."

"What do we do?" Marlie stood outside the bathroom door. Behind it, they could hear water running in the tub—and a noise like quiet moaning. "Do you have a key for this door?"

Ruth shook her head. "We need to let Katie be. If she wants to talk to us, she'll find a time."

Marlie stayed by the door for a while longer. She watched Ruth, Rick, Solomon, and all the cats except LG leave. She wasn't sure what to expect. Katie hadn't taken advantage of their ride home to bare her heart.

"But then I didn't do such a good job keeping my big yak shut either," she said to the cat.

LG curled up by the door, her paws tucked beneath her. Wise eyes looked up at Marlie as if to say it was okay. They'd wait.

Katie finally emerged from the bathroom while Rick was in the kitchen pouring coffee. She walked past Marlie to stand beside him. Marlie had been dozing in a kitchen chair and, though startled to wakefulness, held her tongue.

"I'm sorry," Katie said.

He nodded, never looking up. But even if he had, she was already gone. In the living room, she lifted her fingers, acknowledging Ruth and Marlie, who had followed her, but keeping them at a distance as she walked across the floor and up the stairs. She had gone through the bathroom medicine cabinet searching for the bottle of cough syrup, but wise to the ways of alcoholics, Ruth had removed that when Charlie had moved in. Katie hesitated outside the short man's door, then remembered Ruth warning Charlie she would be keeping an eye open for a hidden bottle.

So, she's probably searching his room on a regular basis, Katie thought. Crying herself to sleep seemed to be her only option.

Chapter Forty-Eight

Early the next morning, Marlie rose to leave for her first day at Norwich University. Katie, Rick, and Ruth were already seated at the table.

"I didn't hear you people get up," she said.

Rick put a plate in front of her, his signature breakfast. Two bright yellow egg eyes over a smile of bacon, home fries circling like hair, and toast point ears with jelly dot earrings. Marlie laughed, tears sparkling on her lashes.

"You guys," she said.

Katie looked haggard, as if sleep had eluded her, but she was dressed for work, as was Rick. They talked about what Marlie expected at Norwich, how much money the Schoolhouse Yard Sale had earned over the weekend, and debated if Monique would be bringing the baby goats into the house while Amos was away. Then Marlie loaded her suitcase and a tin of Ruth's date bars into her car. Before she pulled out of the driveway, Katie stepped up to the door.

"You were right, and I was wrong." She hesitated, looking up Lover's Lane the way she used to go with Poppa, looking for new adventures. "I'd like to say I learned my lesson. But I don't know about that. I do know that going to the AA meeting twice a month isn't helping me. Maybe I need a different kind of counseling. There's a meeting in Charlotte every Thursday evening. I'm going to be going there as well."

She looked down at Marlie's sad eyes.

"You should really think about if you want to be around me."

Marlie gave a teary laugh. "You dope. Sometimes you just can't do it alone.

Talk to us, me, Rick, and Ruth. Stop shutting the door. Think about it." She blew a kiss. "I'll see you soon." And she pulled away.

"Now what?" Ruth asked, waving enthusiastically as the car disappeared.

Behind her, Katie and Rick looked at each other.

"We need to talk," Rick said.

They were both late for work that morning, and Ruth arrived at Grace's house after nine.

There had been a lot of tension in their short and heated conversation. Katie agreed to go weekly to the AA meetings at Woodman Hall, and those in Charlotte as well. Before she left the house, she called Corporal Derrick and asked him to pick up the diaries.

"Will you go with me to talk to Sheriff Lewis?" she asked. "That way, I can explain it to both of you at the same time." *And I won't have to be alone with him.*

He agreed. Rick said it was a start but put Katie on notice.

"I never expected living here would be so stressful. I'm an old guy."

* * *

When Katie got ready to leave work at the end of the day, she called Father Metevier.

"No, Mrs. O'Brien has left for the day," Father Metevier said, "and I didn't see the boy."

Katie drove down the Richmond Road, turning off on Gil Anthony Ridge Road, not headed for Corrapell, but into the small trailer park. She'd felt a chill from the time she'd passed CVU. Clicking on her directional, made her feel even more apprehensive. She didn't want to go down that road.

For the first time, the dooryard of the derelict mobile home the O'Brien's lived in was dry. Mrs. O'Brien answered the door, face flushed, but pleased to see her.

"Yes," she said. "Isaac is here. We're moving, so he's packing his things. I'll get him."

The two little girls stayed in place, watching Katie with shy eyes until their brother sent them away.

"So, you're moving," Katie said as they stepped outside.

"Yeah. Father Metevier got us an apartment in the village, and the folks from welfare are helping us get set up and moved. My mom is thrilled to pieces."

Isaac sounded a trifle embarrassed. Katie couldn't tell if it was because of the Father's help or the mention of the welfare agency. It didn't matter. She had her own things to say.

"That's good, Isaac. You'll be somewhere safer, you know, where you'll have neighbors and all."

"I have to go back to school." He looked away, towards the woods. "Father Metevier said I can either go back and enroll in the Voc Tech, or GED. He don't care, one or the other."

"So, what's your choice?" she asked.

"Don't know. I've got a church sponsor and I'll be meeting with him this week. I'm not sure how that works, but I want to see."

At Katie's questioning look, he added. "Like a Big Brother."

"Cool. I wanted to talk to you about Doctor Reveck."

Isaac's shoulders rose towards his ears. She hurried on.

"You might have heard he was captured. I'm not sure what's going to happen from there, or with Mrs. Reveck, or Corrapell. I wish I knew. But you should know that it's still rough for a lot of people, myself included. I still have nightmares."

She hadn't meant to admit that, but at the relieved look on his face, she concluded he, too, was having some issues. Her confession let him know he wasn't alone.

Maybe I'll mention to Father Metevier, Isaac's Big Brother should talk to him about counseling, she thought.

"Then, there's the diaries," she said. They were leaning on her pickup with the sun warming their faces. "Having them is what took us to the doctor. He might have been free a lot longer without them. But here's the deal. I had to tell Corporal Derrick about them. I'm giving them to him tomorrow when we meet with Sheriff Lewis.

"Isaac, I'm going to have to tell them how I came to have those books. I'm willing to bet dollars to donuts, they're going to want to talk to you about them."

"I know," he said. "I told Father Metevier what we did, that you had them. He told me you'd do the smart thing, and the two of you would make sure I didn't go to prison."

Katie didn't look up, but she had a moment's surprise.

Crafty old coot.

Isaac pushed off the truck. "I gotta go help my mom. The welfare people are coming first thing in the morning. But, hey, Katie, I'm good. I think."

She gave him a little punch in the arm. "I bet you are."

She was late getting home. Everybody was waiting for supper. Charlie came out of the bathroom steamed red and freshly shaven.

"And it's not even Saturday night," Katie said with a laugh as he hurried through the kitchen and headed upstairs.

"It's because he's helping Father Metevier's housekeeper move tomorrow morning." Ruth laid plates on the table. "I think he's sweet on her."

Katie was ladling chicken stew out of the crockpot where it had been simmering all day. She stopped in mid-scoop.

"Mrs. O'Brien? Really."

"Yup," Rick said. "And he's got it bad."

Chapter Forty-Nine

Katie had hoped to meet with Corporal Derrick prior to sitting down with Sheriff Lewis. It was not meant to be. When she pulled into the municipal lot in town, Derrick was already walking up the steps to the side entrance of the sheriff's office. He waved at her to join him.

Inside, they walked past Brad, seated at Angus' desk. Though he greeted the trooper, the deputy ignored Katie.

Twit, she thought.

She made sure the door was closed behind her before she pulled the diaries out of her tote bag and explained to the two law enforcement officers how she had acquired them. Derrick had known the books and the tell-tale postcard existed since her call to him from the Saint Johnsbury barracks.

With each sentence, Lewis' face soured more. Katie knew he was losing the edge he thought he'd be able to hold over her. Though this was not the way she'd wanted to do this, it was the right way.

"That's all I've got to add," she said. "But I'd like you to tell me you aren't going to dump all over Isaac."

"He's a minor," Corporal Derrick said. "He'll be afforded protection accordingly."

Lewis' lips pressed together, but he nodded in agreement.

"Am I going to get charged or arrested?" she asked.

"That remains to be seen," said Sheriff Lewis.

She was dismissed, unsure if she would be in trouble down the road, but relieved that for one time she had done something right. Marlie was supposed to call her on Wednesday evening to let her know how everything was going in her training. Katie couldn't wait to tell her what she had done.

That afternoon, while she was enjoying her day off and cleaning cat boxes, she received a call from Attorney Costello's office.

"Can you hold for Mr. Costello?" the woman asked.

Katie waited. It was short, but it felt a lifetime long. He had information regarding the Revecks. She knew he probably also wanted to vent his frustration at her behavior going to the Seven Dwarfs Motor Court and her subsequent beating on Doctor Reveck.

"This is where we hear if the cat poop hits the fan if Reveck charges me with assault," she told LG while she waited for the lawyer to come on the line.

"This is all very cut and dry, Katelyn," he said. "The State's forensics evidence combined with Gary Reveck's confession in front of seven law enforcement officers added an unexpected layer to this case. The Medical Examiner's report states that given the condition of Holly Guptill's remains, it's impossible to tell how she actually died. The toxicology report is inconclusive. The case is going to end up in the court system. Given what Doctor Reveck did to you and his wife, it's not going to be open and shut for him. Beyond that, Doctor Reveck and Sheila Wesley, a.k.a. Reveck, will be charged with destroying evidence, compromising a death scene, and mishandling a corpse, among a few minor charges. Doctor Reveck is also being charged with kidnapping and unlawful restraint in the second degree of both you and Sheila Wesley.

"It's not attempted murder?" Kate was surprised, as that was how she considered it.

"Not at this time," Costello said. "To go there, we have to establish that he knew the two of you were going to die if he left you there. According to his statement, he said you told him it was okay; you'd talk to the police for him and knew he had every intention of notifying the authorities where you were when he was safe. But before he had a chance, he heard on the news that you had been rescued."

"Are you kidding me?" Katie was flabbergasted. "He's lying!"

"You and I know that. There are others who feel the same, I'm sure. I can't see that anyone else would believe him. But I've seen stranger things happen in a courtroom."

"What did Sheila say?"

"Ms. Wesley remembers nothing from the time she drank the coffee until she woke up in the hospital."

"Are they communicating?" Katie asked.

"Not to my knowledge."

"The other charges Reveck will have to face are all connected to Corrapell, which is a state case and not of my concern. He's not my client. I think it's safe to say the good doctor will be going away for quite a while."

"And Sheila?"

"That's a fish in a different pond," Costello grunted as though lifting his stout body from a chair. "Depending on how badly the state wants to charge Doctor Reveck, she might get away with time served and exoneration if she appears as their witness. I don't know where she'll go, but I'm sure she won't be in your neck of the woods." He paused for a moment before adding, "My concern is that Gary Reveck will use your…emotional response…as part of his defense, and we need to talk about that."

"You mean when I attacked him?" Katie asked.

"Hence the reason for my call. I would like you to drop by my office Thursday afternoon around three so we can go over what happened. Until that time, and forevermore, you are not to reference the occurrence as an attack. It was then and will forever be exactly what I termed it. Your emotional response to suddenly seeing the man who abducted you and left you hidden away beneath that mobile home. Do you understand?"

Katie agreed, told Attorney Costello how to reach Marlie, who witnessed the event, and then said, "Last question. Does this mean that both I, as owner of the Gypsy Copse, and Amos Surrette are cleared of all wrongdoing in Holly Guptill's death? And if so, will Sheriff Martin Lewis be giving a public apology to Amos for all the nasty rumors floating around that, let's face it, he started?"

Costello laughed until he wheezed. "Oh, Katie. I sincerely doubt Sheriff

Lewis will ever admit he made a mistake."

Chapter Fifty

Katie filled the tub with clean hot water, courtesy of the new well, and had a good, long soak while LG nestled in the sink. Later, she walked down to the Dean farm, where Ruth was working in the truck garden alongside Grace and Monique, who was mostly sitting on a stool, rubbing her belly.

"Are you taking the baby goats in the house?" Katie asked.

Monique blushed. "I did once. When Amos found out, he went through the roof. They're getting big really fast and less like puppies. I call them Eenie, Meanie, and Mikey. And the little buggers ate my tomato plants. Right after Amos told me they couldn't come in the house anymore, he and I scrubbed down the kitchen and living room. Then," she said with a little blush, "we started putting together the nursery. It's pretty exciting."

They all cheered. Then Ruth and Katie walked up the slope to the farmhouse.

"What's going to happen now, Katie?"

"Well, obviously, I'm not working at Corrapell anymore. Marlie and I may be involved to some extent in the Reveck trial. I'm not looking forward to that."

She stopped at the site of the old bunkhouse. Rick, his friends, and Raymond had made a good start on the new chicken coop. Rolls of wire, some twisted and rusted, lay strewn on the ground. It didn't look as if there was enough to create a good-sized chicken yard.

The day she arrived back here from Illinois, her plan had been to sell the farm and move on. Yet now, there was a pig yard, duck house, chicken coops, and a garden that needed tending. Eyeing the messy coils of wire, she considered trying to untangle them.

As if in answer to her thoughts, Ruth said, "Dorothea told me the people that bought the Ash house dropped off all the drapes from downstairs, and there were a lot of them. We should go over and see if we can get enough to redo the living room. Maybe the parlor, too, before Marlie comes back in two weeks."

"Two weeks," Katie said with a sigh and a smile. Looping her arm through Ruth's, she pulled the older woman along with her. "Yeah, let's go look at drapes and maybe baby clothes as well."

Acknowledgements

Every new book brings a list of old and new people into an author's life. New hands helping. Old ones, supporting. There are so many, and if I miss mentioning you, I am truly sorry, but believe me, you were appreciated.

My family, partner, friends, all who listened to me talk it out, backtrack, and rush off in a different direction, thank you.

Level Best Books, Verena Rose, Shawn O'Reilly, Harriette Shackler, who believed in me, thank you.

Bruce Robert Coffin, who showed me the way, thank you.

Lisa Matthews, How to Kill your Darlings, (reason I have a new computer), thank you.

Tom at Computer Tutors who helped me find the manuscript when I lost it, and gave me direction, thank you.

Bellamy Gayle, Deb Well, Christine Chenaud, reading, offering advice, and critiquing, thank you.

Shawn O'Reilly, cover art. Pizzaz Girl, thank you.

The librarians, fans, all the readers, huge thanks!

Where would I be without you? Just a long line of words, and no one to share with.

Thank you all!

About the Author

DonnaRae Menard began writing in junior high school and has been scribbling since. She is the author of the An It's Never Too Late Mystery series. A 1970's suspense featuring Katelyn Took and 17 cats. The Woman Warrior's series, historical fiction, The Waif and The Warlord, fantasy, Detective Carmine Mansuer series, set in Boston, Mass. Dropped from the Sky, It takes Guts, Willa the Wisp, and several short stories. She splits her time between Vermont and New Hampshire, has an affinity for odd jobs, and rescued cats. Check out her website donnaraemenardbooks.com. Find her on Facebook.

SOCIAL MEDIA HANDLES:
  DonnaRae Menard @ facebook
  Twitter @donnaraemenard

AUTHOR WEBSITE:
  donnaraemenardbooks.com

Also by DonnaRae Menard

Currier of the Dead Series
The Morality Issue

An It's Never Too Late Series
Murder in the Meadow
Murder on Eagle Drop Ridge
Murder in The Village Proper

The Woman Warrior Series
In the Shadow of Pharaoh
Strength of the Mayan Leopard
Wu-Lee

Gwen Hanson Series
Dropped from the Sky

Shorts
Dreams of a Mad Woman
It Takes Guts

Children
Willa the Wisp

Fantasy
The Waif and The Warlord

Thrillers: Detective Carmine Mansuer Series
Patterns
Hunters

The Lynn Steeve Series
Beneath the Fountain

286